JAWBONE HOLLER

Mace Thornton

MASCOT
BOOKS
an imprint of Amplify Publishing Group

www.amplifypublishinggroup.com

Jawbone Holler

For more information, please contact:
Mascot Books, an imprint of Amplify Publishing Group
620 Herndon Parkway, Suite 220
Herndon, VA 20170
info@mascotbooks.com

Cover illustration by Marco Primo

Library of Congress Control Number: 2023914654
CPSIA Code: PRV0224A
ISBN-13: 978-1-63755-998-7

Printed in the United States⁻

A NOVEL

JAWBONE HOLLER

MACE
THORNTON

MASCOT
BOOKS
an imprint of Amplify Publishing Group

CHAPTER 1

Late Fall 1857

SKEDADDLE
SEASON

PERRY ADAMS PULLED A FLASK of rum from his hip pocket, raised it to his lips, and choked down a spicy swig of bitter truth. Hard knocks were prodding him closer to a decision to skedaddle. As a bead of sweat rolled down his cheek, he wanted to believe that this long, sweltering summer working in his father's Indiana corn field would be his last. Perry had guzzled more than his share of hardship.

Perry was a devoted worker with a keen intellect. His body had been chiseled by the relentless work needed to coax abundant corn crops from his father's land. This year, as harvest approached, something was amiss. Sip by sip, liquor was shoving anguish to the front of Perry's mind.

Perry had discovered rum as an elixir to brighten his disposition while he worked. He liked it. But lately, that revelation had transformed into a fixation. He needed it. Rum was fueling a boiling kettle of self-destruction. It was becoming his grindstone that sharpened a two-edged sword. On one side, it honed a slice of fleeting serenity while mangling the other into a jagged edge that ripped everything in its path. On the brink of his twenty-third year, Perry's relation-ships were ablaze, and he was straddling the bonfire.

The most significant misfortune that propelled Perry to indulge in what locals referred to as "kill-devil" rum was the relentless backbreaking toil on Stewart Adams' farm, where his father ruled as taskmaster and tyrant. Whether toting water, hauling manure, or wielding a machete to chop weeds until his palms bled, Perry stood always at his father's beck and call.

This day marked Perry's fifth anniversary of working at Stew's farm outside Salt Spring. While the farm would one day be his, spending the next thirty years of life in the misery of that certainty made him question whether that legacy was one of promise or prison. Calloused hands and broken wishes roused Perry's hunger for change.

Restless spirit aside, nature had been kind to Perry. His looks surpassed the ragged ends of his disposition. Bold cheekbones, sky-blue eyes, and a well-kept crop of blondish hair set his appearance above most. Perry's sculpted physique revealed the frame of a young man poised for a yet discovered opportunity, his destiny awaiting in the shadows. Perry stood six-foot-two and carried a muscular one hundred ninety pounds. His physical presence opened doors his temperament could just as quickly slam.

After making his final round of chopping weeds from the cornfield, Perry wiped the sweat from his brow with a red bandana and stuffed it into his back pocket. The scorching heat overwhelmed him, surpassing even the effect of the rum as he stumbled toward completion. After the last chop, Perry tucked the handle of his machete into his other back pocket, and began to wobble home, each step more dreadful than the one before it.

Perry was quickly reaching a breaking point and packing a saddlebag to flee his woes tasted better with every additional gulp of kill-devil rum. It fed an inner longing to chase the glow of a distant fire, stoked by the hope that a change of scenery might also salve his emotions.

"The bastard isn't going to win. Not today, Pappy," he cursed his father for the dire condition that weighed heavily on his broad shoulders.

Stew Adams was harsh on his son, but his disposition took a turn toward cruel after the death of his wife had plunged him into the dismal life of a widower.

It had been a dreary November night years prior when Mary Katherine Adams had passed with the fever. That evening father and son had sat by her bedside in the glow of a lantern. Hand in hand they watched her wither.

"Pappy, what will become of us with Mama gone?" young Perry had asked.

Stew hadn't answered. He had sat in silence, staring into the emptiness. Mary Katherine's death was the only bonding moment they had experienced, and grief enshrouded it. From that moment, the chasm between father and son grew to become unbridgeable.

Mary Katherine, always wearing a smile of confidence under a white, lace-trimmed bonnet, had sheltered Perry from Stew's stormy manner. After she died the loss paralyzed father and son. To escape, Perry would sit in silence, clutching the bonnet for hours—on the front porch, in the barn, in a nearby cornfield. Anywhere as long as the angry old man wasn't around to deliver his wrath. He usually wasn't. Instead Stew had eased his grief with a bottle of 'shine.

Since those days, coming home always presented danger to Perry. It typically ended in a shouting match—and sometimes a physical altercation. The trail of abuse continued, even after Stew pledged an oath to sobriety and Perry had become an adult.

Perry kept Mary Katherine's bonnet on his bedroom dresser. From it he'd drawn strength after each blowup he had with Stew.

Lumbering home after this latest long day of fieldwork, Perry mumbled a litany of grievances against his father. The one that lingered was how Stew had denied him a chance to leave the farm five years earlier. Perry had sought a blacksmithing apprenticeship in Kentucky. While Stew was right, damn sure the lad was overdue for a healthy dose of responsibility, sending Perry on the road was not in his best interests or those of his farm. Stew's denial was less than nurturing.

"Get your ass into the field, and don't come to my house until your work's done. I see you still haven't shed the cloak of a mama's-boy." Perry recalled the interaction word for word. "Your mother's long gone, and she's not coming back to save you. Don't even think about letting your shadow darken my threshold until you've plowed the last row."

Perry had wanted to put up a fight, but after investing his body, mind, and soul in the farm's success, he had no fight left to give. He knew Stew would judge his surrender a sign of softness. As Perry returned home that evening, Stew had stormed out to meet him, head shaking and finger pointing.

"Boy, you're not goin' to amount to piss."

Five years ago. That's when Perry had first discovered the bottle, but only recently the abuse had begun to take its toll. Now not even kill-devil could lessen the sting of the daily scalding he took from Stew.

"Five years of inglorious shit, all for naught," he slurred aloud. "I have nothing to my person and even less to my name."

After that realization Perry decided his return home on this fifth work anniversary evening would be different. It was time to make an unstated stand. This evening there would be no grand entrance. No official surrender to make him a target. What could have been just another long day in his unbearable life, this anniversary evening filled Perry with resolve.

On his trek home, Perry pondered what life would be like had his mother survived. She had not only been his parent but in every sense of the word, his guardian. Through the oak branches that lined the lane, he heard her empowering voice whispering familiar words.

"*Chin up. Chest out. The bold and daring win the day.*"

The problem was, Mary Katherine wasn't there. A tear rolled down Perry's cheek. Broken and close to unsalvageable, Perry had run out of choices. As he reached the barn and began to unpack his tools, he saw Stew.

In his hands Stew held a rifle that reflected the lantern light. Stew raised the gun to his shoulder and blasted a shot into a haystack against the barn's rear wall. Perry jumped back. What was Stew's intention? Still muddled by the rum, Perry wasn't sure whether to fight or run.

Stew held the rifle arm's length toward Perry. "It's been five years. This is for you. It's a top-of-the-line Burnside. You've shown me something I never expected. For the better part, you've grown up. The success of this farm may rest on my shoulders, but it's also been placed on your back. For that I am most thankful."

Perry shuddered and did a double-take. He took the rifle in hand and admired its ebony sheen.

"I think you understand now the bitter flavor of hard work makes the rewards taste that much sweeter. The old place ain't perfect, and neither am I, but I don't have horns protruding from my forehead. I just know what needs to be done. I'm broken, and I need your strong back to set this place up for success."

Stew stepped toward Perry and slapped him on the back in appreciation. Perry flinched.

The rifle's deceptive glow danced across Perry's eyes, but he saw it was yet another manipulative move by Stew to keep him chained to the farm. Stew viewed the gift as a shifty investment. The rifle's value would be more than offset by Perry's continued work.

Perry reasoned, if the old man was in a giving mood, why not accept it? It certainly would not ease the physical and emotional scars gashed by Stew's constant lecturing and scolding, but the gun would definitely come in handy.

"The rifle wasn't necessary, but I'll take it," Perry said, forcing a half-smile. "I'll continue to work in your fields, Pappy. My only request is that you give me ample freedom to live my life as a man."

"I'll not make any such promises. As long as you live under my roof, you'll abide by my directives. Happiness is fleeting and overrated, assuredly followed by misery. You must know that by now. You'll work like a dog, dawn to dusk."

Stew's mood seemed to turn dark.

"This farm's the best chance you got. Like nobody else, I'll tolerate your failures because even with your flaws, you're my farm's only hope. But, Perry, you must give up the rum. Alcohol almost killed me, and you're heading down the same path. If you can't live with that, you should hit the road now and save me the aggravation of digging your grave."

"I'm tethered here, like a canary's confined to a coal mine," Perry said. "I fear you'll never turn over the reins. I doubt this will ever be my farm. Try as I might, I can't do this much longer, Pappy. It's killing me from the inside out."

"I've been thinking about beef cattle," Stew threw out a lifeline. "Building the best bloodline in the state of Indiana. I'm not sure you're up to the task, but I'm willing to give it a shot."

"Well, Pappy, I know all the hay haulin' and shit scoopin' would fall on my shoulders. Does it really make a difference?"

Perry looked away from his father's stare and ran his eyes along the length of the rifle barrel. Even with gun in hand, inside, Perry had nothing left to give, including forgiveness.

As the growing season dragged on, it was endless and unpaid, as expected. The old man hardly lifted a finger. Stew's talk of bringing cattle to the farm was yet another lie. The broken promise sucked Perry deeper into a whirlwind of anger. If he had to work this hard, he wanted to do it for himself. He could not wait another thirty years to taste the sweet rewards of hard work. He felt doubly a slave, to his father and, increasingly, to his flask of rum.

The only bright spot that kept Perry in Salt Spring was pure-natured Violet LeDoux.

At best Violet was marginal but pleasing enough to satiate his desire for physical companionship. With coppery brunette hair and freckles dotting her cheeks like the evening stars, even by Salt Spring standards Violet still only a notch above average. Perry contemplated expressing his love, but something always seemed askew. From a more discerning angle, Violet was a bit horse-faced and cackly voiced, flaws that Perry had found easy to swallow. Violet was convenient.

Perry considered Violet his flickering beacon, but realized she could also be his breaking point. As Saturday night approached after a long day of field work, Perry lubricated his mind with a bottle of rum and sought out Violet's companionship.

He rustled the bushes outside Violet's bedroom window, and she quietly hurried to meet him. Perry was drunk and amorous, and Violet was intoxicated by dreams never to ensue.

"Oh, Perry, I've been praying for your visit this night," Violet whispered as the two walked hand-in-hand toward the barn, their usual spot for late-night romance.

Violet pressed her torso tight against Perry, and it lit his fuse of passion. She kissed him and enjoyed the familiar taste of rum on his lips. Perry did not mind in the least. Rum enhanced her appeal.

"Violet, I have been waiting all day to see you," Perry slurred. He pushed Violet into a pile of blossomed clover hay.

After an hour, the two bid silent farewells for the night.

Ample work in the cornfield awaited a hungover Perry as the morning sun broke over a nearby hill. He had been working in the field for two hours when he saw Violet walking toward him down the adjacent road. She ran to meet him.

"Did you mean what you said last night?" Violet asked. "That we should get out of this town and strike a path of our own?"

Violet's screeching voice added to his hungover irritation. Her arrival in the cornfield puzzled Perry. His agitation exploded. As sweat poured down Perry's forehead, he knew his true intent to leave, but staying here and farming for Stew might be preferable to having Violet as a partner, in travel or life.

"All I remember about last night was we had a pleasant time."

"A pleasant time? A pleasant time? Perry Adams, you talked about forever. I gave myself to you."

Violet threw up her arms in anger and turned her head in rejection.

"I'm sorry, Violet, I don't remember. If I said any of that, it was hayloft talk. This ain't gonna happen."

Violet's body shook. Her face melted in despair. Her dream shattered into a thousand shards. Violet turned abruptly and ran from the field, her chorus of squawking cries fading as she disappeared beyond a hill.

Perry wasn't sure what to make of the drama. With a slight dash of remorse, he digested it the best he could. If what she had said was true, Perry knew he would have little choice. Out of honor he would either need to marry Violet or get the hell out of town.

As Perry finished his workday, the scene with Violet continued to weigh on his mind, as did the decision he faced.

Entering the barn to put away his tools, he was met by Violet's brothers, Carl and Lance LeDoux.

Toad-ugly Carl grabbed Perry and knocked him to the ground with a broad-side body blow. Lance, the younger of the two, yanked Perry up by the arms and held him while Carl delivered kicks to the groin, fists to the face, and punches to the gut. Carl flashed the glowing blade of his knife in Perry's bloody face.

"Mess with our sister again, you pigeon-livered bastard, and you won't have another chance to exercise the tools of your manhood," Carl hissed. "Violet's devastated. If she tells us you've been prowling around like a barn cat in quest of a haystack mouse, Lance and I will return as the rabid dogs of your night-mares. You'd better pray she doesn't end up pregnant."

Perry realized the whole affair between himself and Violet, and now her brothers, stunk like rotting fish in a scrap heap. Everyone smelled it but nobody wanted to do anything about it until it grew to be unbearable. Perry realized it had become time to put some fresh soil atop the pile.

Overall, Perry's behavior took on the same rancid qualities among members of the Salt Spring community. Most folks had been inclined to brush it off as a young man blowing off steam. But over the next two-week period, starting with the incident with Violet's brothers, a series of mysterious calamities had become a pattern.

A rock had been hurled through a window. A split-rail fence had been kicked down, resulting in the loss of cattle. A barn had mysteriously caught fire.

Toward the end of the ruinous string of events, townsfolk whispered about the angry young son of Stewart Adams. Was he responsible? Other than the substantiated claim about his mistreatment of Violet, nothing else was really verified. The growing accusation, however, was that when Perry was drunk, he showed little regard for their sentiments or possessions. It was past time for the community to turn the stinking scrap heap. The town elders were asked to do something to encourage Perry to hit the road and to put safeguards in place to ensure he never came back.

Over the next few days, during extended periods of sobriety, Perry grew aware of his growing reputational crisis. He felt helpless. The desperation fortified his growing ambition to leave. Untamed as a wild stallion and gruff as a grizzly, Perry's bitterness approached that of his old man, the last person he wanted as a role model.

The conflict with the LeDoux brothers had been the last straw. It had added the last slosh of kerosene to Perry's blazing choice of hitting the road. His bruised face and sore ribs were the last ingredients in a rancid hobo stew. Perry made plans to rid himself of Violet, her brothers, his father, and all the other carping fools who lived in Salt Spring.

Where would he go, and how? A month earlier Perry had clipped an article from the local newspaper about untamed territories in the West. The article had captured his mind. He'd squirreled it away in the barn under a stack of old feed sacks. The morning after his run-in with the LeDoux boys, he pulled out the old clipping and read it aloud: "Without any doubt whatever, Kansas is destined to be acknowledged 'the garden spot of the world.' Her excellent and easily cultivated soil, delightful climate, and her position as the great center of the United States, will give to her an importance and secure for her a propriety of which her enterprising citizens may justly be proud."

The story had promoted Kansas Territory as "The Land of the Future," and now that sounded good to Perry—a place to farm for himself, to establish a family, to thrive. Worthy goals if he could get there alive.

Late that night by the glow of a kerosene lamp, Perry wandered the kitchen, gathering a few items, a pot, a pan, and a few utensils he considered essential for life on the run. He scavenged through a drawer where he had seen Stew hide a bag of coins. He grabbed the entire bag. So as not to wake up the old man, he carefully placed the items in a burlap bag and cinched it up. He snuffed the lamp and sneaked out the front door.

Perry limped to the barn, still sore from the earlier run-in with the LeDoux brothers.

The barn was Perry's haven. After carefully opening the door, Perry struck a match and lit a lantern. He removed a leather saddlebag hanging from the wall. Perry stashed the bag of coins and utensils into the bag. He jammed in a small satchel of beef jerky. With a length of hemp baling twine, he carefully tied up a bedroll and several hand tools for his journey.

He also gathered three prized possessions: his new rifle and a box of cartridges, a bag of seed corn left over from the previous year's planting, and a brass nautical spyglass that had belonged to a great-great-grandfather rumored to have been a pirate. As Perry gathered the items, he felt like a pirate too.

Scratched into the brass patina of the spyglass was the phrase, "Avast! Pay attention."

One thing Perry did not pack on that moonless Indiana night was his flask. He pulled it from his back pocket, took a final whiff of its remnants, looked at it with regretful ambivalence, and hurled it with a clank against the back wall of the barn.

Perry fastened a halter around the neck of his father's mule, Luke, and snuck him out of the barn. Perry loaded the mule's back and crept from the barnyard with no crumb of remorse for mule-napping or thievery. He came by it naturally. The great-great-grandson of a pirate stealing from the great-grandson of a pirate . . . It was pure symmetry.

Perry had raised Luke from a colt and considered himself the animal's better keeper. To signify his level of endearment, Perry called him Lukey. Perry looked over his shoulder a final time as he led Luke away from the farmstead where he had grown up, had said a last goodbye to his dying mother, and had gone to battle with his father. After that he did not look back.

Like a shadowy apparition, he exited the farm gate. His goal was to make twenty miles a day, sometimes more, sometimes less. Accounting timewise for hazards, and he was certain there would be plenty, was an inexact science.

Perry whispered in the mule's tall ears, "Lukey, this escape is the only tonic that's going to cure the predicament I face here in Salt Spring. The entire world's against me. But I'll show 'em all. I'll fight, scratch, and dig until I build a new home, harvest corn from my land, and sprout a family of my own. I just hope we can make it."

He was certain Luke understood every single word.

CHAPTER 2

Fall to Winter 1857

TREACHERY AFOOT

Perry took guarded steps as he led Luke those first days along the frontier trail. Sweat rolled down Perry's face, his arms twitched, and his stomach ached. He chalked up the vomiting and restlessness to the anxiety of his trek, unaware his afflictions were the stages of withdrawal from rum.

Like the future that lay before him, the trail was not always wide-damn open. Perry fought off suspicions the few souls they met along the way were outliers and miscreants. Still he gathered the gumption to smile, figuring them not too different from himself, or more appropriately the lad he left behind in Salt Spring. He moved his eyes side to side to ward off vulnerability. If varmints laid in wait, he would approach them with the attitude of a pirate. As time passed, his steps grew steady and strong as he attacked the path ahead.

Any peril could be a life-and-death matter, not child's play, nor youthful indiscretion. Solitude along the trail strengthened his resolve. During moments of calm, Perry thought about his past. He'd disrespected his father. He'd wronged

Violet. His weakness for demon rum made him unfaithful to himself. A higher level of self-awareness took hold.

After two weeks on the road, he stopped at a trading post in Illinois. Digging into his bag of coins, he bought another box of cartridges for his rifle and some feed corn to give Luke an extra boost for the remaining trail. He also splurged on some ground coffee for the pot he had stolen from Stew. He conserved the rest of his money for Kansas Territory.

Three days west of the trading post, Perry found a small clearing protected by boulders and trees. He gathered smaller stones and stacked them into a fire ring. He pounded stakes into the ground and rigged a lean-to shelter braced by the trees. After a restful night, Perry stoked the fire and boiled water from a nearby stream for coffee.

As he was about to pour a cup, a distant disturbance broke the morning air. Through his spyglass Perry spotted three men approaching. Were these ne'er-do-wells or merely travelers on a mission? He recalled the inscription on the spyglass—*Avast. Pay attention.*

Smoke from his campfire had betrayed his location. As they drew closer, Perry cupped his right ear to better hear their conversation.

"You approach the campfire from the front, and I will flank him. If there be spoils for gain, we shall quickly butcher the holder and be off to greater glory," the chilling words lifted by the morning fog.

As a pirate's great-great-grandson, Perry appreciated the bravado of anyone attempting frontier freebooting. But as the one about to be freebooted, possibly butchered, Perry took offense. Each hair on his forearms stood at attention. He would not become a victim of plunder and murder. He put away the spyglass and braced for conflict. From behind an oak, he shouted a warning.

"State your purpose on this trail." His tone startled the bushwhackers. Luke lowered his ears to the threat and let out a blood-curdling neigh.

The three men, shocked by the greeting, jerked their heads upward in unison as if attached by a single nerve. Their eyes shot toward the direction of the voice from their would-be victim. They looked young, even younger than Perry.

"Why, sir, we come but to share the warmth of an early morning fire, maybe a cup of coffee, and to forewarn of perils that lie ahead," one of the varmints shouted back.

Ahh, horse shit, thought Perry. He overheard their true intentions. These buzzards were not about to curtail his dreams.

"The only peril you should think about, sirs, is the lead poisoning from the barrel of my carbine that will afflict your asses," Perry replied.

The invaders quickened their march toward his position. Perry shouldered his Burnside rifle and drew a bead. A shot rang out and winged one of the lads in the arm. Recognizing the peril the young men scattered like a nursery of flushed raccoons.

Perry shouted after them. "Don't come back again. I'd take no pleasure in the death of the wicked, but I will assuredly send you to plunder the pits of hell."

Perry turned to calm his mule, who continued to jump about like an overgrown field mouse. He reached out his hand and stroked the mule's jaw.

"It's OK, boy. They won't be back. All cowardly plans seem favorable until someone adds a dose of adversity."

For days after that incident, Perry kept his senses sharp and his eyes peeled. While growing in confidence after his run-in with the rascals, every few miles, he paused and retrieved his spyglass to scan the horizon. He stopped and paid attention. While the youthful rascals did not return, traversing this path toward his promised land continued to carry a measure of jeopardy.

The spyglass already paid its first dividend on the trail. This was not the first time the instrument had come to the aid of an Adams. The spyglass had saved his great-great-grandfather Matthew Adams. It was rumored, but never clearly documented, Matthew had sailed the seas around the West Indies and the young British North American colonies as a first mate to a mysterious man by the alias of Edward Thatch, better known as Blackbeard.

Perry knew the story well. While the only ears to hear it were his own and Luke's, Perry spun the yarn under the shade of a maple tree.

"Blackbeard was a bad guy. His ship, the *Queen Anne's Revenge*, was armed with forty cannons of various sizes. He expected all aspects of running the ship to function in only one way—his. Anyone challenging that authority was forced to make a final leap from the short end of a long plank."

Luke's ears perked up.

"Blackbeard was a generous fella when divvying up the spoils of plunder. The stakes were high but so were the rewards. He even allowed crew members to drop off their shares with family members during visits to port. But he demanded that crewmates return to the ship. Those not doing so placed themselves and their families in danger. Once a crew member, you couldn't just leave. Once you were in; you were in for life. If not, you were hunted down like a stag in the fall."

Luke shook his head from side to side as if he understood.

"My great-great-grandad decided to leave. I guess that's where I come by my rambling ways. Anyway, the pirate ships blocked the port of Charleston with cannons blasting. They captured two civilian ships and the innocents aboard them. Now most of the pirate crews were ill, which was not surprising, given their indulgent lifestyle. They probably drank a lot of rum. So, the ransom Blackbeard wanted to release the innocents was a chest of medicine. Can you believe that, Lukey? They waited a full week, but the medicine was delivered. There were a few incidents, but none of the innocents were killed. They were freed, mostly unharmed, but stripped completely naked." Perry chuckled.

Luke let out a snort.

"Here's the best part, Lukey. Grandad Matthew had witnessed enough. He broke the rule and abandoned ship. He was willing to take a risk, just like us. He made a break for it while the fleet was anchored about ten miles from Charleston. He only had himself to worry about and he was willing to risk it all."

"During a foggy, full-moon night, Grandad quit, but before he left, he loaded up a sack full of pirate treasure. He flung that sack over his shoulder and shuffled along the deck so the sack wouldn't jingle. Kinda like what I did to Stew, God forgive. He made his way to a dinghy, lowered it into the water, shimmied down the rope, and off he went. He was careful not to splash until he was a suitable distance from the ship. He set the treasure bag aside, plopped the oars into the water, and rowed with furious strokes toward land and a new life. They say Matthew belted out an English sea shanty he learned aboard *Queen Anne's Revenge* to keep the cadence of his rowing steady and strong."

By this time Luke had lost interest until Perry broke out in song.

"Now rid' the waves, my fair-faissd lad,
And ne'er a day will yau be sad.
So haul the sail till the day yau die.
Yaur saul 'twill float' to heaven nigh."

"My family said Grandad Matthew sang that song while working on his farm in Indiana. Our whole family knows it by heart. Matthew made it to land early one morning, and he hid under a fishing pier. He feared he would be a wanted man, and he didn't want to face a noose any more than he wanted to walk Blackbeard's plank, so he was really careful. He looked across the shore with this very spyglass. There were dogs barking and roosters crowing but no people. It was his lucky day. He flung the loot bag over his shoulder. It was warm, so he rolled up his shirtsleeves. Bad idea, because on his arm was the tattoo of a chesty mermaid in full frolic. He pulled down his sleeves. After the stores opened, he got a haircut and bath at the barbershop. He bought some farmer clothes, a buckboard wagon, and a team of horses."

Luke had lost interest yet again, but Perry rolled on.

"Grandad knew Blackbeard would be on his trail, so he quickly loaded up on provisions at the general store and blazed a trail north and northwest toward the Carolina low country and the rugged western territories. Blackbeard's men never found him, and that's why I am here today. So, you see, Lukey, it's in my blood. Wanderlust and adventure, what could possibly go wrong? At least we don't have a band of pirates chasing us, but I have Grandad's spyglass just in case."

Luke snorted and got to his feet. It was time to move on.

Perry was proud of his great-great-grandfather's swashbuckling days. Perry's aim was the same—to become a new man. It was an inherited trait. "Avast! Pay attention" was the mantra that led the way.

While Perry kept the spyglass always at the ready, in spite of his nagging angst, the trail offered no more calamities carried by human rogues. The trail running across Illinois and into St. Louis was not without adversity from the natural elements.

Perry walked for weeks, across the sleeping prairies of late autumn, through frost-crystal swamps, across cold and unforgiving tributaries. Fatigue weighed on him like a millstone. Hunger bit into his innards. He reached inside the saddlebag for a strip of jerky, but it was all gone. He was relegated to living off the fat of the land. Perry ate what he hunted, fished, or foraged, whether furry, feathered, or slimy. But all the time, Perry was sure to scout out a patch of grass for Luke.

For several nights Perry heard the howls of coyotes cutting through the prairie breeze. Luke flared his ears.

"Don't worry, Lukey. Those rascals are chickenshits, but we need to be ready for anything."

The coyotes' howls signaled they had sniffed out Perry and Luke as invaders. If hungry enough and sufficient in number, the coyotes could do more than howl.

Luke jumped about jittery. But with each howl, his legs stiffened, and his tail twitched. He snorted through his nostrils and lowered his ears. He bellowed a blood-curdling warning. It was a throaty bawl, lower-pitched than a horse. The sound signaled Luke and Perry's whereabouts to the pack. Perry kept the campfire blazing in hopes of keeping the scavengers at bay.

Perry ran his hand along the length of Luke's head, from the base of his ear down to the end of its chin. It pacified the animal. It was the least a friend could do. Perry repeated the stroke time and time again. Ear to chin. Ear to chin. Ear to chin, all along the length of Luke's jawbone.

Perry sang to further calm Luke. It was a paraphrased rendition of the chorus from Stephen Foster's "Old Folks at Home" with an intentional brogue accent. "The whole wide world 'tis sad and dreary, everywhere I roam. Oh, Lukey, how me heart grows weary, far from dem old folks at home."

While Perry certainly did not miss home or the old folks there, the ditty, along with the calming rub down the length of the mule's jawbone, did the trick. Luke closed his eyes.

Life along the trail had a similar effect on Perry. With each passing day, he laced his boots a bit tighter. He paid more attention to the smaller details, like finding just the right type of firewood for the night. He thought about things that he had never considered before, like loading the pack on Luke's back with softer items against the animal's hide. Each action owned intent. No longer was he the carefree rabble-rouser of Salt Spring. Extending his hand to arm's length, the shakes were gone. Kill-devil rum was a former temptress. The stubble of a reddish-blond beard was the only other sign Perry was making peace with himself.

"Relax, Lukey," Perry said in the glow of the campfire, loaded rifle at his side. "Things will be better in the morning."

Sleep overcame the trail mates, and the fire's flames sank into a bright amber glow. While the howls had vanished, a sudden rustling among nearby stands of prairie grass startled Perry. A chorus of growls cut the air. Along the periphery of the campfire's glow, several sets of glowing eyes darted to and fro. Perry grabbed his gun as three animals dashed in for their expected kill. Perry saw right away that these were not the coyotes they had heard all evening. These attackers were gray wolves.

Luke jumped to his hooves and let out a siren bellow. Two of the wolves sank their fangs into Luke's haunches. He kicked at the animals and connected. One flew into the fire's coals before darting into the darkness. Luke launched the other like a cannonball beyond the light of the embers. Both reported with wild howls of agony.

Perry put his finger on the trigger, but before he could get off a shot, another wolf lunged at his upper leg and gashed a rip in his dungarees. Perry whirled toward the aggressor and fired a fatal shot into the animal's chest as it made a fatal leap toward him.

Luke swaggered frantically as pain from the two bites set in. He crouched in a defensive posture within the glow of the campfire during the six seconds it took Perry to eject and load a new cartridge. The wolves retreated to the edge of the campfire's glow. Perry shot again, hitting another member of the pack in the head. He reloaded, and as the remaining pack members circled in retreat, Perry sent a final volley in the dark direction of their tails.

The wolves left, their cries of defeat diminishing in the distance. Perry reloaded the gun before stoking the fire. In the fire's light, he ran his hand over Luke's wounds. One barely left a mark, but the other had ripped into the meat under his hide. Perry tore the sleeve from his shirt and applied it to the wound with pressure to staunch the bleeding.

The cloth stuck to the wound, and Perry turned his focus to returning Luke to the calmest state possible after the attack. Ripping the cloth reminded Perry of one item he forgot to pack for the trail—his mother's white lace-trimmed bonnet. How could he have been so careless? He peered toward heaven, and a calming reassurance fell over him. Chin up, chest out . . . He knew Mary Katherine was along for the adventure.

Perry chucked more wood to rekindle the campfire's blaze and propped his head against Luke's shoulder. But the remainder of the night was restless. Every sound raised alarm. Perry worried about whether Luke could handle the trail ahead. He was unable to replenish any energy for the next day's trek.

CHAPTER 3

Winter 1857

PERSISTENT PERIL

After a fitful sleep, Perry's eyes jolted open, realizing the wolves that attacked Luke might have carried rabies. By morning it was Luke who rested his head against Perry's shoulder. Perry gently nudged the animal awake. Luke stood, and Perry poured a canteen of water over the cloth that covered Luke's wound. He gently peeled off the cloth. It did not bleed, and Perry gently inspected the area where fangs had ripped Luke's hide.

For the next week, the wound, while healing, was an ongoing concern, but Luke was walking without impairment. It was make-or-break time. Perry continued to wake in the middle of the night at the slightest sound. Luke's condition was only one reason for Perry's concern.

Perry's stomach growled with a pang of hunger. He dug his hand into the bag of seed corn but immediately had second thoughts. First the move might lead to an intense case of the bloody flux. Second it would also severely curtail the seed supply with which he would sow a brighter future. He considered the adage: To prosper, one must not eat their seed corn.

When he hit St. Louis, Perry spent a few coins on food and bulk provisions for the trail—some cornmeal, lard, and salt. At the very least, a survival diet of corn dodgers would sustain him. He saved the bulk of his coins for his final destination, where he would purchase a plow and other tools to break the soil and lay down a seed bed.

Perry followed the Missouri River west of St. Louis. About twenty miles west, he walked through a plantation in an area called Gumbo Flats. He saw a white man supervising slaves who were bringing in a late fall harvest from fields in the river valley that appeared to be composed mostly of sand.

"Good day, sir," Perry shouted across the field. "Looks like you've had some flooding."

"Yes, we have. The river's a beast along these flats. It can wash away the topsoil and leave nothing but sand," the man replied. "We're lucky to have a crop at all this year."

"I'm just passin' through. Hope to make it to the territory and set up a farm there."

"Be careful. The path west is uncivilized, and truth be told, it's not too safe around these parts either. An older farmer neighbor of mine went missing some weeks back, and they still haven't found him."

"Sounds tragic."

"He was a mean sumbitch, especially when he was drunk. Some think he might have wandered off in a stupor and fallen into the river. Others think his slaves might have killed him. A white man can't be too careful these days. His son's running the place now. He's one of those enlightened types. The first thing he did was grant all his daddy's slaves their freedom. There was one named Moses who I would have gladly bought from him. He was a strong slave and smart too, but he also had the spirit of a dove. But the son gave Moses his freedom, and Moses and his son headed west chasing the same cockamamie dream you're houndin'. None of us could believe it. He just let all of 'em go. Now he actually pays a number of the former slaves to work for him. He pays them! What has our world become?"

"Well, I'll be on the lookout for this Moses and his son when I get to Kansas, but I'm not much more than a slave myself."

"Ahh, horseshit, my friend. You're white, and you got a mule. Even in this topsy-turvy world, what else does a man need, other than blessings for the road ahead? And I extend that blessing to you."

As Perry departed the sandy field, he pitied the captives. Their conditions were worse than even his while working for Stew back in Indiana. Perry scooped up a handful of the sandy river soil and let it fall between his fingers. It blew in the wind. How, we wondered, could crops even grow here?

"This won't do," he told Luke. "We're gonna find us some deep rich soil, and I certainly will not hold any man to do work I can do myself."

The next week passed like a month. By the time he reached central Missouri, winter laid its frosty hands across the hills and valleys along the river. Perry was tired, but he pressed on. He knew it would be a long, barren winter, but he wanted to find a location that offered the promise that would come with spring.

"Every day is a blessing." Perry kept repeating the mantra aloud to maintain inner courage and strength to move forward.

After two more weeks, Perry reached a flourishing frontier town named Roubideaux, the last stop before crossing the river into Kansas territory. Again he invested only a few of his coins in necessities. Perry, as stubborn as a mule himself, was determined to save his fortune to finance the planting of corn the following spring, and Luke would be there to help him.

At a store called Mixon's Trading Post, Perry slid a few Flying Eagle pennies across the counter to a man named Marcus for a copy of the local newspaper. Above the few other basic survival supplies, it was his only splurge.

Perry walked out the door and loaded the few basic items onto Luke's back. He folded the newspaper and tucked it into his saddlebag. As an educated man, reading was Perry's connection to current events and political thought. Reading was the only good life habit he'd picked up in Salt Spring. Now that he was on the doorstep of the fabled western territory of Kansas, he once again read the item he had clipped from the *Salt Spring Dispatch*. He would welcome any and all additional information he could get his hands on.

Kansas Territory lay just across the rolling river. Perry was in a hurry, but he stopped for a quick chat with a couple locals outside the Trading Post.

"Greetings, gentlemen. Do you know anything about the land that lies beyond the river?"

A bespeckled man spoke up. "It's hilly over there, but it's good soil, and it's up for grabs, that is, if you are content with bein' a squatter. Right now it's all government land, and it's not for sale."

That assurance was all Perry needed to hear. He could make a go of it as a squatter. It was the endorsement for which he was hoping. He firmly planted in his mind the idea that Kansas Territory would be the destination of his corn seeds. He still did not know the exact location any more than the day he left Indiana, but it was about time to find out. He led Luke down a path toward the riverbank.

Reaching the wide and rolling river, Perry grabbed Luke's halter and pulled him aboard a vessel that barely qualified under the definition of "ferry." It was little more than a log raft tied together by rope with a primitive steam engine hammered to the plank deck. He feared the craft might fly apart in the Muddy Missouri's swirling backwaters before they could set foot or hoof on the new land.

The river crossing was much like their trek thus far. Set a wide target for the destination. Jump on. Ride it out. Hope for the best.

"Hang on, Lukey. It's going to be a bumpy ride."

The river set a border between the state and the territory as well as a buffer between pro-slavery Missourians and territorial settlers as strident in their ethical opposition. Though Missouri was a Union state, tensions ran high. Settlers to Kansas Territory from both camps flooded across the border in hopes of influencing the slavery status of the fateful land.

The inclinations of an Indiana Free Soiler branded Perry's soul, but he did not wear the label on his sleeve. More pragmatic than partisan, he read about pro-slavery guerillas sacking the Kansas town of Lawrence and slaughtering innocents the year before. Later that same year, newspapers across the nation sensationalized the revenge doled out for that butchery by abolitionist John Brown, a sunken-eyed, free-state zealot, who assisted in killing five innocent men during an incident known as the Pottawatomie Massacre.

Some folks in these parts sanctified Brown as a modern-day Moses, with the Ten Commandments in one hand and a rifle in the other. While Perry shared Brown's biblical belief in an "eye for eye and tooth for tooth," he was more respectful than Brown of the commandment stating, "Thou shalt not kill."

Unfolding his copy of the *Roubideaux Gazette*, Perry read tales of men, women, and even children prosecuted at the end of a rifle barrel due only to their suspected thoughts. His newspaper clipping from Salt Spring said nothing about this turbulent environment. Perry decided it was best to disconnect from the opposing regional doctrines of free vs. slave. All he wanted to do was farm.

But by the time he stepped foot in Kansas Territory, hatred between pro- and anti-slavery partisans set the table for conflict that split the region at the seams. Kansas was bleeding, and whether he knew it or not, the rising border tension would influence each of Perry's life decisions moving forward.

After Perry and Luke survived their harrowing river crossing into Kansas Territory, they continued their journey for twenty more miles into the periphery of the wild, perilous, and tumultuous region.

Nearly a month and a half after leaving Salt Spring, Perry's eyes greeted a glowing horizon that included a peculiar rising of distant hills. Glacially deposited and windblown loess river bluffs hugged the Kansas side of the river as it meandered east and north before running due south to Roubideaux.

Perry retrieved his spyglass and raised it to his eye. He peered at the bluffs from three miles away.

"Look at those hills, Lukey. They roll into each other like a rumpled quilt on a bed of oat straw."

Perry's prairie-trained vision could not break focus. The closer he got, the faster his heart beat.

Perry approached the base of the first bluff. He wanted proof this place might hold the prime matter of his future life. Was this beauty transient, as was the case with dear, fair-skinned Violet LeDoux, or was it enduring? Not a drop of liquor had touched his lips since the day he'd left Indiana, so unlike his dealings with Violet, his judgement was uncompromised.

Perry dispatched his shovel and dug a test hole into the dormant grass to measure the intensity of the topsoil. The frost had not yet sunk its claws into the soil. He dug five holes. In each one the topsoil ran more than three feet deep. At the last spot, Perry dug his fingers into the earth and grabbed a handful of rich, dark soil. He squeezed it between thumb and forefinger to measure the texture. The resulting ribbon that feathered out from his thumb showed a perfect combination of soil mixed with decaying stems, leaves, and crawly things. The consistency reminded him of bread dough mixed with oatmeal. It was a gritty, lightweight, porous soil, not too clay-like or too sandy.

With ample proof in hand, Perry shouted in delight as if he had struck gold. "Eureka!"

Seeing the excitement, Luke ran to Perry and nudged his snout into Perry's ribs, as if to signal approval.

Perhaps to summon good fortune, Perry rubbed Luke's forehead. All the signs were positive. Not only was the soil deep, but it was rich in structure to retain moisture and feed his crop. Such prospect. Such fertility. Such fortune. Perry stopped digging.

No longer a prairie man, after nearly a month and a half of travel from Salt Spring, Perry left his Hoosier days behind in distance and memory. Amid the rolling bluffs of the Missouri River, Perry and Luke stopped walking.

"Every day's a blessing, Lukey. This is the end of our trail."

The words were as foretelling as the hills would be foreboding.

Perry officially wore the label of squatter, though a precipitous one. He was eager to assert his rights as such. Land, with rich, windblown glacial soil, was here for the taking.

While other had pioneers ventured further into this rugged territory and settled in regions flatter and sufficiently cleared by nature, there were no signs of humans in these hills for miles and miles. As Perry scanned the scenic vista, he thought his eyes were likely the first of European lineage to do so. This unsurveyed land, though owned by the government, was his to tend as long as he maintained a productive presence. While he had no formal rights beyond those of a squatter, he would plant the seeds Luke had hauled all the way from Indiana. Here Perry would invest his labor on his own behalf, rather than out of familial obligation. Here, we would sow the kernels and harvest corn along the steep hillside slopes and flatter meadows of this rolling paradise.

Concluding the long journey in the icy heart of winter, Perry chose a clearing uphill from a clear-running creek. He had no materials with which to build a shelter, so Perry improvised. He grabbed his shovel and started to dig into the hillside. Shovel after shovel, his arms ached as he excavated a cave-like hole. He axed and sawed through smaller hardwood trees. He sank some upright, like adjacent fence posts, to provide an entrance structure. He used smaller branches to bridge the posts. Upon those rafters, he placed his unfolded copy of the *Roubideaux Gazette*. Atop that, he scooped dirt, moss, and leaves to spackle the gaps between the paper and branches. As primitive as the shelter appeared, it would have to do.

On the verge of exhaustion, Perry scratched and dug a similar shelter for Luke. It resembled a rough, lean-to shed, fashioned from logs and the boughs of nearby scrub cedars. The dugout would shelter Luke as best as possible. It too would have to do.

The first night, with Luke tucked under the lean-to, Perry stared into the darkness from the void of his own shelter and pulled every stitch of fabric at his disposal tighter to conserve his body heat. His head rested on the sack of Indiana seed corn.

The next morning demanded additional action. Perry gathered rocks and built a campfire ring close to the opening. He dragged a week's worth of dry wood to the shelter, cut it into lengths and stacked it outside the entrance. Perry grabbed his shovel and dug deeper into the hillside. If one living being generated almost enough body heat to ward off the frigid Kansas night, two would even be better.

That night, after building a blazing fire close to the opening, Perry pulled Luke into his own shelter, and the two slept next to each other like they had on the wide-open Illinois prairie.

While that night was more bearable, each grew colder and longer, brutal to man and beast. Perry was determined to persevere and not allow the harsh elements to define the tenor of his life in this land of promise.

As weeks progressed, conditions for Perry and Luke deteriorated beyond desperate. Perry's back ached for a full week after he dug into the river bluff for the crude shelters. The sting of winter in the hardwood forest ate into his resolve. An issue ever greater than the cold was the fact that they had run out of food. Perry foraged across the hillsides. From the creek-side bank, he plucked cattail roots, which he sliced and boiled into a soup. He found several pine trees and harvested the nuts from their cones. Perry gathered acorns from a nearby oak. Once soaked and softened, they provided some gritty nutrition. Perry searched for grubs in rotting logs. None were found. Perry fired his rifle into treetop squirrel nests, hoping a furry rodent would fall. None did. The land refused to yield its fat.

Matters grew worse when the snow fell with a vengeance. Traces became inches. Inches became feet. Calories that could have been foraged were buried. There was no winter thaw. This was no place for a temperate flatlander.

Inside the shelter's darkness, Perry rested his head against the warmth of Luke's shoulder. Once fleshy and full, Perry now felt the animal's bones. Sleep continued to be elusive as the pangs of hunger spiked Perry's stomach.

The next morning, deep in the hibernating hardwood forest, Perry clung to reality as the fangs of winter bit into his ears and fingertips. There was no way to retrace the path that led to his current condition or Luke's. While his dream was within reach, would this be yet another failure? He thought about going back to Roubideaux but didn't want to relinquish this prime location to anyone who followed. He was also concerned about he and Luke surviving the trip.

Perry's thoughts turned to his mule, who was also starving and freezing. Perry dug through the snow, hoping to find patches of dormant grass for Luke. All he found was leaves, and they offered no relief for Luke from the stark starvation that raised ribs all along his sides. Luke whimpered in agony as the will to live slipped from his body.

The clutches of profound and hopeless suffering crushed both Perry and Luke. Perry could stand it no more nor stomach the sound of his friend wailing in misery.

In desperation Perry reached out and ran his hand along the length of Luke's jawbone, like so many nights before, from ear to chin. The stroking calmed Luke, but it was fleeting. The animal was being consumed from the inside out. Perry looked into Luke's eyes and hugged him around the neck, tears unrestrained.

Perry retrieved the Burnside Carbine from the dugout shelter and loaded one of his last cartridges.

"Lukey, you are the brother I never had." Perry was barely able to say the words aloud.

Perry did what he agonizingly had to do. A split second later, a blast rang out and the act was done.

Perry urgently skinned the mule, threw a rope around a tree limb. and hoisted the carcass safely out of reach of any scavengers. While the coldness of winter kept the meat from spoiling, mule meat was not exactly venison. These were days of desperation. In the last days of winter's reign, Perry resorted to sucking the last bits of nutrition from the strips of rawhide peeled from Luke's carcass with his axe.

Without Luke the nights were colder and riddled with guilt. Perry's decision to sacrifice Luke kept him alive that first winter but just barely. Perry kneeled to ask for forgiveness. As the snow melted, and with the mule meat gone, Perry foraged into the first weeks of spring.

Weeks later, as the frost vacated the soil and the morning sun shot through the budding branches of spring, Perry gathered Luke's bones for a proper burial befitting a cherished friend, not a mule. Perry dug a hole sufficiently deep to ward off scavengers and carefully sat the bones in the bottom, all except for one. As a remembrance, he kept Luke's jawbone—the one part of the animal that when stroked brought calm from the storm for both the mule and Perry.

To consecrate Luke's untimely demise, Perry looked out across the valley. In the ginger dawn of that spring morning, Perry held the mule's jawbone high above his head and asked for a blessing.

From his days as a church-going lad, Perry knew the power of the jawbone was biblical. Samson wielded the jawbone of an ass to slay 1,000 foes. If the Holy

Spirit extolled power upon one jawbone, why not two?

"Most holy God, grant to Lukey the eternal peace you impart to all your four-legged creatures. Let your spirit live through his jawbone. Create in this holler a fitting memorial to him through the eternal blessing you have so charitably created through richness of soil, beauty of landscape, and promise for bounty. Amen."

Perry christened the valley below him Jawbone Holler.

The name stuck.

CHAPTER 4

Backstory to 1856 to 1857

THE DELIVERY
OF MOSES

MOSES WATSON'S SHOULDERS WERE AS WIDE AS A BULL'S. Muscles rippled from his bones, but life's long road etched scars across his body and face. Despite his hard appearance, Moses carried a soft spirit. The first to offer a hand and the last to leave a job until it was done, his work ethic was as spotless as a prize rooster before the county fair.

Moses perfected the ability to coax a plant, whether corn, hemp, or hay, to prosper in the sandy but fertile bottomland and he was just as skilled at managing the breeding and care of farm animals. He worked a team of horses pulling a plow, as well as managing the finer art of animal husbandry, but he was as gentle with the beasts of burden as he was with livestock kept for the farm's supply of meat, milk, and eggs.

From cradle to grave, Moses's fate was tied to this land with which he shared a common definition. He was one of River View Grove's valuable capital assets. Moses Watson was a slave.

After the land, Moses was the most treasured property of Bert Manchester.

Moses's qualities and capabilities returned value to River View Grove, which hugged the Missouri River in Gumbo Flats west of Saint Louis. He carried the Watson last name of his father, who took the name of a previous master prior to being sold to Manchester. River View was Moses's birth spot and he thought, his final resting place.

Moses had no expectations about leaving the farm. Attempting to do so presented a clear hazard. As a slave master, Manchester was a harsh man. He was keen to the slave law and the teeth it contained for enforcement. The penalties for runaways were stiff. Manchester's son John was an attorney in Saint Louis, and the old man boasted he would pursue justice to the end if required to retrieve his rightful property.

Manchester relished that Moses and all the other members of his slave stable would judge their haggard lives at River View highly preferable to the physical perils of being on the lam and the probabilities of being beaten or lynched as runaways.

Manchester was anchored to a traditional plantation way of thinking. He was quick to strike with his whip, regardless of whether the living target of his anger was breeding stock with four legs or two. They were all animals in his eyes.

Manchester treated the slave women with brutality, especially when he saw one who sparked his lust. He never knew their names and treated them all with the same disregard.

On one particular night, Manchester summoned one of the more petite women to the big house.

Immediately, he grabbed her by the arm and led her to the bedroom. He tied her down with rope, and to heighten the thrill he got from his victim's fear, he slowly drew out a knife and ran it sideways down the length of her leg. The message was obvious.

"Do exactly as I say, or you'll feel the cutting edge."

On several occasions, when the women were noncompliant and chose to resist, Manchester had resorted to the knife's edge to convince his concubines. More than harm it was the fear factor that drove his satisfaction.

The unfortunate recipient of Manchester's lust always bore bruises and rope burns, sometimes cuts, the following day. On many nights, shrieks of pain from female voices were carried by the night air, concealed from no one, from the big house to the slave quarters. There were no secrets about Manchester's cruel ways, and as the master of River View Grove he never tried to cloak them.

While Moses and the other men deeply hated Manchester for his actions, they never uttered a single objection to his transgressions. They knew better.

Manchester bragged he made a wise business decision to keep Moses, rather than sell him down the road when he hit the age of highest value. Moses grew into the most skilled and sturdy member of Manchester's slave stable.

"Boy, you're making me money every damn year," Manchester said. "I only wish I owned a full stable of bucks just like you."

Manchester demanded that Moses select a mate from the stable of ten women slaves. The directive was not out of appreciation. Manchester knew what Moses could not hide; he carried the proper physical and character traits to increase and enhance the slave crew from within the farm itself.

Moses did not expect such attention from Manchester. He always kept his head down and did his work to not draw any kind of attention from the dastardly master, good or bad.

"Yessir, Master Bert," was Moses's answer for every directive. "I'll do you right proud, Master Bert."

Moses selected a pleasing but shy slave woman named Sally to be his partner.

"Miss Sally, Master Bert has ordered me to select a suitable mate," Moses said. "If you are willing to entertain such an arrangement, I shall choose you. But should you have any misgivings, I will turn my attention elsewhere."

Sally was slender with delicate features. Her deep-brown eyes had been on Moses for as long as she could remember as he worked the fields and tended livestock with care and compassion. Sally was quick to accept the proposition, and it presented the positive dividend of keeping her out of Manchester's painful clutches and nights in his big house.

"I'll gladly become your mate and bear your children," Sally said.

Though their match and duties were bound to old man Manchester, this pairing became more than that for both. Slaves could not marry, but Moses considered Sally his mate for life. Together, and with the Manchester slaves gathered 'round in the candlelight of night, Moses and Salley promised their love. Together they jumped over a ceremonial broom the other slaves placed in their path. It was a symbolic rite originating in their ancestral West Africa to ward off evil in their lives together.

At first Manchester was jealous Moses selected one of his favorites. He leered at the couple as Sally routinely greeted Moses with hugs at the end of the workday. The old man resented Moses for making the choice and regretted he simply did not assign Moses a more homely and sturdier mate. Manchester withheld his own advances on Sally to keep his male slave content, but a furor built inside him.

Over the years Sally and Moses increased Manchester's slave stable by three sons, each carrying the potential to be as sturdy and conscientious as their father.

"You're as prolific as our prize bull," Manchester said. "But just remember, boy, you aren't the first bull to visit that pasture, and what a fine pasture it was."

The knowledge that Manchester had forcibly raped Sally for his own sick pleasure ate at Moses's soul. He said not a word.

Manchester's demeanor was gruesome and backed by his penchant to deliver a lashing and his harsh treatment of every living, breathing thing on the farm. Through force he always maintained the upper hand. But nature had its own way of leveling the field.

Weeks of rain upriver spawned a summer flood that widened the river's flow from bluff to bluff. On the first day, Manchester stood on his porch as his life washed away. The flood drowned the summer crops and claimed most of the farm's animals, except for two cows and one strong workhorse. The flood buried the most productive crop acres under a deep blanket of barren river sand. Manchester's barns and slave quarters were all washed away. The big house was reduced to rubble, but its foundation remained standing.

Manchester rounded up and chained his investment in human capital and rode out the flood for two full weeks in canvas tents erected in the forested high ground overlooking the flats. The financial impact on River View was insurmountable, and it teetered on the edge of insolvency. Manchester determined his only choice was to liquidate a good share of his assets, not his land, but his slave holdings. He drank from a jug of whiskey the day he delivered the news to Moses.

"Boy, I have come to the realization I must take drastic action," Manchester slurred drunkenly. "This will involve my slaves you think of as family. As much as I hate the act of shipping your woman mate for the preservation of my own memory, it will be done."

That was the darkest day of Moses's life.

"Master Bert, you don't need to do this." Moses blanketed his words in a submissive tone. "We can rebuild. I'll rip the bottomland to bring the topsoil back. I don't want to see you give up on your lifetime of hard work."

Moses had overstepped his bounds.

"Boy, damn your hide. I have made my choice. It would take years to reclaim the fields. I don't have years to wait. My decision's final," Manchester said, taking in a deep chug of the whiskey.

"Master Bert, there's another way. I'll save the farm for you."

"When I say something's final, I mean it. How dare you question me? The fact that you think of your offspring as a family is hideous enough. You are all my property. Your disrespect has earned you forty lashes."

"But, Master Bert, my wife and my boys are all I have. My sons are mere teenagers. We can make a go of it here, sir, with hard work and a measure of faith."

"She is not your wife, and you do not hold your boys, I do," Manchester shouted, taking another swig from the whiskey jug. "I warned you to never again address me in such a subordinate tone. Remove your shirt. Embrace the walnut tree."

Moses knew exactly what to do, and he did it as he was told. He placed his arms around the tree's trunk and prepared for the promised retribution. Manchester corked the jug and dropped it to the ground as he furiously drew forth his bullwhip.

Each of the lashes from Manchester's whip cut deeper into the skin on Moses's back. After a full forty lashings, Moses fell to his knees in pain, a stream of blood rolling from his back and down his sides.

"Get up, boy. You deserve twenty more. This time I want you to count them out loud for me. After that you will recite an oath that you will never again rebuke your master."

After the additional lashings, Moses's back was as raw as beefsteak, but he stoically hugged the tree to not give old man Manchester any sadistic satisfaction for his cruelty. Manchester picked up the whiskey jug, uncorked it, and poured a stream of the vicious liquid across Moses's shoulders and back. The burn was deep and unbearable. The pain cut Moses to the bone. On the edge of consciousness, Moses barely construed his master's next words.

"There's high demand for field hands in Tennessee. I'll have the woman and the two youngest bucks transported to the Memphis auction tomorrow. As for you and the oldest, you'll work in tandem, dawn to dusk, to reclaim my topsoil from the river's ruin. You better hope your efforts bear fruit, or your oldest son will be the next to go."

Grueling work did not worry Moses in the least, but the devastation of his family being sold and dispersed to parts unknown was more than he could accept. While Sally was not his wife in the eyes of the law, she was the woman with whom he jumped the broom. It was a pledge for life, cut short by this cruel action of Master Bert. He vowed to break any law to get her back. This act overshadowed all the other hateful things the old man did over the years. Moses smoldered with sorrow, but hatred quickly took ablaze.

Manchester's attorney son John, who arrived from Saint Louis to survey the flood damage, witnessed the entire merciless episode. A bit younger than Moses, John was in his late forties. He saw his father's deterioration over the years. John detested the hard-hearted man his father became after the woman of the house, his mother, died during a cholera outbreak years before. He pitied Moses and grew to despise the old man.

Moses and John had practically been raised as brothers under Mrs. Naomi Manchester's doting and watchful eyes. Prior to her marriage, Mrs. Manchester was a schoolteacher. Her commitment to sharing Christianity led her to the unacceptable societal transgression of teaching Moses to read alongside John.

Due to this intense education, Moses was articulate, an inappropriate trait for a common field slave. But Moses never exercised his superior vocabulary among those he did not know or could not trust. Around most folks, white and black, he played dumb. Old man Manchester pretended he didn't know. He ignored the interaction encouraged by his wife. Naomi ruled the roost, and the farm was her inheritance, not his. But whatever goodwill that might have remained between the elder Manchester and Moses had been stomped out long ago, by actions such as sixty flesh-ripping cracks of the bullwhip.

During Moses's period of recovery from the lashing, John opted for an extended stay in the tent overlooking the flooded site of the big house.

"A few shelves are still standing in the foundation. I know there's medicine along the wall. I will fetch some salve and other treatments and bring them to you."

Moses was appreciative, yet silent to the younger Manchester. Moses always considered John much different than the old man. John possessed a scale of good and evil, both sensible and sure. Neither did it hurt that during their younger years John had always treated Moses as his equal or at least near to it. Moses trusted John. In those earlier days, Moses called John, Mister John-Man. John referred to Moses as Watty, a child-like shortcut for Watson, and he still did.

Moses's remaining son Gabriel, the eldest, felt a similar connection to Mister John through stories shared by his father. At night, Moses taught his sons to read.

At seventeen years of age, Gabriel was still a boy in years, but physically he was a man-child. Moses taught him all the slave codes of the day.

"Never rebuke your master even if he strikes you, never look a white lady directly in the eyes, never let a white man know you can read, and never use big words," Moses told him. "But there are times when all men must be at peace with themselves."

In hushed tones, beneath the shroud of the moonlit night, Moses told Gabe repeatedly about the concept of "finding one's maroon." Word had spread throughout the states that communities of runaway slaves had established maroon communities far away from the masters who had chained them, where they could live and die as free men.

"Let me tell you about maroons, my child," he would say. "Maroons are established by men like us, but these men found their road to freedom. They carved out their own havens, hidden in the folds of the land, far from the watchful eyes of the masters. These men haven't just run away; they have woven their dreams of independence. Among the winding rivers and forested hills of the new territories, through the stars of difficulty, these men have built their own maroons. Never ever give up the dream of finding your maroon, Gabe."

The desire to find maroon ran deep in Moses' blood, but the circumstance he faced made such a dream seem beyond the horizon.

"I will never give up on the dream," Moses told Gabe. "But if I had it to do all over again, I would have taken all of you and fled years ago. That would have been my maroon. I just never believed Mr. Manchester would sell our family down the road. Even if that time never comes for me, I pray for you my son that you will find the peace and contentment of maroon."

The thought soaked deeply into Gabe's being. In the dream of finding maroon and other wisdom shared by his father, Gabe was obedient to the call, but on occasion he spoke words better left unexpressed.

Gabe's heart broke the day his mother and brothers were carted off to never be seen again. It was a deep pain inside his chest, unlike anything he ever felt.

"I'll find a way to get even, even if I'm lynched for it," he told Moses. "Whether or not I find my maroon, I prefer facing a storm head-on, papa. If you try to run, it catches you anyway."

"This evil act is not one we can remedy by taking physical action of our own," Moses replied. "If there's any maroon connected to this moment, Mister John will provide it."

Several days after the old man shipped the three members of the Watson family to Memphis, Moses seized an opportunity to petition the younger Manchester for help.

"I feel I have no recourse against your father's assault on my family, but I do hope you'll be an advocate for the best situation possible," Moses told Mister John.

"Watty, I'm certain the old man has become unhinged. I could not stop his shipment of Sally and your sons to Memphis. Being a man of considerable means,

I even offered to buy them so I could set them free. He scoffed at the idea. Said something about standing up for principle. Now, deep inside, I know their whereabouts will be untraceable in the Deep South, and for that, I'm most miserable.

"The status you and Gabe face here is also on shaky ground after the Supreme Court ruled in the Dred Scott case. Basically, they said you aren't citizens of our nation due to your African descent, and here in Missouri that is doubly true. It was a clear instance of licking the boots of slave owners. But I do think there is hope and I'm going to help you leave this place and this wretched old man."

"Mister John-Man, I couldn't consider such a notion. This is my life, and whatever meaning is left to it, I'll be gratified, as will Gabe, to live it out here at River View."

"I'll hear nothing of the sort. A good many of your fellow slaves who have previously worked in a free territory have filed freedom suits down at the local courthouse. Some have even won. Since you have worked here all your life, I don't think you'd qualify, but I have means at my disposal in my law office for drafting freedom papers that will pass for authentic. The documents will serve as tickets for you and Gabe for a better life beyond River View. Even though the Supreme Court has muddled the entire issue of allowing territorial settlers to decide the fate of slavery through popular sovereignty, I firmly believe Kansas Territory is your best bet. Free-soilers are flooding into that frontier land, and I think there's a good chance for freedom."

"Your father will hunt us down and have us lynched before we get there."

"He's my father only by blood, but not by allegiance. I remember as a young man, after Mom passed, he grew angrier by the day. I remember going with him to the fancy bank down at the stockyards, walnut molding, marble floors and even indoor plumbing. We took coffee at the little café inside the bank and dad excused himself. I know he wanted to check out the extravagant bathroom fixtures, but when he came out, the door behind him swung closed. On it was a big sign that said 'GENTLEMEN.' I remember being angry when he went in there. He had no right. He was a man, but he was never gentle."

John continued, "From that day until now, I've witnessed his cruelty, even against my mother though she scared the living daylights out of him. As a grown man, the backside of his hand has crossed my face. While teetering, my respect for him as my father has never allowed me to raise a hand, but I'll make sure he does nothing to harm you further. I have a case of evidence to support beyond doubt that his callousness to men of all races is due to the frailty of his mental condition. I've tolerated it long enough. I will no longer appease him. If he raises a fuss or drafts a posse against you, I have the legal tools to have him committed to the Fulton asylum. Give me a week, and I'll return with your passports to freedom in hand."

With one remaining workhorse to aid in the task, for the entire next week, Moses and Gabe began the arduous task of scooping sand, reclaiming the farm fields from the flood damage. They toiled with shovels to the point of blistered hands to rehabilitate the corn fields buried deeply in river sand.

The day of his return to River View, John handed Moses a leather satchel with two notarized letters of freedom signed by him, though he was not the valid owner. John also gave them enough currency to start a new life at their destination in the territory. He presented Moses a map to the first stop of the underground railroad, which could lead the two men to the relative safety of Kansas. Reaching the first house safely held the key.

"Guard these documents with your life, for your survival will depend on them," John said. "Take the money to buy the necessities for farming. Squatters, even those who are freedmen, are welcome in Kansas Territory. And from this day forward, Watty, you have solid verification in hand should anyone challenge that you and Gabe are free. I cannot ever deliver your sons or your wife Sally back to you, but I will do everything I can to deliver your freedom."

"Mister John, I cannot thank you enough," Moses said, mentally noting John called Sally his wife. "I appreciate your kindness, but are you sure these papers are good enough?"

"They aren't fool proof, but they are sufficiently sealed, notarized, and certified. Even if a question does arise, the fact that you bear the last name of Watson will make it difficult for anyone to trace you and Gabe back as runaways belonging to the Manchesters of River View Grove. But someone in your situation can never exercise too much caution."

"I'll repay you the money. I pray you'll be able to rein in your father."

"The old man is not right in the head. I've seen the steady erosion. I will do what I must. As for you and Gabe, you must leave in the dark of a Friday night," John continued. "The next newspaper will not publish until Monday. That is the earliest date the old man would be able to publish a notice of your getaway, but I'll work to ensure that does not happen. Just in case I have also started proceedings that will assuredly consign the old man to the state's care. If you ever have an opportunity, wire my office of your safety. And please, Watty, for old time's sake, you can call me John-Man; no mister needed."

"Thank you, John-Man," Moses said.

John responded, "Godspeed, Watty."

Gabe was hesitant when Moses filled him in on the plan.

The morning of their planned departure, Old Man Manchester was making his rounds. His final stop was in the far riverside field to inspect the progress Moses and Gabe had made.

"You boys better pick up the pace. We got fall crops to plant and we don't want to . . . "

As the old man turned to point out a particularly sandy patch of land, Gabe raised the blade of his shovel high in the air and brought it down with fury. The blow smashed the old man's skull. Blood splattered across the sandy soil. Moses stood motionless, paralyzed in horror. Gabe finished the job with five more blows from the shovel's blade.

"Son, what have you done?" Moses screamed. "You just sealed our death sentence."

"I thought it was time to seek my maroon, Papa. It was too risky to leave loose ends untied," Gabe said calmly. "Papa, we're right here by the river. The river gives, but the river also takes away."

"We both had plenty of reason for this, my son, but the timing could not be worse."

With no one else in sight, Moses and Gabe strained to load Manchester's corpse into the wagon. They hauled it to the river's edge and splashed it into the rolling current. Hungry carp, catfish, and snapping turtles would finish the task of concealing the murder.

Moses and Gabe possessed convincing papers certifying their status as freedmen, and after Manchester's murder, any hesitancy about leaving vanished. However, the old man's disappearance on the same day as their escape would definitely arouse suspicion. They stayed another two weeks. Nobody would ever figure they were responsible.

The day following the killing, John could not find the old man. He inspected each tent and searched high and low across the river bluffs. He approached each slave about the old man's whereabouts. A few had seen him making his rounds, and he appeared drunk, but other than that, nobody had a clue. He asked Moses and Gabe.

"Watty, did you see the old man yesterday? I can't find him."

"We saw him. He came by to see how the sand removal was going. Forgive me for saying this, but he was drunk as a skunk. We tried to convince him to go home, but it just made him angry. The last thing I wanted was to feel the crack of his whip, so we watched him go on his way toward the river."

By the end of the week, John surmised the old man's drunken bender led him toward the river's muddy banks where he must have slipped to his death.

John informed Moses and Gabe as they toiled to remove sand from the topsoil.

"I appreciate that you tried to talk the old man into going home. I suspect he's gone forever but we never found his corpse," John said without emotion.

"It'll take the court a while to do a proper estate hearing and declare the old man's passing, but it's all a technicality. They already have the paperwork I filed to have him committed, so it shouldn't take long."

"John-Man, in spite of your misgivings about your father, Gabe and I are most sorry for your loss," Moses said.

"Appreciate that, Watty, but the father I used to love and respect died many years ago," John said. "I, no doubt, will be the new owner of River View. And while it might be a bit premature, I grant you your freedom. Since I was the one who signed your freedom papers, they are now quite valid, just a little early. But still, you best be careful on the trail. With one misstep, even a freed slave can end up in the flames of hell. Make sure you guard those papers, and to be safe, you should stick to the secret path to Kansas."

The tenuous escape plan to freedom became more real, but Moses and Gabe exercised caution. As John instructed they hitched a ride on the secret underground railroad system, hop-scotching their way from safehouse to safehouse across the slave state of Missouri, mostly at night. The final night they hid in a stable in Roubideaux owned by a man named Marcus Mixon.

They took no chances until they reached the frozen banks of the Missouri River in the dim, pre-dawn hours of the next day. Their only choice was to walk across it.

The river froze over, but not solidly. In the sun's waking light, it was hard to determine at each step if pieces of ice might shift in the river's flow. As they crossed Gabe's leg sank up to the knee in the frigid waters. Such a slip could have meant a cold and certain death. Moses grabbed his son by the coat sleeve and pulled him back. Step by step the two inched closer to a new life in a new land, one far away from Gumbo Flats and River View Grove. Though Kansas was no-man's land, an unfamiliar jolt of freedom hit both Watsons broadside as they stepped foot onto the territory's soil of liberation. Not only were they free men, but also in a land where slavery did not rule. Before taking five steps, Moses and Gabe fell to their knees, father hugging son, tearful joy streaming down their cheeks in what would be their first communion in the full spirit of maroon.

CHAPTER 5

1858-1859

FRIEND OR FOE?

DURING THE SOLITARY CEREMONY to commemorate Luke's life as a devoted mule, Perry's eyes spotted a clear meadow in the valley below. It was the perfect location for a homesite.

On an initial excursion away from the holler, in the early spring days following his long winter of struggle, Perry secured the tangible materials for farming and construction of a proper home. The only choice at that time was the trading post in nearby Roubideaux, Missouri. Without Luke by his side, the walk took him a day and a half, but if he could acquire a wagon and team, he expected the return trip might take half that time.

Once again, to save money for his transactions, after walking the twenty miles from the holler, Perry took the familiar ramshackle, steam-powered ferry across the Mighty Missouri. He recalled the first trip with Luke, and it dipped into his well of emotion. If only he had not taken the last leg of his journey from Indiana. If only he had not crossed the river, Luke might still be by his side. His paranoia about wintering in Roubideaux and possibly losing his squatter land was a big miscalculation that cost him dearly.

Perry gathered his sentiments as he reached Mixon's Trading Post. A slate shingle hung from the building's bold pine façade priggishly proclaiming, "Marcus Mixon—owner and proprietor."

As Perry ambled through the front door of the trading post, he startled everyone by shouting what would become his trademark greeting to shopkeepers.

"Here from the holler. Who wants my dollar?"

As the patrons scattered, an earthy aroma of frontier and rotting hides mixed with a sickly fruity fragrance of civilization greeted Perry. The smell blasted his nose like hot fumes from a blazing forge. A vast array of goods lined the shop. The selection was impressive, even for an established frontier town. Burlap bags of flour and sugar were stacked shoulder high along one wall. Crates of potatoes and onions, traded for that morning, sat near the door. Wooden shelves held cans of salt pork, lard, buffalo pemmican, and tins of fancy spices, none of which Perry had heard of except black pepper and salt. One shelf held an array of kettles, pans, and utensils made by the local blacksmith. A young mother, two children in tow, was looking through fabric bolts. Fresh beaver pelts hung on one wall from pegs. Behind the glass counter, which held penny candy, chewing tobacco, tinned tobacco, rolling papers, and pipes, stood Marcus.

Wearing arm garters like a blackjack dealer, Marcus, a squat and balding man, looked capable of teaching a lesson or two about wheeling and dealing along the frontier. In addition to the trading post, Marcus owned the stables.

"I reckon you must be Marcus," Perry said as Marcus looked up from behind the counter.

"Sure am, sonny. And who might you be?"

"I'm Perry Adams, and I come to you as an honest farming man in search of a square deal," Perry said.

"And a square deal you shall have," Marcus said. "How might I fill your order?"

The proprietor's eyes reflected wisdom that most people were quick to underestimate. Marcus liked talking about trivial matters. It was part of the grand theater of negotiating at Mixon's Trading Post. Marcus was a pragmatic merchant. Perry suspected it was merely a cover for making a buck.

"Where you from, Mr. Adams?" Marcus asked.

"I farm in the hills about twenty miles west."

"Hm, a Kansas squatter. You didn't happen to stroll through here early last winter, did you? As I recall, the only thing you bought was a newspaper. Guessing you must be keenly interested in the politics of the day, but I prefer to talk about the weather. My clients tend to be polarized on topics other than the sun, the rain, and the temperature. I try to steer clear. Something that might make half my customers happy would just piss off the other half."

"I prefer talking about the weather myself, Mr. Mixon. My success depends on it, and yes, I did stumble through your shop last winter to pick up a paper on my way to the territory. I was in a hurry."

"It was a really grim winter. I'm surprised you survived. As I recall you were traveling light, and you didn't even bother to stock up on provisions."

Marcus and Perry were happy to keep the conversation confined. Perry suspected Marcus's sentiments ran deep with conviction, especially on slavery, but it was a secret for which he did not push.

After the initial chitchat, both men got down to business.

"I know exactly what I need, and then I'll be on my way," Perry said.

"I hope you've kept your mind open to some good-spirited haggling. That's what makes the world go 'round here at the Trading Post."

After meandering through the store, Perry pulled out his sack of gold coins and bought a copper-trimmed wooden plow. The plow, which Perry named Old Woody, was not the nicest plow on Marcus's garrisoned lot, but it was the one he could afford. He also bought some building materials and a wagon with side boards. To pull the wagon, he visited Marcus's stable and bought two Belgian draft horses, Beulah and Barney, and the saddlery necessary to bond the horses and wagon as one.

With the big purchases out of the way, Perry bought a cheap pocket watch, a large keg of freshly forged nails and a suitable hammer, a cookstove, a kettle, a smithing anvil and bellows, and some pig iron.

"I should have bought all this stuff last year before the winter set in, but I had no idea about the hardships I'd face. Kansas winters are much worse than those of southern Indiana," Perry said.

"Well, better late than never. I like a man who gets down to business, especially if he's buying more than a newspaper and a sack of cornmeal," Marcus said. "I'm going to remember you, Perry Adams. I just raked in one of my biggest sales of the month. You're welcome back anytime."

"Oh, yeah, Marcus. I'd like a newspaper too."

Perry's list completed, he took stock of his remaining coins. He had just enough in the coming weeks to invest in a floppy-eared blue-tick hound dog named Archibald and a lactating milk cow named Butter. As a whole the breeding pair of horses, the dog, and the cow never came close to the sum of the bond he'd shared with Luke.

Archibald became his housemate. It was lonely in the holler, and the floppy-eared hound acted much like a person, as convincingly as Old Luke. Almost.

Perry had much work ahead. His priority was to break ground in a clearing with the wooden plow and plant a crop of corn. As the seeds sprouted and grew, over the course of the summer months he worked tirelessly to build a sturdy log house and hand-dig a spring-fed well. His final summer project was a log-hewn barn. It had ample storage for native grass, a smaller crib for corn, and protection from the elements for his animals.

All this planning and investing aligned with his grand strategy for success. The wooden plow with copper trim sufficed the first year. The Indiana corn seeds he dropped into the furrows of the deep territorial soil sprouted, and a surprising number of the corn stalks produced gargantuan ears.

It took Perry the bulk of the summer to finish the shelters, but by the winter's turn, he was ready. He had learned lessons the hard way. Preparation was an obsession he now wore like the mariner's albatross. Never again would the natural elements lay him so bare and desperate.

Perry also made the wooden plow work for a second season, when he broke land on another nearby meadow. But as he walked behind the plow, behind his team of horses, he had to pause every ten yards or so to scrape dirt off the plow face. Perry's ultimate goal was a self-scouring John Deere steel plow. He hoped to buy one with proceeds from his first two crops. The day of his visit to Mixon's Trading Post, Marcus had a couple of the nicer plows on his lot, but the price was simply too steep.

Progress came slowly, even when powered by a two-horse team, but Perry was as progressive as any of the early sodbusters in Kansas Territory. He lusted for that John Deere plow. He'd seen one of Deere's plows in action during a field demonstration back in Indiana. Hooked to a team, or even a single horse, the plow could slice through the soil like the bow of a river steamer cutting an upstream current.

But Perry was patient. He notched two bountiful growing and harvest seasons in '58 and '59. God smiled on the holler. From the ears of corn that resulted, he reserved seed from the best and sold the rest at the granary in the nearby settlement of Lowland. The settlement, seven country miles south of Jawbone Holler, was a frontier boomtown that took instant root in 1858 due to an influx of eager settlers, tradesmen, and merchants. A short-line connection of the Palmetto & Roubideaux Railroad that ran from the Missouri River's western bank solidified Lowland's place on the territorial map.

After those first two years, life became far different, more comfortable and secure, not only on the farm near Jawbone Holler, but also in the boomtown of Lowland. The number of residents grew to 527, not counting dogs, cats, and goats. Lowlanders were a cohort sufficiently diverse in talents, from banker to doctor to shopkeeper to blacksmith. The diversity enriched the community's steady growth.

Nestled in a broad valley, Lowland was less than an hour wagon ride from Jawbone Holler. At first, the residents were cautious around Perry. Many arrived with the purpose of casting the territory as a dominion of like-minded free-soilers. They branded him an outsider to their more civilized ways. Perry's success of tying a ribbon of triumph around the frontier river bluffs was insufficient for inclusion. During his visits to town, Perry tried hard to fit in. He shared with all willing to listen the stories of his Indiana roots, his journey, his travails of that first winter, and his story of Luke. Takers were few. It all fed into the same kind of insecurity he left behind in Indiana.

The strategy of openness backfired. Instead of a growing understanding, many of the good people of Lowland added their own narratives around the story of demented pioneer Perry Adams. They shared and embellished stories, some true and some fables, of his arrival and survival. The tale of his mule-eating ways grew mythically. Some began to speculate that during his odyssey from Indiana, he had also consumed several fellow pioneers. Some said he was birthed in a cave, raised by a mother wolf.

Residents scrambled—not toward or away from, just scrambled—every time they saw Perry approaching from afar. Perry noticed the aversion. It created a negative level of self-consciousness he drove away with rum in his former life. It bruised his spirit. He did not understand.

Many of the townsfolk privately revered Perry for the challenges he had faced, but most remained reluctant to express it, choosing the same kind of respect one extended a timber rattler, admiring its handsome sheen but well outside of striking distance. A few residents clung to the stale legends and focused only on his choice of mule meat that desperate winter. When hearing his bold greeting to shopkeepers, they replied out of earshot, "Fool, fool, hide your mule."

Many referred to Perry as the wild-eyed Hoosier, tiptoeing up to but stopping short of it being a term of endearment.

Perry overheard his nickname. He did not quarrel with the Hoosier part and knew it to be derived from a native word meaning man of the corn. And growing that crop was his passion. Unlike back in Salt Spring, he sprouted a deep admiration for everything related to growing the crop—how its leaves whistled in the wind, its earthy smell during pollination and the strands of silk that peeked out of each ear resembling the tresses of Rapunzel.

But Perry was not a fool. It would be easier to work with the citizens of Lowland than plow them over. But he knew they would never understand the desperation of that winter or that Luke had been more than his mule. Much like the disciple after whom he was named, Luke had been his caretaker.

Perry pledged he would commemorate the martyred mule that saved his life by devoting himself to succeed on a farm where Luke would have been perfectly at home. The crowning feature of Perry's warm home was a limestone fireplace with a red hearthstone and a rough walnut mantle. Using a couple of bent nails, he hung Luke's jawbone above the fireplace as a perpetual reminder. The only item that could have hung with greater reverence was his mother's white, trim-laced bonnet, but that was an item he was sure he would never see again.

Each time he viewed the memorial to Luke, Perry rededicated his life to working that land with the deep topsoil and growing corn in tribute.

Perry did not want anything to come in the way of his primary intention—to succeed in farming. He vowed to never be hungry again and to never stray from the holler for more than a few days at a time.

If only the townsfolk of Lowland knew the full story of his dedication to success. Instead, they continued to buffet Perry with an attitude of scorn. He was nothing more than an unhinged mule eater. On a sunny afternoon in Lowland, he found out why.

While passing on a board sidewalk, Perry glanced up at a shop window. Looking back at him was a haggard man with a long, dirty reddish-blond beard and unkept shoulder-length hair. His knees weakened at the sight of himself. He took a step back. Perry's appearance, a matter of pride back in Salt Spring, had eroded in the hills. Perry slapped himself upside the noggin. Could the disgust and mistrust among the townsfolk be rooted in the fact he was too focused on his pursuit of farming to care about how he presented himself? Turning on his heels, Perry set an immediate course toward Norman Smith's barber pole.

"Mr. Smith, do you think you could help a young man out?" Perry said as he walked into the shop. "It's time for me to clean up my appearance."

"Son, from the looks of it, I'd say your need for a clean-up might be older than the hills you are farming up north."

"Let's do it right. Cut the beard and hair. Give me a shave. And I could use a bath. I want to show the folks around here there's nothing to fear. It might be the tonic I need to fit in."

By the time Smith completed his cutting, it appeared that two medium-sized animals died on his barber shop floor.

"Wow, Adams," the barber said. "This has to rank up there as one of my greatest masterpieces."

The handsome Perry Adams was back and ready to begin a charm initiative on his new town. After buying a new set of work clothes, he walked down the street to see the reactions. There was no cowering, no scattering. Nobody knew it was him. The women of town gazed at him with aroused interest.

Perry clapped his hands and walked into the hardware store. He needed a pair of pliers and a splitting maul. For good measure he belted out his shopkeeper greeting. "Here from the holler. Who wants my dollar?"

Looking up expecting to see the scruffy Perry Adams, store owner Max Jenkins nearly fainted. He was greeted by a striking young man, one who would garner attention walking down any street in any town.

"Adams, is that you?" Jenkins asked.

"It's the real me, Max. Whatcha think?"

"While it might be shallow for me to say, I think your reputation is about to turn for the better."

Perry's reclaimed looks didn't stop him from having fun with Max and the other shopkeepers. He continued to wrangle his trades with the shrewdness of a possum and was not afraid of anyone knowing it.

When Max told Perry the new tools cost a total of $3.50, Perry looked away and began to walk out the door without a word. At the threshold he spun around on the toes of his boots.

"I reckon I can keep using the tools I have, Max. But what if I were to offer you $3?"

"Done," Max replied.

The shopkeepers were no match for Perry's negotiating prowess. But they learned to do their best to earn Perry's dollars.

Instantly, Perry enjoyed an atmosphere of near celebrity rather than scorn. Like magic there was growing respect for the fetching young man who came with little and prospered through the sweat of his brow, the hard-bargaining ways of a patient riverboat gambler and a constant eye toward innovation.

No longer would Perry cling to survival through social isolation. The growth of his emotional maturity begged for a greater connection to the entire world around him, including whatever connections Lowland might afford. Heck, he might even start looking for friends, maybe even a wife.

The day Perry met Daniel Buchanan, Lowland's first constable, he struck up a friendship with the most important man in the village. The people had elected Constable Dan by a popular vote in the fall of 1859, after settlers determined they rightly deserved to be governed by the rule of law, rather than by any man bold enough to exert control. While capable of enforcing either, Dan committed himself to laying down the law.

The only real matter Dan and Perry held in common was physical stature. Both were brawny men, but Dan was more than twice Perry's age. Dan sported bold features, a nose that jumped from his face, one long eyebrow that extended above one eye to the other like a woolly-bear caterpillar, and graying mutton-chop sideburns. He always wore a black leather vest, attached to which was a bold tin star. The contrast was intentional. Above all else Dan was a patriot. He was a decorated veteran of the Mexican-American War. His job was to protect his people and do what he could to preserve the Union. There was never a doubt about who was in charge.

At first sight Perry was impressed by Dan's intrepid profile. But for a good amount of time, Perry kept his distance. During visits to Lowland over the next months, Perry considered a heartier endorsement of the lawman. But before he could endorse Daniel comprehensively, he needed to assess the constable's grit. That came in the spring of 1860.

"Greetings, Constable Dan," Perry said in a forward manner when meeting the lawman by happenstance after hitching his team outside the Lowland dry goods store. "I know we have not been subject to a formal introduction, but I'm . . . "

"You're the one and only Perry Adams, I suspect," Dan interrupted. "I have heard all about you, Mr. Adams, and I have heard about your famous mule too."

"I hope in a good way. I'd like you to think of me as an ally. But first I hope it is not too presumptive on my part to get to know you a little. I'd like to know more about the fabric from which you are tailored before I cede to you the power of enforcement over my person in this fair burg."

"Why, Mr. Adams, I can assure you all men within these limits are held to the same standard. How exactly might you want to take a gander at the origin of my humble threads?"

Perry delivered a mischievous grin toward the constable. "I'd like to measure you up a tad. How about we match either wits or brawn? I will defer to you to pick your poison, constable."

Dan erupted in a full belly laugh at the suggestion.

"A challenge based solely on chance would be pure folly. Surely, a test of logic would be far too basic, both of us being men of superior intellect. Though, a trial whose basis is a feat of strength would be biased in your favor since you are but half my age. If you insist on such a tournament, however, my choice is a spirited match of arm rasslin."

Dan knew exactly his chances in the challenge he proposed. He had been crowned arm wrestling champion while riding with General Zachary Taylor during his service in the Mexican-American War. If he could best a throng of more than 3,500 other challengers, surely he could better this single but sturdy frontiersman.

Perry's anticipation bounded on the edge of elation, himself being crowned arm wrestling champion several years prior on a day he was drunk at the Orange County Fair back in Indiana.

"Challenge accepted. And what should be the venue for such a spectacle?"

Both men knew the contest had to be staged in public to secure the proper validation of Lowland's citizens.

"How about the yonder oak stump, the one on the far side of this dirt street, opposite the boardinghouse?" Daniel proposed. "And we shall request the crier to spread word up and down Main so the result can be properly documented for posterity. How about today, high noon?"

The oak stump was like an extension of Daniel himself. It was the location where he had delivered a fiery oratory to townsfolk about his qualifications for the post of constable. His familiarity with the stump might balance the scale of youth tilted in Perry's favor.

With confidence overflowing, Perry agreed to the terms. The showdown was set.

Townsfolk, both common and distinguished, gathered 'round the old oak stump at the appointed time. There were aproned shopkeepers, the editor of the fledgling *Lowland Ledger*, teachers, doctors, and other curious onlookers.

At high noon, the two men broke through the crowd of inquisitive spectators and strode up to the stump. Daniel extended his meaty forearm for the challenge, and Perry met the action in kind. The men locked hands and the Honorable Judge Virgil Merriweather, after consulting the time on his golden pocket watch, held their locked hands in check above the stump. As the minute hand hit exactly high noon, the judge shouted, "Commence!"

The two men exploded with fury sufficient to shatter both of their forearms. The onlookers also expected such a gruesome outcome. They watched the action with the same fervor one might observe a carriage crash.

A minute in, trauma flooded both men's faces. The crowd gasped and awed as momentum meandered back and forth, back and forth, a matter of inches in both directions.

One minute became two, and two became three. Sweat of struggle dripped from both of Perry's brows and Daniel's singular variety. Three minutes in and neither competitor drew a clear advantage.

Daniel mustered an assault that rocked Perry from his well-leveraged stance, but Perry held steadfast. The muscles of his forearm quivered. As quickly Perry summoned a wave of might to rival Atlas. His forearm pushed back Daniel's advantage and the two men were locked once again in a straight-up stalemate.

Both contenders grimaced in raw agony. When would this end? Four minutes became five.

The fortitude of both men locked the crowd in a trance, as five minutes became six.

While stationary, the oak stump vibrated. Neither Perry nor Daniel could establish an advantage. Their arms were locked in a throbbing impasse. Neither rendered a flag of surrender. The credibility that might be won or lost that day was too precious to throw in the towel.

At the full seven-minute mark, 12:07 exactly on Judge Merriweather's pocket watch, audible whimpers leaked from both distinguished foes. The judge stepped in to propose a merciful armistice, concerned either man might succumb in a fit of overexertion.

"Gentlemen, you have both proved a worthy opponent to your counterpart. I propose this match be declared a draw, with full measures of honor and glory retained by both parties."

Perry's eyes dripped with perspiration. He aspired for an end to the pain's intensity. Dan looked back with a gaze that signaled his vigor was also exhausted. Dan nodded. Perry nodded back.

Judge Merriweather delivered his compassionate verdict. He ordered the two men to break their contested grasp and to end their agony. At exactly thirty seconds after 12:07 p.m., both Daniel and Perry were eager to comply. They broke contact in an instant. Both laughed uncontrollably, insanely spurred by a common rush of adrenaline.

"Ladies and gentlemen, you all know your constable, but you might not recognize our other handsome competitor," the judge shouted. "He's none other than the gentleman we used to call the wild-eyed Hoosier. Perry Adams."

The crowd broke out in wild applause and shouts of amazement.

"With the authority vested in me, I hereby declare this match an even-up draw." The judge grabbed the wrists of both men and raised their arms high in the air.

The onlookers exploded with another roar of jubilation. Though it was a draw, never had they seen such a dramatic event inside the freshly drawn limits of their town.

The two men embraced in a bearhug. Mutual respect jumped from their exhausted faces.

"How about a rematch down the road?" Perry asked his new friend without wanting to hear an affirmative answer. "I bet we could sell tickets."

"Not on your life, Adams." Dan chuckled. "There ain't gonna be no rematch."

Perry's right arm trembled, but he managed to smile back at Dan.

"Even though my arm feels like death itself, you know what, Daniel, every day is a blessing."

"Indeed, it is," Dan said. "Indeed, it is."

Dan's fifty-three years of wisdom were always at Perry's disposal. Despite the cult of notoriety created around the two men that day, one of Dan's foundational points of mentorship to Perry was to always take the high road. That was especially true since being renowned by the citizens of Lowland was not always a positive quality.

The two men were destined to celebrate many triumphs as their little corner of Kansas Territory flourished. Neither wanted those blessed days to end.

CHAPTER 6

Summer 1859

A SQUATTER'S PERIL

ON THE SAME AFTERNOON of his arm-wrestling draw with Constable Dan, Perry's arm still ached from the encounter. Perry hit the trail north to Jawbone Holler. He took a different route this day, hoping to find a workable shortcut. After topping an unfamiliar hill on that fresh course toward home, Perry spotted a tail of smoke rising from behind a small hill. Still a good two miles from home, he blinked his eyes twice. The sight was shocking. Who, besides himself, could be looney enough to set roots in this part of the untamed wilderness?

Stopping dead center at the hill's top, Perry surveyed the scene below. A modest cabin and barn and a small outbuilding with smoke rising anchored the clearing. It was hotter than blazes. With there being no logical need for a fire, the smaller structure had to be a smokehouse. Perry could smell the meat even two hundred yards away.

Fetching his trusty pirate's spyglass, Perry could clearly see close to a dozen head of dairy cattle, a perfectly matched team of horses, a pen of fat hogs and some miscellaneous chickens running to-and-fro.

The shadowy outlines of two men darted from behind a tree. Perry approached the homesite with caution. In this situation, he was the one who wore the boots of a trespasser. If Perry indeed had neighborly squatters a mere 20-minute hike from his own domicile, it might be the hospitable thing to introduce himself.

Perry was intentional about signaling his arrival, so as not to startle the inhabitants into a defensive action. He shouted a loud, "Git up!" to Beulah and Barney and the team plodded down the hill toward the farm site.

A booming voice greeted Perry a mere fifty yards from the home.

"Hello, stranger, what brings you to our farm?" the voice asked.

Stepping from behind a towering black walnut tree were what Perry identified only two minutes prior as two shadowy figures, but he could now plainly see the figures were men—Black men, one young and one considerably older. The more senior of the two held a rifle and fired a warning shot into the air before pointing the gun in Perry's direction.

"No need for alarm, sir. I think we are neighbors," Perry said, expressing his friendly intentions as clearly as possible. "The name's Perry Adams. I am a squatter about two miles due north of here over a couple of river bluffs. I stopped by for an introduction. May I approach?"

The older man with the gun motioned Perry forward. Before Perry could descend his wagon, the man approached Perry with the gun still pointed chest-level.

"The name's Moses Watson," the man said. "This is my son Gabe. What do you need, sir?"

Perry could not believe his ears. This had to be the same Moses he had heard about during his walk through Gumbo Flats during his own trek to Kansas.

Moses and Gabe both wore the typical clothes of farmers—denim and cotton with rugged leather boots. Moses was in his late fifties, and Gabe was less than a full two decades. While Moses's weathered face and graying hair made him appear older than he was, his physical presence showed he was a hard worker.

"I do not mean to disturb your peace," Perry said. "Like I said. my farm is twenty minutes to the north. I took a new route home today from Lowland. After I saw the smoke, I simply wanted to acquaint myself with neighbors to whom I was oblivious. I can't believe we have not met until now. The folks in Lowland never mentioned you."

"Approach slowly, mister," Moses said. "We have been to Lowland several times, but we're always prudent about our visits. A Black man in these parts can't be too cautious."

"I guess you can't, but I have always found mighty things are possible when expressing faith, no greater than the tiniest mustard seed," Perry waded in carefully.

"We've got no mustard here," Moses said, motioning for Gabe to approach the conversation. "And the only faith I have is in knowing that most white men wrongly believe they are of a superior race."

"I have nothing to hide from you, Mr. Watson. And I certainly do not consider you or your son inferior in any way. But I must confess that during my travel here from Indiana, I walked through some plantation land west of Saint Louie in a place called Gumbo Flats."

Perry saw Moses and Gabe look at each other in shock. Gabe whispered in Moses's ear.

"I don't like it. What if he's a vigilante? What if he knows about old man Manchester?"

"There's no way in hell," Moses whispered back.

"Mr. Adams, why don't you go ahead and tell us more about your trip through Gumbo Flats?" Moses said.

"Well, I heard about a freedman named Moses Watson and how he was the hardest worker west of the Mississippi. I heard how you earned your freedom and even about your goal of coming here to Kansas to farm."

"Who told you that?"

"A farmer who was a neighbor to the plantation where you worked."

"What else did this fella happen to say about me?"

"Well, that was it, really, other than you and your son left for this glorious land of freedom and that I should make your acquaintance if we ever met. I find it hard to fathom the thought that we are actually neighbors."

"Mr. Adams, either this is a grand coincidence, or you are a great liar.

Which is it?"

"Well, Mr. Watson, I don't make a habit of lying. It's bad for the soul."

"We better explore your story a little further, Mr. Adams."

"I think you gentlemen must have arrived in these parts a bit before me. I arrived in the dead of winter and practically starved and froze to death."

"Oh no, don't tell me you're the mule eater," Gabe blurted out.

"Well, yes, I guess that's what some people in Lowland called me. Wild-eyed Perry Adams, the Hoosier mule-eater."

Gabe gave a hearty laugh.

"This really is hard to believe, but it's so strange I can't help but believe you're telling the truth," Moses said. "OK, Mr. Adams, come on over and join us. Sounds like we need to get to know each other a little better, since we're neighbors and all."

"Glad to oblige. From the looks of your farm, I might just learn a thing or two about becoming a successful practitioner of agrarian science."

Moses lowered his gun. Perry said all the right things to at least secure an audience with the two men.

"Mr. Adams, I'm sure you understand we can't be too careful. There are ruffians about. If you are indeed our neighbor, we should make your acquaintance," Moses said, now speaking more eloquently than a freed slave should. "Gabe and I have seen far too much injustice in the world. Accusations against men of our color can materialize from thin air."

"Whatever do you mean, Mr. Watson?" Perry said. "I know you and your son aren't fugitives. Have you committed a crime of some kind?"

"No, sir, we have not," Gabe chimed in. "My father has never so much as lifted a finger in anger, though he has many reasons to have done so. We hesitate to go too far out on a limb for any white man in fear we might be found hanging from a limb ourselves."

"That's quite enough, Gabe," Moses scolded his son, fearing that the impetuous young man said too much. "The point is: being Black men, we must not take chances."

"Nobody should take chances in our contemporary world," Perry said. "I hope you will accept my greeting."

Perry walked slowly closer.

"By the looks of your fine farm here, I think we must be three peas in a pod when it comes to agrarian pursuits. It looks like you have progressed in your efforts a bit farther than me. You have a fine herd of livestock and a handsome poultry flock. I am envious."

"I grew up looking after someone else's animals," Moses said. "Gabe and I are now doing that on our own behalf. We are claiming our maroon."

"Yes. The point is you are both free men, regardless of the color of your skin," Perry said. "But even if you were fugitive slaves, I believe a man is a man. I have no respect for any law running counter to that notion. Why did you decide on this location?"

"We are indeed free men," Gabe blurted out. "We've done nuthin' to disrespect any man's law."

Moses shot Gabe another look of caution.

"We have all the proper freedom papers," Moses said. "Glad to show them to you."

"Nah, I don't need to see them. Like I said, it doesn't matter to me," Perry said. "But why Kansas?"

"Gabe and I came to start our own farm. We knew we could do it here. You might think it folly given my advanced age, but I am not as old as I look. I want Gabe to learn all the finer lessons of animal husbandry. This is a fresh start and an opportunity to do what we know best away from any restrictions that might be imposed due to our race. After I am gone, I hope it will be something for Gabe to call his own."

"Sounds like we are all in the same boat. I came here to start a new life, away from the prejudices held against me for my checkered youth. I'm doing what I do best—raising corn. I also have a small menagerie of critters, but nothing to rival the Watson operation. And please call me Perry. I have been called much worse."

"Folks who know me best have always called me Watty, so I think you can drop the formal salutation too, Mr. Perry," Moses said, warming to Perry's approach.

The muscles in Moses's forearms rippled as he motioned Perry forward. Moses looked capable of bettering both Perry and Constable Dan in a match of arm wrestling. His skin was medium but weathered darker by hours under the sun. Moses's neck was as thick as a small tree trunk and his jawline was square and strong. While Gabe's skin was lighter, similar to a black man of Cajun heritage, Moses had passed all the other traits along to his son. After the initial tepid greeting, Moses carried a more affable disposition, almost jolly; not exactly the temperament of a man who once toiled under the prejudicial bullwhip of a white master.

"You say you have been caring for critters all your life, Watty. Was Gumbo Flats always your home?" Perry asked.

Moses was light on details.

"Born and grew up about fifty or so years ago in Gumbo Flats. Lots of rich bottomland when it's not buried in river sand. It was a wonderful place for field crops like corn and hemp when the river didn't flood, but almost always suitable to the practice of animal husbandry."

Moses lowered his guard with an elevated level of eloquence. He crept toward a higher level of trusting this white visitor. "Gabe and I both were born on the farm where we worked, on the unfortunate side of the institution of slavery."

A bitter distaste for slavery bit Perry's tongue, but even now his vocal opposition to it often depended on the audience. It was safe to express his thoughts to Moses.

"I find slavery to be the greatest sin on our nation's extensive list of ills. Read in the newspaper about Congressman Lincoln from Illinois. He believes a man should be endorsed to freely rise to the level of his talents, not limited by the color of his skin, or, for that matter, his choice of religion. I also read that he may be in line for his party's nomination for president, so in spite of all this uncertainty, we may be in store for a change down the line when the territory votes."

"You will help decide that, but not Gabe and me. Even with all the wisdom I have stored under this gray hair, I am still less than a man under terms of current law, undeserving of even the right to check a ballot. Gabe and I are less than welcome as freed men within the bounds of many states where such a concept is despised, including our very own Missouri. I have several very compelling reasons to go back there some day, but not sure I would dare to do it alone."

"For more than a half century, I was owned like a barnyard animal. I brought Gabe into that same world. The man who set us free did so after his daddy passed, and the farm became unsalvageable due to the flood a couple years back. Though there were some good times, it was more often a bad place to live, and the old man was the devil incarnate. His son, with whom I grew up as a sprout, set us free after the old man passed."

Moses continued, "After granting us our freedom, the son pointed us west, toward Kansas Territory. It seems like a lifetime ago. He even grubstaked us with a handsome sum to invest in the tools for our new life of freedom, which we did through a gentleman in Missouri secretly sympathetic to our cause."

"It's too bad all white folk aren't like that," Gabe jumped in.

"But each and every day, Gabe and I have much to regret in the matter," Moses said. Gabe looked nervously at his papa. What was he about to say?

"In a fit of craziness, the old man sold away my wife and Gabe's mother and my two other sons. Shipped them to the Memphis auction. Their final destinations could have been anywhere in the Deep South. We keep them in our prayers each night, but we fear we will never see them again. We will never give up. After our nation overcomes slavery, as I hope it will, we will go find them."

"I hate to admit it, but at least for now, I have kin I don't care to see again, but at least for me it's a choice," Perry said. "I admire both of you for your passion to eventually find your family."

"Thank you, Mr. Adams," Gabe said, warming only slightly to Perry. "But that's what makes us different. You do have a choice."

"Whatever happens from this point forward, I know I will never fully give up, but right now the situation feels so hopeless," Moses said.

"The one thing we both knew, Mr. Adams, was we had to get the hell out of Missouri," Gabe said. "The laws governing slavery there are so strict that we could be forced back into bondage with little notice, in spite of our freedom papers."

"The old man saw us as little more than work mules," Moses said. "Missouri was no place for slaves or freedmen."

Perry found it ironic that Moses compared himself in slavery to a work mule. Perry had just as fervently considered his mule, Luke, as being quite human. The perverted contrast imprinted a blunt realization on his soul.

"I'll never judge you or Gabe on any aspect of your physical appearance, but if you choose that judgement for me, I will understand completely. Many of my people have not been righteous."

Since Moses provided a few select features of his past, Perry did the same, but in much more detail. He included the misdirection of his youth, the spell cast over him by good rum, his father's denial of blacksmith training, and every last detail about his many tribulations during that first desperate winter in the holler. He even told Moses and Gabe in detail about his beloved mule Luke and his desperate decision that first frigid winter to dispatch Luke from the misery of starvation, which saved his own life. He told them about the jawbone he kept as a remembrance of Luke and his decision to name Jawbone Holler in Luke's honor. He also shared his longing for the acquisition of a new John Deere plow.

Over their shared tales of triumph over tribulation, on the very first day, Perry and Moses bonded. Gabe remained skeptical.

"I will always view you as river bluff neighbors, and hopefully as equal partners in occasional barter, unless your combined years of negotiation skills are better than mine," Perry smiled.

"You got yourself a deal, young man," Moses said. "I hope our dealings might expedite the timeframe for you acquiring that plow."

"I thank you for that sentiment. An alliance we shall have. I'm guessing you and Gabe could prosper even more if you had some bushels of my corn as feed for your herds and flocks. I am occasionally in need of meat and eggs. Plus I have a dairy cow myself. Named her Butter, but her milk output is dwindling. I think she needs to take on a new calf. Do you think we might acquaint her with your fine bull?"

"After we get to know each other a little better, perhaps that can be arranged," Gabe chimed in. "I believe we might be able to work out some kind of barter for that and other common transactions beneficial to both sides, even though you are not one of us."

Moses shot Gabe a stern look.

"The point here, Gabe, is that Perry is very much one of us," Moses admonished his son.

Perry appreciated Moses's wisdom and his acceptance. Moses embraced him in a way that the people of his own race in Lowland initially had not. Perry also grew to appreciate the brash but astute business sense shown by Gabe, who was not even as old as Perry.

Moses invited Perry inside to join himself and Gabe for an early supper, including cornbread, fried taters, garden tomatoes, and a hunk of smoke-cured country ham. Perry accepted. The meal was the best one Perry had partaken since leaving Indiana. He was his own cook and not particularly good at it.

"Watty, if you cured this ham yourself, our future barters simply must include such a prize, even if infrequently," Perry said.

"I did and it most certainly will," Moses said. "Glad you like it."

After the meal Moses and Perry sat in the shade of a willow and discussed the finer points of farming while Gabe tended to chores. It was as if they had been lifelong business partners. Perry recounted the additional struggles he encountered with the folks in Lowland. Watty recounted the bigotry he and Gabe experienced at River View Grove. He stopped short of showing Perry the scars on his back. Perry would never know about old man Manchester's demise. The stories they shared were so soulful that neither Perry nor Moses were sure who had experienced the most serious tribulations.

"We have survived to excel in our current conditions," Moses said. "The future is what we make of it, Perry. With a mutually beneficial arrangement, however, we can reach our destinations twice as fast."

Perry agreed. He arose from his seat under the willow and told Moses he would see him again soon, with Butter in tow to meet her new beau. He shouted a goodbye across the barnyard to Gabe.

"You're always welcome to cross those bluffs and pay me a visit when you need a distraction from your routines. Not sure I can match the fare you put before me tonight, Watty, but I will certainly do my best to return the favor of satiating any hunger or thirst either of you might have. I can make a delicious plate of chipped beef and gravy with biscuits."

The two men shook hands, calloused from hard labor but in distinctly different shades of pigmentation. Perry began to walk back to his wagon, belly full and spirit lifted. As Perry looked back, he saw Gabe approach his father and speak, but he only heard mumbles.

"I think he could grow on me. Seems to be an honest and likeable fella . . . for a white man," Gabe whispered.

"Have a little faith in humanity, son. Not everyone is like old man Manchester."

Perry ruffled the reins, and his team headed back toward Jawbone Holler, where he tended a corn crop primed to yield long and full ears. This might be his best crop yet.

It was a steamy, late July afternoon, and the thunderheads built overhead like gigantic bolls of cotton. The southern breeze puffed a steamy breath across the river bluffs and a blustery northwest wind that delivered a chilling exhale collided far above the tops of the hardwoods.

The sky grew an indicative mix of gray, tan, and green. The clouds cut through the sky like a clipper ship. A brewing storm ached in Perry's bones. He gathered the animals and tucked them into the relative safety of the barn. Perry went out and sat among his corn.

Swirling winds sliced through the corn stalks like a machete. Perry put his head in his hands. All he could do was watch as nature shredded his crop.

The clouds cut loose, and a furious down blast flattened a third of his first field in a matter of minutes. The rain followed. Drops were as big as bullfrog tadpoles before losing their tails. At any other time, the rain would have been welcome, but this was a gully-washer, in places cutting ditches as wide as a wagon track.

Hailstones bigger than silver dollars floated as lightly as the drifting seeds of dandelions, blown parallel to the horizon by vicious straight-line winds. They smashed and slashed at least another third of the cornstalks to submission. Still sitting at the edge of the field, Perry examined his conscience for misdeeds deserving of this wrath. He could find nothing, at least lately.

The storm lasted less than fifteen minutes, but Perry would have sworn it dragged on for more than an hour. A mere quarter hour of misfortune wiped out a massive chunk of the progress nature built over the previous three months. Perry figured the tempest cut his crop in half in the blink of an eye.

At that moment Perry thought Moses and Gabe might have made a better decision to be practitioners of animal husbandry, rather than tenders of crops. Livestock could weather a storm of that severity with little difficulty. The chickens might be a different story, but at least they could move to shelter, unlike a vulnerable stalk of corn with roots held hostage to the full wrath of nature's anger.

The notion of switching agrarian pursuits was fleeting.

Upon further consideration, this event was one of those act-of-God moments. It had not been a punishment for some unknown moral transgression. The rending incident was simply a matter of misfortune. Sitting in front of a blazing fire that evening, Perry questioned why there were good years and bad years, but few between the two extremes. He stood and went to his front door. He searched the starlit heavens for an answer. While he had seen crops destroyed before, this was his first personal taste of the bitter porridge.

After a sleepless night, a profound sense led Perry back to the Watson farm. He needed to see firsthand how his new business partners handled the travails of the storm. Did their dairy herd seek shelter? Did their hogs crawl into their shed? Did hail plunk any of their chickens on the head so they ended up in the stew pot?

Perry's slump showed the physical and emotional exhaustion of the last two days. First it was the physical trauma from his friendly contest with Constable Dan. Second it was the mental duress of seeing much of his corn crop flattened. He needed to talk it out. He was hoping the Watsons would oblige. Regardless of the length of a business relationship, one must always look out for his partners and Perry's trip was as much about making sure Moses and Gabe were on solid ground after the storm as it was about his need to find solace from his own pain.

Some of his downed green corn would be a suitable feedstuff for the Watsons' herd of pigs. After the break of dawn, Perry hitched up his team and drove them to the field's edge. He gathered a full wagonload of hail-battered stalks, many with ears snuffed out like partially burnt candles before reaching their potential.

Half an hour later, he reached the Watson farmstead. But something on this morning seemed quite different from his first visit. The cattle were still in their barn. The pigs were stacked side by side in their shed, and the chickens were still nested. Moses and Gabe were nowhere in sight, nor were their horses. A billow of smoke rose from the smokehouse, so Perry figured they must have run into town to deliver a few of their country-cured hams. Perry took a familiar spot in the shade of the willow and waited for their return. He drifted off to sleep.

A couple hours later, Moses and Gabe and their horse-drawn team arrived at the house. The outstretched form of a man laid beneath the willow. Some manner of tragedy must have struck the man, Moses thought.

"Would you look at that, Gabe? I think there's a corpse under our tree." He approached slowly to see that the seemingly lifeless man was Perry.

"Mr. Perry," Moses said in a whisper. No response. He raised his voice. "Perry Adams!" he shouted.

With that Perry awoke in a start.

"Where am I? What time is it?" He regained his bearings and snapped to attention.

"Watty, I am so glad to see you. I was beginning to think you and Gabe might have been spirited off by a band of border ruffians."

"I don't believe that for a second, Perry. You were sleeping like a baby—and a well-fed baby at that. How did you weather the storm?"

"I figure I lost half of my crop, if not more. I came over to see if you and

Gabe experienced ill effects. Looks like things are in good order. I, sir, am as thankful for your fortune as I am troubled by mine."

Moses shook his head. "Welcome to the life of a farmer. Nobody told you this would be easy, did they?"

"They certainly did not, but neither did they warn me of the severity of Kansas storms. I am sure you and Gabe have seen worse, but how do you cope with a situation that is so negative and so final?"

"Perry, I have witnessed cyclones and floods, famine and bloodshed. I have seen men in chains. I have watched trials, beatings, and lynchings, all because of the color of a man's skin and his yearning to be free. The cries of slave women being raped. The bullwhip snapping at my back. I have been separated, maybe forever, from my wife and family. Compared to all that, Perry, a storm of any size is just small potatoes."

CHAPTER 7

Spring 1860

THE PRIZE

EVEN WITH HIS LATEST CORN YIELD cut in half by the hellish storm the previous summer, Perry counted his blessings. He scratched out a return that allowed him to scrape by. Things evened out over time. During his first several harvests, Perry loaded wagon after wagon of corn for delivery at the Lowland granary. Each time he stashed into his pockets a small stack of bank notes and Gold Eagle coins. Not that he did not trust his fellow man, but he hid the money under a wooden shipping box that doubled as a table. One night he brought out the money and sifted it through his fingertips as he counted. He was financially ready to pull the trigger on one of the biggest gambits of his life; the acquisition of one of the finest farming tools in the world—the steel John Deere plow.

Without the plow, Perry did not consider himself a true farmer, but the fact he could afford it meant he had already succeeded.

Perry was more than comfortable dealing with the manager of the granary and a few other merchants in Lowland, but for big purchases, Perry wanted to trade with no one other than Marcus Mixon. He prepared to make a day trip back to Marcus's trading post on the eastern bank of the Missouri River. He even had enough money to make the river crossing by the nicest ferry to serve the west bank of the Mighty Missouri. It featured a bold steam engine and two smokestacks. His condition had changed considerably since he and Luke made their first westward crossing on a cold wintry day in '57. The only choice Perry had then was that rickety steam ferry fashioned with logs and rope. His solo crossing that next spring, with Luke only a soul-stirring memory, was better.

It was a new day. Spring was in the air and sealing an amiable transaction at Mixon's Trading Post required all the haggling skills Perry could muster. He thought about the words he would employ during the negotiation. From his first deal, he knew Marcus was a cunning negotiator. It would take crafty dealing by Perry to better Marcus. Perry had dealt with Marcus during his foundational trip, when he did not fully know what he might need. Advantage Marcus. This time, however, the target of his desire was as clear as daylight itself. Playing coy would be the formula to win that Deere self-scouring steel plow. Striking such a bonanza would allow him to till more land in less time and sow more seeds of prosperity.

Perry made his plan. After dealing with Marcus, not before, he would stop at the Outpost Tavern for a sip of rum. It was just down the street. Perry was aware of his penchant for spirits. He had not consumed a single sip since his Indiana days. That had been miles ago in his process of maturation, but the demon of drink always loomed large on the horizon of his mind. Surely, a couple years of growing up, buffeted by privation, would make such imbibing a celebratory but temporary matter.

With those plans in mind, he hitched Beulah and Barney to his buckboard wagon and headed toward the now well-worn trails eastward toward the amber dawn and the Roubideaux trading post.

Along the journey his mind turned to the structure of his life itself.

Perry wasn't much into sentimentality. He was a practical man. Certainly, his history begged against thinking of family as a warm, accepting unit. But Perry, his life settled in the holler, was too solitary for solace. Though the family history he knew from his youth begged otherwise, Perry was lonely. He pined for the sensible efficiency and permanence that might accompany a family unit and his soul craved additional grounding and companionship.

Though he constructed secure shelter for himself and his animals, something was still missing. Plus, should a scribe one day put quill to parchment to record the proceedings of these days, the dialogue would indeed be less than inspirational with one human voice in a brabble with only neighs, barks, and moos.

But on a more corporeal level, Perry missed the pleasure of simply being a man. For the first time since he plucked the petals from Violet LeDoux's innocent blossom, he missed the touch of a woman's hand. Perry did not consider love an essential ingredient. On a fundamental level, success on a farmstead required more than two hands. Perry acknowledged that the notion unto itself was so like his father's way of thinking, but it was simply time to think about finding a mate and starting a family. Love, he reasoned, could come later.

As he reached the riverside ferry on the far bank opposite Roubideaux, Perry dispatched his brass spyglass tucked snugly behind his right suspender. Raising it to his right eye, he found his target destination—the trading post. It had been far too long.

A stench of frontier sewage and rotting carp burned Perry's nostrils as he paid the ferryman and onboarded his team and wagon. The folks in Lowland described the Missouri River in summer to be too thick to drink and too thin to plow.

On this occasion, the crossing was enjoyably smooth. The ferry floated along the water's surface. As he disembarked the ferry, Perry guided his wagon team straight away to the trading post. The shingle was still hanging. He genuinely admired Marcus, but he also was as keen as mustard to the fact Marcus drove a hard bargain.

After hitching his team to a street-side post, Perry walked through the establishment's wide-open double door. While focused on the essential task of buying a new plow, unlike his first visit to Marcus's enterprise three years ago, Perry would do a little browsing afterward. As usual the trading post was well stocked and smelly.

The plethora of selections made Perry's head spin. He would tend to the provisions later, as his heart was set on one bullseye—a John Deere self-scouring steel plow. He walked straight through the establishment, trying not to glance at any of the distractions of civilized life. Past the licorice and peppermint candy sticks decorating a countertop. Perry ignored the brick-like plugs of chewing tobacco and cans of snuff lining the wooden shelf behind the counter. He snubbed the pitchforks, the buckets, and the steel-jaw traps. In the fortified lot on the back side of the store, Perry spotted his quarry. It glimmered in the sun.

As he closed in on his target, his old acquaintance Marcus Mixon greased his way into a casual conversation. His slippery smile broke Perry's trance. As Perry recalled, Marcus's personality was as big as his stable barn. As usual, Marcus was indifferent to the issues swirling around the border states, except for the fact that conflict was bad for business. He was a pragmatist as long as it secured a return on his investment. But there was also something new and peculiar about the shopkeeper on this visit. When he spoke, Marcus's words spilled out of the side of his mouth.

"Howdy, Mr. Adams. It's been a couple of years, but I never forget a customer. Made a run over to Lowland recently and I've heard the tales of your struggles and your triumphs. How can I help make your life better?" said Marcus, sticking out a hand to welcome Perry as he would any returning customer. "How's the wagon and team holding up? I hope the nails have come in handy to hold your shelters together. We've chalked up great growing seasons as of late. Is that old wooden plow still busting clods to your liking?"

Perry paid no heed to the small talk and tried not to gaze at either Marcus's distorted mouth or the shining plowshare. Staring at the former might have been interpreted as an insult. Gawking at the latter would have offered Marcus a clue Perry was enamored of the plow and surely sabotage his bargaining position. Though in the corner of his mind, he was impressed by the merchant's memory.

Perry had matured through adversity since the last time he had visited Mixon's Outpost. He had also soaked in valuable life lessons from his new mentors, Moses Watson and Constable Dan. This time he would not be taken in by Marcus's big-time tactics. He would get that plow, he would get it at a fair price, and he would assert himself as a true farmer in every sense of the word, including wheeling and dealing.

"The growing seasons were great, Marcus. But last summer I experienced a little showdown with a hailstorm. Took half of my crop, but I persisted, never-theless. My team is hitched outside. And Old Woody, the copper-trimmed plow you sold me a couple years back, is still busting clods with reckless abandon. Thanks for asking."

For a split second, Perry looked at Marcus and the slight deformity at the corner of the merchant's mouth. And for too long he allowed his wandering eyes to focus on the object of his desire. For full dramatic effect, and in fear his cover was blown, Perry pointed at the John Deere plow with a disdainful finger to signal his contempt and disinterest.

"Is this the best plow you have? I thought you'd have something better." Perry's heart raced like a quarter-horse at the thought of using the plow back home.

Marcus warmed up his pitch.

"Well, yes, it is. But you told me the old wooden plow was working great. If you are interested in this beauty, it's one of the best plows you can find west of Saint Louie."

Perry would no more travel to Saint Louis for a better model than he would pay his father for the items he took years ago. Neither was in the realm of possibility.

"Old Woody is doing fine. Cuts through the earth like a knife through warm butter," Perry delivered the half-truth line with studied confidence and a tad too much rehearsed enthusiasm. "This old model here though is not exactly what I wanted to replace Old Woody, but how much are you asking?"

"This is last year's model, but unlike the wooden variety, you won't have to stop your horses every ten feet to knock off the clods."

In the process Marcus sent out a warning shot to challenge Perry's con. "I may be able to extend you an attractive proposition since you are a return-ing customer and all. What do you say we come to terms around $20 and call it straight up?"

The offer sounded more than fair, but Perry winced for dramatic effect after hearing the phrase roll out of the corner of Marcus's mouth.

"Why, sir, I think that a mighty steep fee for such an implement of yesteryear.

What say we settle at $15?"

Marcus broke into a wide grin that showed no distortion at all. He met Perry's drama with an act of his own.

"I shan't make such a deal for that trifle amount, sir, for it would be genuine frontier robbery. The best I can do is $18.50."

Perry scratched his chin. What would be his next move? How could he seal this deal in a way offering no sense of triumph to Marcus, with whom he would also have to deal in the future?

"I will tell you what, Sir Marcus. I like you and think you're an honest broker. I'll offer $17 for the plow, and if you throw in a sack of flour, a box of cartridges for my rifle and a wrapper of peppermint sticks from your countertop, we'll strike a fair agreement."

Marcus initially shot back a frown, but it twisted into a perfect broad smile once again. Even at that low-ball rate, he would turn a profit and make overhead.

"Why, Sir Perry, you indeed drive a hard bargain, but one I shall accept. But I suspect you might be a wily thespian."

"Not really, Marcus. I'm the great-great-grandson of a pirate."

At that point it mattered not to Perry that his ruse had been exposed. He shook his head and smiled. His dimples emerged like the first dandelions of spring.

Perry turned serious and chose his words carefully.

"Marcus, may I ask what happened to your mouth since the time I saw you last?"

"Around a year ago, a horse kicked me. The sumbitch kicked me so hard it snuffed my candle for a couple of days!"

"Damn, that kick must have been a real slobber-knocker," Perry said.

"Yeh, Doc Anderson down the street said I had nerve damage, whatever that is. He said it would come around, but so far, no such luck. I was so desperate I bought a bottle of tonic from the traveling snake-oil salesman. He told me some medical men derived it from the finest nectar extracted from a combination of nuts and twigs with immaculate healing properties. Quite frankly, it tasted like dog crap. But, as you can also see when I smile, the defect melts away. It's better than a magician's trick."

"A great reason to greet each day with a smile, Marcus. And why not? Every day is a blessing."

"Agreed. Smiling not only conceals my affliction, but it has become somewhat of a necessary philosophy for my life."

"And the belief every day is a gift from God, has become mine," Perry responded. "Next time I see you, Marcus, I pray you are fully recuperated. Now, if you'd excuse me, I have some more trading to do."

The two men looked at one another with newfound respect, and they shook hands. While civil and amiable on the outside, both harbored strikingly identical notions in the wrinkled creases of their minds. "I bettered you this time, you poor bastard." Both knew they would meet to haggle again another day.

CHAPTER 8

Spring 1860

SETTLIN' UP

Before settling the full invoice with Marcus, Perry gathered a bag of sugar, a sack of potatoes and onions, a can of lard, and one shiny new bowie knife cased in a bull hide sheath. Up to this point he used an axe for most of his cutting tasks, even those he tried not to remember. While the axe was sharp, it was awkward and heavy. Owning a genuine bowie knife, one with a clipped-point blade, was more necessity than luxury.

The knife and the food provisions rounded out Perry's springtime needs. He had milk from his cow Butter, corn meal he crushed from his own crop, and wild game—venison, and an occasional raccoon he'd harvested with the able help of his housemate Archibald, the floppy-eared hunter.

Perry's favorite wild game with which to stock his pot was the red-tailed squirrel. He and Archibald took many trips up the holler to a tall burr oak tree. It was the grandest tree around, and as Perry walked up hill, Archibald barked excitedly along the way. The squirrels scurried above them, hopping limb to limb high in the treetop canopy. They congregated at the top of the hill in the last tree before a clearing, the big burr oak.

Perry brought the butt of his rifle to his shoulder and pulled the trigger three times. On each occasion another meal fell from the tree. Perry knew the value of conserving the wild game around him. He could have picked off a dozen or more of the bushy-tailed targets in the towering burr oak tree, but he took only what he needed to fill his kettle. Stewed squirrel was the best. Not a bit gamey and all red meat.

Perry topped off his gleaning of nature with a pan of gravy and a bounty of edible forest goodies; wild greens, morel mushrooms, black walnuts, and later in the year, in-season berries and wild fruit like apples, pears, and paw-paws. He also had the choice of walking two miles to the Missouri River in pursuit of a muddy catfish. The river ran east past Jawbone Holler before making a thirty-mile bow-like bend to the north and jagging immediately south past Roubideaux. Perry never went hungry again, and with the coveted plow in hand, he was set for a productive spring laboring in the fields of Jawbone Holler.

In the late afternoon sun, Perry loaded the provisions and the prized plow onto the buckboard wagon. Around the plow he looped a chain secured with a bulky lock like one might see on a primitive jail cell. He spread out a sheet of canvas to conceal it from prying eyes. He did not care about the fate of the provisions, but the last thing he wanted was to have the plow stolen before he could even break soil with its glorious, shining face.

He stuffed the wrapped peppermint sticks into his shirt pocket and threw the bag of flour into the bed of his wagon. Triumph in hand he howled out his farewell. "Here from the holler, and you, Marcus Mixon, got my dollar."

Marcus broke out an ear-to-ear smile as he watched Perry drive his wagon away.

A cheerful warmth rose in Perry's being. He had sealed a deal akin to an act of piracy on the high seas. Blackbeard and great-great-grandpa Matthew would have been proud. In addition to succeeding in farming, he had succeeded in the trickier art of frontier agribusiness. The steel plow was his and for a great deal to boot. Had there been a tattoo parlor in sight, a bare-breasted mermaid surely would have taken up residence on his shoulder. He fancied the notion of himself as an erstwhile pirate. He belted out the chorus from that old English sea shanty he'd heard so many times back in happier days in Salt Spring when family folklore was the evening's fireplace topic.

"Now rid' the waves my fair-faissd lad,
And ne'er a day will yau be sad.
So haul the sail till the day yau die.
Yaur saul 'twill float' to heaven nigh."

Perry ruffled the reins and bade the team of Beulah and Barney onward with the dusk glowing on their backs. He repeated the shanty verse three times from the helm of his buckboard wagon. Perry was in the mood to commemorate the productivity of a notable day. Plus it was getting dark, and he had no place to go this evening. Back in Jawbone Holler, Butter was locked safely in the barn with plenty of hay, grain, and water. Moses would be checking on her. And as added protection, Archibald was sure to put up a ferocious fight against any cowardly varmint that dared even think about entering his domain. When not acting out his usual playful demeanor, Archibald was fierce when necessary. But he would be upset about Perry consigning him to the barn with Butter. Perry took a deep breath. All was safe at home.

Traveling at night back to the holler was not an option Perry considered, even on the most urgent of nights. Not only would crossing the river at twilight be perilous, even aboard the best ferry, but the trails back to Jawbone Holler took on an extra measure of danger after dark. Cliffs and ponds could jump out of the landscape like a bay quarter horse in full sprint. The wise and prudent decision would be to ride out the evening inside the Roubideaux stable, on a bed of hay alongside his wagon, his team, and his precious cargo. After visiting the stablemaster and rendering a fee for a night inside the monstrous shed, Perry drove his team down the street to the Outpost Tavern where he wanted to partake in a celebratory nip of rum, or maybe two.

After hitching his team in a location he could clearly see from inside the tavern, Perry pushed open the swinging doors of the bar with the posture of an accomplished man. It was time to celebrate. Taking two steps in, an overwhelming stench of cigar smoke, sweaty armpits, hair tonic, and what could only have been stale beer greeted him. It was a dark, dank, musty place; a miserable setting for prolonged attendance.

The hubbub of the bar melded multiple simultaneous conversations into a singular cloud of cacophony. The plinking sound of the corner piano broke barely above the dull roar. By the evening light pouring in from the swinging doors, an attractive young woman with flowing ebony hair sat behind the black and ivory keys. She looked more like a librarian than a barroom musician. Her face was as striking as the library images Perry had seen of the *Mona Lisa* but more delicate and finely sculpted.

Perry damn near fainted. He could see that the pianist drew joy from her musical calling as her full-bore smile illuminated the entire room. Her fingers danced across the keys like a miniature ballerina springing from a music box. He tried ridiculously hard not to notice her, unaware that was the same tactic he'd used an hour before when the plow was his object of affection.

But Perry was a man on a mission. He was unaware that another quest would soon eclipse his pursuit of rum. He sauntered to the bar rail and flung down a coin that jingled across the bar top.

A sheet-painted sign behind the bar announced Smit's beer was the preferred brand of the frontier. The prospect of rhyming the word "shit" with that brand name made a smirk cross Perry's face. Perry wasn't a beer man, and the opportunity for satirical poetry about Smit's beer causing the "shits" was as rich as the boundless sea.

Perry preferred spicy rum. It dropped a pleasing sensation on his taste buds. But any rum would do. He remembered sampling beer back in Indiana. It smelled like horse piss. It also tasted as he imagined horse piss might. The after-effects left him feeling quite crapulous, and he wretched for hours.

Perry blamed his genetic passion for rum on his pirate lineage. On this occasion, a nip or two might be a fitting test of his growth and moral character.

"Set me up, barkeep. One shot of the tastiest rum you have on the shelf."

Bartender Pete Fontaine had his hands full, marshaling beer for the majority of his thirsty beer-drinking patrons. Pete was a rough-and-tumble sort. A waxed handlebar mustache shot out beyond his bushy mutton-chop sideburns and his chest was thick like a barrel of beer. He possessed more than adequate heft to serve capably as bartender and bouncer if the customers grew unruly. Pete and his wife Lucy owned the bar.

Pete was guarded with a lot of his opinions because, like Marcus, he knew these were divided days along the bloody border region. There was no need to alienate any patrons whether their sentiments leaned pro or con. But being the piss-cutter he was, Pete was not above asking others about their opinions in a very pointed way. Pete could see arguments on both sides. It was in his nature.

Pete was the son of an underprivileged white sharecropper on a cotton farm near Jonesboro, Arkansas. Each year, the man who owned the land extended to Pete's dad credit for seed to grow a crop and food to feed the family. The landowner charged rent for the use of farming equipment and draft horses as well as the cramped shotgun shack the family called home. The day for settling up the bill was always a matter of dread.

Even in good years, they barely scraped by. Some years the gap was unfillable and was carried forward to the next. Sharecroppers were peasants serving the man in the high castle. To lessen the family burden, Pete toiled as a youngster alongside his mom, dad, brothers, and sisters. During those early days, Pete's daddy praised him by saying, "Awesome job, Petey Possum." Pete liked the rhyme and adapted it as his own.

For Pete and his family, survival was seasonal, but he grew up a proud son of the south. He only had a bare minimum level of education, but he was a student of life. He never set foot in a fancy planation house nor did he want to, yet he respected the men who collected such wealth, even those amassing their fortunes on the stooped backs of others, white and black alike.

Pete yearned to be like those southern gentlemen with the big houses. Sharecropping got in the way of that dream. There was no way to get ahead. When he hit adulthood, he took to the road with a gunnysack of earthly possessions and headed east.

Pete didn't make it far before he hit the banks of the Mississippi River. Pete acquired employment as a blackjack dealer and waiter on a riverboat. Eventually, he saved a stake large enough to quit his job and become a customer. Pete's game was poker. He once justifiably killed a man for dealing from the bottom of the deck.

Pete was also known to frequent the roulette wheel. Pete was a habitual winner. He parlayed his winnings into a stake of sufficient size to make himself an independent business owner.

He traveled upriver looking for opportunity, but Saint Louis proved too ritzy, refined, and socially closed for a man with new money and sharecropper blood. He hit the trail west to explore the frontier towns along the river and territorial border. Pete found Roubideaux. More accurately, being unwilling to cross the border into the untamed Kansas Territory, Roubideaux found Pete.

He struck a friendship with the frontier town's established trading post proprietor, a man named Marcus Mixon, who coached Pete on the finer points of business dealings, both ethical and those more on the side of opportunistic pragmatism. A dollar was a dollar, Marcus told him, whether gained honestly or through advantageous bargaining. With the many lessons he learned while stocking the wooden shelves of the trading post, Pete built his own business, a combination bar, frontier grill, and gambling parlor known simply as The Outpost.

Pete spoke in a slow and distinct southern drawl, even when angered or excited. He was in his mid-forties, slightly balding and of average height. In addition to being barrel chested, he had enormous arms and a pooch of a belly from oversampling his own wares.

The only other distinguishing feature Perry could see on Pete was a tattoo of a playing card on his left arm—the ace of spades, the death card. Perry knew better than to ask and Pete did not volunteer. Pete remained proud of his southern heritage, but not so enamored that he would take up arms on its behalf.

After not securing the bartender's attention, Perry tried again.

"Barkeep, a shot of rum for me," Perry repeated. "The best ya' got."

At that, Pete looked up from the tap pouring at full stream with Smit's beer. Perry thought for a second time about reciting the poem about Smit's to the bartender, but he recalled the advice bestowed by Constable Dan: always take the high road. Perry didn't want to get off on the wrong foot with this burly bartender.

"This here's beer country, friend. I only have one bottle of rum, but it's all yours. My name's Pete. There ain't many rum drinkers in these parts." Pete stretched for a dusty bottle from the highest shelf. "Guessing you ain't from around here."

"Oh, very much so. The folks over in Lowland call me Perry, the wild-eyed Hoosier, but now I am every bit a part of Kansas Territory as the flowering cottonwood seeds that bury the ground like snow in the middle of spring. Rum is part of my heritage. My great-great-grandpappy was a pirate."

"Okay," Pete thought, *"so the guy's a pirate who knows his trees. What other knowledge might be lurking in this fella's brain? Smart as a whip or dumb as a rock?"*

"Perry, your name rings a bell with me. Are you that fella I heard about who walked through three states to reach Kansas Territory on nothing more than a wing and a prayer? If so, I've heard tales about you from the Lowland folks. Is it true you were so ill prepared for your first Kansas winter that you dug a hole to survive with nothing more than a shovel, an axe, and mule meat, or is that just a tall tale?"

"Everything you heard was probably true. That was a dark, abysmal winter. Desperate measures were needed. Since then I've been clearing and cultivating the bluffs about twenty miles due west. Growing corn in topsoil deeper than the river itself."

"It really is an honor to meet ya'. Marcus told me a few details about all your struggles that first winter too. He admires you and your gumption. But since you raise corn and all, why aren't you a bourbon man?"

"I prefer a drink that doesn't burn like the infernal blazes of hell as it navigates past my gullet."

The barkeep put a larger-than-normal shot glass in front of Perry and uncorked the dusty rum bottle.

"We call that the shot heard round the world." Pete grinned, pleased with his flair for frontier marketing.

But Pete still had questions about the fabled man from the Kansas Territory. He'd heard all about the first winter and a somewhat accurate account of how Luke the Mule had met his demise. Pete also knew that many of the settlers in those parts were rock-ribbed abolitionists. Despite the harshness of his share-cropper upbringing, his sentiments leaned slightly in the opposite direction. He wanted to know which side of the ledger Perry claimed as home.

Before pouring rum for this stranger, Pete launched an interrogation.

"A good many of the newcomers to the territory come for opinionated reasons on slavery. Would you be one of those like-minded rambles?"

Perry flinched. He seemed taken aback by the direction of Pete's loaded question. Given the rising number of cross-border raids, burnings, and murders, the question could not be evaded.

Perry weighed his words. He knew his answer would be like walking through a field of quicksand, placing one foot cautiously before the other, assessing the ground's firmness before applying weight. He would declare his stance on the institution of slavery in a diplomatic but forthright manner, while not betraying his kinship with his new business partners Moses and Gabe Watson.

"Well, sir, I can honestly tell you while I do have a clear-cut position on the issue, I came to the territory for one reason only: to become a farmer. It is the solemn truth that I could have kept going into the hinterlands, but the land directly west of here was too good. The possibility of farming my own land, and good land to boot, was why I set up camp."

Perry briefly considered his opinion about slavery, but he did not share his sentiments with Pete, a bartender he just met from a slave-friendly state.

Perry considered one man's ownership of another to be a moral wrong, especially when determining who owned whom was based on the color of a man's skin. His reading on the topic revealed that even the founding fathers tiptoed around the issue.

He also read the full text of a three-hour speech Abraham Lincoln had delivered in a place called Peoria back in the autumn of 1854. Throughout the oration Lincoln had laid out logically the economic, legal, and even moral reasoning why slavery should be opposed. The problem that had stuck in Perry's mind was Lincoln did not feel a conviction sufficient to label himself an abolitionist. To complicate the matter further, Lincoln confessed he was uncertain about how to manage the slavery question within the scope of that day's political structure.

Lincoln had traveled to the embattled territory of Kansas and spoke on the steps of the slapped-together courthouse in Lowland, on Dec. 1, 1859. It had been a frigid day, and Perry had not been able to pry himself away from the warmth of his fireplace for a chance to hear the golden-throated orator. He'd later regretted that decision as short sighted and selfish.

After the event Perry had read in the *Lowland Leger* that about fifty townsfolk packed inside The Honorable Virgil Merriweather's courtroom as the Illinois politician spoke for two hours, laying out logical principles as to why all men should hold the freedom necessary to rise to the level of their talents, regardless of the color of their skin. Again, much to Perry's disappointment, Lincoln had stopped short of making a black and white indictment of the institution of slavery, opting instead to repeat his belief that the union must endure, either with or without slavery because, as he had stated the year before, "A nation divided against itself cannot stand."

Perry drew from Lincoln's border-state diplomacy and responded to Pete's pointed question.

"The simple truth of my own standing on this issue is not what you want to hear. Farming is what brought me here. Farming is my sole concern. If only for a second, however, we could place ourselves in another man's skin and see through his eyes, the souls of all men might be transformed. To see men in chains whipped to within an inch of their death. To see trials, beatings, and lynchings, all because of the color of a man's skin and his yearning to be free. To see all that through his eyes might indeed offer a moment of conversion."

Perry stopped talking.

The answer was sufficient. Pete hoisted the rum bottle toward Perry's face in a half-hearted salute.

"Awesome possum. Here's to you, Perry Adams. I just never thought of it in that way."

Perry asked a few questions of his own.

"You a married man, Pete?"

"Sure am. See that bobbing blond-haired lass in the back kitchen? That's my Lucy. She's a real spitfire. Been married for a while now. She's my partner in all life matters, business and matrimonial. Working on starting a family, but no luck so far."

Pete told Perry he first met Lucy while working at Mixon's Trading Post and overseeing construction of the Outpost Tavern.

"She grew up here, but her family came from Pennsylvania along with a whole wave of German immigrants," Pete said. "They came like all the rest of us, to uncover opportunities here in the American frontier."

"Why else would we have come?" Perry asked.

"One morning she came strolling into the Trading Post. After looking up at a bare shelf, she shouted at Marcus from across the store, complaining there weren't any cans of smoked salmon. She even asked him if she could expect to see any in her lifetime."

"That's pretty spunky."

"It was, and the answer Marcus gave her did not sit well. He said he could only stock 'em if they catch 'em and can 'em. Her reply to Marcus was, 'How hard can it be?'"

"Oh, my! What did Marcus do?"

"Well, it gets worse. I was trying to stay out of the way, just minding my own business. She saw me stocking shelves and practically sprinted across the store. I was up on a ladder, sweat dripping from my forehead. She looked up and asked me if I was Marcus's smoked salmon guy. She called me bucko and told me I needed to knuckle-down. She was in such a tiff her curls were bouncin' side to side. I knew she was flirting, but even to this day, she denies it."

"I have been familiar with bold women in the past, but it didn't really work out," Perry said.

"I met her brashness with a little bravery of my own. I looked her in the eyes and said, 'Ma'am, I'll do my best, especially for you. If I could go down to the river and catch you some salmon bare-handed, I'd do it, but salmon, I fear, do not thrive in the Muddy Missouri.' Then I went a step further. Asked her if she was always this spirited, or did her cuteness fizzle out as the day wore on. She looked right back into my eyes and said that was something I was going to have to discover on my own. So, I did."

Pete continued, "And from that day forward, we were inseparable. After we married, she even helped me put the finishing touches on this place, as well as becoming the business manager and cook. Me? Well, I'm just the bartender and customer relations guy."

"And it was all because of smoked salmon, or lack thereof," Perry surmised. He looked toward the kitchen where Lucy was banging pans and scurrying like a flushed rabbit.

"Yup, smoked salmon."

Pete tipped the rum bottle, and out of it gurgled a golden nectar. "Hope to get a chance to meet her, Pete. Sounds like an admirable woman."

As the rum poured, Perry's mouth watered. Though he knew he was tempting fate, he wanted to put himself through this moral assessment as much as he wanted to celebrate his victory over Marcus earlier that day. Perry took the shot glass in hand and sipped it like it was a thimble of honey, savoring each sweet and spicy note as it splashed his palate.

"If one shot can be heard round the world, Pete, two would likely be audible on our majestic moon," Perry said with the same cheesy panache dished up by the bartender. He told himself two was the limit, and after his years of isolated sobriety, a strange emotion of regret rose from within.

Pete poured the second shot and took Perry's coin in return.

Perry's mind raced, but during a vacant moment, he turned his head and glanced out the swinging doors. He took a deep breath after making sure his wagon and its precious payload remained secure.

Perry stuck his nose inside the rim of the second shot glass to savor the familiar spiced sweetness of the sugarcane-derived liquor. He slammed it in one massive gulp.

Familiar piano notes sprinkled the bar's smoky air. The pretty lady with the flowing black hair—the same one who looked out of place in this frontier bar and whom he tried so hard to ignore minutes earlier—was playing the chorus section from Stephen Foster's "Old Folks at Home." Perry could not believe his ears. A melancholy memory of Lukey crossed his mind. She played the tune at a more frenetic pace than the mellow version he sang years earlier to calm his mule on the open prairie.

Perry's tolerance for alcohol was at low tide, and being in the celebratory mood as he was, Perry could not help but sing with the lovely pianist. The throaty howl of his voice cut above the dull roar of the other bar patrons.

"The whole wide world 'tis sad and dreary, everywhere I roam. Oh, Lukey, how me heart grows weary, far from dem old folks at home."

The bar fell silent as the handsome man drinking rum ended his song of solitude. Except for one snarling man with bushy eyebrows, the entire bar exploded with applause. The young pianist arose to accept the adulation, and Perry immediately saw that in addition to her outward beauty, she had long legs.

Pete looked up in shock and amusement. The distraction caused him to spill a full mug of Smit's that created a current of suds down a full third of the bar top's length.

Pete looked at Perry and belted out a deep, guttural laugh.

"Not sure if that applause was for the piano player or you."

Perry blushed. He had slugged down two shots of liquor, but after singing the chorus he was as sober as a church mouse. Remembering Luke and then all his troubles in Salt Spring, he no longer felt an urge for more.

"Wow, that's quite a voice." Pete chuckled. "How about a shot of rum on the house?"

Perry looked back and smiled, but his eyes expressed a tale akin to spying a ghost, or maybe it was his past.

"No thanks. If I were to have one more, it would surely be a shot I would only regret."

Perry passed the test but wasn't sure whether it was due to his memory of Luke or the familiar melody born on the wings of the angelic pianist.

Perry looked up for a moment toward a table near the end of the bar where two patrons stared back at him. One of the patrons exploded from his chair. The other grabbed him by the shirtsleeve and yanked him down. Perry saw a whisper take place between the two, but could not make out the words.

Unheard by Perry were the words, "In due time. In due time."

CHAPTER 9

Spring 1860

BUT FOR THE GRACE OF GOD

SEEING THE MISPLACED LASS PLAYING the upright dance-hall piano at The Outpost Tavern sprouted new thoughts in Perry's mind. He was instantly smitten by the lady with the ebony locks. Even across the smokey bar, he could see her facial features were as delicate as the first lilies of spring. Her face was long, but not displeasingly so, her eyes and lips were delightfully slight. Her nose was but a whisper. She wore a gray linen dress collected at the waist by a deep blue ribbon. So prim. So proper. All in all, Perry judged her as flawless. Not horse-faced at all. Her grace at the piano, the way she moved her hands along the keyboard and how her head glided from side to side with each passing verse made Perry think her lineage surely sprang from the British Isles.

The young woman's flowing crop of jet-black hair remained a mystery. He imagined it might have been inherited from a lusty horde of Germanic raiders or a daring gang of ancient Celtic warriors, either of whom might have sewn their seeds among the innocent misses living in the coastal hamlets.

After the thought passed, Perry's head lurched with a sudden start when

Barney snorted an audible warning outside. Perry's head seized into another level of consciousness. His thoughts tumbled over a cliff of sheer panic. His dream of the pianist was broken by the urgent realization he had neglected to check on the safety of his plow. Dread flooded his mind as he sprang from the barstool and sprinted out the bar's double doors.

His concern was well founded. It was nearing dusk, and a shadowy figure slumped near the end of his wagon. Both Beulah and Barney were visibly shaken by some kind of commotion.

Perry snatched his rifle from under the wagon seat and crept cautiously toward the street end of his wagon and the shrouded plow. He drew the rifle to his shoulder and shouted.

"Who goes there? And why are you snooping around my wagon when clearly it is cloaked for a purpose?"

A shaky voice shot back, and a feeble head popped above the wagon's tailgate.

"Wha? I dint mean any offense, misser," the prowler responded with an incoherent slur. "I'm jus lookin' fer another trink. I wuz thinkin' there might be a bottle or two of beers under the canvas. Please don't shoot me," the intoxicated man begged. "I jus want one more trink, and I done run out of coin. Jus one more trink to cap off me night."

Perry laughed on the inside. Just a harmless and innocent drunk, but was there really such a thing? At the very least, self-harm was being committed. He recalled his many drunken episodes back in Salt Spring. Unlike this fella he doubted the folks back home would have considered him harmless or innocent due to his archive of destruction.

"Ahh, hell, my friend. Come back into the bar, and I'll buy you a tankard to cap off your evening, but you know that stuff's bad for you, right?"

The drunk nodded, and Perry was simply happy the threat had been nothing but pure folly.

The man, Jeptha Nichols, was a slight and jolly fella. He was shorter than average with a sunken chest and pot belly. He was bow-legged, and he bounded to Perry's side but with the gate of a man slowly dying from the inside out. The two men slid back into the bar, hoping to be unnoticed.

Perry pulled Jeptha to the bar and asked Pete to pour him a mug of Smit's. Pete frowned but nodded his head. Jeptha Nichols wore out his welcome on most nights by panhandling among the paying customers.

"Ok, Jep, this'll be your last one of the evening," Pete said. "I want you to go back to the boardin' house and sleep it off, or would you rather Lucy come out here and lay down the law?"

"I promis, Petey. Don't bother Miss Lucy. Jus one mor, and I'll hit da road," Jeptha slurred, snuggling the mug in both hands like a fragile treasure. He staggered to a stool at the end of the bar.

Pete hated to feed into Jeptha's addiction, but it was the best way to stop the drunk's panhandling. It also showed Pete a bit more of Perry's character. A man aiding a struggling soul rather than judging him was agreeable in Pete's book. That led Pete one step closer to his belief Perry indeed was an honorable man.

Perry was tempted to make his exit, but piano music was still being played. He reclaimed his spot at the bar and returned his attention to the lovely pianist. But now, instead of rum, Perry opted for a syrupy glass of sarsaparilla. Perry wanted to keep his wits. The drink was not intoxicating and much sweeter than rum, often a mix of squeezings from mysterious tropical roots along with cinnamon, vanilla, sugar, and other various ingredients, depending on the whim of the mixer.

"Jep seems harmless enough," Perry said. "But I fear he's standing on the precipice of tragedy. How in the hell did he ever get himself in such a habitual state of inebriation?"

"It all started when his wife left. Up to that point, Jep owned the local sawmill, then the Mrs. up and left and took up with a certain trading post proprietor."

"Ahh, hell, Pete. You're not talking about Marcus, are you? I'm not sure whether the ladyfolk would consider Marcus a catch, but maybe if you throw in Marcus's Trading Post."

"Yep, but Marcus couldn't help himself. She threw herself at him, and, well, you know Marcus. When a good deal smashes him in the face, it's hard for him to say no."

"Shit, that's sad. So, what about Jep's sawmill?"

"Though Mrs. Nichols was the one who caused it all, the judge awarded her a chunk of the place. Her lawyer demanded she was entitled to an immediate cut of the business assets to start her new life. It was the only thing Jep had to his name. He had no choice but to sell. His whole life of hard work and, poof, 'twas gone in a flash."

"Still, he should have received a handsome chunk of money for his sweat equity in the sawmill, right?"

"He sure did, but what's the old saying? Idle time is the devil's tool or something like that. Jep took up the unfortunate vices of gambling and drunkenness. Both failings occurred in tandem, and they did not mix. Now, most days Jep thinks he's a genie," Pete continued. "Either that or he's playing a clever con on all the rest of us."

"A genie? You mean like from the *Arabian Nights*?"

"Yup. I try to balance the situation as best as I can. I worry about Jep. I fear the worm of alcohol has eaten into his brain, but the fact he's here means he's not freezing in some dark alley."

"If he thinks he's a genie, does he grant wishes?"

"On occasion, but it requires handin' him a shot or a beer. I don't feed into it, but others do. While it might be amusin' to some of my patrons, I don't see the humor, and it really pisses Lucy off. Jep's become the local freak show."

"Did he gamble his money away?"

Pete raised his hand and pointed at one of the poker tables in a dimly lit corner of the Outpost.

"Yep. He lost it all one drunken evening playin' five-card draw at that very table against some grifters up from Westport. If there's one thing I know, it's card gamblin'. I can spot a shark a country mile away because I used to be one. I warned Jep. He told me his genie forces empowered him to see through the cards. He was holdin' a full house, jacks over kings. His genie eyes tricked him into the belief the only fella left held nothing but a jack-high straight. Turned out to be a straight flush. Jep lost everything."

"The genie in Jep must be color blind," Perry said.

"I tried my best to intercede, but at the card table, a fair hand is a fair hand. And I try to keep my customers happy, whether they're locals or swindlers passing through. There was just no way I could save Jep from his genie self."

Perry looked down the bar. An intensified level of pity flooded his emotions. Jep the genie was nursing his beer, looking pleased and appearing not to have a care in the world. Old Jep didn't have much to worry about, except for maybe the origin of his next pint.

"Damn, that is one sad story, Pete. There are plenty of tales of tribulation all along the frontier trail, but it's hard to measure up to Jep's."

"He works menial jobs during the day, like scoopin' horse shit at the stable and sweepin' the floors here, at least when Lucy and I have a profitable week and we don't feel like doin' it ourselves. He works half the day so he can drink all night until he feels transformed into his genie self. When his money runs out, he resorts to panhandlin', grantin' wishes in exchange for handouts."

As troubled as Perry was about Jep's downfall, he was even more perturbed that he might have misjudged Marcus.

"All during the time I have been dealing with Marcus, I thought him an honest and upright man. How could he steal another man's wife? But, then again, who am I to stand in judgment? We all have a few ghosts in our graveyards."

"I think you can still think of Marcus as a stand-up feller. He didn't cause the break-up, and after about six months, he threw her out of the house. His conscience got the better of him as Jep's life spiraled out of control."

"There was also the little issue that the former Mrs. Nichols insisted on imposin' her will. It was different for Lucy and me, but Marcus was set in his ways. It wasn't that he was afraid of the changes she was demandin' for him, but when she started tinkerin' with changes at the trading post, Marcus saw the light."

"She wanted to stock the shelves of the tradin' post with items that might appeal to women, like frilly petticoats and lace stockings and such," Pete continued. "As a married man, I can appreciate that she was trying to spice up life around here. But the last straw was when she secretly invested a whole week's worth of tradin' post sales to order two dozen bottles of fancy French perfume, imported via ocean steamer all the way from a place called Toulouse and transported here aboard a Wells Fargo stage."

"Damn, that probably hurt old Marcus worse than the horse kicking him in the mouth."

"Old Marcus about lost his usual peaceable demeanor. It was an untenable position. He had to recover the loss for two months. It was a costly ordeal. The former Mrs. Nichols got the boot and appropriately so. She's been disgraced, reduced to slinging hash over at the Pitts House. But she still hasn't apologized to Jep. Not a peep."

Perry offered a final thought on Marcus.

"Trust is a big issue for me. The folks over in Lowland are quick to judge. Most of the men are either pigstickers or honey drippers. There's not a happy medium and they are quick to share their opinions. At times, I feel beset by peril akin to walking through a den of pit vipers. The folks smile at my face, but I always fear that when I turn my back they will draw their horrible blades. At least Marcus is the devil I know."

"Marcus is far from bein' the devil. In order to live inside our skin, each of us needs to consider a higher cause. Just know that Marcus admires you, and there's a lot about him you don't know."

Pete took another look down the bar at Jep and shook his head in sympathy.

"I've witnessed Jep's downfall. But it's a busy Friday night, and I don't have time to harbor any lingering notions of sorrow. I have bartender duties to conduct, and there's not much you can do once Jep hits full genie mode."

To coax his paying customers to stay even an hour longer, Pete fired up The Outpost's kerosene lanterns and placed a few thick candles on tables around the joint. He was willing to serve his clientele as long as they were eager to spend their money and enjoy the followship, a good many at the risk of their own household bliss. Faces around the bar caught a flickering of the well-placed flames.

The fair pianist continued to pound out tunes in the background. Of all the profiles in the Outpost that evening, Perry was sure the most stunning face in the candescence was found at the keyboard.

It had been a long day, during which Perry finalized a good many deals. His mind drifted away from Jep's genie incarnation. In spite of life being driven by a series of harrowing turns, Perry began to think about a turn of his own. Living life alone carried no appeal. The thought cut furrows into the depth of his mind.

Perry's intrigue with the magnificent pianist's splendid rendition of "Old Folks at Home" captured his mind. He construed it as nothing less than a sign of destiny. Her beauty drew his intense fascination. He vowed an introduction was in order, but rashness was not a becoming quality, especially in the way he wore it. While Perry wanted to explore what made this captivating and talented woman tick, the evening had slipped away.

"Pete, it's been a long and challenging day. I appreciate the delight of our sprouting camaraderie, but the hour is nigh for my retreat. I need to secure my horses and wagon and the new plow I just bought from Marcus. The stable is as far as I am traveling tonight. I have a few more topics to delve with you, but those matters will wait for tomorrow. Nothing too weighty. Mostly about the merits of delightful music and pretty women. I can meet your Lucy too."

Pete flashed Perry a knowing look. Perry's infatuation for the delicate pianist was as obvious as a pounding hammer.

"Lucy and I swing the doors open for business at the crack of dawn every Saturday mornin'. Always like to serve Lucy's ham and eggs to the early-risers. Lucy tells me the more business we can attract, the better we can spread our fixed costs and realize a superior rate of return on our investment and labor. I leave the number stuff up to her."

"Lucy must be quite astute at business. I bet she could even give Old Marcus a run for his money."

"She's the best, but for God's sake, don't ever talk to her about Marcus and his inability to stock smoked salmon." Pete laughed. "She gets all riled up anytime smoked salmon's the topic of conversation."

"Really? Smoked salmon really sets her off? I'll have to file that away. I sure hope to meet Lucy in the morning after sunrise breaks over yonder hill."

"She'll be workin' the kitchen, which to this day continues to be free of smoked salmon."

Perry arose from his stool, tossed Pete a tip and delivered his trademark yell.

"Pete, I'm here from the holler and you got my dollar!"

"Awesome possum," Pete replied.

Perry told himself the rum had nothing to do with his boldness, but he waited for the pianist to finish her song before making his exit. He sauntered across the barroom floor to where Jep retreated into the suds of his beer.

"Say, Jep, why don't you take tomorrow off? Sleep it off and go calm your mind under that big willow shade tree down at the river's edge."

Perry handed Jep a few folded bank notes. The value of such a gift exceeded the wage Jep could make in a full week of floor sweepin' and shit scoopin'.

Jep's words were hobbled but humble.

"Tank ya, stranger."

Jep's eyes sparkled, and they practically shouted the appreciation of a genie just escaped from a magic lantern.

"I tink I'll grant ya' a wish."

"My only wish is for every day to hold a blessing for you, Jep. Don't let anyone get in the way."

Jep's fall had been a hard one, worsened by the fact Mrs. Nichols's rise in the opposite direction came largely at his expense. To make matters worse, on her way back down, she did not bother to pick Jep up. He might forever be a genie.

As Perry continued his exit, he puffed out his chest as he walked past the piano.

"Ma'am, the name's Perry Adams," he said and tipped his hat to the lovely pianist. He placed a gold coin as a tip in the beer mug atop her upright piano. He also left one of the wrapped peppermint sticks he'd bought at Marcus's. It was one fluid motion. The pianist's eyes lingered for three seconds beyond a level of comfort.

She smiled at Perry.

A strange feeling shot through Perry's chest, and he smiled back.

That night Perry walked out of The Outpost Tavern and up to the hitching post with a stinging sensation in the pit of his stomach. His skin tingled from head to toe. He had never experienced such a feeling in matters related to poor Violet back in Salt Spring.

Perry was buzzing as he untied his team of horses and set out for the stable for a much-needed night of rest and, if possible, to sleep off any lingering side effects of the devil's rum. Perry wanted to ensure clarity, both in body and thought, for the next morning's conversation with Pete. He still had work to do.

Perry coaxed Beulah and Barney carefully into the sanctity of the barn's expansive interior. He unharnessed the horses, scooped them a night ration of ground corn and filled a trough of water. Perry fetched a pitchfork from the tack room. He heaved five fork-loads of oat straw into the bed of his wagon and crawled under the canvas tarp next to his plow. Looking up, the ceiling was as high as the old world's grandest cathedrals. In the humble tone of an amazed farmer, Perry said to his team, "I bet we could store a lot of corn in here."

In the glow of a kerosene lantern, Perry's final thought before drifting off was that tomorrow beckoned another day of opportunity. A quite unexpected matter begged for his sober attention. He rolled over in the oat straw and a smile of contentment reflected off the burnished face of his new self-scouring plow. Perry was too exhausted to notice.

CHAPTER 10

Spring 1860

DISCOVERY DAY

Awoken by a feral rooster's crowing before the sun crawled over the eastern horizon, Perry opened his eyes with his face vividly reflected in the polished face of his treasured plow. He felt satisfaction in that waking moment. Beulah and Barney were still partaking in morning slumber. He left the animals and his cargo within the secure confines of the livery stable. Perry consulted the stable hand about the arrangement in exchange for a generous tip.

Feeling no ill effects from a bit of indulging the previous night, Perry was now driven by hunger. He panged as much for information about the pianist as he craved sustenance to break his morning fast. He exited via the stable's roadside door and walked two dusty blocks to The Outpost.

Spring songbirds—goldfinches, robins, orioles, cardinals, and chickadees— flitted, darted, and warbled as they tweeted out their morning anthems. Three apple trees rooted next to the wooden sidewalk exploded in full blossom. Drawing near The Outpost's swinging doors, Perry saw it was *the* place to be this morning. Buggies and horses and wagons crowded the dirt street in front of the bar. Customers came for Lucy's ham and eggs, served up with a healthy serving of gossip.

This early morning crowd at The Outpost was buzzing. It was the social gathering of the week.

When Perry walked in the swinging doors, The Outpost's interior had been transformed. White linens and stick candles adorned each table, even the poker tables, touches that were set in motion by Lucy, who was in the kitchen cracking eggs and flipping cast iron skillets. Life was simple during this weekend special. The only item on the menu was ham 'n eggs. The only option was with cheese or without.

Perry took a seat at the bar, like the night before. He was happy all the other patrons, men, women and even some children, chose the fancy tables.

"No piano music this morning, Pete?" Perry frowned his disappointment.

"We try to set a different ambiance on Saturday mornings, Mr. Adams. I hope you're not too forlorn."

"I tend to create my own misery because of my hopes, but once I set my eyes on a goal, I keep ticking along until I reach it."

Pete raised mug after mug to the beer tap. Each one contained about two inches of a red liquid in the bottom before being topped off with Smit's.

"What in the world are you doing there, Pete? Did your dishwasher forget to scrub your mugs?"

"I'm servin' up a magical concoction I offer to the Saturday morning patrons of my fine establishment. I call it 'mater beer or tomato juice and beer for you more refined types. Got a special price on Saturdays, but I offer it on demand, any day, any hour."

Pete continued as the frothy foam of the mugs took on a reddish tint.

"It's a magical elixir. Quite effective at relievin' hangovers. Pourin' them up straight outta the tap is the best way to go. No mixin' needed. Just salt the top, give it a little swirl, and you got the perfectly measured 'mater beer."

"I'll be damned. Who was the evil genius who devised such a recipe?"

"Did it myself. I consider it my contribution to frontier society. Came up with the idea back during my blackjack dealin' days . . . sort of. I served drinks to the gamblers between my dealin' sessions on the riverboat. One day a fella ordered a beer and the guy sittin' next to him ordered a glass of 'mater juice.

While I was totin' 'em back to the table, the riverboat smacked head-first into a sandbar. Sent a jolt through the cabin that almost rocked me off my feet. I kept my balance, but in the hullabaloo, some of the 'mater juice splashed into the beer. Shit, Perry, I couldn't serve it, so I drank it myself. It was damn good. My tastebuds 'sploded with satisfaction."

"What a stroke of fortunate happenstance. I think I'll try one."

"Oh, I guarantee you'll find it quite delectable. Once I became a gambler myself, it was my drink of choice. Helped me keep a sober edge at the poker table, while all the other fellers were guzzlin' beers left and right. Right after we opened this place, I convinced Lucy it'd make a perfect breakfast essential. The legend of 'mater beer at The Outpost grew from there."

Perry leaned forward on his barstool, elbows on the bar. "I'm starvin', Pete."

"We only got one food item on the menu. Just let me know when you're ready."

"I'm ready." Perry tilted his head toward the kitchen and shouted far louder than necessary so Lucy could hear it above the clattering of kitchen pans.

"Three scrambled eggs topped with cheese, but instead of ham, I'd like mine with smoked salmon."

"Oh, shit, you've done it now," Pete said.

Lucy exploded from the kitchen and stared Perry in the eyes across the bar.

"Are you the Adams guy Pete told me about?" Lucy asked, energy shooting from her eyes like lightning bolts.

"Why, yes, ma'am, I am," Perry said.

"Don't ever mention smoked salmon to me ever again. The reason I'm here is because of the lack of smoked salmon at Mixon's a couple years back. Long story, but it's how I met this guy," Lucy said, nodding to Pete.

"Oh, I know the story, ma'am. That's why I placed my order. I just couldn't wait any longer to meet the one and only Mrs. Fontaine."

"I tried to tell him, but he did it anyway," Pete said.

The corners of Lucy's mouth turned upward and the fire in her eyes transformed to warmth.

"You son-of-a-gun. Just to get me out here. We'll talk more later, Adams, but I gotta get back to the kitchen. Enjoy your eggs and ham. Pete, remind me to get even with this guy later." Lucy skipped back to the kitchen.

"OK, thanks for that, Perry. Just know, she'll get even. Since that introduction's out of the way, what'll you drink? And please don't say rum."

Perry smiled and scratched his dimpled chin. "No rum this morning. Think I'll try one of those Smit's with 'mater juice. My imagination tells me it must cut the level of distaste of the beer alone."

As he waited, Perry surveyed the room, hoping he would spy the young maiden who played the previous night's piano. The piano was there, draped with a lace tablecloth to make the place feel a little classier. She was nowhere in sight. Perry continued to scan the room. Pete knew exactly who Perry was looking for.

Perry's eggs arrived piping hot, too hot to eat. He slugged down a gulp of the 'mater beer, which was not objectionable, and looked across the room once again.

"Not only do we not have music this morning, but my pianist will not be making an appearance this morning either," Pete said.

"Whatever do you mean? I'm just here for the food and conversation." Perry took a bite of the fluffy eggs and washed it down with a swallow of 'mater beer.

"Yeh, right. Just like you were here last night for the music. Don't try to horseshit a bullshitter. I was beginnin' to think you were a forthright man. Now I'm not so sure."

"In response to your well-pointed implication, I am afraid to admit you have unmasked my true motivation," Perry said sheepishly, before adeptly changing the subject. "How does Lucy make these eggs so fluffy?"

"Cream. She stirs it into the scrambled eggs to the point where it froths. Now, enough of your misdirection. What do you want to know about my piano player?"

"Why so abrupt, Pete. I thought bartenders were supposed to be more hospitable. The longer we talk, the more money we spend, right?"

Perry looked at Pete. Like his partial parable about his stance on slavery, Perry began to spin a yarn about his interest in the piano player's talent. He was certain Pete could see through it like a spider web. Perry's mission was to not get entangled in the silken threads and become the spider's next meal. He kept his intentions transparent but his words nebulous.

"You know why I'm here," Perry said, confessing but not coming entirely clean. "And it really isn't about the scrambled eggs."

Pete shot Perry a knowing grin.

"She plays the piano here five nights a week. Has Saturday mornin', Sundays, and Monday night off," Pete began.

"I really like how she plays," Perry said, still trying to not break into jail. Perry took the conversation forward with one more precipitous step. But he weighed his words as politely as one might ask a war hero how he lost a leg.

Pete's attention was divided, listening to Perry with one ear as he began drawing beers for a table of customers who were drinking in the morning experience.

"So, friend, is she a relative, a younger sister, perhaps? What details might you share with me about this establishment's talented musician? She seems as out of place here as an opera singer in a coal mine."

Pete cocked his ear toward Perry and looked up, trying to ignore the unintended slight of his fine establishment, which Perry had just compared to a dusty, dark coal mine.

"I can tell you for a fact she is very much out of place here. I'm not sure why I am tellin' you all this because I usually don't make it a habit to divulge details about colleagues. You're still pretty much a stranger to me, but I do feel empathy with you and know if I called you a crazy bastard, you'd probably take it like water off a mallard's back. The young lady is definitely not my younger sister, but Lucy and I guard her like she was our younger sibling."

Perry respected the answer, and he waded in for another carefully measured query.

"It is the simple truth. I admire her choice of music and her ability to interpret it with elegance." Perry balanced his works as carefully as a banker guards his gold. "Is this her full-time vocation?"

"Nah. She's an underpaid schoolmarm. The fact that she even sets foot in this place is a secret held tightly by me and everyone who walks in my door. That's how much they appreciate her. She teaches over at the Benedictine Mission School, but if anyone raised a fuss about her playing the piano here, they'd fire her in a heartbeat. I'm a gambler at heart, Perry, but I don't like to leave anything to chance. You might say I hedge my bets just a tad. Every quarter I deliver a cask of fine Italian wine directly to one Father Eugene McCord. He runs the place and appreciates the gesture very much. You might call it my contribution to the Benedictine Community."

"But as for my piano player, she is a devout Catholic woman, very much dedicated to the church. But she's also as innocent as a lamb frolicking in a sunlit meadow. I don't think she understands her affiliation with this establishment might be frowned upon."

Lucy came back to the bar after the orders subsided.

"Let me guess, this backwoods fella here likes our piano player."

"Oh, hell. I guess there's no foolin' a woman," Perry said.

"Right you are, Mr. Adams. Just like Pete has told you, she's a beautiful and delightful girl, which you already know, but she is also very strait-laced and devout. What religion I do get usually comes directly from her. This week she told me about some biblical woman named Mary of Bethany. Actually, it seems a bit eerie because Bethany is also her middle name.

"As she told me, during a visit by Jesus at the home she shared with her sister, this Mary of Bethany sat at Jesus's feet and did nothing but listen to his teachings while her sister Martha did all the work connected with his visit. Spiffing up the place. Preparing a meal. Stuff like that. Mary's inclination to do nothing but listen really ticked Martha off. When Martha complained about being stuck with all the work, Jesus told her that Mary was doing the only thing that mattered. The more we talked about it, the more I knew I was Martha and she was Mary. She said the story was her private message from heaven to only be concerned with loving and serving the Lord. She considers her teaching the same way. It's her calling. Well, that and the joy she brings to others through her music. She really is the full package. I'm not sure you measure up."

"You might be right, Miss Lucy. I know you don't owe me a thing except possibly a bad turn for my smoked salmon comment, but I would like to find out."

Pete scratched his chin and went into more detail about the Benedictine monks who built the mission school in Roubideaux.

"They got here a little before you. But they were a bit wiser. Stopped their journey in early summer, before that cruel winter set it. They live under the Rule of St. Benedict. *Ora et labora.* Work and pray. It's their holy promise to pray and work each day for the Glory of God."

Pete said the Benedictines were like jacks-of-all-trade monks, while other Catholic orders often had a singular, core pursuit to which there was always fanatical dedication.

"Whenever and wherever the Benedictines see a need to build the community, they dig in and do it," Pete said. "Wherever their holy quests took them and whatever the task at hand might be, they tackle it with devotion and solitude. Work and pray. That's what they do."

The dark-robed priests were skilled at expanding their reach, in both state and territory, like they were on a crusade for every frontier soul, Pete explained. They mined large blocks of limestone and erected a monstrous abbey high on a hill overlooking the Missouri River near the settlement known as Brenner. They established parishes, large and small. They farmed the rich bottomland next to the river, and they prospered as a community through prayer and work. Establishing educational missions in the outlying area was one of their core works, and if that work upset those more predisposed to other education-focused holy orders, so be it.

"The only problem with the Benedictines is they expect the laity who teach and work beside them to share the same hallowed dedication to all aspects of the monastic ethic of work and prayer," Pete explained. "The wages are so paltry the joke around here is they also expect the lay people to uphold the sacred vow of poverty. And that explains why your favorite teacher is also a barroom pianist. She needs the extra job just to pay rent."

"She lives upstairs, above my kitchen," Lucy said. "It certainly is not expensive, but it is all she can afford. She's been banging on those piano keys for a couple of years now. She has bought into the Rule of St. Benedict. Work and pray. And it's a good thing because she has no time to do anything else. I doubt she'd have time for you."

"Ouch, that hurts, but do you mean to tell me I am down here talking with you two, and she is a mere forty feet from me at this very moment?"

"That's what we're tellin' you," Pete said. "She's probably up there right now in full recital of the rosary. Either that or she's finishin' a good night's sleep. Anyone who works as hard as she does deserves to sleep in on a Saturday mornin'."

"Either of those options is certainly good for the soul. One more question. Does she currently have any beau interests?"

"Are you kidding me? The only menfolk in these parts are coots or hermits, of which you are the latter. She does not have time for men," Lucy said. "The only relationship she might have right now, in addition to herself and her work, is the man upstairs. While I must admit you do possess striking looks, I'm not sure that God is a competitor that even you can intimidate."

"Don't be so hard on him, Lucy," Pete said. "Perry, I will see what I can do if you think you're up for the challenge."

Perry popped a smile wider than the river, his giddiness as audible as a bell tolling for Sunday mass. He considered Pete's offer to make an introduction a generous one.

Lucy fired a final salvo at Perry as she turned to return to the kitchen.

"Just don't stink up the opportunity if Pete makes arrangements. I'd hate for smoked salmon to be the less odorous option of the day, but then again, I still don't have any. Now, gents, Martha is being called back to the kitchen. The orders are starting to stack up."

"I'm up to the challenge, Miss Lucy. Nothing but best behavior from me from now on, I promise," Perry said.

Reaching the kitchen, Lucy shouted over the roar of the bar, "I'm going to hold you to that, but I'm still not sure you are right for her."

"So, when can I try to make this happen?" Pete asked Perry.

"Not this trip, Pete. I need to clean up first. I don't want to scare her off or appear overconfident or overly eager. But I swear to you, as sure as my middle name is Samuel, my intentions are unsullied. But I am still at a disadvantage. God knows her name, and I still do not."

"The name's Millicent Longworth, but we all call her Millie."

Without a doubt Pete could see Perry held deep admiration for Millie, and he hadn't even formally met her yet.

"I only tell you that because I believe your intentions are honorable. Don't prove me wrong."

"Thanks, Pete. I don't believe I have heard music as sweet since my Grandpa Elijah took me to Indianapolis for a bit of culture. But, ruse aside, Miss Millie is a beautiful woman and one I'd like to get to know a little better."

"Glad to hear you finally admit it. I'll tell you what. You go back to your humble little holler and get your crop in. Come back to see me and I'll find a way to make a right proper introduction. I'll make sure Lucy is hitched to the wagon as well."

"You got a deal, Pete. Oh, and just to let you know, on my way out of the bar last night, Millie smiled at me."

"That's a good omen. Millie works so hard, both day and night, she hardly has the energy to even acknowledge most people. That, my friend, could be a portent of promisin' things to come."

Perry finished his eggs and ham and chugged the last of his 'mater beer. He looked up at the door to the room above the kitchen. He could only imagine the young lass still asleep in her bed, but for now, that would have to do.

"I will see you next month, Pete, after I get my corn planted. Work and pray. But, brother, you better stock up on your sarsaparilla fix'ens. I'm done with the devil rum. But I can't rightly say I will ever be able to kick my habit for a pleasant tune on the piano or, for that matter, pretty schoolteachers."

"Awesome possum," Pete replied.

Perry arose from his barstool and bid his new friend Pete farewell. After waving at Lucy, he walked back to the stable with a noticeable spring in his step. He paid the stable hand for the extended stay and extra feed and water for Beulah and Barney. He hitched up the team and started his day-long return journey to the holler with plow and provisions in transport.

Perry had fields to plow and corn to plant. Confident this would be a better year and the hailstorms would pass him by, he could not wait to put his new plow into service. He also began work in earnest to draft his introductory script for the day he would meet Miss Millie Longworth.

CHAPTER 11

Spring 1860

A SINGULAR
FOCUS OR TWO

PERRY REACHED JAWBONE HOLLER by midafternoon. Beulah and Barney were exhausted from the long day trip back from Roubideaux and Perry moved quickly to relieve them from the wagon. He approached the wagon and gently scooted the plow toward the tailgate. Then, carefully cradling all 243 pounds of the plow with a bearhug at the plowshare and moldboard, he gently lifted the prize and sat it inside the barn.

After that, Perry checked on Butter and Archibald, who was annoyed about his exile from a comfy bed in the house. Perry grabbed a bucket and moved on to milk Butter. The cow's udders were overflowing, due to inattention during Perry's trip to Roubideaux. As he milked Butter, Perry munched on one of the remaining peppermint sticks while imagining Millie doing the same.

As Perry turned her out to the barn-side pasture, he thought it was time to find Butter a boyfriend, at least for a temporary affair. That was a matter he'd already arranged with his bartering partners, Moses and Gabe Watson. He would make a trip to the Watson farm later in the week.

After offloading his food provisions in a storage room in his house, Perry relaxed a spell. Though he was tempted to take the plow for a spin right then and there, Perry waited until the following morning to give his new plow a field test. Work to prepare his cornfields would begin tomorrow.

During his respite Perry used the evening hours to begin drafting in his mind the words he would deliver when first introduced to Millie. "It's a pleasure to meet you, ma'am. Maybe you remember me from the peppermint stick I left on your piano . . . " The words fell flat. He would have to work on it.

Dizzy with anticipation, sleep was elusive.

Morning broke with a western meadowlark belting out a familiar multi-syllable song through the early morning air. So shrill was the sound that it reached Perry's eardrum as he enjoyed the last minutes of comfort from the oat straw mattress atop the self-fashioned split log bed inside his house. The pitchy serenade served as Perry's reveille to start his working day. And what a working day it was.

Perry had plowed his fields that fall with Old Woody. And the cooper-trimmed wood plow did an admirable job of turning under the unrealized promise of hail-smashed corn stalks. Now that it was spring, with the devastating visions of the 1859 crop turned to clods and memories, Perry was ready to tackle the task of spring plowing, the last step in preparing the seedbed for the corn crop of 1860. The field had to be cross-plowed, perpendicular to the direction he walked during the fall, to help ensure a suitable seedbed. He could not wait to put the John Deere steel plow through its paces.

The anticipation made Perry's heart race. In the morning light, he quickly donned his dungarees, a flannel shirt, and his leather work boots. He practically danced to the barn to prepare Beulah and Barney for a long workday, and to hitch them up to the tool he still viewed in the same manner a child might admire a new toy drum on Christmas morning.

Perry led the horses to the field's edge in anticipation of seeing a miracle of modern agriculture performed on his own squatter acreage. After all the harness components were in place, with the horses to the front, the plow and Perry walking behind, he braced himself for what he anticipated would be a breathtaking show of agrarian ingenuity.

He slapped the reins, shouted at his trusty team to, "Git up!" and off they went. About fifteen feet in, the plow face bit fully into the earth, sending waves of rich, black soil into the area adjacent to its path. It was a miracle. The furrows rolled off the shining plow face slicker than the sales pitch Marcus Mixon had used to make the deal.

Perry and the team worked the entire day, stopping only for water and a nibble or two to reclaim their energy. By the end of the day, the entire field was wearing a black cape of freshly turned earth. Not once did Perry need to halt the team to bust a clod off the plow face. It was his dream come true. With this boost of productivity, he would soon have the means to think of other matters in life, such as love and family.

The results were equally astonishing the next day in the last field. Seed bed prepared, Perry waited impatiently for the mercury to rise in the thermometer to plant his crop. Too early tempted the killing last gasp of a late spring frost. Too late enticed the arrival of intemperate heat of an early summer that would suck the moisture from the seedbed and stunt the crop's germination. Perry chomped at the bit with even more intensity than Beulah and Barney when they hit their stride, but he waited a couple more days.

A quick run over to Roubideaux to check on Pete, Marcus and Jep entered his mind, but moreover, he could also steal another glance at Millie. Such a move would be folly given the demands of planting. Signaling his intentions to Millie would have to wait.

The vacant corners of his mind began to wonder. Would she remember the night they exchanged smiles? Would she recall him accompanying her with all modesty abandoned when he belted out his slightly modified chorus of "Old Folks at Home"? Would the calling cards of gold and sweet peppermint he left on the piano top rekindle a spark of her memory? He did not want too much time to pass. The questions drove Perry mad. He needed a distraction.

The next day he got one in the form of Moses Watson, one of his new bartering partners, who came to call. The diversion was a welcome one.

Moses and Gabe had visited the farm on a couple of occasions before, but this visit by Moses alone was a surprise. As Moses's perfectly matched team of horses pulled into the clearing near Perry's house, Perry was completing his morning chores. Archibald came running to meet the visitor, ears flopping and tail wagging.

"*Uh-roo-roo-roo,*" Archibald barked.

"Good morning, Watty, this is quite the surprise," Perry said. "I see you still know your way back here to Jawbone Holler, even without Gabe as your navigator. I am pleased to see you."

"I hope I might be able to take a fresh look at your place during planting season and see how far your field work has progressed," Moses said. "Gabe is holding down the fort at home, but I want to maybe take a gander at that plow you had planned to acquire."

"You and Gabe are always welcome, and I do have something I'd like to show you."

Perry pulled back the canvas covering the steel plow. Its face radiated in the morning sun.

"Take a look at this beauty," he said, nearly popping the buttons off the front of his shirt in a display of pure pride.

"I've read about them and even used one during my days of captivity. It is indeed a marvel of ingenuity."

"Better yet, you have to see how it works this generous topsoil."

The two men walked to the edge of the first field where Perry had prepared a seedbed as royal as a king's festival table. Moses bent at the waist and gathered a handful of dirt. Like Perry had done years before, he squeezed it between his thumb and forefinger to form a ribbon of organic prospect.

"Oh, that's good soil, Perry. It's no wonder you have become successful in raising corn. But for Gabe and me, we will stick to our livestock. The work's constant, but a lot less painful if things go awry."

"I'm not talking about any crop perils at this point in the year. I don't want to tempt fate. But I do hope to bring Butter over within the next couple days for a visit with your fine bull."

"Ah, you're a busy man this time of year, Perry. Why don't you let me tether Butter to the back of my wagon, and I'll take her with me today? She'll be in good hands, and frankly, Chester needs the company, regardless of what Gabe thinks. My cow herd is heavy with calves, and old Chester is getting little to no attention."

"Why, that's a mighty generous offer, Watty, and one I will accept. Why don't you come inside, and I'll stir up some chipped beef gravy and biscuits with a side of fried morel mushrooms."

"That, sir, I will do as well," Moses said.

As the men entered Perry's house, Moses's eyes were drawn to the mantle above Perry's fireplace. He recalled the story about Luke that Perry had shared the first day they met. The long white jawbone above the mantle could be nothing other than the relic jawbone of that magnificent animal.

"Is this the jawbone you have preserved of that marvelous mule that saved your life?"

"Yes, it is. Take a close look if you like."

Moses carefully lowered Luke's jawbone from the fireplace and ran his hand along its length.

"Really must have been a magnificent animal. The way you continue to honor his life is quite remarkable."

"Old Lukey is the only reason I made it here in the first place, and my survival that first winter would have been quite impossible without him."

Moses returned Luke's jawbone to its place of honor. Perry started a fire in his cookstove and began to prepare the meal. As Perry fumbled with utensils, Moses could see cooking was not Perry's strong suit, but he waited patiently as the conversation continued.

"Watty, during my last trip to Roubideaux, a young woman captured my heart. I didn't really meet her, but I sure hope to do that soon."

"Is this the kind of woman who might join you here on the farm?"

"Yes, I believe so. Any words of wisdom?"

"If she captures both your heart and soul, you should move with urgency. If only one, it still might offer a foundation on which to build. but leave nothing to chance. Her answer might be yes or it might be no, but boldness is always a marvelous educator along life's path. The path that led me to select a mate was mandated, but I will never regret the brave choice I made in Sally."

After all had been prepared, the two men supped on the best food Perry knew how to make.

As they were finishing, a loud commotion echoed outside. The beating of horse hooves punctuated by a rifle blast. Perry stepped to the door to see four horsemen approaching the farmstead at a rapid clip.

"I think it's best you stay here, Watty," Perry said. "I need to see what this commotion is about. This could spell trouble."

Perry went to the doorway and was greeted by four men wearing bandanas across their faces. If that wasn't enough to signal their hostility, their words reinforced it.

"We hear you're a squatter in these river hills. We're here to ensure your intention is merely that, and you're not a sympathizer to the abolitionist heresy," said one of the men, clearly the leader of the goons, pointing his rifle in a menacing way toward Perry's house.

Border ruffians, Perry surmised. Surely, neither Marcus nor Pete would have given up any information that led these cowards to his threshold. Both his heart and head wanted to trust that notion. Perry regretted that he had not been sufficiently inconspicuous during his recent dealings in Roubideaux. And certainly, singing a song in such a public setting as The Outpost might have sparked an interest from someone harboring malicious intent.

"You hidin' any runaways?" the leader demanded. His hollow eyes and bushy eyebrows could not be shrouded by his bandana.

Perry swung his head for a quick look inside at Moses, who was quite unruffled by the event.

"I beg your forbearance, Watty," Perry whispered to his friend, "but I think it might be best for me to lead the discussion."

Moses nodded in agreement.

"Yes, sir. The name's Perry Adams, and I have come solely to farm these hills. You can look around to see the seedbeds I have prepared. You can search my barn. My farmhand and I have much work to do as we prepare to impart the seeds for this year's corn crop."

"Your farmhand, you say? He wouldn't be a darkie, would he?"

Perry chose his words with the precision of a sharpshooter, which by that time in his life, he was. Survival in the woods demanded it.

"Yessir, he is a man of African descent."

Perry spun a tale that might satisfy the men with malicious intent. He was notably vague, not wanting to provide too much helpful information.

"That would be Willie Jefferson. Acquired his services about a couple weeks back during a trip over to Roubideaux, the same day I bought my new plow. Willie's a hard worker and as essential to the success of my farm as the plow."

"Do you own this man?" the masked intruder asked from the saddle.

"As you likely know, the Territorial Legislature passed a bill last year precluding me from technically being his owner," Perry said, thinking the inclusion of the word "technically" might create some sway in the aggressor's mind. "Once we hold a territorial vote, however, that's likely to change."

Perry grasped in desperation to feed the prejudice held by the horsemen. His soul ached from the need to dramatize in such a sinister manner, but he and Moses were outnumbered and at a clear disadvantage.

"Let's gaze upon your man," the hideous, bushy-browed horseman shouted.

Perry beckoned to Moses, who came to the door carrying an inappropriate but necessary deferential posture given the crisis of the moment. Perry could see Moses was scared shitless. Moses played the part to perfection. Perry was sure Moses had considerable practice in this technique of deception.

The four men laughed in unison as Moses appeared at the door. How could such an aged man be helpful as a farmhand? Hatred dripped from their bandanas and shot from their eyeballs.

"Why, Mr. Adams, it's right progressive of you to allow this man inside your own home. Should he not be a resident of your barn instead?" the leader cracked with another challenge to the sham Perry so convincingly portrayed.

"Why, yes, sir. That's a valid observation. But as I stated, we have much work to complete, and it's simply a matter of the master's convenience. I need him strong for the day, and to preserve my own energy, I asked him to fetch his own vittles from my residence instead."

Perry was on a roll, though again, his mind objected, almost to the point of physical pain, to his necessary choice of the word "master."

"Mr. Adams, I reckon that's good enough for me, at least for today. But if we hear any whisper of this story being a lie, we'll be back, next time in the dark of night with torches aflame. And, Adams, the next time you visit Roubideaux, don't befriend the drunks. And there better not be any singing with the pretty pianist."

Perry muttered under his breath, "If you assholes come back, you better bring an army."

Perry perceived the masked rider's words as an insult, but he also unraveled a clue as to who this bushy-browed infidel might be. The rogue must have been in The Outpost the night he sang to the young lady at the piano. Perry also interpreted the latent threat of the parting words as a clear sign additional armament would be on his near-term shopping list. A rifle only did so much when it came to the matter of self-defense. He needed a pistol to strap to his leg. This item would be bought in Lowland, rather than in Roubideaux, which might not be as hospitable as he once believed.

The men whipped the reins of their horses and rode off as quickly as they arrived. Perry breathed a sigh of relief. Moses trembled at his core. He wiped the sweat from his brow and steadied his legs; the incident reminding him of the brutal events that transpired at River View Grove.

"If those bastards weren't as worthless as teats on a boar hog, I don't know who is," Perry said.

After the intruders' departure, Perry was ashamed of the tenor of the scam he pulled off. The deception itself was not objectionable, but that was not true for the prejudicial way he was forced to assign his bartering friend Moses the false and subservient identity of fieldhand Willie Jefferson. Moses was a freeman in all aspects of the territory. Perry rationalized this had been one of those instances when the edict of riflery weighed with heavier authority than the laws of the land.

"Don't despair, Perry. You did only what you had to do to ensure our joint safety. I take no offense. I have seen their type before. A man of similar ilk owned Gabe and me."

"I most regret my delivery of the word 'master.' It rolled with ease off my tongue. Too much ease, I must add. As I have stated, Watty, if you are not my equal, you are indeed my superior. Our hatred of slavery rivals only our love for farming. I still have not learned all the lessons you have soaked in through experience both as slave and freedman. If there is a debt owed, it falls on my side of the ledger."

If there was any fiber of doubt remaining in Perry's mind about his stance on slavery, this incident set it free like a quail flushed from a thicket during a morning hunt. Coupled with hearing the firsthand stories from Moses and Gabe about their experiences with the brutality of the institution, Perry crossed the border in his mind. Perry was now a solid abolitionist.

In spite of the concerns over the union expressed by Abraham Lincoln, elected President of the United States that previous November, the house was divided against itself. The state of the union as it existed simply could not stand.

And, if indeed the ruffians returned, Perry vowed they would have hell to pay. You don't mess with the great-great-grandson of a pirate. He swore he would put a bullet right between those hateful, bushy brows. If not taken by surprise, he would have done it that day.

After the intruders left Jawbone Holler, they rode horses due south to meet the main trail back to Roubideaux. They spotted smoke rising over the ridge and rode to check it out.

Gabe was outside tending the animals when the four horsemen approached. When they pulled their bandanas over their faces, Gabe stood tall and defiant.

"Young buck, who are you and what do you think you're doing?" the bushy-browed leader snarled.

"The name's Gabe Watson, and this is my farm."

"A Black man shouldn't be taking up land that belongs in the hands of a white man. I think you're a runaway. We're gonna take a couple of minutes and dig through your bullshit."

One of the men carried a rope. On the end was tied a noose. Gabe's heart raced. He broke out in a full-on sweat. For one of the first times in his life, he chose his words carefully.

"Yessir, I'm a freed man. Got papers to prove it."

"Not interested. What matters is the fact you are a stain on the landscape, presenting yourself as a free and independent farmer. You should mount your horse and ride away from here to pursue something more proper for a creature of your race."

Gabe thought quickly about a response.

"While a freedman, I also work for a gentleman a couple bluffs to the north named Perry Adams," Gabe said. "I provide him labor whenever he demands it."

The mask leader chuckled and looked around at the shrouded faces of his cohorts. "Well, that right there is kinda funny. We just left the Adams place. He's got another man there who does the same, but on a full-time basis, almost like a slave. He never mentioned you at all. Why are you lying to us?"

Justified by their perception of Gabe's tale, the men encircled him.

A thug reached out a gloved hand and grabbed Gabe by the shirt.

"I think you owe us an apology, you lying asshole," he said.

Gabe was not going down without a fight. He'd killed one white man. He could do it again.

Gabe took a swing, landing a right fist to the aggressor's chin. That was the only blow he could deal before the men grabbed him and shoved him to the ground. The hollow thuds of boot to body were audible as they kicked him in the ribs, the legs, and the head. Their blows were relentless.

Dazed and bloody Gabe staggered in and out of consciousness, vaguely aware the men remounted their horses and galloped away. Gabe drifted back to awareness, and a tingle of blood ran down his chin. A prickly sensation nipped all around his neck. The men had slipped the noose over his head and left the rope beside him on the ground.

Gabe survived, but the ruffians sent a clear message. In these parts the only place for Black men was slavery. It was a mindset Gabe had experienced before, and he had slain it.

CHAPTER 12

Spring and Summer 1860

THE FAITH OF A FARMER

MOSES SHOOK LIKE THE TAIL OF A TIMBER RATTLER, more agitated by the incident with the ruffians than Perry. It struck him way too close to his past life. If the bastards visited Perry, could they also have visited his own farm? If so would Gabe's short-fused demeanor bring harm to his son? He needed to find out. Moses firmly shook Perry's hand, and his team hit the trail south over the bluffs. Butter followed along, tethered to the wagon's tailgate by a soft cotton rope.

As Moses's horses drew close to the farmyard, Gabe sat on the ground near the willow tree, knees bent and hands interlocked around his shins. Moses jumped off the wagon as it moved forward. He ran full speed to embrace the bloody mess that was his son. The sight raised tremors of anger down Moses's spine.

"Oh dear God, what have they done to you, Gabe?"

"I'm gonna be fine, Papa," Gabe said, fighting back tears as pain shot through his body. "It was four ruffian bastards. Accused me of lying about not being a runaway and didn't care to see the freedom papers. Said this was white man's land. I had no right and should leave."

"Son, I am sorry I've led you to this place," Moses said, gently embracing his injured son.

"You did the right thing, Papa. This is our maroon, or at least it should be. And I tried to talk my way out of it as gently as I could, but they were hell-bent on making an example out of me. Left behind this noose as a lasting reminder. They grabbed me. They were going to string me up, so I fought back. That's when they knocked me down, kicked the snot out of me, and left me with the noose around my neck. They said they met you and Perry too."

"We put on a convincing act for them, and they left. There will be retribution here on Earth. We may not be the ones dealing it, but they will pay the price. In due time, son. In due time."

Moses retreated to the house and gathered bandages and rags to tend Gabe's wounds. He picked up the noose and spat on it. With the honed blade of his knife, Moses sliced into the rope, dividing it into a dozen pieces. He put the remnants in the wood box for the smokehouse.

That night Moses wrapped Gabe in the security of a quilted blanket, like he had done so many times in his son's infancy.

"You're my blood, and I will defend you to the death. You did the right thing in the face of mob violence, and I'm proud of you." Before snuffing the lamp, Moses told Gabe that he loved him.

As Moses tended his son back to health, Perry buckled down for the task of planting corn. He strapped a seed bag over one shoulder and swung the handle of his shovel over the other.

Perry marched out for his duty in the first field like a soldier on the edge of conflict. Girded by passion he looked forward to the task, but he also dreaded it.

It was backbreaking and hand-blistering toil. The drudgery included digging hills, spaced at an appropriate interval, dropping in a suitable number of precious seeds and covering each hill with a pat of his shovel. Some farmers watered each hill to encourage germination. Being a one-man operation, hauling the water necessary for that task was prohibitive. Perry counted on the generosity of nature to complete that step. Besides, after the previous year's hailstorm, he figured nature owed him a debt. Planting took two full days of work in his first modest patch.

Perry wasn't exactly a church-going man, but as a farmer conducting field-work, a spiritual connection drew him to God's land. It was a bond not known to the shopkeeper, the barber, or the banker. Perry branded himself a well-intentioned backslider. Baptized at birth, Perry was raised Catholic back in Indiana, where he obediently accepted the sacrament of confirmation. It was a duty-bound faith, forced on him by his loving mother and stringent father. In his maturity Perry accepted that abandoning his faith led him to walk down the path of delinquency back in Indiana. But eventually, that transgression brought him to the miracle that was Kansas Territory. While it had been years since he celebrated the sacrament of the Eucharist, now, as a farmer in his own promised land, Perry's heart was tugged to reconnect, maybe just not in an every-Sunday kind of way.

A layer of protection born partially in faith insulated him from the unexpected cruelties of life, whether in the form of a band of bushwhackers or a more menacing mob of border ruffians. When he needed strength, in a pirate-like way, Perry asked for it. For most ordinary times, Perry barely whispered to the man upstairs. Nonetheless, the day after Perry planted his first field, the rain fell in abundance. Perry bent his knee and offered thanks.

After his second field dried sufficiently, Perry began to go through the same motions. Dig, plant, cover. Dig, plant, cover, hill by hill, until they spanned the length and width of the field. It took him three days to finish his second field. Perry's hands were raw and the pain emanating from the muscles of his back made him feel twice his age. To make matters worse, for four consecutive days, the weather was blistering and dry. Perry grew anxious about the germination of the seeds he deposited in his second field. Would it be pretentious to ask directly for the blessing of rain? On the fifth day after completing his second field, it rained again. For the second time in a span of less than two weeks, Perry bent his knee and offered thanks.

Other than weeding the crops throughout the growing season, either by hand or by hoe, Perry's job was done. The crop was now in the hands of the great unmoved mover. Perry accepted as fact that his faith as a farmer shined brightest during the span of year between planting and harvest. In a way he considered to be typically Catholic, he recalled the tragic hailstorm the season before. Had he done a sufficient job of offering thanks?

Now Perry had new motivation to direct a few soft-spoken words toward heaven. Her name was Millie. When it came to the issue of the young lady, he was not above asking for holy intercession. He even threw in a few Hail Marys and Our Fathers for good measure.

After deciding such action was acceptable, Perry dropped to his knees. He also offered petitions for the other people in his life, both present and past. It became a habitual part of his routine. In addition to sweet Millie, the litany included prosperity for bartering partners Moses and Gabe Watson, strength and courage for strategic ally Constable Dan, honesty and healing of his injured mouth for loyal trading partner Marcus Mixon, forthrightness and honor for buddy Pete the bartender, strength and sobriety for genie friend Jep, happiness and health for his former flame Violet LeDoux, strength of character and forgiveness for estranged father Stewart Adams, and heavenly passage for the gentle soul of departed mother Mary Katherine Adams.

But the primary subject of these prayers was most definitely Millie. Given her affinity for her vocation of teaching as part of the Benedictine Order, Perry also solicited intercession from St. Benedict himself, a man who walked the Earth some 1,300 years earlier.

Benedict had been a hermit for a good portion of his life, not unlike Perry's life thus far in the holler. Benedict even lived in a hole, or in his case a cave, for three full years, extolling sacred counsel to anyone seeking salvation. Monks flocked to Benedict's dwelling for guidance and intercession. Perry, on the other hand, only managed three months in his earthen dwelling that first terrible winter.

Nobody stopped by for a visit.

Soon, as word spread throughout the land of Benedict's miracles, the council of local monks appointed him abbot. During his life, he established more than a dozen monasteries across Italy. Like Perry, both critics and peers scorned Benedict for his overzealous ways. The rigorous rule attributed to him, *ora et labora*—work and pray—aptly applied to a farmer.

While Benedict's rule was strict, the faithful also viewed him as an understanding and forgiving man with a soft spot for the less fortunate and downtrodden. In that spirit, Benedict was known for repeatedly and charitably feeding a raven from his own loaf of bread. Benedict was particularly reviled by one group of intemperate monks, who attempted to poison him. Suspecting the malevolent endeavor, Benedict presented the poisoned bread to the raven with an order to take it far away so as not to endanger neither man nor beast. The raven returned unharmed—a sign it complied with the prophetic order.

Praying to St. Benedict for mediation in the affair of his heart seemed like a natural thing for Perry. Even when his spiritual mind did not focus on Millie, he still found it comforting to commune with the allied spirit of St. Benedict. He required nothing short of a miracle to win the heart and soul of the young pianist, so he made every effort to win heavenly favor. Besides, the day was quickly approaching when he would discover the truth about his prospects with Millie.

It had been a month to the day when Perry packed for his trip back to Roubideaux to meet up with his old friend, bartender Pete, who promised him a formal introduction to Millie. Due to the recent run-in with the band of ruffians, however, Perry made an early morning side trip down to Lowland.

Perry's one intention was to visit Max Jenkins at the local hardware store. Max had all the latest guns in stock and was always eager to make a deal.

Entering the store, Perry snorted out his familiar call.

"Hey, Max, I'm here from the holler. You want my dollar?"

Max looked up from behind the counter and smiled ear to ear.

"I'd be glad to take a dollar or more off your hands," Max said. "How can I help you today, Mr. Adams?"

Perry recounted for Jenkins the run-in with the masked ruffians. He also confessed that his primary intention that day in Roubideaux was to make the acquaintance of a fair maiden. Max sauntered up to the display cabinet stocked with sidearms. The model he recommended was a Colt, single action, five-shot 1855 revolver. Not state of the art, but close to it.

"It's got a good balance, hardly any kick, and allows you to get off five quick shots while any assailant is fumbling to reload. That should prove a worthy weapon for self-defense, Perry. Plus, you can hitch the holster up to your waist and tie it at the leg during normal, everyday use at the farm. You never know when you might stumble across a timber rattler in the bluffs that needs subduing."

"That'll be $18 for the pistol, holster, and bullets," Max said.

"Damn, Max. That's more than I paid for my plow, but I'll take it."

Perry was intent on ensuring his safety. The Colt revolver was the best way to do that.

"Not sure if you've seen Moses in the last couple days, but the same goons that visited your place also made a trip to his farm. Roughed up Gabe pretty bad," Max said. "He's OK, but not exactly the kind of shit you'd expect so close to our civilized village."

"Those bastards. Gives me another reason to be ready for those cowards."

The two men settled up and as Perry turned to leave the store, Max shared a final word of caution.

"Perry, you be careful over there in Missouri. Tensions are building with the intensity of the hailstorm that hit your place last year. Watch your back. There are a good many of those headstrong Missouri partisans itching to go on the offensive for the sake of what they're calling states' rights, and that's even before our territorial vote. Sure, they see the writing on the wall."

Perry took the advice to heart. He loaded five bullets into the Colt, ran the holster through his belt, and tied it to his right leg with the attached leather cord.

"One more thing, Max," Perry said. "When you see Constable Dan, let him know of my recent troubles. I'd do it myself, but I need to make my trek east."

Perry took his time that day on his way over to Roubideaux. He stopped on five separate occasions to get a feel for his new pistol. At each stop he held the revolver eye-high, arm straight, and gently squeezed off six rounds at a predetermined target. His shaky hand grew steady. By his fifth stop, a connection was made. He became one with the Colt pistol. He fired it quickly and with accuracy, like an extension of his hand.

Along the way Perry determined to approach his visit in a manner that was uncharacteristically low key. There would be no singing on this day, regardless of how sweet the piano music or the fair lady playing it might be. Considering his stops for target practice along the way, he made the trip in record time.

After hitching up his horses, his first stop was the trading post to see his old friend Marcus. As usual, Perry focused on one particular item, and Marcus would not persuade him to add to the list. As he walked into the store, sidearm strapped conspicuously to his leg, Marcus met him in the front aisle.

"If it ain't Perry Adams," Marcus said. "I sense a financial windfall. It's good to see you, my friend and loyal customer, in spite of that sidearm on your hip."

Though Marcus extended his hand for a customary greeting, Perry did not take time to shake. Instead he closed in to deliver a bear hug. He was delighted that the move surprised the sprite-like and balding proprietor.

"Marcus, you amiable snake-in-the-grass, it's so good to see you," Perry said with a big smile.

Marcus, fighting to catch his breath, returned the friendly embrace.

"Perry, to what do I owe the pleasure on this fine Friday afternoon?"

Marcus squeezed out his words, still trying to catch his breath after the embrace, but his words sounded quite normal, rather than the airy delivery of a man speaking out of the corner of his mouth due to a horse kick.

"Marcus, your mouth! You have been healed. It's a miracle!"

Perry was sure his prayers had been answered. If God bestowed such a blessing on the less-deserving Marcus, in spite of his sins and transgressions with the former Mrs. Nichols, his own request about Millie might also be honored.

"I have been healed, Perry. Woke up two weeks ago, and my malady was gone. If your prayers were the reason, I am indebted beyond reproach."

"Don't put your money where your mouth is right away, Marcus. While I might be willing to take credit for the intercession with Almighty God for your healing, that's where my favor stops on this day. All I stopped by to acquire is one of those packages of wrapped peppermint sticks."

Marcus's face dropped with double disappointment. Not only was he not going to score a big sale of provisions, but he was all out of peppermint sticks. His next shipment from Cincinnati was not due for another two weeks. The only sweets Marcus had in stock were a few lemon sticks and a few boxes of Whitman's chocolates shipped in from Philadelphia.

Perry wrinkled his brow in disappointment. One of the few tangible connections he had made with Millie, in a way that might evoke her senses as well as her memory, was no longer a possibility. He did not try to hide his frustration. It shook him to the core. He considered it a bad omen.

"Marcus, you can't tell me that. I was hoping to make a gift of an entire sack to a woman whom I imagine is at least twice as sweet."

Seeing the letdown written across the wrinkles of Perry's forehead, Marcus, being the opportunistic salesman he was, quickly suggested an alternative.

"How about a box of these Whitman chocolates, fresh off the latest stage from Philly by way of Saint Louie. I know they're a bit pricier, but isn't that sweet lady worth it?"

Perry weighed the option. When it came to Millie, price was not a matter of contention, but stoking her memory of that first night they spent with lingering looks and smiles was the crucial concern.

"I guess so, Marcus," Perry said. He gladly obliged Marcus for the asking price without the slightest hint of a haggle.

Marcus put the chocolates in a folded paper bag, tied it with a delicate red ribbon, and presented it to Perry.

Perry took the package, embraced Marcus again, and made his way out of the trading post. Looking back, he offered a final comment.

"Marcus, I have a somewhat sensitive question, if you would pledge to honor my confidence."

"Fire away, pardner."

"Have there been any gentlemen particularly inquisitive as to my character and whereabouts?" Perry asked. "Four visitors came to my farmstead in Jawbone Holler a couple weeks back. The ringleader was an especially hostile character with bushy eyebrows. I think due to their stated pro-slavery stance, they might be residents of your fair town."

"A lot of fellas in these parts sport bushy eyebrows," Marcus said. "I have not been approached with any particular queries about you by any of them. I will honor your request of confidentiality in this matter, though. That's what friends are for. You might want to check with Pete over at The Outpost. He gets a lot of traffic and hears a lot of gossip."

"Thanks, Marcus," Perry said. "In case anyone asks, I've acquired the services of a hard-working fieldhand. His name is Willie Jefferson. Makes my work a lot less demanding."

"What exactly do you mean by 'acquired his services?'" Marcus asked, feeling his face temporarily flushed with anger. "You can't own slaves in the territory, and besides, you never would anyway. I know you, Perry."

"He may have been a slave here, but in Kansas he's a paid farmhand. Let's just keep it to the fact that I acquired his services, okay?"

"This Willie Jefferson doesn't happen to have an adult son with him, does he?" Marcus asked.

"Whatcha mean, Marcus? You must be confusing Willie with someone else," Perry said as he spun the tale.

"Umm, right, I must be. Nevermind. Sometimes I think the horse kick must have loosened my brain a bit," Marcus said, fondly recalling the father-son pair of Moses and Gabe Watson he secretly sheltered one evening in his stable, before also providing them the tools they needed for farming at below-wholesale rate.

"Just keep your eyes out for me," Perry said. "I'm not sure who my friends are anymore, besides you and Pete. And, Marcus, I'll continue to keep the well-being of your body and soul in my prayers. Every single day is a blessing, my friend."

Disheartened as he was, Perry took his leave from the trading post with the neatly wrapped box of chocolates in hand. He boarded the wagon and snapped the reins. Beulah and Barney plodded down the street toward The Outpost. It was a sweltering day and Perry hoped he could make it the two blocks to The Outpost before the chocolates melted into a puddle of insignificance.

CHAPTER 13

Summer 1860

THE
CONFRONTATION

Upon reaching The Outpost minutes later, Perry consulted his pocket watch. It read 12:34. With his revolver strapped to his leg, and the neatly wrapped box of chocolates in hand, Perry entered the swinging doors. Since it was a Friday afternoon, Perry was surprised such a multitude of patrons was already doing business with Pete. But, he reasoned, it was a sweltering day and there were thirsts to quench with a detestable mug of that horse-piss brew Smit's, which according to the banner above Pete's bar was still the preferred beer of the frontier.

About half of the bar's tables were packed with Missouri gentlemen peacefully enjoying a mid-day chat and a brew. At the piano's keys was a different gentleman, wearing a bowler hat and a puffy, white cotton shirt rolled up to the elbow, sleeves held in place with arm garters on both sides, like a blackjack dealer. That seemed strange, but he surmised Miss Millie was likely still performing her classroom duties at the mission school.

Perry paid no attention to the men gathered at the tables and walked straight to the bar, even past Old Jep, who was slurping down a luxuriously foamy mug of Smit's. While he paid the other patrons no attention, a tingle on his neck hairs told him eyes were tracing his every move.

Perry sauntered across the room and Pete followed each of his steps. Seeing the sidearm, the bartender wore a look of concern. Pete had heard about the visit to Jawbone Holler by the ruffians.

"Perry, my friend," Pete said in a bold tone loud enough to ensure every ear in the bar heard. "I hear a few rat bastards visited your place in Jawbone Holler. If I ever find out who it was, they will never again slide their shit-kickers across these floors."

Perry could tell that Pete admired his strength of character and saw no peril in expressing that fact to his other customers.

Perry reached out a hand to Pete who grabbed it with fond enthusiasm. He leaned in to Perry and whispered.

"I will not let there be a doubt about the strength of our friendship," Pete whispered.

In spite of the words, Perry could see a look of vexation etched across Pete's face.

"What's wrong, Pete? You look like you have encountered a ghost."

"Nothing's wrong, Perry," Pete said in a tone that, again, only his friend could hear. "There have been whispers among shadier members of my clientele that you encountered a gang of ruffians a couple weeks back. Just to be clear, the rascals never heard a peep from me. I guard my words carefully, but rumors get around pretty quickly, especially when the suds are pouring here in the bar. Word is that you now have the services of a farmhand. A Black man. When did this happen?"

Without revealing too much, though his trust for Pete ran deep, Perry recounted his fictitious story about acquiring the farmhand's services during his last visit to Roubideaux the previous month.

"I trust you, Pete. My need for a farmhand should come as no surprise. I have my hands full. I'll never admit I broke out too much land for my corn crop, but it is more than I can handle myself. He offers me much needed assistance with the plow and the rigors of planting."

"His name's Willie Jefferson," Perry said to complete his tale.

"That all checks out with the stories going around here, Perry. Don't know the name, but I also heard one of your neighbors was beat up pretty bad. I have no idea who the varmints were who made that trip, but I'll continue to beat the bushes for information. If I find out, I'll certainly let you know, for your own protection mostly. If someone's after you, I think it only fair you know their identity."

"I appreciate that," Perry said, once again with a higher level of trust in the bartender. He held up the ribboned package. "I have a small token of admiration I'd like to present to Millie today. I hope you have been able to broker a formal introduction, as we discussed in detail last month."

"Perry, I also have some additional information I need to share, but you better sit down first," Pete said, reaching for the bottle of rum on the top shelf. "Before I tell you, let me pour you a shot."

"No need for that. But I will take one of those Saturday morning concoctions you stir together, that combination of Smit's and 'mater juice. They are quite savory and hide the horse-piss aftertaste of the frontier's finest brew."

While Pete wanted to laugh at Perry's comment as he stirred together the bloody beer, he continued to maintain a dire expression.

"It's about Millie. She's gone. You know the story Lucy told you about Millie's spiritual connection to Mary of Bethany? Well, about three weeks back, she left town to explore a closer connection with Christ through life at the convent down in Brenner."

Perry's heart sank. His head shook from side to side and his voice cracked in misery.

"Lucy and I tried to talk her out of it, but she made up her mind. There was an incident here at the bar, and we think that sent her over the edge."

"An incident? What do you mean, Pete? Is she really entering the convent? Was this a matter she was pondering for a great deal of time?"

"I know it was always in the back of her mind, but this was a snap decision. She talked to Lucy before she left, but I never knew anything about it until it was too late. If I knew in advance, I wouldn't have raised your hopes. Lucy said the first stage of entering the convent is a lengthy one, so you never know. She might come back if it doesn't suit her."

"I believe you," Perry said, still shaking in denial. For a fleeting second, he considered drawing his pistol and depositing a shot cleanly through his own brain, but that fit of self-destruction would not change the situation, just make it much more tragic, especially for him. "I've done nothing over the last month but anticipate this introduction and the conversation I would strike up with Miss Millie. This is my worst nightmare."

Hearing the conversation, Lucy emerged from the kitchen with a cooking mitt on her left hand.

"Perry, I'm so sorry this happened. Millie was quite an emotional wreck when she left. Honestly, I think the two of you would have made a great couple, in spite of my initial misgivings."

Lucy walked up to Perry, placed her mitted left hand on his shoulder and gave him a hug.

"Thanks, Miss Lucy. I wish your words could bring her back."

As Lucy retreated to the kitchen, Perry drew the mug of 'mater beer to his mouth and chugged it to completion.

"As much heartbreak as my life has caused for others, I reckon it was time for some retribution. Pour me another, Pete."

As Pete took the mug and began to tap another round, Perry looked nervously around the bar at its patrons. Men were playing poker and sharing their latest tales of bullshit. A good many rifles leaned against their high-backed chairs. Perry searched for facial details, hoping to not recognize or be recognized himself.

A man with high cheekbones and bushy eyebrows stared directly at Perry from across the bar. He was unattached from the conversation at his table. He just stared. Perry tried to imagine the profile behind a cowardly bandana. Sure enough, this was his oppressor. Perry made a friendly approach, as much as could any man with a revolver strapped to his leg.

Perry walked across the barroom floor as the man glanced toward his own rifle.

"There's no need for that, friend. But I do believe I have seen you somewhere before."

"I think you're mistaken," the coward said. "Don't believe we have ever met."

In the background, the growing commotion across the room drew Pete's attention. He reached under the bar and drew out his own rifle.

Perry continued the conversation.

"You been to the territory lately? I could have sworn you and a few of your buddies might have paid me a visit at my farm a couple weeks back. And after that, you made a visit to young Gabe Watson. What you did to Gabe was despicable. But do you recall the threatening tone you used as you and your buddies rode off from my place? You might recall, dark of night, torches ablaze."

"It's no business of yours where I've been, mister. I don't know you from Adam," the coward said.

"Actually, you son of a bitch, the name's Adams, not Adam."

The other gentlemen seated around the unnamed coward pushed back from the table, their chairs ringing out a chorus of screeches as the legs scooted across the bar's hardwood floor.

From a distance Pete raised his rifle to the ready position for what looked to be sure-fire trouble.

With a path cleared between them, the coward rose from his chair and went for his rifle.

Perry fumbled for his revolver, and the holster strap caught his thumb.

The coward raised the rifle to shoulder level as Perry unleashed the pistol and leveled it in response, as though he'd possessed it since childhood.

A shot thundered across the bar, chased by a second. Men scattered left and right.

Bartender Pete raised his rifle to bring justice to the aggressor, but it was too late. Just before the blast from the bushy-browed man's gun rocked Perry's shoulder, Perry squeezed the trigger of his Colt revolver.

Smoke from the resulting explosion of gunpowder spread an acrid sweetness across the room. As the smoke rose above the table, the barroom erupted in shouts as it became clear Perry's bullet slammed right between the coward's bushy eyebrows. Blood ran from the aggressor's brain. Perry had killed a man.

While it was an act of self-defense, in that split second, a measure of innocence left Perry's body. He failed to notice the blood on his own shoulder.

Pete ran to the scene with his repeating rifle flashing at several of the men who were on the verge of drawing against Perry themselves.

"Son-of-a-bitch had it coming. I hold all of you present responsible to bear witness to this event of self-defense," Pete shouted to the mob. "Stay calm and don't even thinking about going for your guns. If you do, you'll feel the burn of lead from my rifle."

Pete ordered patrons to clear the bar immediately and for someone to fetch the law. Pete meant business as the tattooed ace of spades flashed on his short-sleeved arm.

"He was the reason Millie left town. He was a no-good, pig-sticking bastard. He chose his own fate, Perry. You helped him expedite an end that was coming sooner or later anyway. I'll make damn sure all who were present swear an oath to this obvious act of self-defense, and I will do the same."

"I may merely be a simple, honest farmer, but I do not regret any of my actions. Had he not drawn on me, I probably would have drawn on him. Right is right and wrong is . . . "

His words trailed off.

Pain burnt deeply into Perry's tissue, like a scorpion crawled inside his left shoulder and stung him just above his heart. A warm wetness from the uncontrolled spilling of his own blood ran down his chest. In the blink of an eye, Perry hit the hardwood floor with a massive plunk.

CHAPTER 14

Summer 1860

AFTERMATH AND CONFESSION

THE STABBING PAIN RAN FROM THE top of Perry's left shoulder down his arm and radiated into his chest like a festering snake bite. Sweat ran into his eyes and down his cheeks. His mind was cloudy. He looked around the quiet, white-washed room but didn't know where he was.

Perry's mind wandered as he struggled to regain consciousness, but a few details began to float into his understanding. He had been injured in some manner, but how? Was he run down by a carriage gone astray? Did he fall from a barn roof? Had a horse or cow kicked him? These fuzzy questions haunted his mind.

He remembered. He had been shot. How bad was it and where was he? Was this heaven? Was he about to be judged? Was he ascending the steps of the Pearly Gates, or headed in the other direction? So many questions and no answers. He lay in bed, drifting in and out of a semi-conscious daze.

An hour later, Perry opened his eyes, narrowly at first. It was all a cloud of haze. He vaguely saw several human forms around him, but he did not recognize faces. Voice-like squeals and grunts bounced inside Perry's ears.

Perry forced his eyes wide open, expecting the murky picture to linger. But, clear as day, Pete was standing on one side of his bed and Marcus on the other. Perry focused on Pete, who smiled at him.

"You are a lucky man," Pete said. "He got off a shot to your shoulder, but that's better than getting shot in the gut or the heart. This could have turned out far worse, my friend. If he plunked you anywhere else, none of us would be here in this room now."

Perry did not feel lucky, and who exactly was this "he" who tried to plunk him in the heart? Perry's mouth was as dry as dust. He pointed at the water pitcher near his bed.

Pete poured Perry a glass of water and helped him drink. Perry forced his words. "What . . . was . . . his . . . name?"

Pete and Marcus didn't understand. In his first puff of conscious speech, was Perry wanting to know the identity of the man who'd attempted to take his life?

"He must mean the Doc," Marcus whispered to Pete across the bed as if Perry could not hear.

"Oh, you must mean Doc Anderson," Pete said. He took a chunk of lead off the table and held it for Perry to see. "The Doc pulled this bullet out of your shoulder. It was wedged against a bone. That cartridge must have been a little light on gunpowder or it would have blown a hole clean through you. Doc threw in a sprinkle of morphine, and stitched you up tighter than the laces of a barmaid's corset."

"No," Perry said. "The man I killed?"

Again both men looked at each other in bewilderment across the bed.

"His name didn't matter," Pete said. "He was a no-good son-of-a-bitch. You did this town a favor."

"His name was Charlie Wilson," Marcus said. "He was a hot-tempered asshole with a low boiling point."

Marcus snapped his fingers. "I shoulda known right away it was him you were asking about earlier. I quit doin' business with him. He always found something wrong with everything he bought and always wanted his money back.

I should have known it was him when you came by the store asking about a bushy-browed jackal."

Pete offered another glass of water to Perry, who shook his head. "I kept my eyes on him when he was in my place," said Pete. "A mean streak with the disposition to act. He got what he deserved." Pete took a few gulps of the water. "He wanted to challenge everyone at his first deranged perception of slight. It was always headed for a showdown at high noon."

"He kicked dogs," Pete continued. "Cursed at kids and harassed our womenfolk. He was cruel to Millie. He was drunk as a skunk one evening a couple weeks back. Might have been the same day he came calling on you. Millie began to play the song 'Nearer My God to Thee,' and that's when he became unhinged. Started screaming crazy shit about it being an abolitionist song. He walked up to Millie and called her a sympathizer to the Underground Railroad or some shit."

"We do have such sympathizers among us," Marcus was quick to add. "But, in spite of her tender heart, Millie wasn't directly involved."

"Charlie grabbed Millie by the arm and ripped her dress and petticoat down to the skin," Pete said. "She was humiliated. Inconsolable tears ran down her cheeks. I woulda put a bullet between his eyes that night, but Millie begged me not to. Instead, I kicked his ass out and told him to sober up. Lucy did her best to comfort Millie, but after that evening, she said there was no way she could stay. Her best option was the convent."

Pete continued as Perry was entranced by the narrative.

"Charlie came back the next day and begged for forgiveness. Much against his prevailing character, the dumb bastard got on his knees and begged! This bar was his only real lifeline for stirring up hatred, of which I was becoming aware. While she didn't want to be anywhere near the sumbitch, I made him apologize to Millie from the same submissive posture—both knees bent. She couldn't even look him in the eye. The next day she told Lucy she was leaving."

"Now I wish I would have pulled the trigger instead," Pete concluded. "Surely old Charlie is chained inside the gates of hell at this moment with a hot metal poker sticking out of his ass. I don't think it matters anymore. He's dead, and Millie's gone."

"It certainly matters to me," Perry said. "I wish you would have pulled that trigger too. Maybe she woulda' stayed."

"Old Charlie worked the scales at the granary," Marcus added. "He weighed the wagons coming in before and after unloading. The difference between the two weights determined how much corn the farmer would be paid for. One day a farmer tried to pull a fast one by putting a couple of big rocks in his load of corn. Before his wagon was weighed empty, he threw the rocks aside, so he also got paid the corn value of their weight. Charlie saw the whole thing, and he was madder than a hornet. He yelled at the farmer, 'You play hell!' He pulled the farmer from the wagon and beat him senseless, even kicking him in the head once he lost consciousness. They think he will never fully recover, but if you go to the granary today, there's still a pile of big rocks alongside the scales."

"Charlie viewed himself as judge, jury, and executioner, all rolled into one," Pete elaborated. "He was one of those rule-of-men believers. The bigger and badder you are, the more right you have to trample the less fortunate. He was a bully, Perry. The asshole deserved to die."

Marcus touched Perry's wounded shoulder and jumped in to calm the moment. "Good news is, Doc Anderson got you sewed up and said you can travel home in a few days."

The pain in Perry's shoulder throbbed through him. "Can I?"

Pete took a step toward the bed. "Sure. Doc said."

Perry tried to laugh, but only a choked noise came out. "I killed a man."

"Self-defense or not, you think it's safe? By the looks of that mob, I might be a wanted man in these parts, whether sanctioned by the law or not."

"There won't be any problems from that rabble," Pete said. "I have ways of keeping those fellas in line. I know stories about each one of them that would sink their good standing in the community, and if I must, I will do exactly that. Maybe even worse. You don't need to worry about any of them. I found out Charlie was the one who organized, badgered, and threatened the other riders that invaded your peace. They mostly went along for their own protection. They feared what Charlie might do if they turned him down."

"Our lawman said you're innocent," Marcus said. "He even pledged to carry you over to the river ferry himself if need be."

"That's mighty nice," Perry said.

"He also wanted me to pass along the fact you are always welcome here in Roubideaux. We're a border town, so we have to maintain a profile of moderation. I've recently become a believer in that principle myself. In my book it's awesome possum."

From what he judged as Pete's swing toward a moderate stance on the slavery issue, Perry came clean about the fictional Willie Jefferson.

"While I know this isn't my death bed, gentlemen, I do have a confession to make. That story about Willie Jefferson, my new farmhand? It was all bullshit. I lied in hopes both of you might share it among the riffraff. I meant no offense, but since I had not yet become aware of the ringleader, I couldn't take any chances."

"I guard this information with my life, and I know you will do the same. He's a freedman. Name's Moses Watson," Perry continued. "He and his son Gabe, the one who got roughed up by Charlie and his gang, farm a couple of bluffs south of my place. Both were emancipated on their own accord, and they have freedom papers to prove it. Like me, Moses and Gabe are squatters. They have become my friends."

"Yeh, no offense taken, Perry," Marcus said. "I knew your story was bullshit from the very beginning. I just didn't want to tell you."

"How'd you know, Marcus?" Perry asked.

"No need for you to sweat the details, Perry. I just knew. Let's leave it at that," Marcus said.

"Given that your position on slavery has matured, your story didn't hold any water, but good try," Pete chuckled. "There's no way you would press a man into service, paid or unpaid."

Perry's mind shot back to the oppressive relationship he experienced with his father back in Indiana, where he was little more than a slave himself. Just as suddenly, his mind began to spin on a different cog altogether.

"Where are my horses? Last I recall, they were hitched outside. They need food and water."

Perry tried to sit up in bed, but the pain only allowed him to lie still.

"Don't worry about your horses," Marcus said. "I took 'em over to my stable for room and board. I took care of all the arrangements. They'll be fine for the next couple days."

"I'm appreciative. One more thing. When I'm ready, can you send a telegram to Constable Dan Buchanan over in Lowland? I'd like him to meet me on the far riverbank and accompany me and my horses back to Jawbone Holler."

"Consider it done," said Marcus as he stepped out the door.

Perry had about all of Roubideaux he could stomach, at least for this trip. But he was not one to be intimidated.

"I'll be back. This incident is but a minor setback. Though I am certainly ready to retreat to my holler and convalesce and keep up with my corn crop the best way I can."

"Oh, and that box of chocolates Marcus wrapped up for me to present to Millie. You keep those stashed behind your bar, Pete. Between them and the 'mater beer, we can celebrate our friendship during my future visits. But you might also want to slip one to Lucy on occasion, not that she isn't already full of sweetness."

Pete opened the door and yelled downstairs, informing Lucy that Perry had regained consciousness. Lucy bounded upstairs like a yearling fawn jumping a creek.

"Mr. Adams, I am so glad you are back among the living," she said. "Pete and I are going to do everything we can to let Millie know that Charlie Wilson is no longer walking the Earth. If that was the only reason she left, maybe she'll return."

"I won't hold my breath for that, Miss Lucy. I think it best for my aching heart to move on. Am I right in guessing this is Millie's old room?

"It was the most convenient option at the time. Marcus and I carried you upstairs," Pete explained. "You are in the very bed Millie slept in."

Lucy reached out her arm to Perry. In her hand was a small wooden box.

"In her rush to pack her belongings, she left this behind. I think you should have it."

Perry carefully cracked open the box. Inside was an intricately carved olive-wood rosary.

"I think it'll bring you some peace," Lucy said.

Perry reached out for the rosary and immediately drew it toward his aching chest. The combined toll of losing Millie and killing a man weighed like a pirate's anchor on his soul. The contrasting emotions of grief and gratitude were too much. Tears welled up in his eyes. His whole body shook, sending fresh waves of pain through his shoulder. Uncontrollably and audibly, Perry wept.

"I'll cherish it as long as I walk this Earth, Miss Lucy. Maybe one day I'll have an opportunity to return it to its rightful owner."

The moment crushed the emotions of everyone in the room. While Pete fought back his tears, Lucy began to cry right along with Perry.

Perry would heal physically, but at this moment, he was not sure about emotionally.

Two days later Perry arose gingerly from bed and donned some fresh clothes, courtesy of Marcus, free from the stains of his own blood. Instead of strapping his sidearm to his belt, Perry carried it carefully like a loaf of piping hot bread, not sure he ever wanted to squeeze the trigger again. He walked down the stairs to meet Pete.

"I think I'm ready to ramble on," Perry said, placing the pistol carefully on the bar top. "I know it's not Saturday morning yet, and I know I have been a major annoyance, but do you think Miss Lucy could whip me up some of those fluffy cream scrambled eggs and ham? That would sure provide me the boost I need to get across the river."

"Awesome possum. It's been a genuine pleasure, despite the circumstances, to have you as a guest under this roof. Hey, Lucy, can you make Perry two fluffs and an oinker?"

"When you need to get away for a couple days, I hope you will consider making a visit to the holler," Perry said. "I'd love to show you around the place. If you want, you can even bring Miss Lucy. Oh, and, Pete, how about a mug of that 'mater beer? A palatable dilution of the finest beer in the frontier will surely provide healing to my soul."

CHAPTER 15

Summer 1860 to Fall 1860

CALM AND THE ENSUING STORM

AFTER BREAKFAST THE ROUBIDEAUX LAWMAN accompanied Perry and his team to the river ferry. Using his pirate spyglass, Perry gazed across the width of the Muddy Missouri. He spied a solitary horseman on the opposite bank.

Reaching the river's western bank, Perry, along with Beulah and Barney, disembarked the ferry and rode up to meet the horseman. It was none other than the pride of Lowland himself, Constable Dan.

"I got the telegram," Dan said. "Sounds like we have a lot to talk about."

"That's a gross understatement," Perry said.

As they proceeded side by side down the trail westward, Perry shared the stories of the hostile visit to Jawbone Holler from the band of ruffians, his unfortunate run-in with the notorious Charlie Wilson, and the many details regarding his unrequited feelings for a woman he still admired from afar.

Though admitting he was putting the cart before the horses, Perry confided in Dan the plan he had envisioned was for the good constable to serve as the presiding officiator for a nuptial ceremony. Now he was doubtful such an event between himself and Miss Millie would ever come to pass.

The men reached Jawbone Holler as the sun fell behind the slope of a western bluff.

"Dan, I have an extra bedroll. Why don't you hole up here overnight, and you can hit the road for Lowland in the morning? There'd still be time to prepare for any rambunctious weekend that might be coming your way."

"I'd kind of like to see your place in the morning light, and I gotta see that plow. And after their recent visit to Lowland, I hear from Watty and Gabe that you make a delectable plate of chipped beef gravy and biscuits. You throw that into the mix, and you got a deal."

"Even with this bum shoulder, I think I can still whip together a feast fit for a constable, if not a king. A deal it is."

After supper that evening, Perry lit a couple of candles. The men gathered in front of the fireplace. Constable Dan noticed the jawbone of the amazing mule he heard so much about from the fair citizens in Lowland.

"Is that the relic you have kept to rekindle your memory of Old Luke?" Constable Dan asked.

"It sure is, Dan. There will never be another animal as loyal as was Old Lukey."

"Mind if I take a closer look?"

"Be my guest," Perry said. "A gentle stroke along the length of his jaw brought him great comfort. That is why I have preserved his jawbone as a reminder of what he meant to me. Anytime I feel like the world is heading in the wrong direction, I reach above the fireplace and give it a stroke or two."

The two men slept in peaceful solitude that night, the silence broken only by an occasional snort and snore from Constable Dan. By morning light, after the robust breakfast, which Constable Dan choked down out of respect, Perry showed Dan the animals' barn, the amazing self-scouring plow, and finally, his fields of corn, which again this year looked primed to produce a bountiful yield,

"What do you think of my little slice of paradise?" Perry asked after the grand tour.

"I must admit, you certainly make a much better farmer than a cook. I have never seen a place as grand as this, especially considering the limited number of years you have invested. You should be proud of how you have risen above all the struggles and tribulations you have faced."

"Speaking of men who have faced a multitude of tribulations, I owe Watty and Gabe a visit," Perry said. "Watty is a much better cook than me. Plus he's taken my cow, Butter, as a willing hostage, and I need to retrieve her after a lustful fling with his bull Chester."

"I'll ride along, Perry, then head into town. I'd like to check out the Watson place as well."

Over the bluffs the two rode southward. They reached the Watson farm mid-morning. Moses and Gabe were glad to see them. Gabe immediately reported to Perry in graphic detail the mating ritual between Chester and Butter.

"By May of next year, you should have a newborn bawler in your barn," Moses said. "You'd better make room."

The men took shelter under the Watson's willow tree for no less than two hours. Perry recounted for Moses and Gabe all the events that transpired in Roubideaux.

"Charlie Wilson, the leader of the ruffians that paid a call to us, will no longer spread his hate outside your door," Perry said. "I put a bullet through his head in self-defense."

"I hate to say I am excited to hear that news. I'm glad he's dead," Gabe said.

As the conversation waned, Perry expressed appreciation to the Watsons for loaning the services of Chester.

"What might the appropriate barter be for Chester's stud fee?" Perry asked.

"Given all the extra milk we acquired during Butter's extended stay, I think we can call it even," Moses said. "If what she gave us was diminished output, I'd like to see her when she is in full production. We used some of the milk ourselves and shared the rest with our hog herd. They licked it right up. That is one fine cow you have there, Perry."

Following a lull in the conversation, Dan invited all three men to attend an upcoming town meeting on matters of governance, most notably a statute establishing a clear edict supporting abolition for the town of Lowland, atop the law already passed by the territorial legislature. While Gabe begged off for the need to constantly tend the livestock, both Moses and Perry obliged. They would simply serve as observers and help the constable maintain order if the party were to be crashed by any members of the ruffian horde.

"I understand your need to tend to business, Gabe," Dan said before turning his comments to Moses and Perry. "I know both of you hold strong opinions on the matter, but not being residents of the city, neither of you will be able to cast a vote." Dan conveniently omitted the obvious fact that even with the city's enlightened view, Moses also would have been precluded from voting due to the color of his skin.

"But to make it all official and shit, I will swear both of you in as my deputies. I'll even give you both tin stars for the day." Dan chuckled. "Make sure to bring your guns."

"Sounds dangerous," Gabe said. "You two better be ready at all times."

"I'm not expecting trouble," Dan said. "An earlier poll conducted by the editor of the *Lowland Ledger* shows this vote should be a formality. These days, though, you never know if outside rabble-rousers might try to disrupt an otherwise peaceful proceeding."

After the men accepted the duty, Dan and Perry took their leave. Perry tethered the now-pregnant Butter to the back of his wagon and returned to Jawbone Holler for continued healing of his shoulder and, due to that, the solitary and painful work of tending his corn crop of 1860.

Two weeks later Moses and Perry both dutifully and willingly recited an oath administered by Constable Dan to uphold the law. He clipped tin stars over their hearts. Both men carried out their sworn duties to help Constable Dan keep the order during Lowland's consideration of the codifying ordinance. The meeting went off without a hitch. Lowland officially became a domicile governed under the doctrine of abolition. The fact Dan enlisted the peace-keeping duties of a Black man only added a cherry atop the celebratory cake.

After the meeting Perry returned to the holler and embarked on his daily efforts to prepare for the fall harvest. Each morning Perry stretched out his left arm in the crisp morning air to measure his physical recovery. Deep inside his shoulder, a twinge of pain reminded him of his showdown with the ruthless Charlie Wilson. Perry adjusted the collar of his shirt. He looked down at the bold pink scar stretching from the top of his shoulder to the meat of his chest muscle. Perry accepted the scar as a reminder of his stance against slavery and the ache as a blessing. Several times the pain stabbed him with greater severity, a forewarning of the approach of a severe storm. It was the kind of omen that only a farmer would appreciate.

As Perry focused on harvest preparation, Lucy Fontaine took on a mission all her own. While initially skeptical of Perry's fitness as a mate for Millie, she talked Pete into closing The Outpost for a day trip down to the convent in Brenner.

Upon arrival, Pete stayed with his team of horses in a grove near the convent as Lucy marched with determination toward the limestone building. An elderly nun was stationed at the entry door to greet Lucy.

"Sister, I'm here to visit an old friend, Millicent Longworth," Lucy said.

"I'm afraid Millicent is quite busy right now, preparing our noontime meal," the nun replied.

"I'll wait. I need to pass along some news about her family." In her mind, Lucy expanded the definition of family to include Perry and Millie's friends in Roubideaux.

"Very well. Take a seat on the bench, and I will see about arranging a quick visit. Hope it doesn't take long. We are all depending on Millicent."

Several minutes passed before a younger person appeared down the long hallway. Millie was dressed in white, like a kitchen maid. Recognizing Lucy from a distance, Millie ran to meet her. While their separation had been a mere two months, Millie embraced Lucy like she hadn't seen her in years.

"I have news, and I wanted to tell you in person," Lucy said, still locked in the embrace with Millie. "Come sit with me." Lucy led Millie to the bench by the entryway. They sat with interlocked hands.

"If you've come all this way to share some news, I hesitate to know whether it is good or bad," Millie said.

"I wanted you to know that the despicable Charlie Wilson is no longer walking the Earth."

Millie was shaken. Tears rolled down her cheeks.

"I will pray for God to forgive his soul, but I never could." Millie barely got the words out.

"There was a gunfight inside The Outpost, and Charlie was on the losing side. Not sure if you would remember, but some while ago, there was a young man who broke out into song when you played 'Old Folks at Home.' I'm not sure of all the details, but I think he left you a generous tip and a peppermint stick on your piano when he left."

"I remember vividly. His name was something that rhymed with Jerry, I think. Nobody else ever left me candy on the piano," Millie said. "Who was he?"

"Well, his first name is Perry, and his last name is Adams. A Kansas sodbuster. He was the one who sent Charlie to his grave. Charlie was belligerent about Perry's opposition to slavery, as you know better than anyone. Right after you left, Perry was the recipient of a hostile visit from Charlie on the Kansas side. He and three other guys were wearing masks, and they made all kinds of threats. Next time Perry came to town, he stopped by to see me and Pete, hoping you would be there too. Charlie was in the bar, and Perry recognized him. Perry confronted him and Charlie made the fatal mistake of going for his rifle. He shot Perry in the shoulder, but not before Perry fired a shot that made Charlie nothing but a terrible memory."

"Even with all my prayers, during the still, quiet moments, the memory of Charlie haunts me," Millie said. "God works in mysterious ways. I think he used the incident with Charlie as a call for me to explore the religious life."

"Charlie's gone forever, so you can put him out of your mind. But have you thought that God could be using Perry for you to explore another path? He's recovered from his wound and has returned to the farm, but he asks about you every time he visits Roubideaux."

"Oh, Lucy, while I'd never take solace from the death of another person, even Charlie Wilson, the fact that Perry remembers me lightens my soul. It's been tough here. I came to explore the possibility of joining this holy community. I thought it would lead me to the same kind of spirituality and peace that Mary of Bethany experienced at Jesus's feet. You remember the story?"

"I do, Millie. Pete and I have been wanting only the best for you. He even closed The Outpost for the day to bring me down here."

"Pete closed The Outpost for the day?" Millie questioned in disbelief and made the sign of the cross. "Hell must be freezing over."

A smile broke out on Millie's face. "I have been true to the spiritual cause here. Work and pray. But it's been mainly work with little time to pray at all, at least by myself. It's not what I was expecting. I fear that instead of Mary, I have become Martha, but through no choice of my own."

"Hey, be careful," Lucy said with a smile. "You're talking to another Martha here. There's no shame in that."

"No shame at all, but the drudgery of caring for other members of the community has drained me of some of the zeal I had for religious life," Millie confided.

"It's never too late to change direction. That's our common imperative as women in this modern world. Deciding to change direction is not a sin. You haven't recited your final vows."

As that fall's corn harvest commenced, Perry was neck deep in the task when a lone horseman approached from the east. It was bartender Pete. Perry greeted Pete with a bear hug and an invitation for supper.

"I've been told my chipped beef gravy and biscuits are exquisite, Pete. You might think about asking Lucy to add my recipe to your Saturday morning fare."

"I'll be the judge of that. I'm not accustomed to such a menu for supper, but Lucy might be game." Pete stared at the ground and kicked dust with his boots. He had news for Perry, but he wanted to wait for an opportune moment, after supper.

Perry cut his harvest work short and after Pete handed him a fresh copy of the *Roubideaux Gazette*, the two men retreated to the house to catch up on happenings in Roubideaux. The men engaged in talk about the continued tensions along the border, as well as the larger matter of the conflict between north and south. Pete indicated the demise of Charlie Wilson diminished the level of fervor for the flames of disagreement. Both men sensed deep inside their souls, however, this might be a calm before the storm.

While the discussion ensued, Pete's eyes focused on Luke's jawbone in its place of honor above the fireplace.

"Is that Old Luke?" he asked.

"It is. The finest animal that ever walked the earth."

Pete took a closer look and ran his hand across the length of the jawbone.

"Sorry I never got a chance to meet old Luke."

Returning to the table, Perry dished up for Pete what resembled a pile of tasteless glop atop some biscuits that looked like chunks of granite. Pete dug in with no small degree of hesitation. As his fork sank in, the biscuit, along with a wave of gravy, skittered across the plate, not wanting to be cut.

"Come on now, you must be patient, Pete. It takes a couple minutes for the gravy to penetrate the crust of the biscuit. You must be hungry, my friend."

"I've never heard of such protocol," Pete said, laughing. "I think that biscuit must be allergic to chipped beef."

"Trust me on this; it will be worth the wait."

Perry lowered his fork to test the texture of the biscuit, and it cut clean through to the bottom of the plate. A minute passed.

"Okay, try it now. I think you'll find it passable, even though I have to confess the food here at the Jawbone Holler Café doesn't get any better than this. In fact, this dish is my crowning culinary achievement, at least thus far. I do not have the patience or skills necessary to make anything better."

With a degree of hesitation etched across his brow, Pete lowered his fork for a second time to confront the biscuit that minutes before exhibited scampering tendencies. The fork cut into the biscuit and sunk into the bottom of his plate. He scooped a forkful of the farmer-cooked delicacy and shoveled it into his mouth.

Perry saw Pete frown as his taste buds judged the flavor. The biscuit was way too salty. The gravy was a greasy tasteless paste. Even the chunks of chipped beef tasted like gamey bull meat.

"Mmmmmm," Pete said, not wanting to hurt Perry's feelings. "This beef is indeed delectable. The gravy is hearty, and the biscuits are a delight."

"A delight in what manner, exactly?"

"Delightful in a biscuit kind of way," Pete said quickly.

Perry rubbed his forehead with noted disappointment in himself.

"It's not good, is it?"

"Not so awesome possum. Let's say that one of these days it might be suitable as a side dish on Lucy's menu, but today is not that day." Pete shrugged his shoulders. "With a little bit of perfecting the recipe, who knows?"

Both men were so hungry, however, they cleaned their plates.

"Want more?" Perry asked. "I whipped up an extra batch. Old Archibald will inherit any leftovers, and I hate to make him too greedy of a beneficiary."

Pete pitied the hound.

"I think I'll pass. Plus, I have news to share that I think you might want to hear."

Perry's thoughts raced. Had there been another incident at The Outpost? Was Marcus OK? Had Old Jep sunk to another level in his downtrodden life?

"This should strike you as glad tidings, I think," Pete said. "Millie is back. Lucy and I went down there, and Lucy told Millie all about the demise of Charlie Wilson."

Perry's heart thumped.

"You don't say. For my sake, I hope she doesn't have long legs and a short memory."

"Nah. She remembers you. Just didn't know who you were. And she never asked. During a visit to the convent, Lucy gave Millie the full rundown. She wanted to know more, so Lucy told her about your confrontation with Charlie and how your actions were in self-defense. She even told her all about you, including your name and your successful pursuit of agriculture here in Jawbone Holler. To say the least, Millie was intrigued by the identity of the man who stood up so boldly for a higher ideal she herself supports."

"Lucy shouldn't have done that. Now I'll wonder for eternity about what might have been," Perry said.

"That's not all," Pete jumped in. "While forever to be a faithful Catholic, the level of devotion and the laborious lifestyle of sisterhood was too much for her. Told Lucy it wasn't true to her soul. She viewed it as a defeat. Thinks she's a quitter, much like a puppy after its first run-in with a bobcat."

"I reckon it was good she was able to make that decision, but I'm sad she feels demoralized. I felt the same way when I left my pappy's farm back in Indiana."

"Hold on to your chair, Perry. She told Lucy she missed her students. She missed playing my piano. Most of all she's open to meeting the striking and mysterious bar patron named Perry. She remembered that on one night not long ago he sang a verse during one of her songs and left her a generous tip and a peppermint stick."

"That is truly awesome possum," Perry said.

CHAPTER 16

Post-Harvest 1860

BIBLES AND CONFETTI

PERRY WAS QUITE ON BOARD WITH PETE'S immediate suggestion that they attempt an introduction to Millie during the nearest possible opportunity. There was now at least a suspected level of mutual admiration. Such a recipe might lead to a more promising outcome, unlike Perry's peculiar formula for biscuits and chipped beef gravy.

As much as Perry yearned to deal with matters of the heart, his practicality required him to stay in the holler until he shucked and gathered his corn crop. That required at least another week, maybe two, depending on the weather. It was an essential step to solidify the future of his farm and his own, in addition to that of any young woman who might consider making Jawbone Holler her home.

"You think she will wait that long, Pete? In some cases two weeks is a life-time," Perry asked, not wanting to hear the answer.

"I know she will, Perry. She has done nothing but talk to Lucy about you since she got back. She was probably thinking about you the whole time. You're one of the reasons she came back. She would like to meet you, and the peppermint stick encounter didn't count. But, Perry, do yourself a favor: Don't offer to make her any of those dogshit biscuits with chipped beef gravy."

"Oh, thanks, Pete." Perry grinned. "Give me at least a week or two to finish harvest, and let Marcus know I will need some fresh duds, even a new pair of boots. He knows my size. If he doesn't have any current options, I know he can request it in an expedited manner up from Westport."

"And, Pete, tell Marcus I will burn his trading post to the ground if he doesn't save me a full box of peppermint sticks."

Pete laughed at what Marcus's reaction might be.

"Sounds great, Perry. You might want to pack Millie's rosary. She asked about it."

Pete continued, "Do you mind if I find a pile of hay in your barn for the night? I'd rather not ride the old nag here home in the dark of night."

"I can do better than that, Pete. I have an extra bedroll, and you can snuggle up with Archibald. I insist you join us in the house."

That night Pete passed considerable gas. It kept both Perry and Archibald awake, but Perry knew if he were to talk about it, Pete would just blame the supper.

The next morning Pete was off at the break of dawn. That motivated Perry to hit the field for a full day of harvesting. He also had a new reason to complete harvest as quickly as possible.

The act of harvesting corn was not overly complicated, but it taxed the hands, arms, and lungs. Perry used a leather strap with a metal shucking hook. The strap buckled across the back of his hand with the hook in his palm. In one motion he slid the hook from the top of the ear to the bottom, slicing through the husk before snapping off the stalk and throwing the ear toward the wagon. Occasionally, Perry missed his target and the ear bounced off the bang board before falling into the bed of the wagon.

Perry flung the corn with accuracy, keeping an ear in the air at all times. Perry's development of this skill was essential. He was at least twice as good at shucking corn as he had been back in Indiana. In those days he was lucky to harvest fifty bushels of corn per day. Now his capacity on an average day was one hundred bushels, enough to fill four wagons.

Prior to this season, he stored his ear corn in a section of the barn. This year, during the milder than usual late winter and early spring months, he constructed a corn crib attached to his barn. It was sufficient in size to hold the yield from more than one harvest. He also purchased a corn sheller, a machine that stripped corn kernels off the cob. It would be easier to store shelled corn than ear corn. That created for Perry a distinct advantage in the marketplace. He could keep his corn in storage until prices were more favorable than during harvest season, when most farmers simply took their crop to the granary, where they either sold it for cash or paid additional fees to the granary for storing the crop in hopes of higher prices down the road. It was a risk. A big risk. One Perry took off the table by building his own storage crib.

After harvesting his corn, Perry wrapped his arms around bundles of stalks and loaded them into the wagon. Though not the most nutritious feedstock, Perry counted on the stalks as wintertime fodder and bedding for Butter, as well as Beulah and Barney. He later loaded the gathered stalks into the loft of his barn.

It was a warm, late-fall evening when Perry loaded the last of the cornstalks into the wagon. He got into the wagon's seat, slapped the reins, and coaxed Beulah and Barney down the hill and up the lane to the barn. An orange October moon made its early appearance in the dimming sky. Perry drank in a feeling of accomplishment as he approached the barn. The harvest had been optimal. That was when he noticed Beulah looked as though she made too many trips to the feed trough. She was wide in the middle, much wider than Perry recalled. That could mean only one thing. She would bring him a colt in the spring. Barney turned his head toward Beulah and as if to signal an affirmative answer. He bobbed his head twice and boasted a proud snort through his nostrils.

Immediately after Perry wrapped up harvest, he and Moses were once again summoned to Lowland by Constable Dan for peacekeeping duties. The enlightened citizens of Lowland called a meeting with the intent of doubling down on their abolitionary stance.

While this matter was of high moral importance, Perry almost declined so he could travel sooner to meet Millie in Roubideaux.

Lowland officials set the date of their meeting to draw attention from newspaper reporters from all along the border-state frontier. This meeting, held outside in the public square, was sure to put Lowland on the map. It was a precarious action, given the heightened level of tensions in the region, but the good folk wanted to share far and wide their ethical platform opposing the injustice of slavery.

A half dozen newspaper writers showed up. They sat in a small roped-off area near the stage.

Dan assigned Perry and Moses duties along the outskirts of the crowd.

"Keep your eyes open for potential trouble," Dan instructed. "If anything looks the least bit sketchy, fire a warning shot overhead."

Perry took the north side of the square, and Moses took the south.

As the crowd began to gather, many of the townsfolk grew squeamish. They were solidly behind their convictions but were rightly concerned about the possible consequences.

Presiding over the meeting was the Honorable Judge Virgil Merriweather, much like he did over the grand arm rasslin' match between Perry and Constable Dan. The judge was a bespeckled man with distinguished salt-and-pepper hair. He sported a Lincolnian stove-pipe hat and a black long-tailed jacket. The good judge pulled double duty by also serving as mayor of the boomtown. Standing at his side, quite stoically, was Constable Dan, wearing his trademark black leather vest and tin star over his heart.

Judge Merriweather brought down his gavel on a block of wood in dramatic fashion to start the meeting. Constable Dan made sure his deputies were in place and continued to scan the crowd for any hints of trouble. The area reserved for the newspaper writers was packed with men, pencils, and note pads ready at elbow height.

"Fellow citizens, distinguished members of the press, we gather here today supported by our territorial statutes to put an exclamation point on this enlightened city's abhorrence for the institution of slavery," Judge Merriweather barked out the rehearsed lines with dramatic authority. He raised a black, leather-bound Bible high over his head.

"We also stand before Almighty God in recognition of that institution's basis in race to be in violation of everything heaven holds sacred and moral. This issue has been debated from north to south and east to west. Yet, no ethical mandate has been issued to send this fetid atrocity to its rightful grave. Our forefathers, in their haste to win freedom from the Motherland, failed to live up to their divine mission of decreeing all men are not only created equal but can also live out their lives in accordance with that divine principle. All men must be free to pursue the inherent human right of self-determination. No man should be deemed a possession of another based on the amount of pigment in his skin."

As the judge's fiery rhetoric poured from the platform, Perry and Moses continued to scan the crowd with greater intensity for any signs of mischief or aggression.

"Slavery, as tacitly abided by our powder-wigged ancestors, was and is today nothing less than an unholy abomination," the judge lectured.

As Judge Merriweather lowered the thick Bible to a point covering his heart, a man who blended into the crowd raised a pistol and shouted, "The only abomination is the one standing before me."

A shot rang out.

A puff of dust exploded from the Bible, and the judge fell back. Constable Dan drew his sidearm, preparing for the next shoe to drop. He stood boldly where the judge had been a split second before. The crowd murmured in disbelief.

After the powder flash, several local partisans grabbed the assailant, wrestled the gun from his hand, and knocked him to the ground in a cloud of dust. The man was fully subdued by the time Perry and Moses reached the spot. Moses brushed the other men aside and pulled the goon from the dust and raised his entire body by the neck until the tips of his toes barely touched the ground. Perry abruptly applied handcuffs. Constable Dan rushed to the scene, dispatched the fanatic to the hoosegow, and locked the black iron door.

"I'll deal with you later, Plantation Paul," Dan said, coining his own epithet for pro-slavery sympathizers. "That's what happens when you bring a muzzleloader to a town with a conscience. You don't get off a second shot."

Shaken but unharmed, Judge Merriweather rose from the ground. He waved off the doctor and looked down at the gaping hole in his Bible. The slug destined for his heart blasted its way through nearly all the holy book but not quite. The judge pulled the slug from the tattered Bible and dropped the still-warm lead ball like a tiny hot potato. He scooped up a handful of the confetti created by the errant shot. It drilled a ragged path, from Genesis clean through to the sixth chapter of Revelation, where the Four Horsemen of the Apocalypse began their ride of malice. Judge Merriweather's life was spared by a biblically malevolent miracle.

Raising both hands overhead in triumph, Judge Merriweather waved the shredded Bible with one and let loose a rain of the divine confetti with the other. He also abandoned his well-rehearsed script.

"The forces of darkness are upon us, friends," he stated as calmly as possible for a man just targeted by an assassin. "It is time for our community to raise its voice in a unified cry for justice and freedom. Not only should that be a neutral ideology in our courts of law, but it should also be the basis of law itself. From the standpoint of nature, no man is better than another, regardless of the color of his eyes, his hair, or his skin. Outside of this territory, dare a half-day's ride to our east, a perversion of our singular and universal law of nature still holds sway in law and among public opinion. It is our duty as man, woman and child—to God, our nation, our territory and our city—to halt this travesty, not only at our doorstep, but everywhere it breeds."

The judge collapsed in a heap. Constable Dan rushed back to the stage, kneeled at the judge's side, and waved forward the doctor.

Had he not fainted, Constable Dan knew Judge Merriweather would surely consider this a splendid story for the newspapermen.

And it was. For the most part, the newspapers got it right. Stories were printed everywhere about the attempted assassination of a territorial judge by a lone proslavery fanatic, as well as the aftermath of that incident.

Dan and Perry, in a quick discussion after gathering evidence, including the tattered Bible, noted the juxtaposition of the four horsemen of the apocalypse to the act of calamity their presence halted. The miracle struck both men as eerie.

Later that day, by a vote of 257-5, ballots submitted by Lowland's white men approved a resolution demanding the immediate and unconditional emancipation of slaves in all states, whether they entered the union as a slave or free state.

The next day Plantation Paul was hanged in the town square after a speedy but fair trial.

The news made headlines in newspapers along the border states and beyond.

Afterward Perry and Moses turned in their badges to Constable Dan and headed back to their respective farms in the Missouri River bluffs. Perry had urgent affairs with which to tend. Millie was back, and a long-awaited introduction was in order.

CHAPTER 17

Late Fall 1860

SETTING THE STAGE

BEFORE HE LEFT LOWLAND THE DAY OF THE INCIDENT, Perry wired messages to Pete and Marcus that he would be in Roubideaux in five short days. He reminded Marcus about his need for a suit of clothes fitting for an introduction to Millie.

Though his corn crop was tucked safely away in his crib, plowing was a necessity before the frost set into the topsoil. While bigger matters weighed on his mind, plowing could not play second fiddle. Time was of the essence, for a couple of distinct reasons. Perry was ever conscious of Beulah's pregnant condition, so Barney pulled the plow alone, working twice as hard to rip the fields.

After three days of putting Barney and his John Deere plow through the paces, Perry now hoped he might be absent from Jawbone Holler for at least a couple of days for his grand introduction to Millie in Roubideaux. The morning he left, he made sure Butter had plenty of water, feed, and hay. He also prepared a stockpile of scraps, including a pot of chipped beef gravy for his floppy-eared buddy Archibald. On his way out of the river bluffs, he stopped to ask Moses and Gabe if they could check on Butter and Archibald.

It was midafternoon when Perry hit Roubideaux with the disposition of a miner who had struck a wild vein of silver. Millie's olive wood rosary was in its box, carefully secured in his front pocket. His first stop was Marcus's trading post.

"I have come in search of peppermint sticks, and I am bearing a torch," Perry joked as he entered the trading post.

Marcus met him in the aisle. The place still smelled with a stench of the frontier.

"I got your telegram. I am ready to do business, my friend. I've been guarding an entire box of peppermint sticks, and I think I've picked out an ensemble of attire that might even make you look appealing."

"Ahh, you really know how to make a guy feel confident," Perry said.

"Step into my boutique," Marcus said.

Marcus led Perry past the stinking buffalo hides and beaver traps, past the cast iron kettles and the canned provisions.

"Here we are. Welcome to Marcus's Men's Fashion," he said. "I got a fresh shipment of duds, and I ordered some items with your handsome mug specifically in mind,"

Marcus stepped inside a storeroom and brought out a crate that included a smartly creased pair of trousers, a matching jacket and vest and a fresh white shirt.

The trousers, with tubular legs, were navy blue and checked, constructed of heavy linen with a button fly. A single-breasted vest with a flat collar was the same color as the jacket. The shirt was white cotton, shorter and meant for daytime wear rather than also serving as a nightshirt. It had three buttons down the front and tucked snugly inside the trousers.

Perry tried on each article of clothing and viewed himself in the mirror. The jacket was about an inch too short.

"I will draw in my arms to make them a bit shorter," Perry said. "Does all this work?"

"It sure does, you handsome devil. You don't think I'd set you up with anything less than top-shelf fashion, do you? I had plenty of lead time to gather your order, plus, as you know, I am a consummate professional."

Before Perry could say another word, Marcus, always the salesman, aggressively jumped in with a new pitch.

"While we're at it, how about this handsome tie?"

The tie was thin and silver, made of the finest silk. It topped off Perry's regalia perfectly.

The boots Marcus ordered came in two distinct varieties. He showed Perry a pair of what was called lace-up day-boots, as well as a more practical work boot with a shiny finish. Perry looked at both and opted for practicality.

"I am a simple man. I don't want to put on airs with a fancy pair of day-boots I might not wear another day in my life. In my case, I guess you could call them never-boots. At least I can buy the work boots with the intention of wearing them to town. I like the way they shine."

Perry was a bit unsure despite Marcus's eagerness to make the sale.

"You don't think this makes me look a tad too dandy, do you? I don't want to appear too eager either. It would be a calamity if I scared Millie back to the convent."

Marcus laughed. He had met Millie and judged Perry's taste in women to be impeccable. Of course, he had never met Miss Violet LeDoux, the young woman in Perry's checkered past who ultimately led to his settlement in the territory.

Perry was pleased with his new ensemble. Marcus was elated. This was his biggest sale of the week.

"Now, how about that box of peppermint sticks?" Perry asked. "Or do I need to go out and fetch my torch?"

"Got 'em over here at the counter."

Marcus pulled out a neatly wrapped package, even more striking than the box of chocolates he wrapped for Perry some weeks earlier.

Perry pulled the boxed rosary from his pocket.

"Marcus, could you place this box on top of the other and make it a two-story package?"

"Certainly can. Nothing is impossible here at the trading post."

Marcus placed the wooden box atop the other, dead center. He retrieved a length of red silk ribbon to couple the boxes when Perry interrupted.

"Marcus, I see what you're thinking there; the red ribbon might complement the striped peppermint sticks inside, but I'd like to make a more pragmatic suggestion," Perry said.

"I'm all ears, my sophisticated friend. What do you have in mind?"

"How about that silver silk ribbon behind the counter?" Perry motioned toward the spool. "I think that might not only be a fitting way to bind the two boxes, but afterward I am pretty sure a certain piano-playing schoolteacher might use it to tie back her long black hair."

"Oh yes, my smitten friend. Glad you put the kibosh on the red one. The silver one is perfect, plus it matches your tie."

Perry stood back and admired the package and imagined how Millie's locks might look adorned with the silver silk ribbon in her hair, like a flash of lightning in the darkness of night.

"Marcus, you have outdone yourself. I think you might be outgrowing this stinky trading post. You ought to hop the border and come over to Lowland and become the town's premier men's clothier."

"I must admit I have thought about it, but I am a Missouri man. I can do much more for the cause right where I'm at."

While Perry didn't fully understand what Marcus meant, he stepped forward to settle his considerable bill. He tucked the box of peppermint sticks under his arm and left the trading post with an exterior that was stylish but appropriately modest. Nobody meeting him on the street could guess he had once lived in a hole in the ground and still allowed a floppy-eared hound dog to sleep in his house.

Perry's next stop was The Outpost. It was four o'clock. He hoped it still might be early enough he could have a couple of private moments with Pete.

A sparse crowd of bargoers was at The Outpost Tavern as Perry walked through the swinging doors with the two-story gift in hand. Gentlemen around the tables paid him little attention in spite of his flashy appearance. That suited Perry. He wasn't exactly seeking attention during these troubled times when law and order on the border could merely be a wishful thought.

Pete was busy washing mugs in a tub behind the bar as Perry's silhouette appeared against the backlit entrance. As he was about to welcome the dapper stranger to his establishment, Pete recognized it was Perry.

"Why, Mr. Adams, lookin' all awesome possum. You do not resemble the muleskinner I have grown to respect and admire," Pete said, suddenly thinking that a poor choice of words given Perry's regrettable experience with Old Luke. "Can I pour you a shot of rum or a delectable glass of 'mater beer? You know what they say about Smit's; it's the finest in the frontier."

"Pete, you old buzzard, I have come to make the acquaintance of a fair maiden. I think you might be the party responsible for making that happen. In case you are wondering, the gift is not for you; it's for Millie."

"Perry," Pete tried to appear as despondent as he could, "speaking of Millie, I'm afraid I have some unwelcome news for you. She's not here."

Perry's mind raced.

"Oh no, not again. What is it this time?"

"I am sorry to tell you," Pete paused for effect, "your fair maiden has been delayed."

"Okay, fine, how delayed will her appearance be, exactly? A month? Two months?"

"It's hard for me to say. She wanted to make sure her appearance would not disappoint a certain gentleman farmer she has come to admire from quite afar."

While his act was convincing, Pete was horsing around.

"Pete, you horse's ass, you had me going for a minute. I thought you were about to tell me she reconsidered and escaped my grasp yet again. I was already preparing a regretful mental speech about my loss being God's gain."

Pete laughed uncontrollably.

"Your damsel will be delayed by about an hour. After teachin' those whippersnappers all day, she wanted to freshen up her appearance a bit for you. She's meeting up with Lucy for a quick shoppin' trip at Miss Fannie's Fashion Shop."

"I have admired her for so long in my mind I'm concerned this Miss Fannie of whom you speak might spoil what I already consider a vision of perfection. What's your summation of our situation, friend? Do you think we will see eye to eye? Do you think our personalities compatible?"

"I think you will be as flawless as the matched pair of Clydesdales that pull the Roubideaux fire wagon. It took some time, but so does Lucy," Pete said. "You two are awesome possum."

Perry could feel his anticipation bubbling.

"I think I'll skip the invitation for an alcoholic beverage. My nerves are practically crawling out of my skin the way it is."

"Suit yourself, Perry, but I have seen first-hand the calmin' effects alcohol can have on an anxious man. Old Jep and, of course, that snake Charlie Wilson notwithstanding."

"What exactly are your plans for our piano player on this fine day?" Pete continued.

"Plans? I didn't have any plans. The only three places I have set foot in this town are here, Marcus's trading post, and his stable. No offense, but I'm not sure any of the three venues would be suitable for this splendid occasion. Would a lady of her persuasion expect a gentleman caller to have an actual plan?"

"Right you are, kind sir. As much as it pains my better business sense, being they are competitors against my fine line of Saturday morning fare, we made reservations for two over at the Pitts House. I haven't tried it, but I hear they serve up the best Italian menu this side of Saint Louie."

"I'm willing to give it a shot, if you think that would appeal to Millie."

"I know it would. She has often spoken of visitin' similar Italian restaurants during her youth down in Westport."

"So, does that mean Mrs. Nichols will serve us? I still have a soft spot in my heart for Old Jep, and I'd hate to contribute to her favor in any manner whatsoever. Plus, I'm quite sure all of her twattling will spoil the evening, even before I get a chance to."

"Nope. They are a bit short-handed at Pitts these days. That mercurial bitch high-tailed it out of Roubideaux some months back. Said she was shaking off the dust of this holier-than-thou town and going back east, where the people are honest and don't judge one based solely on their immoral behavior."

"Good for her, I guess. I'm sure Old Jep and Marcus both celebrated that moment with a toast of good riddance."

"They sure did. Marcus picked up the tab, and Jep granted him a wish."

"Oh, one more thing," Pete continued. "Millie's not meeting you here. Lucy and I did not want to expose our customers to the kind of beauty she would most certainly be exhibiting. We'll be meeting her at the Pitts House at straight up six o'clock. I've asked Lucy to come back here and cover the bar for a few minutes. I'll make the elaborate and long-awaited introduction as short as possible, and I'll take my leave. While improper as it might be, I shall leave the two of you unchaperoned."

Perry paused for a moment, considering all the arrangements Pete and Lucy made for the evening.

"You've literally thought of everything; I am afraid I might be in your debt for a lifetime. And right now, I'm not too sure if that's a positive or a negative."

"It's all good," Pete said. "I'm thinkin' of it as an investment in my future. Remember, you still need to help Lucy perfect that ungodly recipe of yours for chipped beef gravy with biscuits."

CHAPTER 18

Late Fall 1860

THE MATCHMAKER REALIZED

PETE NEVER CONSIDERED HIMSELF A MATCHMAKER, but here he was. Introducing a man he'd known for only a year and a half to a young lady, his employee, whom he considered a naive younger sister.

"You better be on your best behavior," Pete warned. "While she lowers herself to play piano here, she's quite respectable. I must add, she's particular in her taste for the company she keeps. The men in this town knew she was beyond reach. But you, my friend, are a complete complement to her perfection."

Perry didn't know quite how to respond.

"Never fear. I understand the importance of propriety and decorum. I am quite beyond approach myself, but that is due more to choice than any intimidation caused by my rippling biceps, fair hair, and striking jawline. Though I did not realize it until recently, I have waited for this moment since I left Salt Spring, Indiana."

"You ain't seen nuthin' yet," Pete assured him.

It was an unseasonably warm late fall evening as the two men approached the entryway of the Pitts House, Perry, with gift in hand. Millie was standing under the awning in full splendor and beauty. Perry practically lost his breath at the sight.

Millie wore a dress of light purple satin that accentuated her beauty. It featured a tight, flat-collared neckline and a delicate pleated top. The fabric gathered to a slender waist with a silver silk ribbon tied in the back into a majestic bow. The light purple satin exploded into a skirt trimmed with silver lace and black trim.

Overall Millie's attire was so stunning Perry almost didn't notice the figure it decorated. Millie stood tall and lean but with a chest that amply puffed the pleats below her shoulders.

Millie also wore a matching purple satin bonnet trimmed in silver lace. It reminded Perry of a fancier version of his mother's cherished headwear that he had left in Indiana. His mother's empowering words echoed through his mind. *"Chin up, chest out."*

Despite the jolt of reassurance, a remnant of doubt drove his thoughts. He might be underdressed and outclassed at the same time. He shook his head and nearly turned tail and ran. Sensing Perry's uneasiness, Pete grabbed him by the elbow, as if leading a grieving soul down a funeral aisle. As the two men approached, Millie lifted her chin and peered in their direction. Perry was awestruck and speechless. His emotions ablaze, never beholding such beauty.

Perry shook off Pete's grasp of his elbow and walked toward Millie but a full stride behind Pete.

"Miss Millie, I'd like to introduce to you Perry Samuel Adams. He's a gentleman farmer from a place called Jawbone Holler," Pete began. "He's an honest man with a kindly heart but quick to defend principle when vital. He prefers not to drink. He cooks well enough not to starve. He has a soft spot for mules and genies. And as you can see, he sports a distinguished profile. He also sleeps with a hound dog and has a fragile heart."

Millie tried not to laugh but let out a shy whisper of a giggle. Though Perry felt slightly betrayed by Pete's unveiling of the mutual admiration between himself and the floppy-eared Archibald, he met Millie's hint of laughter with a smile. He was enchanted, and the tables were about to turn.

"Perry, I'd like to introduce to you Miss Millicent Bethany Longworth, a lady who plays the piano and molds young minds with equal courage. She has toyed with God's emotions, but nary a mortal man. Some might think her a spinster, but I assure you, this is of her own choosing. She has lofty standards for virtue and a low threshold for cruelty. She is cultured in the most appealing aspects of society but detests those who place their own social standing above others. As you can see, she is a beautiful specimen of feminine charm but approachable for a finely chiseled man such as you. I proudly claim her as my self-adopted younger sister."

Compared to Perry, Millie got off sparingly. If Pete's introduction of Millie was half as accurate as the one devoted to him, Perry would surely enjoy spending at least one splendid evening with this fair princess. He was already hoping for more than one evening, but Perry clamped down on his facial expression to not make a public showing of his internal feelings.

"I think my damage here is done," Pete chuckled. "Enjoy your supper and small talk. It's Friday night, so, Millie, if you get tired of this slob, come back to The Outpost and bang out a few tunes. And, Perry, if the poor lass bores you to tears, come back to the tavern because I am sure Jep will grant you a wish for someone more appealing."

As Pete walked away, Millie and Perry looked at each other dumbfounded. What had Pete done? They were like two abandoned puppies stuffed into a burlap bag about to be tossed into the throat of a Missouri River whirlpool.

"Oh, Pete, gotta love him," Perry said with a transparent stroke of admiration for the bartender. "It's a pleasure to make your acquaintance, Miss Longworth."

"It's nice to meet you, Mr. Adams," Millie shyly joined the conversation. "Miss Longworth is what my students call me. Please, Perry, call me Millie."

The ice was finally broken.

"Pete is certainly one in a million," Millie added. "And I can't say enough about Lucy. They are the big brother and sister I never had. They've saved my life on more than one occasion and in more than one fashion."

Perry reached for the brass handle of the thick oak door of the Pitts House.

He swung it wide and gestured a gentle introduction for Millie to enter.

Millie entered the restaurant and approached the attendant.

"Yes, we have reservations," Millie said. "Pete said he made them under the name of Serendipity,"

Overhearing this Perry laughed.

"A gentleman and a philosopher, Pete is one in a million," Perry said.

Perry and Millie looked at each other, and in unison they said, "Awesome possum."

Still laughing from the moment, Millie and Perry were escorted to a booth by a front-street window. Perry pulled out a chair for Millie and gently scooted her toward the table, where the flames of two candlesticks were dancing a Quadrille.

Perry joined Millie on the table's opposite side. A waiter stopped by to deliver the narrative menu of that night's Italian, by way of Missouri, cuisine— baked macaroni au gratin, spaghetti and sausage balls sauteed in tomato and garlic sauce, or baked chicken with garlic and white cheese sauce. Each came with two slices of buttery bread, oven fired and sprinkled with a delightful combination of garlic and salt.

Millie ordered the macaroni and Perry the chicken. Perry informed Millie that he wasn't much of a wine guy, but he was going to order a bottle of local wine.

"I love the wine they make here. Any other time I'd join you in a glass. But as a teacher, I can't consume alcohol in public. It's a dumb rule, especially at a Catholic school, but it's one I must respect."

Millie opted for a glass of tea, and for the sake of harmony, Perry opted for water. The waiter retreated to the kitchen, where he also doubled as chef.

Perry had so many questions about his table partner. Where would he start?

"Miss Millie, I think it proper etiquette to invite you to share your story of perseverance before I launch into my long-winded tale of woe. But in the spirit of proper manners, I also would like to give you the option."

Millie placed the interlaced fingers of her hands at face level and rested her perfect chin on the resulting bridge. Looking over the dancing candle flames toward Perry, she flashed a smile capable of disarming a regiment of rogues.

"Perry, I am a simple girl in some respects but complicated in others."

Millie started with the basic demographics. She'd grown up in Westport, a rough and tumble place much like Roubideaux. She was the shyest of her parents' five daughters but also the apple of their eye. While they were supportive of her exploration of the convent, since her exit into the laity they expressed concerns about her singleness. She was twenty-three, a spinster, and past the prime of courtship.

Like her now-married sisters, Millie had received a proper Catholic education, having graduated from the Ascension High School for Girls. The devoted story of Mary of Bethany had kept her anchored spiritually. She had a passion for the written English word and an affection toward music that equaled her talent. She preferred the piano but also played the harp and cello with equal skill. She often hid behind her music.

Millie told Perry she had never held fascination for any man despite the efforts of many. What she did not tell him was that she found herself somewhat attracted to the gentleman farmer seated across the table. It tickled her soul awkwardly.

She went on with a few narrative details. She appreciated an occasional glass of fruity red wine and enjoyed foods that struck a balance of savory and sweet. She was still searching for the best way she could serve God and the Church, and that devotion had led her to become a teacher at the Benedictine Mission School in Roubideaux.

She preferred warm over cold, comfortable over formal and honesty over opacity, even if for the sake of emotional security. Social events often left her with a hollow feeling, but she learned to intentionally compensate for her reticence with the flip of a mental lever. Her ego was reserved, but she was driven by calculated ambition. She cherished children and adored dogs.

After hearing the delightful soliloquy from Miss Millie, Perry's was concerned his somewhat checkered past might not measure up.

"Miss Millie, I am but a simple man," Perry began. "But for a good portion of my misspent upbringing in Indiana, my blood often ran hotter than a riverboat boiler."

Perry recounted the tribulations of his early life, his journey to Kansas with Luke and all that transpired.

Very carefully, he admitted drifting away from the institution of church. He had not been to confession nor taken communion in several years due mostly to his remote lifestyle. But he knew the Benedictines had started a mission church in Lowland, and he might start attending. Most of the time, he communed with God in the quiet of the night, the celebratory light of dawn and throughout the duration of his work in God's corn fields.

He told Millie he endeavored to overcome what some considered a hard exterior by exhibiting an inward attitude of blessing and joy. While he appreciated the taste of spiced rum, he had sworn it off, but he did like a good glass of Pete's 'mater beer. He might consider trying a sip of fruity red wine. He appreciated tasty food but particularly admired squirrel stew and chipped beef gravy and biscuits.

Perry explained that he looked beyond the color of a man's skin, and he had killed a man who was overcome by hatred. He would possibly cherish children in due time, but for now he had a soft spot in his heart for hound dogs and genies.

"The thought of Old Jep and his drunken shenanigans makes me smile, but it also makes me feel ashamed for finding amusement," Millie confessed.

Perry could see he passed the schoolteacher's initial quiz.

After the two engaged in no less than a dozen interchanges to solicit more details about their backgrounds and core beliefs, their order arrived. Millie made the sign of the cross and recited a blessing. Perry recognized the common blessing and joined Millie at the end with an "Ayy-menn!" They chatted throughout their supper. And they lingered for an hour after they finished their meals, looking for an excuse to stay even longer.

Perry settled the check and asked the waiter to add a bottle of the wine he intended to order with supper. He wanted to take it home for a special occasion. The waiter and chef soon informed them the establishment had closed for the night. Millie and Perry meandered during their walk back to The Outpost, not wanting the evening to end. Perry presented the two-story gift he guarded all evening. He handed it to Millie and told her the evening had been as splendid as the harvest moon lighting that night's stroll.

Millie squealed with anticipation as she took the complicated package in hand. She untied the silver silk ribbon and asked Perry to tie it around her light purple satin sleeve. The familiar wooden box containing her precious rosary, a graduation gift from her mother, brought joy to her eyes. Whether improper or not for their first date, Millie hugged Perry like she had known him for years.

"Not knowing when or if you were ever coming back, Lucy asked me to hold on to it for safekeeping, as well as a remembrance of the young woman I had never really known. At the time it brought me great comfort for it was the day after Charlie Wilson shot me."

Millie dug into the next layer of the gift. She gently tore the brown paper wrapping and opened the box. It contained a plethora of peppermint sticks.

Millie blurted out a phrase Perry would never forgot.

"This is as sweet a gift as the man who bestowed it on me. That first peppermint stick atop my piano was a sign that fate did hold for me a divine connection of love."

Love. The word had slipped out of Millie's mouth like a late-season grape at a parish picnic, never to be retrieved after hitting the dusty ground. She did not regret the word rolling off her tongue. Perry made note of her word choice in his heart.

As the two arrived back at the threshold of The Outpost, Perry presented Millie the full bottle of wine he'd purchased before leaving the Pitts House.

"This bottle is for a future occasion of my choosing. Keep it safe and store it on its side to keep the cork protected."

"Thank you, Mr. Adams. I will keep it safely in the drawer of my dresser."

Perry explained his plan to spend the night with his horses Beulah and Barney in the stable. To his surprise, Millie said she might like to meet them one day. Perry bowed at the waist and kissed Miss Millie on her delicate piano playing hand. She looked at him with a twinkle of stardust in her deep green eyes and kissed him on the cheek.

"I thank you for one of the most pleasant evenings of my entire life."

"Perhaps we might do it again soon," Perry suggested, feeling the bravado of the moment.

"I think perhaps we shall," Millie said.

Perry admired her as she walked away. She looked back and smiled at him over her purple-satin shoulder tied with the silver silk ribbon.

CHAPTER 19

Late Fall and Winter 1860

THE CUSP OF COURTSHIP

WHILE IT REMAINED AN UNSEASONABLY WARM morning jaunt to The Outpost, the streetside trees were shedding their leaves. The songbirds had vacated their nests for even warmer southern climates. But on this morning, the essence of springtime floated all around Perry. Pete had not yet replaced the seasonal swinging doors with the stable and insulating wooden variety. As Perry entered the bar, it once again had been transformed into a venue resembling a French café, complete with tablecloths and fancy candles. His heart danced at the sight.

Patrons were wall to wall, and the flurry of activity overwhelmed Pete. Perry found a spot at the bar. Bustling to and fro, Pete paused in front of his friend.

"How did the evening transpire? Are you a married man or a confirmed bachelor?"

Perry blushed at both questions.

"It went well," Perry stated in an unfussy tone. "We enjoyed a splendid meal and even better conversation. She hugged me and kissed me on the cheek."

"Sounds like I need to lecture that young lady about extending such improper gestures."

"How about some of Lucy's creamy eggs and ham and a 'mater beer, Pete?" Perry asked.

As Perry bellied up to the bar, Lucy overhead her name.

"Good morning, early bird," she said. "Hope you're not expecting a worm from my kitchen."

"You never disappoint, Miss Lucy. So, how about knocking on Miss Millie's door to see if she might like to join me?"

"I'm not sure you should do that, Lucy," Pete said. "After hearing about Millie's forward deeds of the evening prior, I harbor some concerns about the welfare of my friend, Perry. She kissed him on the cheek."

"Oh my, what a scandal," Lucy said.

Perry laughed, saying, "Ahh, come on, Lucy. Just do it."

Lucy left the kitchen, climbed the stairs, and knocked on Millie's door. Before a count of five, Perry could see the door crack open and Lucy jump inside.

In the privacy of Millie's room, Lucy wanted to hear details about the previous evening.

"Perry's downstairs. He would like you to join him for breakfast. So, I take it the evening was a rousing success?"

"It was a splendid evening. He's such a gentleman and a bit handsome too. "

"Yeh, not bad for a hermit."

"I think my decision to leave the religious life might have been for the best, but I guess only time will tell."

"All I can tell you is that Perry is practically glowing this morning."

"Oh my," Millie blushed. "I had a very nice time and there might have been a spark or two. I suspected he might be here this morning for one of your breakfasts, so I picked out an outfit that I thought might work. What do you think, Lucy?"

"I think he will be even more smitten."

A minute later Miss Millie bounded down the stairs in a bright, flower-printed linen dress, appropriately announcing the weekend. She claimed a seat at the bar beside Perry.

"Good morning, kind sir," she said.

"Care to accompany me in a plate of Lucy's famous eggs?" Perry asked, knowing already the answer would be yes.

She nodded to Perry, and Perry nodded to Pete, holding up two fingers to Lucy.

Lucy brought over two plates abounding with similar mounds of ham-speckled heaven, along with two sets of silverware wrapped in white linen napkins. Pete poured Perry a 'mater beer.

Millie made the sign of the cross and bowed her head in prayer. Bowing his head, Perry joined her. He'd never prayed in a bar. The prayer was brief on a Saturday morning.

"I see you have taken up drinking in the morning, Mr. Adams. Did the prior evening disturb you so?" Millie asked in full jest.

"Not at all, Miss Millie, I have to travel back to the farm for work today and hope to be there this afternoon to tend to my herd. I require both types of energy, solid and liquid. But I'll tell you what, if you might entertain the notion, I shall return in a fortnight in hopes you can show me some new destinations in this town."

"A fortnight it will be," Millie replied with a sparkle in her deep green eyes. "I would be thrilled to do that."

Perry was ready to proclaim a budding courtship in both heart and mind.

After finishing his eggs, he kissed Millie's hand and expressed a gentlemanly farewell.

"Every day is a blessing, Miss Millie," he said. "And sometimes, the evenings and mornings are too."

Perry reached across the bar, shook hands with Pete and waved to Lucy, who was scurrying in the kitchen.

"I shall return in a fortnight," Perry proclaimed, like a valiant knight of old. He headed to the stable to retrieve his wagon and team.

As Perry crossed the river, a line of clouds passed overhead. The temperature dropped a full twenty degrees in a matter of minutes. Perry shivered as he sat in the wagon in his work clothes with no coat. If the temperature got much colder, he'd have a hard time getting home. Perry hated the cold.

Reaching Jawbone Holler that afternoon provided needed relief from the elements. He checked on Butter, who had ample feed and water remaining. Her pregnant belly was well pronounced. It looked as though Moses or Gabe must have also milked her during a visit, much to Perry's relief. He welcomed the liberation from such a task on a such a gray and frigid day.

Perry and Archibald beat a straight path to the house. Before Perry could stoke up a fire in the fireplace, he noticed an item in the middle of his kitchen's log table. It was a country-cured smoked ham wrapped in cheesecloth, courtesy of the generous Moses Watson.

The two weeks until his next visit to Roubideaux lumbered by like an overloaded freight train to Lowland. But finally, the day arrived for his return to Millie's side.

It was a Friday evening, and Millie was waiting anxiously at her piano, biding her time, pounding out tunes that abetted the drinking mood of The Outpost patrons.

Perry entered the solid wood doors of the bar that kept out the wintry cold and saw Millie dutifully earning her pay. Millie had tied her long black hair into a ponytail with the silver silk ribbon from Perry's last visit.

"Howdy, Miss Millie," he said. "Nice ribbon! Looks like you might be ready to hit the town."

Millie nodded in affirmation.

He walked up to Pete. Pete poured him a 'mater beer and Perry slugged it down.

"Pete, I'm going to steal your pianist this evening, if you don't mind."

Pete begrudgingly signaled his approval.

"I'll have her home an hour before closing time, so she can serenade your late-night patrons down the home stretch," Perry said.

"I'll hold you to that," Pete said.

Perry and Millie found a frontier restaurant on the far side of town and enjoyed a meal of beef and potatoes, in addition to a deeper conversation about the future. Upon returning the lovely Millie to The Outpost, as usual, Perry bid her farewell at the door. Before leaving, he looked deeply into her green eyes for a serious matter of discussion.

"Millie, I have been thinking during the drag of the last two weeks. If you are favorably inclined—and don't object to the whirlwind nature of my advance—I would like to visit every fortnight throughout the winter months."

"Mr. Adams, the last two weeks have seemed like an eternity," Millie said, swiftly kissing Perry on the cheek. "I do believe the formality of your regular visits throughout the winter will lift my soul."

From that moment forward, with an informal visitation plan in place, the pattern of Perry's visits to Millie ensued. Pete and Lucy were pleasantly lenient and even asked the piano player who acquired the gig during Millie's dalliance with the convent to rejoin the staff on a part-time basis. He was not as classically polished as Millie nor as pleasing to the eye, but this was not a hoity-toity auditorium in New York. It was a frontier bar.

Beulah's final trip to Roubideaux helping to pull Perry's wagon came right before Christmas. She was heavy with a spring colt. During that trip Perry acquired a ruggedly handsome buckskin quarter horse gelding named Buck, whom he tethered to the rear of the wagon during the trip back to the holler. Buck was his chosen mode of transport for the remainder of the winter, as Beulah and Barney were nestled in the barn. Perry did not want to risk losing the colt or Beulah. The rigors of the winter trail would be burdensome.

Perry's trips to Roubideaux aboard Buck made the trip time shorter, and he considered that another positive. Perry hated winter, so any decreased time in the weather was welcome. But he continued to make a resolute sacrifice to brace the elements in order to experience morsels of time with Millie. Of course, he would also enjoy the fellowship by reconnecting with the rest of the Roubideaux gang, Pete and Marcus. Old Jep, of course, would be present, drinking himself into oblivion, all the time granting wishes to those willing to fuel his stupor, including Perry, to whom he still referred as "Stranger."

The trips continued under this ad hoc pretense. During Perry's subsequent trek in early March, he put forward some life-changing ideas. With trees in full bud corresponding with the return of the songbirds, Perry formalized his plan to woo Millie. He requested that she consider the prospect of a proper period of courtship.

"Perry, you have made me the happiest woman this side of Saint Louie. I graciously accept your proposition," she said.

Pete and Lucy were equally pleased. If Millie was informally their adopted younger sister, they reckoned it might one day make Perry their adopted brother-in-law.

Given the continued border tensions and Millie's sentiments about slavery, Perry first had to get Millie out of Missouri. Nothing against Lucy and Pete, but in Lowland, a slug of new houses was available and rent more affordable.

"I've seen how you struggle in this town," Perry said. "Most of the people here struggle with the concept of freedom for all, and you're working your fingers to the bone. Might I suggest a move to Lowland? I think I could secure a small house for the amount you're paying Lucy and Pete."

"The Fontaines have been so good to me. I'd miss my kids, and while playing piano here isn't the perfect venue, I do enjoy it."

"Well, Millie, the Benedictine monks have established a new church in Lowland, and they're building a school too. The school needs teachers. You'll be safer in Lowland. We can always visit Lucy and Pete."

"But what about my access to a fine piano?"

"I have a plan."

Before Perry left Roubideaux, Millie decided a move to Lowland would be logical.

Perry sheepishly approached Pete and Lucy about the notion. Like a shy schoolboy, Perry dragged his feet and lowered his head when he mentioned the plan to the Fontaines. It was like asking parental permission for the hand of their daughter, but they understood fully.

"I've witnessed first-hand incidents of harassment Millie has dealt with over the years from inebriated bar patrons," Lucy said. "The old coots who come in here are usually drunk, hungry, or horny, sometimes all three. I've seen the lascivious and unwelcome glances Millie draws from the rabble in this place. We'd miss seeing Millie on a daily basis, but it might be for the best."

"I just have an ominous sense that things are about to explode around the slavery issue," Perry said. "I think Millie would be safer across the river."

"I hate the idea, but I understand totally," Pete said. "Lucy will probably be able to find a replacement musician to step in full-time, and she certainly could find a new renter for the room above the bar."

"We don't blame you one bit," Lucy said. "Both you and Millie have waited your entire lifetimes to find your soulmates, and this is a situation that begs for urgency. Having her safely tucked away in Lowland would lift a significant burden of concern off our shoulders."

"I appreciate your understanding," Perry said. "This is becoming a matter of necessity. I fear for all of us living along the border, but if there is strife, I am guessing many of the battles will be fought down south or back east. Those of us who live here can continue to keep our kinship regardless of the side of circumstance represented by our residence."

There was growing talk of conscription for men as both sides marshaled their forces. That matter troubled both Perry and Pete, as they were both able-bodied, bright-minded, and within the appropriate age for war fighters. For the union that turned out to be between the ages of twenty and forty-five. For the confederacy there was talk of that age range running from seventeen to fifty. Of course, that would not limit the ability for older volunteers with a partisan pull to one side or the other.

"I have to get Millie out of here, and I fear for your safety as much as mine," Perry said. "Regardless of what happens, Pete, you and I will always be brothers. If a conflict erupts, we must continue to find ways to meet so we can stoke the flames of our friendship."

"You can count on it," Pete said. "Even if all hell breaks loose, I doubt the powers that be will put an end to the telegraph lines connecting both camps. But we might need to speak in code. You know, a special word that establishes the need to gather here at the bar, or at least down by the river."

"I got it. How about sarsaparilla? That will mean meet me at high noon on my side of the river, and we can measure the current level of danger and proceed accordingly."

"You got it, friend," Pete said. "Sarsaparilla it shall be. Not knowing what my future holds, I will let Marcus in on the codeword as well."

CHAPTER 20

Early 1861

THE WINDS OF WAR

SHORTLY AFTER PERRY AND PETE DEVELOPED their strategy about future meetings, the region was thrown into another provocative tailspin. After referenda throughout the territory, it was clear the huge influx of anti-slavers won the day.

On January 29, 1861, Kansas was admitted to the Union as a free state.

Kansans fired rifles into the night sky. Indiscriminate celebrations broke out across the land as news reached the embattled former territory. It was the culmination of an action initially envisioned after President Franklin Pierce signed the Kansas-Nebraska Act in 1854, which granted territorial settlers the right to choose their destiny.

Perry was as jubilant as any on the far side of the river. While Missouri was a Union state, it clung to its pro-slavery tradition. Kansas coming in as a free state provided even more impetus to transport Millie to the other side of the river, where sentiments of most residents were fully behind Kansas' free-state status. But Perry wanted Millie to be happy and secure. He approached another quite urgent matter with Pete and Lucy as a bartering proposition of sorts.

"As you know, Millie loves music, and not any old tune but music she can perform on that piano," Perry said, pointing at the instrument. "If possible I'd like to acquire that fine piece of melodic machinery."

Lucy and Pete mulled the idea for a moment. They had been considering the purchase of a new piano to partially offset the quality difference their patrons might notice after Millie left for good.

"Actually, this old place needs a new sound," Lucy said. "If war comes, this little rat hole of a bar will need every edge possible to continue to attract customers. I sure hope Pete isn't drafted, but if he is, I'll run this place the best I can. Between you and me, Perry, I already do." She smirked at Pete.

"During your next trip here, let's load up the piano in your wagon and you can transport it to Lowland while you still have an opportunity," Pete said in deference to his lovely wife.

"My new calf and colt are due sometime this spring. I'll sell them in Lowland and hand-deliver the money to you, maybe not the next time, but soon," Perry said.

"Awesome possum, it's a deal," Pete responded. "Your credit's good with me, but if not, I'll come over and steal your plow."

With Lucy's blessing Pete walked to Marcus Trading Post that day and arranged for the shipment of a new piano on the next freight wagon from Chicago, by way of Saint Louis.

The deal struck, Perry returned to Jawbone Holler.

In the early days of March, Perry was thrilled that both Butter and Beulah delivered strong and healthy offspring. Beulah's colt came into the world without complication. Butter's calf, on the other hand, needed a little assistance. On a dewy springtime morning, Perry rode to see Moses and Gabe regarding the urgent matter.

"Done it a thousand times," Moses said, "but we need to hurry. Gabe, why don't you come along so you can see your papa in action?"

Reaching Perry's barn Moses rolled up his sleeves and sprinted to Butter's side. He washed his hands and arms before investigating her condition in a more intimate way. Moses reached in his hand to determine the calf's location in the birthing canal. Gabe and Perry stood back and watched. Butter was definitely in labor.

"Everything is in order. We should be able to save mother and calf, but this little fella must be a little bigger than any Butter has delivered in the past," Moses said. "Chester fathers larger calves. That's his only drawback."

Moses reached in his hand again. Two tiny legs appeared. The calf was in the proper position for birthing, but it was not emerging.

"I may need a rope, but I am going to be as gentle as possible and do this by hand."

Moses carefully grabbed each of the protruding legs above the ankle. He pulled gently each time Butter pushed. Perry was amazed. Progress was slow, but finally the calf began to appear, legs, head, and chest. Butter pushed again. Moses gave another pull, and the calf popped out with a splash.

"The miracle of birth," Perry said, wiping his brow. "A fine job, Dr. Watson. I would not have known where to start."

Moses dried off the bull calf with a burlap bag. After a minute it wobbled to its feet.

"That's a strong calf. I think he takes after his daddy."

Perry beamed like a proud papa himself.

"It looks like I might be giving you fellas a run for your money in the livestock department. Not only do I have a colt from Beulah, but now also a calf from Butter, both robust and healthy."

"We've already had eight new calves and seven new litters of piglets," Gabe said. "Not counting our new baby chicks, who are already scratching around in the yard for worms, I think you have a way to go. I hope you were taking notes. I sure was."

"Life is a constant process of learning and your papa's an outstanding teacher."

"Bringing new life into the world is my favorite part of farming," Moses said. "It keeps me going during the doldrums of winter."

"I'll tell you what kept me going this winter," Perry said. "It was that country-cured ham you dropped off. It was a welcome addition to my dinner table. I even altered my recipe to become one for ham gravy and biscuits. Why don't you come to the house? I'd like to make you both a meal if you have time."

Moses noted that the gravy was notably better, with a hint of smoke and salt. The biscuits, however, were still hard as rocks, but they were delightful because they were baked with neighborly kindness.

As the men ate, Perry updated his guests about what he'd heard and read about the rising border tensions.

"The situation is reaching boiling point. This whole matter of statehood, and free-statehood at that, has extremists on both sides crawling from beneath their partisan rocks to express hatred for the other side. In relative terms, you both are a lot safer here in Kansas."

Perry continued, "Know that I might be conscripted to become a combatant in the days ahead. If that happens, I am hoping one or both of you can keep an eye on my place, and if possible, make room for my animals."

"That all goes without question, Perry," Moses said.

"The only other thing I would ask is for you to make a place for Archibald inside your home."

"Done deal. It sure seems like a lot of men are being backed into corners and have developed attitudes like badgers. The tendency is always to sharpen one's teeth and claws in a moment of crisis and it sure sounds like we are heading in that direction. If you get called up, Perry, we will take care of everything here. Well, I can't speak for Gabe, but I feel far too old to even think about joining the fray. Glad to help here at home since you'll be fighting for my forever freedom. In my book, that's more than a fair trade for any services rendered. There aren't enough country-cured hams in the world to repay the debt."

"Perry, as soon as you get your notice, you let me know," Gabe said. "This is a cause I'm willing to die for, and I'll volunteer if I can serve by your side. It's personal. I've seen far too much injustice and am forever in wonder of what has become of my mother and brothers because of slavery. I will fight for my father, my missing family, and myself."

Perry assured Gabe he would keep him informed. After breakfast Perry rode with the Watsons back to their farm and departed for Lowland.

Perry made many arrangements to ensure Millie's happy transition. The house he rented was small but comfortable. He visited Father Linus Carrigan at the mission church and inquired about how he might rectify his current standing to become a regular parishioner. He also mentioned the convenient fact that he was in contact with a highly qualified Catholic schoolteacher.

After returning to Jawbone Holler for a couple more days, Perry prepared for his late March trip back to Roubideaux to transport Millie and her belongings. He needed his team of horses to pull the wagon, but there was one slight problem, a frolicking colt. Perry hitched up the proud parents and, with the young horse riding in the wagon, he headed to the Watson farm.

"Gentlemen, could you look after him for a couple of days? I'm taking his momma away for a bit. Headed to Roubideaux to pick up Millie and her worldly possessions. I've found a place for her in Lowland, and I'll be carting both her and her belongings on this trip. About the colt, you'll need to bottle feed him, but I know milk's not in short supply here."

Moses and Gabe quickly agreed. They were pleased to hear Perry was removing Millie at least a decent distance from the neighboring slave state. A girl with her abolitionist convictions had no business staying in Roubideaux when the winds of war came blowing.

"I'll be dropping by the trading post while I'm there to stock up on a few provisions," Perry said. "Can I pick up anything for you before my return?"

"Nothing for me, Perry, but I do appreciate the offer," Gabe said.

"It's been a good spell since I have enjoyed the pastime of chewing some fine plug tobacco," Moses said. "Several bricks of that God-awful stuff would be appreciated. I enjoy the leisurely pursuit of a good tobacco spit."

"Glad to do it. It's on me. Just take care of my colt."

Shortly after Perry reached Roubideaux, most of Millie's worldly belongings were loaded into the wagon.

"We need to make sure to pack stuff around the edge because I have one more item to load into the middle," Perry said.

"What is it?" Millie asked.

"You'll see."

Perry guided Beulah and Barney on a direct route to Pete's Outpost Tavern.

Once arriving, Lucy supervised while Pete, Perry, and Marcus teamed up to load the old familiar piano onto the wagon. It was now Millie's. Around it they placed the remaining pieces of Millie's life. The bottle of wine from their first date was dutifully wrapped into the softness of a cotton blanket.

"Pete, I'm going to have to extend that loan on the piano for a bit. The colt and calf aren't ready for sale yet, but don't worry, they're growing like weeds," Perry said.

"Like I said, Perry, your credit is good with me," Pete said.

Millie was thrilled to have her own piano. She hugged Perry around the neck.

"It shall be an inseparable part of my life. At least I will have that," Millie said.

Lucy pulled Millie off to the side and whispered in her ear. "He'll come around. Even in this world, I know he will."

After situating Millie and her piano safely in Lowland, the sound of plinking notes quickly made it to the seat of his wagon as he left for the day. On the way home, Perry stopped off at the Watson farm to deliver five plugs of chewing tobacco he promised to Moses. He thanked the father and son for watching after Beulah's young colt and he headed back to Jawbone Holler for some focused fieldwork.

These days turned out to be the final breath of calm. Two weeks later and this entire trip would have held much greater danger. A wretched storm of war split the nation, Union and Confederate, north and south, slave and free.

In April 1861 the Confederate States of America lit a fuse of rebellion during an offensive assault of Fort Sumter, South Carolina. The entire world, for partisans of both sides, would never be the same. The attack came after President Lincoln refused the southern states' efforts to secede. In turn, southern leaders demanded U.S. troops immediately vacate the fort, located on the outskirts of Charleston. This was a demand Lincoln rebuffed. South Carolina was the backyard of the benefactors of slavery and state's rights. Why not, they calculated, make Fort Sumter the site for a headline-grabbing showdown?

The two sides crossed the line and were now expressing their grievances through blood, animosity, and resentment. In some regions commerce ground to a halt, trumped by hatred. In the frontier border regions, trade, communication, and transportation continued, just to a far lesser degree, before the flow of commerce dried up altogether.

In this part of the world, where the map of the brand-new state of Kansas appeared it had been bitten in its northeast corner by some matter of celestial ogre, the Missouri River became the great divide. It was a bizarre situation, given Missouri's status as a Union state. Many souls on both sides of the muddy river shared not only lineage but also similar cultures and dialects, but the river effectively partitioned them by mindset, each in brutal opposition to the other.

Hatred and rivalry demanded the stated allegiance of citizens on either side of its banks. The peril in not picking a side presented a risk even more calamitous than the hidden remains of a river snag waiting to bite into the hull of a passing steamboat. Not voicing one's allegiance could lead to an immediate beating, shooting, or lynching.

But, as the river took, it also gave. In the dead of winter, with its muddy skin partially frozen and in places deceivingly thin, the river afforded the opportunity for runaways brave enough a gambit to escape from the surly bonds of slavery. Many brave souls crossed the river's ice floes on foot. While many negotiated the course to liberty, some souls punched their tickets to freedom by plunging through the cracked ice to a final and eternal destination. Perry still had no idea Moses and Gabe were two of the successful brave souls who had made the crossing several years earlier.

Perry found tatters of his heart and soul dispersed on both sides of the river. On one side was the land and the woman he loved. On the other, twenty miles away from Jawbone Holler, were the traces of his existence and the tracks of his friends in Roubideaux who endorsed his survival.

During those desperate and uncertain days following the war's outbreak, Perry kept his mind occupied with visits to Millie in Lowland and by preparing the seedbed for his 1861 corn crop.

A full month after Millie became a new resident of Lowland, snuggled in the extreme northeast corner of the new free state, she made her abolitionist position official by swearing an allegiance to the cause. Shortly thereafter her proficiency at those old familiar black and white keys eclipsed even the point of virtuosity. Her love of music grew through what was now the sheer joy of performance, rather than being a job she fulfilled to ensure a shelter over her head.

During his visits to Lowland, Perry saw and heard the difference. Millie's strokes of the piano keys were more graceful and more precise. At the same time, her spirit and her music seemed to meld as one, a mixture of spiritual exuberance and the bliss of fulfillment and purpose. Her talent at the keyboard earned her numerous friends among the several feminine social circles of Lowland. Millie Longworth, the courted lady of wild man Perry Adams, was a local celebrity. She no longer hid behind her music; instead she celebrated it as much as it announced her arrival.

Perry had put off the inevitable about as long as he could. The day was getting close for Millie's first visit to the Holler. It was time for them to have a peek at the kind of future and life they might have in Jawbone Holler. After more than two months in her new home, and after the muddy trails north became passable by wagon, Millie had a date to see the life Perry cultivated among the hardwoods and serpents.

Outside her small wood-frame house on the south side of town, Millie took Perry's hand as he pulled her gently into the seat of his buckboard wagon. By now it was a dusty and bumpy ride, one Millie savored with each rut in the trail.

The first stop was the Watson farm, where Perry went through an appropriate introduction. She heard about their struggles, including the mystery location of the rest of their family members. She also heard about the exploits Moses shared with Perry. Millie hugged both Moses and Gabe with deep emotion and in hope that one day their family might be reunited. Out of habit, Gabe did not look her in the eyes.

Reaching the farmstead, Millie met Butter and the infamous, floppy-eared Archibald, about whom she fought off a tinge of jealousy due to the license he enjoyed in sharing a common roof with Perry.

"*Uh-roo-roo-roo*," Archibald barked a welcome to Millie.

"So, this is it, Jawbone Holler. It has become such a fabled place in the depth of my mind. I was beginning to think it nothing but a myth of your imagination."

"Oh, it's quite tangible, and I have the scars and calluses to prove it."

Perry began his laborious planting exercise that morning, while Millie stayed at the house to be amused by Archibald. The wind blew briskly on the fresh spring morning, to a degree so chilly that Millie and Archibald quickly sheltered in the house. The two developed an instant bond.

Above a bright red hearthstone, Millie's deep green eyes were drawn to a peculiar shape that was bleached by the sun. Above the fireplace mantle was the long and almost mystical jawbone of Luke. She admired it from afar, not thinking it proper for a lady to touch the relic. The jawbone glowed with a luminous aura. Thinking of the tragedy of Luke that Perry had described, for a good half hour Millie broke down and wept.

When Perry returned from the field later that afternoon, he was greeted by a banquet fit for a king. Millie had discovered the provisions and whipped together a meal of fried ham, mashed potatoes and gravy. Perry knew right away that if he saw this betrothal through, he would surely need to buy some larger work trousers.

With the sunlight inching toward the horizon, he and Millie hastened their departure and climbed aboard the wagon for the return trip to her new, but what she hoped was her temporary home in Lowland. After a teaching position was posted at the new mission school, Father Carrigan offered her the job. She would begin her new duties in two short days.

"So, what did you think of the place?" Perry asked upon their arrival at her

Lowland home. "Would it be suitable for your throne, my fair lady?"

"I could not envision a more regal setting. Its majesty is beyond reproach. This is testimony to the fact your sweat, toil, and worry have all been worth it."

Perry bid her goodbye with a kiss on the cheek and boarded his wagon for the journey back to Jawbone Holler. Finally, he was the man he sought with every endeavor of his life. Perry won the heart of a woman who would make him a better man in all aspects of the word. Perry puffed out his chest. As the sun dipped below the western bluff, for the first time he carried the profile of accomplishment.

CHAPTER 21

1863

DELIVERING
LEGITIMACY

IN SPITE OF HIS SELF-ASSURED STATE, fleeting moments of uncertainty, kindled by a doubt of legitimacy, continued to burn the fibers of Perry's mind. Branded with the classification of squatter, any accomplishment he labored to achieve up to this point might be fleeting. He was farming government land.

As the war raged in locations from Aquia Creek and Bull Run in Virginia, to Blues Mill Landing and Springfield in Missouri, Perry kept his head down. He continued to plant, tend, and harvest his crops. As a squatter, he could only claim this rich black topsoil as long as the prevailing wind of governance blew in the right direction.

On May 20, 1862, President Lincoln put an end to Perry's uneasiness when he signed the Homestead Act. The law opened a massive tract of government-owned land for private farmers. One of the motivations behind the law was to encourage homesteaders to settle the new territories and eventually bring them into the Union as free states.

In addition to being aligned with the act's unstated motivations, Perry met all the legislated requirements. He was head of a household. He was several years older than twenty-one. He had been working, in all, as much as 120 acres. The new law said he could claim 160 as his own. All he had to do was "prove up" his claim, a matter he considered as easy as husking an ear of corn with his leather shucking hook.

He socked away many times the amount of money required for the filing fee that would be paid after his five years of proof. His intention was to live on the land and make additional improvements above and beyond those he had already made. Proof of farming the land was easy to obtain. He had witnesses to his yearly investment in challenging work and determination. He was a confirmed ally of the United States. He fit all the criteria.

The law also contained a provision for the purchase, after six months, of up to 160 acres for the paltry rate of $1.25 an acre. He selected a different option, which was a pledge to invest five years of work and improvements on the land. Jawbone Holler was his destiny. Perry wasted little time filing his claim.

While Moses and Gabe both held concerns about their freedom papers passing muster as proof for homesteading, Perry encouraged them to complete the endeavor. He served as their witness for the essential requirement of "proving up" the claim.

Constable Dan even toyed with proffering a claim in the river bluffs between the Watson farm and Jawbone Holler. But even given the level of vigor at his age, his true calling was behind a badge, rather than behind a plow. He stuck with his peace-keeping duties in Lowland. Perry and the Watsons, though, continued to work as a team to build common strengths and eliminate shared vulnerabilities.

During the final weeks of 1862, there were rumblings as to a change in semantics for the war. Officially, on January 1st, 1863, President Lincoln issued the Emancipation Proclamation. It stated that all persons held as slaves within the Rebellious regions were free. No longer could the war be viewed by any sympathizer to the Union cause as one to merely put down the southern secessionists. Even though many southerners argued the point, this was now in common perception a war to end slavery. Slave holders in the pro-Union, pro-slavery state of Missouri were given a free pass.

With that shifting horizon in focus, Perry continued to concentrate on three matters: Millie's safety, Millie's happiness, and raising the best corn possible. He patiently waited for his conscription notice to serve in the Union Army. He, and consequently Millie, had already waited for two entire years and corn crops. During a conversation at her Lowland home, he came clean regarding his true intentions.

"Millie, as much as I would prefer to end this courtship for the next stage of our relationship, I can't bear the thought of leaving you a widow of this war. The burden on you would be too great. If God's plan includes a full life for me, as well as an enduring and fruitful bond between the two of us, I believe it most prudent for us to observe from the wayside this ongoing conflagration with the necessary levels of patience and virtue."

Perry navigated the murky waters with carefully chosen words.

"Perry, I have waited my entire life for you. If it's written in our joint book of life, we shall become united in marriage, I will put my ambitions for such on hold for a more opportune time. Deep down, I believe it's all part of God's universal plan."

This extension of the courtship between Millie and Perry ran in opposition to the standard norms for such a process. Most courtships ran for no longer than a two-year duration, during which time a decision was made to formalize or abandon the relationship. Due to the uncertainty created by the Civil War, their courtship had already run through the duration of two and a half calendars. Lingering doubt by Perry was not what caused their extended circumstance, but instead it was due to the ambiguity of life caused by the war. Their aligned view was that this war created a provisional world.

The commitment Millie and Perry made never strayed in mind, body, or soul, neither wandering in flesh nor wavering in spirit.

The tormenting spirits of Perry's stress-fueled dreams were just as resolute.

Each night Perry jolted awake, his nightshirt drenched in sweat following a vivid nightmare he divined as Revelation's Four Horsemen of the Apocalypse. Clothed in scarlet britches and equipped with guns, swords, and torches, the four specters rode apparitions with thundering hooves emitting the fire of hatred and the steam of vengeance through their flaring nostrils. The vision plagued his soul. He was tempted to fetch a bottle of rum. Perry could have dismissed the nocturnal confrontation had the dream only transpired once, but for three consecutive nights, every detail of the dream was replicated exactly.

In the gloam of evening, each of the red-legged horsemen rode stallions of vengeance toward buildings in full conflagration. With bodies of young and old strewn about the streets, the mounted avengers wielded rifle and sword against a horde of evildoers responsible for the slaughter. The horsemen slashed and blasted until the silence of justice prevailed. Whatever innocence that lingered in Perry's spiritual constitution was snuffed by the apparitions of divine judgement.

Haunted by the repetition of the nightmare, it was later that week during a visit to see Millie in August 1863 when he heard the news as it wafted among the dusty streets of Lowland. A Missouri bushwhacker named William Quantrill led a posse of ruffians down the streets of Lawrence, Kansas, burning, looting, and raping. Two hundred Kansans were murdered. Men and young boys were yanked from their homes and put to death before the weeping eyes of wives, daughters, mothers, and sisters. And in the shock and grieving of the wretched aftermath, the women witnessed torches raised to their homes.

Perry and Dan both rationalized only a stroke of random fortune spared Lowland from a common doom. Like Lawrence, Lowland was a bastion of abolitionist doctrine. The righteous citizens even made a public event out of driving that point home, and if not for an earlier appearance by the Four Horsemen of the Apocalypse in the Bible held by Judge Merriweather, he would have fallen to an assassin's slug. Pure happenstance was the only condition preserving his dear Millie from a fate mirroring those of the tragic women of Lawrence.

The newspapers printed stories of how Quantrill justified the sacking as an act of godly retribution for an incident in the Missouri town of Osceola almost two years prior. While much water traversed under the bridge in that amount of time, Quantrill and his men insisted on pumping the runoff back upstream. Quantrill's rationalization for such an atrocity was contrived at best and premeditated at worst.

Whatever the justification, Perry burned with anger.

"Defending our state and responding to this rebel atrocity really chaps my ass," Perry shared with Constable Dan.

"I'm allied with your spirit of conviction," Dan replied. "We shall not sit idle, waiting for such a travesty to visit the streets or the women of our town. We must take swift action to send a transparent and direct message that actions such as what occurred in Lawrence will be repaid with no less than a two-fold reprisal."

Dan explained to Perry how the news of Quantrill's raid resulted in the rallying of forces under the banner of the notorious Jayhawkers. Perry heard of the fearsome regiment and the panic they cultivated in the hearts of Missourians, regardless of their leanings on the issue of slavery.

Dan further explained the regiment's structure. Combatants were all volunteers, not officially sanctioned, although considered part of the Union muster. While many fought out of sheer allegiance to the cause, and in defense of their homeland, some had checkered pasts. It was alleged that Jayhawkers were guilty of atrocities against Missourians on par with those of Quantrill and his raiders, including theft, arson, and summary execution. One brigade of Jayhawkers specialized in mounted warfare. They rode in unity of conviction and appearance, each member wearing britches of scarlet.

The literal interpretation of Perry's nightmare struck his intellect like a bolt of cogent lightning. The Jayhawkers were the mounted horsemen of his recurring dreams. They were the red-legged avengers.

Perry's decision to enlist with the Jayhawkers was contemplative but also immediate. With the lives of Millie and himself in limbo, his decision was to deliberately alter the narrative of his life, defend abolitionist principle and exact an appropriate level of reprisal against the Rebels. Loyalty also led him to fight on behalf of his friends the Watsons. One matter of which Perry was certain; heaven itself ordained this decision through the prophetic imagery of his recurring dreams.

Millie's reaction to the news of Perry's decision was calm acceptance and empowerment.

"My heart shall ride with you. You must follow the lead of your soul, and when you return, I will be here to heal any wounds your spirit might endure."

Perry rode north to see the Watsons and to tell them of his decision to join the fray. Under the shade of the willow tree, Perry waded in to announce his emotional decision.

"Watty and Gabe, I've been waiting for two years for the call of conscription, and one never came. This conflict has occurred during my days of mortal being for a reason I can no longer ignore. There must be judgment against the forces of evil, the Union must stand, and slavery must be wiped off the face of our continental nation. Our Kansas is bleeding, and I feel obliged to do everything in my power to clot the horrible wound. I feel compelled to fight for you."

He looked at Moses. A drop of unexplainable sweat ran down Moses's scarred cheek.

"I am hopeful while I am gone you might team up to manage my animals, and as best as you can, tend my crop while I am gone. And please check in on Millie while I am away. I will forever be in your debt."

"You are wrong, Perry. We will forever be in yours. Your call to this purpose is unimpeachable. If I were but a few years younger, I'd saddle up with you. But these bones feel as old as these hills, and they've already lived through a good amount of campaigning for the cause. If God were to grant me a way to go back in time, I'd take the offer, but I fear I must keep my battle plans confined to producing what I can within the confines of my farm to aid your war effort."

Gabe stood to make a bold announcement of his own.

"Mr. Adams, I won't be tending your animals or weeding your crops. Papa is going to have to do that alone."

"Whatever do you mean, Gabe?" Perry asked. "When Confederates capture Black Union soldiers, they either send them back into bondage or lynch them onsite. The stakes are understandably higher for you and so are the dangers."

"Even knowing that, I've made up my mind. I'm going to ride by your side," Gabe said. "If anyone has a good reason to volunteer for this conflict, it's me. I hate slavery. It's empowered the Confederacy with a license for legitimacy. Slavery's robbed me of my mother and brothers. And while I harbor hate toward only a few men who've directly assaulted and destroyed the family I love; I think I'll take some semblance of retribution against any of those Rebel bastards that rise against me. I'm certain I'll see in their faces the reflection of old man Manchester."

Moses was not prepared for his son's announcement, but the words did serve to stoke a flame of pride within his heart. The only regret ricocheting through Moses's mind was he had already lost his wife and two sons to the demon of slavery. The possibility of losing his last son to men fighting to defend the vile institution was horrifying, but he understood Gabe's eloquence in making a stand.

"Gabe, the mere thought of losing you to those Confederate bastards is horrifying. But I understand your commitment to place the importance of defending the cause of freedom before the sanctity of your own life."

The process for enlisting required Gabe to produce proof of his freedom. His papers were packed and ready to go.

"If I were to lose the last certain member of my bloodline, it'd be the death of me, regardless of how just the cause might be," Moses said. "Perry, I know you are only a bit more senior than Gabriel, but I ask you to look after him as best as you can."

"If this all comes to pass and conflict becomes a tangible part of it, I certainly will, Watty. I will place Gabe's safety above my own."

"I am perfectly capable of looking after myself, gentlemen," Gabe said. "But Mr. Adams, I am willing to keep my eyes peeled for any hazard that might be headed your way. You will be in good hands with me."

Perry could see Moses's pride in his son, just as easily as he could perceive Gabe's overconfidence that he could get the job done.

"That kind of cock-sure attitude reminds me of my younger days back at River View Grove," Moses said. "Why don't we say you will both look out for one another? And while the two of you are protecting each other, I'll do everything in my power to preserve the advances we have made here and Perry has made in Jawbone Holler."

Moses and Gabe both extended Perry handshakes, but Perry responded with bear hugs.

"I will let you know when it's time for us to saddle up, Gabe," Perry said.

Perry was prepared to meet any fate God might have for him on the battlefield, so he wanted to see the people who meant the most to him before he headed into the mystery of awaiting darkness.

Perry and Buck made a quick trip to Roubideaux to see Marcus, Pete, Lucy, and Old Jep once more.

He stopped at Marcus's and bought some additional cartridges for his rifle, a box of peppermint sticks for Millie, and a couple bricks of plug chewing tobacco for Moses. Marcus was elated to see Perry, but something looked different about him. Marcus was wearing a toupee.

"Marcus, what the hell is that? Did something die atop your head?" Perry asked. "Looks a little like a gigantic rat or a small possum."

Marcus appeared unsure whether to laugh or be insulted.

"You are welcome to offend the proprietor of this fine establishment at your own risk. But you never know when prices might go up accordingly."

"In that case, Marcus, I'd like a box of cartridges for my rifle, a box of your best peppermint sticks, and a couple bricks of plug tobacco."

"That'll be $500," Marcus said with a serious delivery.

"Marcus, your hair looks quite handsome. It should be the talk of the town, including all the available womenfolk for miles around."

"Thank you, Mr. Adams. These items just went on sale," Marcus said. "That'll be $5."

"You are as handsome as you are wily, kind sir. But I do have some news I would like to impart. I'm enlisting as a volunteer with the Jayhawkers."

"That doesn't surprise me in the least, Perry, but why the Jayhawkers. They are a bunch of marauding renegades as far as I can tell. Wouldn't you better serve the cause and seal your safety by joining the Union regulars?"

"It's a matter of urgency, Marcus. The Jayhawkers are ready to ride for the Union and so am I."

"Well, keep your head low, my friend. You have more to consider than yourself."

"You can count on that. I have never had so much to lose in my entire life, but that's how strongly I believe in the cause."

Perry moved down the street to see Pete and Lucy. Even before he entered the swinging doors, misplaced piano notes told him the new musician at The Outpost was substandard, as was the piano. Lucy had borrowed the piano while awaiting a permanent replacement.

"I see you have replacements for Millie and your old piano," Perry said.

"Replacements for either aren't possible, but we are doing the best we can," Lucy said.

"We long for that old piano and the musician who played it," Pete said.

Perry's tone grew serious.

"I've come to say my goodbye, at least for a while. I'm getting called up, by conscience, not by conscript."

"You mean you're volunteering?" Pete asked. "You joining the Jayhawkers?"

"Yup, that's what I'm saying. Before I go, I wanted to stop by to see whether you were still here yourself, and maybe have a 'mater beer."

"Oh, I'm still very much here," Pete said, stirring up a 'mater beer for Perry. "With any luck I'll stay here with Lucy throughout the duration of the war, but I never know when my notice to serve might arrive at my doorstep. I'm not inclined to go looking for trouble. And given the inclinations of this state, I'm not sure into which side I might get drafted. As much as I'd never target men of your persuasion, part of me prefers not to raise a rifle against my southern brethren. But either side is going to have to come get me. I ain't going voluntarily. Is my old piano player aware of your decision to volunteer?"

"Yes, she is. This is a decision we made together. If the goblins of war fail to suck me into an early grave, we'll be able to move forward with our lives, and if goblins shall prevail, Millie will be free to select her new path."

"I hate to even bring this up, Perry," Pete said. "But if you were to marry before your service and something were to happen, I think Millie would receive widow's benefits. Have you thought about that?"

"We've discussed the matter forward and backward. We think it best to wait until after my service, however long that might be. But if the goblins do come calling, you might even get your piano player back."

"While Lucy and I would benefit from such an outcome, that, my friend, is a wish I'll not cast on the evening's first star. If you need anything, shout

'Sarsaparilla' and I will follow through on our pledge. Godspeed, Perry Adams."

Meanwhile, Jep sat at the end of the bar with a small stack of coins in front of him that diminished with each mug Pete slid his way.

"Hey, Jep," Perry said. "Here's a dollar. Why not order some food from Lucy's kitchen?"

"Tanks, stranger. I already cided that for t'day I'm takin' my food in liquid form. Can I keep the d'llar?"

"Of course, you can, if you tell me my name."

"Yur Petey's stranger brutha, aren't you?"

"Well, yes, I guess you're right in spirit, if not in fact. And the name's Perry Adams."

"Okay, I'll 'member ya nex time, Jerry. My wish for ya is safe passage fer the dangerus journey ahead. Tanks fer the d'llar, whoever ya are."

Perry accepted the reward from The Outpost's genie. He shook Pete's hand and hugged Lucy before taking his leave of Roubideaux and heading back to Lowland on his quarter horse, Buck. Before he committed himself to the action, he sought the counsel of his mentor Constable Dan regarding the Jayhawkers.

Many people, including the border-state newspapermen, contended the Jayhawkers were a rag-tag regiment, not the least bit more organized and just as rogue as the rival bands of Missouri bushwhackers. The way Dan and Perry saw it, the observers and the newspapermen got it wrong.

"I am convinced this is the ordained decision," Perry said during a cross-table discussion with the good constable. "The expression on Watty's face when I told him I was going to join and the fiery response from Gabe to also join the cause were the last bits of evidence I needed. I'll volunteer for the Jayhawkers by next Tuesday, the breaking of our next full moon."

"Gabe is a solid young man with a personal cause worth the fight. I will say nothing to dissuade you or Gabe from your decisions. But don't you think for even a fleeting moment I am going to let you two have all the fun killing those pro-slavery puke bastards. We'll ride together as Jayhawkers, a three-man crew carrying individual missions of retribution, reprisal, and redemption."

"Dan, you're quite past the age of conscription," Perry said, not intending offense or humor. "Even Moses is staying behind to care for our farms. This issue means more to him than life itself. As his contemporary, don't you think Lowland needs you here, keeping peace on the streets?"

"That may be true, but I'm insulted by your insinuation, Mr. Adams. I am not past the age of volunteering, and I'm able-bodied and as mentally alert as a jackrabbit on coffee. If I need to prove my worth, I'd be more than glad to ask Judge Merriweather to preside over a rematch of our arm rasslin' feud."

"Not on your life, you old fart," Perry said, laughing for the first time in five days. "But, Dan, would you ride out to make sure Gabe is ready and properly documented and bring him with you? I'd do it myself, but I want to spend my last few hours with Miss Millie."

"I'll get him in the morning," Dan said.

"Thanks, and, Dan, know I am honored to have both you and Gabe ride by my side and protect my flank as I protect both of yours. We three shall ride together as the Lowland Jayhawkers."

CHAPTER 22

Late Summer 1863

WILLING CONSCRIPTS

PERRY AND MILLIE SHARED A TENDER NIGHT of passion prior to his departure to join the Jayhawkers in Leavenworth, Kansas. Not knowing if or when they would ever see each other again, the soulmates engaged in a final embrace. Fate would determine whether there was a future between Millie and Perry, and whether that span might be weeks, months, or eternity.

Perry strapped his rifle to his saddlebag scabbard and handed Millie his loaded Colt sidearm along with a bag of money containing the savings he had accumulated.

"Use this gun only in an unthinkable time of desperation," Perry instructed. "But use what you need of the money. I was not going to leave it at the farm to be plundered by roughians."

Their last words before Perry's departure went unspoken but between their souls.

Perry ascended the saddle. He stuffed his credentials, in the form of his recent application for homestead, inside his saddlebag. Perry rode off on Buck to meet Dan and Gabe.

Dan's credentials included the certificate signed by Judge Merriweather bestowing the title of Constable of Lowland, Kansas Territory.

Gabe's credentials were his freedom papers.

Proving one's identity was part of the deal prior to swearing allegiance to the Jayhawkers. It was the best way to ensure pro-slavery insurgents from Missouri could not infiltrate the regiment to conduct any acts of murderous sabotage, which would surely deliver the promise of a self-destructive and immediate death sentence.

Perry, Gabe, and Dan rode for hours through hardwood forests that finally broke open to grassy hills, vails, and meadows. An encampment for recruits sat about two miles from the formal walls of the garrison of Fort Leavenworth. The three Lowland-area warriors approached the camp nestled among a grove of maple trees. On the edge of the grove, more than a dozen armed sentries guarded an entrance. At the initial checkpoint, the men were asked to produce credentials attesting to their identities, in addition to stating their preliminary allegiance to the cause.

A sentry, not more than a teenager, read over the documentation produced by the three men for what seemed like an hour. Reverting to the turnstile, he returned the documents to Perry, Gabe, and Dan.

"Everything looks to be in order, Mr. Adams, Mr. Watson, and Constable Buchanan." The sentry continued, "I have a couple more questions. First, in small, medium, and large, what are your uniform requirements, and what, if any, are the specialties you might possess for war fighting?"

Constable Dan went first.

"My uniform size is large. I am a skilled marksman and possess some skills in man-to-man physical engagement. I previously served under General Zachary Taylor during the Mexican-American war when I was arm-rasslin' champ. I know the laws of our land backward and forward."

Perry jumped in immediately amid Dan's puffery about his arm-rasslin' feats.

"Like the constable I am a large and possess impeccable marksmanship skills. I am physically stout and of the highest moral character. I have also battled a certain arm-rasslin' champ to a draw."

Gabe followed his two elder compatriots.

"Like any farm boy, I am a steady shot. I am competent in animal care and have skills in evasive mobilization. I'm a medium."

Evasive mobilization? Perry and Dan shot each other a look of bewilderment, wondering what Gabe might have meant. Gabe liked to talk. The longer you knew him, the bigger the words, often much to the chagrin of Moses. They brushed it off as little more than that.

The young sentry stepped away for a consultation with a gathering of older men, some with the stripes of senior officers on their sleeves. He returned after ten additional minutes with standard-issued items; pairs of bright-scarlet britches, regular Union Army-issue jackets, Sharp's rifles and Navy revolvers, bayonets, and sabers for all three men.

The trademark scarlet britches were constructed from a wide range of materials, from bright crimson carpeting to silky red drapery. Perry and Dan suspected the material had been stolen during preceding Jayhawker raids of Missouri border towns. They did not ask.

Perry declined the Sharp's rifle, preferring his own Burnside carbine, but Dan and Gabe both accepted the items.

"After you swear your oath, your horses will become property of the U.S. government," the teenager said. "The Union will compensate you for your horses and your service. You'll be under command of Lt. Colonel Daniel R. Anthony, and your field commissions will be at the rank of Captain for Constable Buchanan, given his prior service, Sergeant for Mr. Adams, and Private for Mr. Watson. Thanks to all three of you for your service to the Union and the Jayhawkers."

"Sentry, I have a request," Dan said. "I'd like these two men to serve in my unit, given our common abilities as sharpshooters."

"I will pass that request up the ladder of authority, Mr. Buchanan. Are you prepared to swear an oath of allegiance?"

All three men nodded in the affirmative.

Sergeant Perry Adams found himself once again, like in Lowland several years ago, under the authority and jurisdiction of the man he knew as Constable Dan. Gabe was disappointed in his assignment, but he was encouraged Constable Dan requested his service.

The three men quickly donned their uniforms. Dan retained his black vest and badge, which he wore under his Union jacket. Perry tucked his brass pirate spyglass into the pocket of his red britches. Gabe found his uniform to be a bit too large, but he was pleased with the official look. The three men tossed their civilian clothes into an accumulating stack of wooden crates under the shade of a nearby maple. Also left behind were the mental vestiges of their civilian identities.

The sentry escorted the men to a table where a Bible lay open to the sixth chapter of Revelation, verse ten. "O Sovereign Lord, holy and true, how long before you will judge and avenge our blood on those who dwell on the earth?" Like years before, during the assassination attempt on Judge Merriweather, Perry and Dan found the coincidence of Revelation Six nothing short of divine.

While vengeance partially drove all three men to this point, they counted on God to deliver his ultimate judgment and revenge on the souls of evil men. Protection of homeland and opposition to the unjust institution of slavery were the tenants tilting their scales of justice as well as their motivations prior to swearing their common oath.

Colonel Anthony earned his rank, but that did not prevent him from a good deal of self-promoting showmanship. He went to great personal expense to commission the striking of several hundred unauthorized Jayhawker Medals of Bravery. They were awarded at opportune times to raise morale among the troops and, as importantly, to provide himself a spotlight moment of leadership publicity. Anthony always set the tone. He insisted on administering the oath of allegiance to all recruits worthy of a battlefield officer's commission. He extended the same courtesy to Perry and young Gabe.

He held the open Bible between them, invited all three men to place their left hands on the open scripture, raise their right hands, and repeat his words, phrase by phrase.

"I do solemnly swear I have never borne arms against the United States since I have been a citizen thereof; that I have voluntarily given no aid, countenance, counsel, or encouragement to persons engaged in armed hostility thereto; that I have neither sought nor accepted nor attempted to exercise the functions of any office whatsoever under any authority or pretended authority in hostility to the United States; that I have not yielded voluntary support to any pretended government, authority, power, or constitution within the United States, hostile or inimical thereto. And I do further swear that, to the best of my knowledge and ability, I will support and defend the Constitution of the United States against all enemies, foreign and domestic; that I will bear true faith and allegiance to the same; that I take this obligation freely, without any mental reservation or purpose of evasion; and that I will well and faithfully discharge the duties of the office on which I am about to enter, so help me God."

Each man repeated the oath as directed by their commanding officer, concluding with the phrase, "So help me God." They were now official members of the Independent Mounted Kansas Jayhawkers.

The Jayhawkers were guerilla fighters. They were fierce and they stood by their just cause. As much as anything, however, they were fighting for their families and their land.

"After we survive this ordeal of service, remember you have another holy obligation to perform," Perry reminded Dan. "Once we are delivered back to Lowland, you will be required to officiate a matrimonial ceremony."

"I swear my personal oath to you, as my ally, my friend, and my kindred brother," Dan said.

"Younger brother," Perry reminded.

"And I am the youngest brother of all," Gabe added.

The men joined the organized ranks as a team. They would defend each other's backs.

The men quickly learned they joined the campaign as fresh recruits for the purpose of establishing new companies—H, I, and K—to resupply the full Jayhawker regiment stationed at Corinth, Mississippi. Even before engaging in action, this plan ran counter to the men's stated convictions of defending the homeland. The idea of taking the fight to Johnny Reb was more appealing to Gabe but barely.

The troops gathered for reveille and were organized into the three companies. Captain Dan Buchanan was assigned the charge of Company H, as in, "Give-'em-HELL," he boldly proclaimed. Dan told them their call to charge would be three words, "To the stars . . . " The phrase was a truncated version of the Kansas motto, "To the stars through difficulties." The untranslated Latin phrase, *ad astra per aspera,* had been promoted as the embattled state's motto by a character Constable Dan knew all too well: U.S. Senator and Magazine Editor John James Ingalls of nearby Atchison. He endorsed the motto, saying, "The aspiration of Kansas is to reach the unattainable; its dream is the realization of the impossible."

With the lone exception of Gabe, companies "H" and "K" were comprised of mostly poor white farmers; company "I" was made up of 120 freedmen of African descent. With similar motivation to Gabe, the former slaves were destined to carry added ferocity in battle linked to the principle of freedom itself. Their motivation in this war rang out like a trumpet on judgment day.

The next morning the newly formed companies of red-legged Jayhawker volunteers prepared to cross the Missouri River at Leavenworth for what they expected would be a weeks-long ride to Mississippi.

Nearly four hundred in all, most of the Jayhawkers, whether black or white, were fresh off the farm and still quite green. While they were equipped with lessons of survival they acquired on their farms, their real military training would happen along the trail south.

They never got the chance to turn south, let alone cross the river.

On the outskirts of Leavenworth, before they even reached the river, they ran head-first into a rag-tag brigade of Rebel infantrymen joined by units of Missouri ruffians. The Confederate horde, eight hundred in all, crossed the river from the east at night and awaited in ambush. They outnumbered the

Jayhawkers two to one.

As the mounted Jayhawkers topped the last bluff, before descending to the river, sustained volleys of gun and cannon fire erupted. Some twenty horses and several riders fell after the opening barrage. Those soldiers not thrown from their horses, including Perry, Dan, and Gabe, dismounted immediately so they could dig in and reload from the ground. The horses, including Perry's horse Buck, scattered to the wind.

The only other advantage held by the Rebels was the element of surprise, but that was spent with that first flash of gunfire.

The biggest factor in the Jayhawkers' collective favor was the strategic fortune that they held higher ground. The rag-tag Rebels would have to slug their way uphill on foot, their backs against the river. The Rebel leaders neglected to fully consider the area's geography. It became a distinct disadvantage that served to even-out the disparity in numbers.

Taking cover behind a glacial boulder, the three Lowland allies used their keen eyes to pick off hapless Rebels at an alarming rate. Perry considered them less deserving of life than the squirrels he and Archibald hunted in the big burr oak tree back in Jawbone Holler. Gabe envisioned old man Manchester behind every Confederate uniform.

Buoyed by the inflated hope that came with their superior numbers, the Rebel force continued to press forward as their comrades fell all around them. The Rebel advance took a toll on those outmanned and underexperienced red-leggers unable to find adequate cover.

After the Jayhawker officers had adequate time to organize their troops, their coordinated series of return volleys against the Rebel front forced the invaders to pull back and regroup. These same types of advances and retreats by the Rebels transpired over the course of three full hours.

The horrific shrieks of those struck by slugs or cannon balls pierced the summer air. A growing number of dead bodies were stacking up on both sides, along with the number of wounded who were likely bound for the same fate.

Men from both camps staggered or crawled around the hilltop and hillside in agony and shock. Those not shot through their vital organs hung on to the vestiges of life with missing arms and legs.

Perry, Dan, and Gabe continued to plunk individual targets from the Rebel force with precision and speed. A majority of the shots fired from their rifles were kills.

Wave upon wave of Rebel infantrymen continued to charge the Jayhawker line. The red-leggers had no need to give up their advantageous high ground, so they hunkered down, lessening the Confederate advantage with each passing charge.

Hour after hour the onslaught continued. By midafternoon the Jayhawkers dispatched five hundred of the Rebels. During that same duration, about two hundred Jayhawkers succumbed to Rebel fire. Finally, the Rebel officers issued a resounding call among the ranks for all the remaining three hundred troops to storm the ridge at once.

The three Lowland men braced each other for the day's decisive action.

"How much longer can they keep this up, Dan?" Perry shouted between lethal shots.

"As long as the officers think is fit, or until they make a break in our line." Dan reloaded his rifle.

"They're relentless," Gabe said. "But I hear my papa's voice in my ear with each shot. Seek your maroon, Gabe. Seek your maroon."

Fetching the brass spyglass from a long pocket of his red-legged britches, Perry looked downhill to see the approaching mass of Rebels, each hooting out a horrifying yell that drifted uphill in the humid air.

"Here they come, fellas, make yourself ready," Perry shouted.

The advancing Rebels were within a mere twenty yards when the call went out among the remaining Jayhawkers to affix bayonets, a sign the battle had eroded into a brutal affair of life-and-death, hand-to-hand combat.

As Perry stood to position what he called a pigsticker atop his rifle, a Rebel soldier bounded over the rock with pistol in hand. As the gray-clad warrior sprang, Constable Dan shot him through the heart. The man fell at Perry's feet, a scrawny youngster with nothing more than a peach-fuzz beard.

As Constable Dan turned to squeeze off that fateful shot, another Rebel sprinted around the far side of the rock. He leveled his rifle and fired a shot that hit Constable Dan in the middle of the stomach. Dan crumpled like an old rag doll. From a distance, Perry saw his friend fall, but he was too far away to assist. He let out a scream, "Daaaaan!"

Perry saw the Rebel lurch forward in a final attempt to finish off Dan, and then there was another blast. Perry turned his head to see that Gabe had just leveled a fatal shot through the Rebel soldier's forehead.

Perry saw Gabe rush to Dan's side and just as he reached his friend, a slug smashed through the muscle of his right thigh. Perry saw Gabe fall to the ground in agony. Perry realized it was now his turn to come to the aid of his friends, much to his own peril. He rushed to the scene and knelt at Gabe's side, ripped some cloth from his uniform and tied a tourniquet around Gabe's gushing wound.

With Rebel bullets whizzing past his head, Perry scooped Gabe up and carried him twenty yards uphill, placing him behind a broad tree trunk at the edge of the grove.

Upon his return Perry shifted his eyes left and right and he had lost his bearings. He could barely digest the surrounding fray. All hell had broken loose. No longer could he distinguish the place where Dan had fallen. Everything looked out of place. A surge of adrenaline drove Perry onward to meet the enemy. Within a matter of seconds, he was locked in separate close-quarter fights with three different Rebel regulars. He bayonetted the first two and shot the third. Perry still could not find Dan.

Perry looked to the grove's edge to ensure no Rebels advanced on Gabe's position. He was astonished to see the injured Gabe in a prone position behind cover of the tree's trunk, firing shots with his service pistol, plunking Rebels left and right like it was a shooting gallery at the county fair.

Perry looked down at his own hands and arms. They were covered in blood, most from the Rebels he had slain in close quarters. He was unaware blood also covered his face, from forehead to chin. Neither did he know the full extent of blood on his matching scarlet britches, but he could feel a thick dampness on both his legs, blood from the men he'd killed.

As suddenly as the first attack of the day began, the Rebel officers ordered their buglers to blow the notes of retreat. Bodies of the dead from both sides, and the still-seizing bodies of those who would shortly join them, were stacked on both sides of the Jayhawker line.

Out of the more than twelve hundred combatants that day from both camps, there were no winners, but more than 950 losers experienced the eternal finality of earthly death. Six hundred and fifty of those fell wearing the Rebel gray, and three hundred wore the scarlet britches of the Jayhawkers.

Of the 250 surviving souls tasting the blood of war on this day, all wretched from the depth of their stomachs regarding the idea of firing even one more shot. What was remaining of the rag-tag Rebel force retreated with urgency down the long hillside bluff. The Jayhawkers did not follow. Perry saw field medics beginning to cart off the wounded, including Gabe, for treatment deep inside the grove. The unwounded Jayhawkers who could still walk fell back to their original position among the hardwoods, where now-dead recruits had pledged their oaths of allegiance the day before.

Seeing that Gabe had been carted to safety for treatment, Perry began to scour the battlefield one more time in search of the site where Constable Dan fell. He retraced his adrenaline-fueled movements some fifteen yards back to the original glacial boulder where the three Lowlanders dealt a quick and accurate death to more than forty Rebels among their three rifles. As Perry searched among the bodies at the foot of the boulder, he spied the figure of a man flailing his arms in distress. It was Constable Dan. Perry could see that his friend had suffered the worst possible outcome of any casualty of war. Constable Dan was gutshot.

Perry could also see that not only was Dan bleeding from his abdomen, but as he approached his friend he knelt to position Dan on his side. It was then when Perry realized the aggressor's bullet had cut a direct path severing Dan's spinal cord.

CHAPTER 23

Late Summer 1863

TENDER MERCY

As Perry recalled from an earlier conversation with Bartender Pete, being gutshot was the worst fate one could experience on the battlefield. Somewhere between the states of life and death, it was the most awful of both worlds. A victim knew immediately they would die, but that end would come slowly, draining life ounce-by-ounce, from the innards out. The best outcome was for the specter of death to come prior to the arrival of buzzards or other scavengers, who would begin to feast on the body of the victim while conscious.

Looking down at Constable Dan, an immediate stab of guilt pierced Perry's soul. The three Lowland men pledged to always have each other's backs; to serve as safeguards for each other in case of any unseen attacker. Constable Dan upheld his part of that deal. He dealt a quick death to a young Rebel who closed in on Perry. But while Perry was fully involved in conflict to ensure his own survival, he let his awareness stray from the task of guarding the flank of his friend. That's when the storming opponent broke around the glacial rock to fire a blast with eternal consequences.

Kneeling beside the squirming torso of his friend, Perry's sense of reality had been displaced by shock. His entire state of awareness went numb. It was as though he saw the scene but wasn't really there. After rolling Dan on his side to evaluate the wound, Perry struggled to squeeze out the words.

"Dan—Dan, what can I do? How can I provide aid?"

"You are here, Adams. I fear there is nothing you can do to prolong my breaths in this word because I am drowning from the inside out. I daresay that if we are to ever engage again in arm rasslin' it shall happen upon a golden stump in the vast unknown above."

Immediately removing his jacket and cutting it into a series of tatters with his still-affixed bayonet. Perry took the resulting cloth strips and applied them to the gaping bullet wound at Dan's midsection.

"Don't give up. I'll save you."

As Perry knelt by his friend's side, Dan explained what led to his grim condition.

"Johnny Reb over here had a moment of fortune while I was fully engaged in other matters," Dan murmured, omitting the fact that the matter of the previous moment had been dispatching the attacker that closed in on Perry. "His moment of luck was fleeting. As he was closing in to finish me off, our young friend Gabe shot the bastard through the skull."

"I saw it transpire."

"Where is Gabe?" Dan asked.

"He was shot through the leg; right after his bullet spared your life. But, oh, Dan, it should not have gotten to that point. I fear I've violated the pact we established for mutual protection. I've dealt you an ultimate betrayal."

"Never fear, Perry boy. We are all responsible for our own person, first and foremost. You were simply performing the most basic function in nature, preservation of self. If you'd succumbed under fire, it would've put us all on the edge of a cold, dark, and premature grave."

"I've forsaken you," Perry shouted in regret. "And now the ultimate payment for your decision to befriend an inattentive ally has come due."

"There is no need to fuss," Dan stammered between bursts of abdominal pain. "Gabe was there to deliver on the pact."

"In no way can this be considered a beneficial situation, Dan. I've defaulted on my end of this bond, thus jeopardizing the future contracts we planned to put in force."

"You did your part, Perry. You saved Gabe by getting him to the tree line, and before that Gabe saved me. But I fear his heroic action to save my life may merely be a transient victory. I'm gutshot. But I feel no real pain because the mercy of God allowed the bullet to also sever my spinal nerve.

"As my fate heads toward an ultimate demise, I need you to let young Gabe know his action saved my life. You must also let Moses know how his son came to my aid. But now I see the Four Horsemen approaching, Perry," Dan said, now clearly in a state of shock. "My sword might strike a blow in defense against them but doing so would only seal for me a fate of eternal damnation. Neither can I send myself to the great beyond with the lead of my own pistol. It'd surely be a transgression for which I could not ask forgiveness. I need you to strike this blow of mercy on my behalf with the knowledge that forgiveness remains within your mortal grasp."

Perry was not sure he understood the flood of words his friend uttered.

"What do you mean, Dan? I have no further blow to strike against our enemy."

"I seek your prosecution of an act of ultimate mercy for both my body and soul," Dan said. "End this before the buzzards hasten to my side. You must give me a final push over the waterfall of eternity. For the sake of pity and my own eternal grace, I need you to end this. I need you to end me."

A torrent of emotion smashed Perry across the entirety of body and soul. Constable Dan was asking Perry to set in motion the ultimate act of mercy from his physical and emotional torment. There was no hope for a gut-shot man, especially one unable to move.

"No, Dan, no, I can't do this. I won't do this," Perry said. "I will, however, remain by your side, fending off the scavengers until you make your passage."

"Perry, for your own preservation and to uphold an oath I swore to precious Millie, you need to vacate this battlefield as much as I do," Dan said. "I have made my peace with God. I beg you to dispatch my soul to its creator with swiftness and grace."

Perry reached out to grasp the hand of his friend. He placed his other hand on Constable Dan's cheek, from a point extending from his ear to his chin, along his friend's prominent jaw line. Not knowing what else to do, he recited the Lord's Prayer.

Perry's tears flowed unrestrained. He offered Constable Dan a final moment to speak with God.

Constable Dan looked deeply into Perry's blue eyes and a sense of peace enveloped his wounded and dying body. Dan closed his eyes for the last time.

Unholstering his Navy pistol, Perry did what agonizingly he had to do. And a split second later, the act was done. Constable Dan's soul was delivered. The dreaded action was merciful, but remorse hit Perry. Each nerve and fiber of his body wretched with mourning.

Perry lifted the remains of his lifeless friend and carried Constable Dan to the shade of a nearby oak. He walked back to the original recruit encampment and retrieved a shovel. Returning to Dan's side under the shade of the oak, Perry began to dig.

The gravesite overlooked the majestic flow of the river below. As songbirds sang praises from the mighty oak's branches, the tranquility of nature flooded the moment. Perry finished digging. He gently lifted Dan's body to remove the bloody jacket of the just-commissioned captain of Company H. He removed Dan's black leather vest adorned with the shining tin star of a constable. He folded the vest so the tin star rested on top and set it aside the grave.

Perry lifted Dan's body and gently lowered his friend into the place of rest. He gathered Dan's Union Army jacket and placed it over his friend's chest. He folded Dan's hands into a gesture of prayer and in the hush of the afternoon, Perry shoveled in soil, resulting in a mound.

"Earth to earth, ashes to ashes, dust to dust," Perry said. "Lord, I commit the body and soul of Dan Buchanan into your heavenly keeping. Grant him eternal peace and watch over him until the day of my arrival."

The mighty Dan Buchanan, Constable of Lowland, Kansas and Captain of Company H of the Independent Mounted Kansas Jayhawkers, was at peace.

Young Gabe Watson was maimed. Perry was numb.

Perry fashioned a cross from branches of the presiding oak and pounding it into the mound of dirt with the Army shovel. He collected his rifle and saber, the brass pirate spyglass, and Dan's black-leather constable vest. Perry walked bare-chested and emotionlessly back to the recruitment camp.

He stopped at the location where the medics set up a treatment area. He found Gabe, who was receiving treatment for his wounded leg. It looked as though he lost an unhealthy amount of blood. Perry approached closer. Gabe was teetering on the edge of consciousness, but he recognized Perry.

"The docs say I was lucky," Gabe said, with a slow and labored delivery. "The bullet cut a clear path through my leg muscle, missing bone and most major arteries. But I've lost a lot of blood."

As suddenly as Gabe captured the vision of Perry by his side, the young man lost consciousness. Medics scrambled to administer aid.

The other surviving souls of companies H, I, and K of the Independent Mounted Kansas Jayhawkers gathered under the shade of the maple grove. Many of the men had wounds wrapped in whatever cloth could be best fashioned into bandages. Most of the wraps were blood-soaked. Hardly a man was without wound or blemish. Moans of agony drifted with the breeze of twilight. There was no segregation among black and white. These men became one body through the experience of a shared horror. Every set of eyes stared into the empty distance. Their physical bodies were present, but they forfeited their spirits on the field of conflict.

The Battle of Leavenworth was neither won nor lost. It was simply a bloody purgatory resulting from the hatred of one man for another. Perry communed in shock with the other lost souls amid the shared venue of agony and despair. He said an audible prayer for the recovery of young Gabe.

In the distance one of the officers began to provide a casualty update. The numbers painted a win for the Jayhawkers. The report fell on ears capable of hearing but not listening. Though only gone for a week, and still aware of his commitment to ride with the Jayhawkers, Perry was already feeling the pull of an inner beacon back to his regular life in Jawbone Holler as well as to the side of Miss Millie.

The night crashed around the camp, encasing it in a shroud of pain and exhaustion. The only sound echoing among the maples was the stuttering call of a solitary male whippoorwill defending its territory. The sound seemed symbolic to Perry. Was this the soul of Constable Dan standing sentinel over his comrades-in-arms, sounding a call of vigilance against the possible onslaught of another Rebel attack?

The Rebel force was as demoralized by this campaign as his surviving red-legged brothers. The Confederates would not return to this site anytime soon, but every far-off crack of a limb created a shock of alarm through the corners of Perry's mind. Sleep eluded the beleaguered remnants of what had been reinforcements for the Independent Mounted Kansas Jayhawkers. What might their condition have been had they reached the foreign land of Mississippi? Likely more preferable than this one.

As dawn brought a new day to the river bluff camp, Perry was already wide awake when the sound of reveille's bugle signaled the call to another day. He went to check on the condition of young Gabe. A nearby medic reported Gabe was still unconscious, but he was expected to recover. He was transported to the Fort hospital for additional care later that morning.

In less than twenty-four hours, Perry's outlook shifted from one of anticipation to one of shock and denial. One of his Lowland friends had been severely wounded, and the other was dead. It was a day much like the previous evening, with shadows of death and destruction etched into the forehead wrinkles and creases of the survivors' faces.

By midmorning the senior commanding officers emerged from their command tent as a unified body. Four of them began to walk through the besieged dregs of the camp. Their steps were slow and deliberate, as it appeared they might be taking stock of the troops for additional action. From person to person, the officers meandered from one struggling warrior to the next. Colonel Anthony carried a look of sorrow on his face as he individually assessed the damage sustained by his band of recruits. He carried the box of shimmering gold Jayhawker medals hanging from silk, crimson ribbons. Anthony bestowed the medals on troops who looked as though they would survive but appeared closest to slipping over the precipice of existence. It was a delicate decision. Anthony could clearly surmise they were still little more than dirt-poor farmers who were only partially efficient at doing what they did on a regular basis. As soldiers their capabilities going forward were minimal at best, yet during the previous day's call to duty most performed in a manner deserving of commendation.

Whether or not he chose to award a Jayhawker medal, Anthony stopped to talk with each of his men. After moving on to the next soldier, the previous one, if physically able, gathered his will to stand and walked to a specific spot in the grove. By the time he reached Perry, more than half of the camp's ninety-seven survivors had gathered as a squad.

What was this all about? Could the colonel actually be gathering able-bodied troops for an additional campaign to scout out the whereabouts of the enemy force?

"Sergeant Adams?" Anthony began. "You performed admirably and heroically on yesterday's field of battle."

At that moment, bloody, bare-chested, and beleaguered, Perry felt as much a hero as the floppy-eared Archibald might feel after having chased down a defenseless young rabbit. It was in his nature of survival. Perry arose to meet Anthony's words. He saluted the officer.

"No need for formality on such a day of grieving," Anthony stated. "My field spotters tell me you single-handedly eliminated some twenty of the enemy, either through marksmanship or hand-to-hand struggle. And you have emerged no worse for wear."

Perry tried to feel proud of what the colonel proclaimed as a grand accomplishment, but all he could think about was the death and sorrow he created for twenty families on the other side of the conflict.

"More meaningful than any medal I could bestow, I think it fitting to recognize you with a battlefield officer's commission," Anthony said. "It's clear to me there's a fitting command post for you down the road, but that's likely in another man's war. I'm conferring with my superiors as to the fate of these assembled companies, at least what's left of them, and I await their reply."

Perry did not know what an appropriate reaction to Colonel Anthony's words might be. Hollow isolation weighed heavily on his heart. He abandoned his best friend and his other friend's son was critically injured. He lost his horse and almost his own life.

"Yes, Colonel Anthony. Thank you for your words of appreciation," Perry said.

"Adams, the aftermath of this campaign has left the hillside strewn with stiff and bloated comrades, and it's a situation we must remedy, for the sake of their honor," Anthony stated. "Can you lead a detail of men to load the hallowed dead aboard wagons so we can transport them to a final resting place nearer the formal walls of the garrison?"

"Yes, sir, I can do that," Perry responded. "It is the least we can do given the sacrifice each of them invested in the cause."

Colonel Anthony saluted Perry and moved on to the next troubled soul.

Perry walked toward the spot where he, Dan, and Gabe had sworn their oaths to defend two days prior. The stacks of civilian clothes were still piled in crates against the maple tree. He searched through the items and finally found his cotton shirt and work trousers. Perry put them on. Even if his days of soldiering were not through, he could at least pretend he was preparing for another day of work among his corn back in the holler.

The task of loading the bodies of the dead took most of the day. A similar duty was also being undertaken by the Rebel side. It was a surreal day. After the manifestation of death and destruction between the two sides, they worked in parallel to clean up the aftermath with an air of indifference. But Perry remembered they were all Americans. It was as if both sides wanted to wipe the slate clean, never to remember what transpired on the bloody hillside at the Battle of Leavenworth.

At the end of the day, Perry reported back to Colonel Anthony the task had been completed.

"Colonel, there is one matter I need to raise. It's about the body of my fallen friend, Captain Buchanan. I buried him yesterday below the boughs of that great oak at the top of the bluff. He saved my life in battle, and I considered it my duty."

"Captain Buchanan was a fine man, Adams," Colonel Anthony said. "I am sorry he yielded his soul in this campaign. His performance in the heat of yesterday's battle was as commendable as yours."

"Colonel, I wasn't worthy to even shine his boots. I buried his body near where he fell," Perry said. "He might enjoy the majestic view of the river, but I do not want the presence of his grave to go unnoticed. Would it be possible to dispatch from the fort a proper marking for his final resting place?"

"Consider it done, Adams," Colonel Anthony said. "A man of his fortitude deserves at least as much recognition as can be offered by an appropriate slab of granite. I will ensure he is memorialized in a fitting manner."

"Thank you, Colonel," Perry responded. "Even greater than the cause for which we took up arms, Dan was a man worth dying for. He already served his nation once. I am overcome by the realization it was him, rather than me, who paid the eternal sacrifice for our cause. While his earthly remains will ceaselessly be joined with this lonely hillside, I want to ensure his legacy is revered. He deserves to be remembered, not only by those he walked among as a civilian but also the sons and daughters of their sons and daughters."

"One other thing, Colonel," Perry continued. "Private Gabe Watson. He was the young Black soldier fighting beside us. He killed as many enemy combatants as Dan and me. Even after he was shot through the leg, he continued to fight on at risk of bleeding out himself."

"Yes, Sergeant Adams," Anthony interrupted. "I was aware of his valor as well. He was still unconscious when they carted him to the Fort Hospital. I could not thank him for his service, but I awarded him a Jayhawker medal. I sent it with the medics to pin to his pillow in his recuperation bed. His father will be proud."

CHAPTER 24

Late Summer 1863

DISCHARGE FROM DUTY

THE HEALING OF BODY AND SPIRIT TOOK TIME. It had been several days since the battle, but already the Jayhawker survivors of the Battle of Leavenworth appeared stronger and more resilient. As the dawn of yet another day broke over the bluffs on the opposing side of the river, the men were served a breakfast amid the maple grove. The offerings included the best the battlefield cooks had to offer. The menu of the makeshift mess hall included cornmeal griddle cakes with syrup, cornmeal mush with butter and coffee.

This wasn't regular bush-raised coffee, like the kind sold at Marcus's trading post, as Perry had grown to appreciate. Since coffee was in short supply for the men fighting for the unity and survival of the nation, the Union resorted to a variant brew. This was something the cooking detail referred to as conflict coffee. It was concocted from the beans of a soy plant. The cooks explained the "soybeans," as they called them, were roasted by the bucketful in a large wire basket over an open campfire. As the beans reached a color of medium brown, they were dumped into a massive cast-iron kettle and tamped with a large wooden pestle until the resulting grind held the consistency of coarse sand. The cooks said conflict coffee was quite high in protein, necessary for the regeneration of muscle tissue and nerves. The soldiers all agreed due to the massive destruction to both mind and body they experienced, this conflict coffee was worth a shot.

The mere mention of soybeans by the cook caused Perry's mind to wander for a moment, back to his farming life and his corn crop in the holler. When reading up on agronomic topics during his visits to Roubideaux, Perry had become aware of studies about soy as a potential cash crop for farmers currently raising corn. He recalled that soybean plants magically supply some of the organic growth matter required for a strong corn crop. If true, when planted every other year instead of corn, Perry suspected this might decrease the need for fertilizing with manure and save him hours shit-scooping labor. But, he wondered, how in the world might he harvest these little beans, with a scythe like wheat perhaps? Perry surmised harvesting the little buggers must be the reason this co-called miracle crop had not yet been planted in addition to corn throughout the states along the border frontier.

After the fleeting distraction from his inner guilt, Perry's mind returned to the steamy cup in front of him. The fact he was beginning to think about topics other than war, Dan's brutal death, or Gabe's severe injury was a good sign. During Perry's first encounter with this hearty conflict brew, he detected a nutlike aroma steaming from his tin cup. His nerves were still in shambles from the harrowing events of the previous days, so, like the other soldiers, he decided it worth a taste.

Perry's tastebuds fooled his mind. This really did taste like coffee. It surprised and delighted his battlefield palate. If he ever returned to Roubideaux, he would certainly ask Marcus to stock some of this conflict coffee on the shelves of his provisions section.

Perry forked into a generous bite of the cornmeal griddle cake and syrup. He savored the cornmeal mush with butter. It wasn't exactly a heap of Lucy's ham-speckled scrambled eggs, but it was better than his own chipped-beef gravy and biscuits. For the first time in days, Perry was hungry. He was already starting to heal.

After the satisfying breakfast, a command was given that in exactly one hour all survivors of companies H, I, and K of the Independent Mounted Kansas Jayhawks were to move as a singular unit to the confines of the fort, two miles away.

At least half of the men visited the accumulated stack of civilian clothes they deposited under the maple tree days before. The clothes went flying as many of the survivors ridded themselves of the bloody garments of war. They longed to forget the hellacious experience. Adjacent to that stack was a growing accumulation of bloody scarlet britches and standard-issue uniform jackets.

The men marched to the fort dressed in a hodge-podge of civilian and army apparel, looking more like a band of vagabonds than a company of accomplished fighting men. These farmers had not marched as an organized parade a day in their lives.

Upon reaching the fort, Colonel Anthony was waiting. His aides prepared what looked like a patriotic gathering more appropriate for a politician's campaign stump speech. The motley survivors stood at attention and saluted in unison as the colonel took the platform. Anthony saluted them in return.

"Men, I cannot express to you the gratitude I personally feel for the brave and honorable service you have provided the cause," the colonel stated. "Not only did we strike a harsh and disproportional blow to the body of our traitorous enemy, but we also achieved a significant victory for the state of Kansas and the cause we hold so dear. The traitors now know better than to bring the conflict to our soil. Though new and untested recruits, as Jayhawkers, you used the skills you possessed as farmers, stablemen, and laborers. You drove the oppressors to the threshold of hell. You repelled the evil forces of the devil himself. The Union and all who support a communion of free states from sea to sea owe you a debt of gratitude."

Perry and the other Jayhawkers waited for what they expected would be an announcement from Colonel Anthony of their next assignment. They were guessing a new call for recruits would go out, and as soon as they assembled another three hundred, they once again would attempt to cross the river at Leavenworth and head south.

"I have personally wired regimental headquarters and the office of Secretary of War Edwin Stanton to inform them not only of your brave and valiant service to the Union—but also of the incredible loss of life and mental hardships of these past days. While never pleased by the death of one American, Union or Confederate, black or white, they took notice that 650 members of the traitorous enemy force were dispatched, with us losing fewer brave and noble Jayhawkers. Realizing the extreme duress under which you were forced to operate only a day into your service as volunteers, I have been ordered to grant all ninety-seven of you a full, unconditional, and honorable discharge from the Jayhawker Regiment. Go home to your families and farms and raise the best damn corn, cattle, and pigs, knowing your labors will fortify not only our state but also the glory of our blessed Union."

A roar erupted from the assembled mass. They were soon to become former soldiers, but in their hearts, they were forever Kansas Jayhawkers. As battered, bruised, and hopeless as they appeared, the men exploded in a chorus of joy, laughter, and tears. They were going home.

While others were celebrating, Perry sought out the location of the Fort hospital. He had to find out about Gabe's condition. He was ushered to the door by a fresh-faced private. Entering the infirmary, he asked for the whereabouts of a young Black soldier with a leg wound. Perry walked through the long row of cots, where medical personnel swarmed like a hive of hornets around white soldiers. He was pointed to a back room, where there appeared to be a dozen filled cots staffed by one overwhelmed black nurse.

"Ma'am, I'm looking for a young man named Gabe, Gabe Watson. He has a leg wound."

The nurse led Perry to a cot at the end of the row. Gabe's leg was wrapped in white linen from hip to knee. Pinned to his pillow was a scarlet-ribboned Jayhawker medal.

"Gabe, can you hear me?"

Gabe pried open his eyes and recognized Perry.

"Perry, you survived," Gabe mumbled in a morphine-induced daze. "How about Constable Dan?"

Perry cut to the chase.

"He didn't make it, Gabe, but he lived longer because of your heroic action. You are a brave man and a hero to boot. You served your cause and your country well. What do they say about your condition, Gabe?"

Gabe fought back tears for Constable Dan.

"I remain a little groggy. I can't remember a lot of the past week. They say I lost a lot of blood. I'm lucky to be alive. The bullet that ripped through my thigh was forgiving in that its path was true, but it took a brutal toll. I'll recover, they tell me, but it could be some weeks before I'm healed enough to go home."

"Thank God," Perry said. "We've all been honorably discharged, and we are free to go back to our farms. You will be back as well but let them heal you up first."

"I woke up, and this little medal with a red ribbon was attached to my pillow," Gabe said, pointing toward the Jayhawker Medal of Bravery. "I think it must mean I lost a lot of blood."

"It means that and much more, Gabe. Much, much more. I will leave for Jawbone Holler as soon as I can, probably walking home, but I will give a full report to your papa that you were injured, are fully on the mend, and will be home as soon as possible."

After leaving Gabe and the hospital, Perry was struck by the unequal conditions devoted to the care of the soldiers, depending on the color of their skin. Was this the cause for which he had fought? He struggled with the notion. It made him miss home even more. The need to extricate himself from the military took on a bold, new urgency.

It had only been less than a week, but Perry was ready to leave. He felt remiss he had not made any meaningful connections with the other men who threw their lives into the breech on that majestic but bloodstained hill overlooking the Missouri River. That situation changed as the men milled around, still in a gleeful state of shock following the Colonel's dismissal of their obligations. All that was left was the paperwork. That's when he met Joe Henderson.

Joe was a farm boy. Joe was a former Hoosier and a member of Captain Buchanan's "Give-'em-HELL" H Company.

After finding they shared a common connection to Indiana, Perry exploded into conversation with Joe.

Joe was homesteading a Kansas farm west of Topeka, near the settlement of Auburn, located at the foot of the wide and rolling Flint Hills. Joe had arrived in Kansas two years prior. He broke out a few acres to grow wheat, but his impassioned focus was raising cattle amid the ocean of head-high prairie grass, a natural mix of bluestem and switchgrass. Through and through, Joe was a stockman. He and his wife were raising two sons, and he missed all of them dearly.

Once they discovered their Hoosier upbringings, almost immediately they identified the towns where they were raised and racked their brains to find a common connection.

"I'm from Seymour," Joe said. "My wife and I came here to raise cattle and support the doctrine of abolition, and after less than a week in the Union Army, I'm ready to go home."

"My name's Perry Adams. I left a little shit-hole Indiana town several years back. I raise corn in the Missouri River bluffs up north of Lowland. Like you I'm ready to beat my sword into a plowshare and get back to the farm."

"Adams? You wouldn't happen to know any of the Adams from over around French Lick, would you?"

"Can't say I've ever heard of French Lick. Where's it located exactly?"

"It's over in Orange County."

"Orange County? That's where I'm from, Joe. Salt Spring."

"Never heard of it, but how is it you haven't heard of French Lick?" Joe asked. "I know a man named Adams from French Lick. For the past several years, he's been raising cattle. Have you ever heard of a man named Stew Adams? Bought some breeding stock from him a few years back. He's established a quality bloodline of cattle."

Perry's jaw dropped.

"I know a Stew Adams from Orange County. He's my father, but he lives in Salt Spring. So, did this French Lick you know start as a trading post?"

"Sure did."

"Is there a series of hot sulfur springs known for their healing qualities?"

"Yup, I saw a sign saying such about French Lick."

"And this Stew Adams you know, is he a widower who lives in a two-story house with a big front porch and an enormous barn on the left side of the lawn?"

"That's the Stew I know and that's French Lick you're talking about, not Salt Spring. I heard it used to be called something else a few years back, but everyone was really tight-lipped about the reason for the name change."

"Damn." Perry laughed. "I bet it was because of me. I was a bit of a destructive hellion before I left. The town elders must have changed the name of Salt Spring in hopes I'd never be able to find it again. You didn't see my face on any wanted posters, did you, Joe?"

"Nope, and I'm not a bounty hunter either, Perry, but if you were that notorious, I bet they changed the name because of you. I feel honored to be with the presence of such notoriety."

"Destructive asshole is more like it, Joe. Pappy always talked about raising cattle but never had a reason to pull the trigger because he had me there as cheap and easy labor for growing corn. I hated corn and everything about it. Now that I'm on my own, there aren't many things I love more than corn."

"Is that what boiled your anger to leave?"

"I was tired of working for free. Pappy said the roof over my head was reward enough, not what a young man of ambition wants to hear. So, I packed my saddlebag and left with intent to farm for myself and to put a new roof over my head. Not to go into too many details, but my dissatisfaction in Salt Spring spilled over into the community at large."

Joe bored in.

"So, you really haven't been back?"

"Not since the day I left. Pappy and I didn't see eye to eye. It sounds like my leaving must have kicked his old ass into action to do something on his own behalf for once."

"I've always judged him a pleasing fella. A real straight-shooter. I'd deal with him any day. Plus, he has an impressive line of cattle. I bet he'd love to know you're alive and well."

"I'm not so sure about that, Joe, but I'll send the old buzzard a wire when I get settled in back home. I promise. It might pain him to know I am prospering out here in the Kansas frontier. It might even create a little buzz in Salt . . . I mean French Lick. You haven't heard of a young lady over there named Violet LeDoux, have you?"

"Nope, I don't know any Violets. Was she special to you?"

"A little, but moreover, she was another big reason why left."

Joe laughed. "When you send that wire to your pappy, let him know Joe Henderson from over around Seymour is now in the Great State of Kansas, and I'm carrying on his fine hereditary line of beef cattle out here in the Flint Hills."

"Will do, Joe. Great to meet you, fellow Jayhawker. If you ever make it up to the northeast corner, look me up. I live in a place called Jawbone Holler. It's a longer story than French Lick."

"Will do, Perry. And, as Captain Buchanan would say, 'To the stars!'"

"To the stars," Perry replied in return. "God rest his soul."

The men mustered for one last action as official members of the Jayhawkers. They gathered outside the garrison gate for the best impression they could attempt of a military march. They still stomped about like farmers. In an attempt to keep step, they even sang a popular marching tune—The Battle Hymn of the Republic, wildly popular among troops after being published the year before in The Atlantic Monthly.

"Mine eyes have seen the glory of the coming of the Lord:
He is trampling out the vintage where the grapes of wrath are stored;
He hath loosed the fateful lightning of His terrible swift sword:
His truth is marching on."

The march, as disheveled as it was, empowered the troops. It was liberating. After reaching the camp, twenty of the men rejoined the ranks of the Jayhawkers on the spot. Others gathered their belongings and girded their minds and emotions for a return home. Like seventy or so of the other surviving Jayhawkers,

Perry was done. He gathered his belongings, Constable Dan's vest and tin star, and his certification papers. Perry had a corn crop to tend and a lady waiting to stroll hand in hand.

The war had been a living hell for Perry. How others tolerated it more than a day was beyond his comprehension. He hated everything about it. The way it smelled of rotting death. Its shrieking cries of agony. The shocking visions of dismembered bodies. Life would not return to normal overnight, but eventually it would. It would take some time.

CHAPTER 25

Early Fall 1863

LONG ROAD HOME

Perry served as a Jayhawker for less than a week, but one of those days unleashed a living nightmare on Earth. He figured that single day of battle had aged him a score of years. The several days that followed were as bad. The lingering torment of the battle chomped into his being like a hungry bear fresh out of hibernation.

For the past three nights, nightmares had awoken Perry in a cold sweat of anxiety. He saw Constable Dan clawing his way out of the grave, pointing a pistol to Perry's midsection, and pulling the trigger. There were visions of the Rebel with the peach-fuzz beard being cut down by Constable Dan's bullet and hitting the ground as a mere infant. He saw Gabe hopping to and fro on one leg. There was wave after wave of Confederates, like a hive of hornets, overrunning the Jayhawker line. An apparition of his lost horse Buck galloped off into the horizon, led away by the Four Horsemen.

In reality Buck was gone. A part of Perry hoped he had taken to the wide-open prairie to live out his life in unbridled freedom. The practical side of Perry was satisfied he had been compensated for the fine quarter horse at twice the price he paid.

Immediately, Perry started mapping out a plan in his mind of his trek back to Lowland, Jawbone Holler and the woman of his destiny. It was more than forty miles from Leavenworth to Lowland. He could always buy a horse but doubted any could be had at a fair price due to their wartime demand. Perry figured the walk would take him two days; two days sorely needed as a buffer to begin clearing his mind of trauma.

News of the Battle of Leavenworth reached Lowland in less than a day. The telegraph line was on fire with clicks and clacks. The report was directly from the commander's staff at Fort Leavenworth. In exaggerated effect, the telegram talked of how a ramshackle unit of three hundred freshly recruited Jayhawkers repelled an attack by the Confederate Army that outnumbered them four to one. The gallant Lt. Colonel Daniel R. Anthony joined his men in the trenches and exhibited bravery deserving of a battlefield commission to full-bird colonel. In all, the Jayhawkers obliterated their Rebel foes. The casualty count revealed that nine hundred Rebels fell against a mere two hundred Jayhawkers.

While the true situation was far worse for the Jayhawkers. The day Millie saw a clipping of the story posted outside the Lowland telegraph office, her body and mind went numb.

Was her beloved Perry among the one hundred Jayhawker survivors? The odds were slim, yet she had faith that Perry had survived the strife. Each moment was filled with worry and dread. Sleep proved elusive. Good or bad, she would know Perry's fate in a few short days. She knelt in prayer and solitude inside the walls of the mission church, sending up prayers for Perry, as well as Constable Dan and Gabe.

On the inside Father Linus Carrigan was as devout of a priest as one could meet. True to his Irish heritage, reddish-brown hair shot from his scalp and a hint of freckles dotted his cheeks. Father Carrigan liked to talk about the weather. He had a gregarious sense of humor but was all business when it came to church matters. He ran a tight parish, a matter expected of all priests assigned to duty at the Benedictine mission churches throughout the region. He enjoyed a strong cup of coffee and an occasional tankard of ale. Above all, Father Carrigan had a welcoming soul. Given his outgoing personality and wit, many had a tough time believing he could adhere to the strict Benedictine standard of "work and pray."

Father Carrigan was also Millie's boss man and her spiritual leader during daily mass and beyond. He oversaw her duties as teacher at the Lowland Benedictine Mission School. Shortly after reading the wire dispatch about the tragic engagement known as the Battle of Leavenworth, she sought out the counsel of Father Carrigan.

"Father, my mind is in shambles. I fear for the life of my dear Perry."

"I know Perry, his virtues, and his flaws," Father Carrigan replied. "I have heard his reconciliatory confession and know his wish is to again rejoin the church in full communion. No need to fret, child. Your Perry is a strong man in both body and conviction. If there were a way to survive such a dire incident as what transpired, Perry would certainly be the one to do it. Plus, he has Constable Dan and Gabe Watson at his side. The three will make for an imposing obstacle against the proponents of southern captivity."

Millie tried to take solace in the wise priest's words, but her faith was as unsure as one's footing on a creek-side slab of soapstone.

"I believe we are predestined for a life together, but my emotional constitution is weak. I'm ready for school to reopen for the fall term. It'll help keep my mind occupied, but additional news from the conflict should be arriving sooner rather than later."

"Child, take heed in the words God has ordained," Father Carrigan said. "It was Saint Matthew who told us, 'Do not be anxious . . . but seek ye first the kingdom of God and his righteousness, and all these things will be added to you.' Keep the faith, dear Millie. Keep your mind in prayerful thought. Your Perry is likely on the horizon as we speak."

Millie prayed unceasingly for the return of Perry.

After learning of the Battle of Leavenworth, the citizens of Lowland finally received official word their beloved constable, Dan Buchanan, had succumbed on the battlefield. The news rocked the town's inhabitants. Constable Dan was their champion, always steady and stalwart even when the world crumbled around them.

As she digested the news, Millie's mind strayed from scripture and back to unease. Would news of her Perry's death be included in the next battlefield bulletin to arrive by wire? The only thing she could do was bolster her soul for that possibility. The next day she revisited the mission church and bent her knee to pray with additional vigor.

At the crack of dawn, Perry collected his identification papers, signed his official discharge, and departed the camp. On his way past the officer's tent, he paused to see Now-Full-Bird Colonel Anthony.

"Colonel, if I could have a moment, sir, please take care of young Gabe Watson," Perry said. "He fought like a hero. And please make sure he has his freedom papers for safe passage during his trip home."

"Best wishes to you, Adams," the colonel said. "We will make sure he makes it safely home."

As Perry hit the meadow outside the maple grove, he labored to clear his mind of distress crashing about him like enemy artillery. He was quite ready to put this place behind him. The idle silence of the trek created an atmosphere of healing, but it also permitted the traumas of the past week to flood the bottomland of his mind. Perry did not walk alone. His shadow of guilt was along for the trip.

Perry made significant progress during the first two hours, but a dark and hard driving Kansas thunderstorm rolled into his path. Thunderheads towered across the sky. Perry was hit by the rage of a driving wind. The sky turned an angry green. A sudden calm fell across the land. Perry looked into the distance. He could hear a dull roar, like a wagon train of settlers bumping across trail ruts. Over a distant hill, Perry adjusted his eyes to see a tail descending from a boiling cloud. Perry took cover from a Kansas cyclone.

Perry tucked his head into his shoulders and hunkered down in a swale away from the threat of falling trees. He dug his feet and fingers into the soil as an anchor. Hanging on with all his strength, windblown debris of sticks, rocks, and chunks of grassy soil whistled past his head. The storm's wrath growled around him. His body jolted from the ground. The maelstrom swirled with anger, dealing what Perry interpreted as the wrath of God.

Minutes after the vortex of the storm passed a calmness settled over the landscape. Perry examined his arms. There were a few deep scratches, but that was the extent of his injuries. The closest thing to this Perry experienced was the hailstorm that hammered his corn crop in the summer of '59. It now seemed a lifetime ago.

Still unaware of Perry's fate from the Battle of Leavenworth, Millie leaned into the vigilance of her purposeful prayer. Father Carrigan stood by in case sad news were to come about either Perry or Gabe.

After the cyclone, Perry regathered his resolve and his stride grew purposeful, boot after boot. He made great progress on his walk northward. Through the course of the day he logged about twenty-three miles. Perry shook life into his spent legs. His spirit rose as he climbed a hill before hitting a long stretch bordered by cornfields on both sides.

In one of the fields, several acres of the corn were cut prematurely and stacked into fodder shocks as livestock feed. To Perry they resembled cornstalk teepees.

Not having the comfort of a bedroll, Perry climbed into the middle of a corn fodder shock and began to sleep. He placed Constable Dan's black leather vest under his head as a pillow. It still harbored the dank smell of war. In the dead of night, the sound of thundering hooves bypassed his location. Random words echoed about burning and raiding Atchison. Perry wanted to spring from the corn, shout defiantly, "To the stars," and blast the intruders to kingdom come. Instead of confronting the passers-by, he tucked himself deeper into the cloaked security of the fodder shock. The last thing Perry needed or wanted was more conflict. He saw enough to last at least two lifetimes.

As the first light of day slipped through the corn leaves of the fodder shock, Perry pried open his eyes and poked his head out between a couple of stalks. He wished for a moment that this corn was his. For the first time in several weeks the world was beautiful. Frogs croaked out their raspy songs in a nearby creek. A rain crow's call echoed through the trees. A red-tailed hawk shrieked overhead as it drifted in the wind. The sleepy clouds floated in a deep blue blanket of dawn. The smell of the corn's freshly cut sweetness made Perry sneeze. It reminded him of survival. He was alive. For a moment, worries and guilt stopped hammering his heart and mind. The day signaled an opportunity to start fresh. There was more bounce in Perry's step than the previous day, when he was reminded of his mortal vulnerability by the cyclone that tried to sweep him into the great beyond.

Perry quickened his pace over hill, field, and meadow. He stopped at a nearby spring to replenish his fluids. Minnows flitted through their watery turnpike. He never recalled viewing minnows in such a wondrous manner. The simplest of life forms, of natural elements, of thoughts, flooded his mind.

The distant hills were bursting into song and trees on the horizon beckoned with encouragement. This new outlook all came together under the wonder of God's universe. Perry was going to make the most of his role in it.

Still he walked. The closer he drew to Lowland and sweet Millie, the less his legs ached. No longer was he taking conscious step-by-step strides. His feet floated toward home. With the noon sun overhead, Perry figured he cut the expanse between himself and his love to a mere eight miles. He pressed on.

Millie visited the telegraph office to see if any additional bulletins had been posted about the war. She picked up a newspaper from a shelf inside the office of the *Lowland Ledger*. A story near the bottom of the front page recounted in more detail the brutal toll experienced by the brave Jayhawkers during their defense of the homeland. Three companies of fresh recruits fought like veterans.

Buried in the story was a single paragraph about orders from Secretary of War Edwin Stanton to grant all survivors of the conflict an unconditional and immediate discharge, and when she read it, Millie's heart raced. Could it be Perry was coming home very much alive? Her emotions teetered back and forth like a hummingbird in search of a flower's nectar. Perry could be dead. The thought reminded her to rely on faith. She dropped to her knees in the newspaper office and offered a prayer.

It was three o'clock when Millie made it home. She sat trembling at her piano in an attempt to remove her mind from the crashing tides of emotions. Anxiety stabbed at her soul; despair at her heart. She attempted to calm her mind, but relief was elusive even unto prayer. She could not go on without Perry in her life.

In a moment of insurmountable doom, Millie grabbed for Perry's pistol. She raised the gun to her temple and drew back in immediate shock. What was she doing? She realized the thought was a moment of sheer insanity. If Perry had not survived, she certainly would. She still had her pupils, her piano, and her God. She looked inward for music to pull her from the dread. Millie thumbed through sheet music for spiritual hymns, melodic waltzes, and patriotic marches. Nothing rang true to the moment.

Her hands slid across the keyboard as if directed by a spirit not of this Earth. She did not even realize notes were radiating from the black and white keys until halfway through the first verse. She was playing by heart; a familiar tune she played at the bar called "The Old Folks at Home" by composer Stephen Foster.

As she reached the chorus, a singing voice poured into her parlor like honey over her soul.

"All the world is sad and dreary, everywhere I roam.

Oh, Millie, I am no more weary now that I'm with you at home."

It was Perry Adams, not his memory, his heavenly spirit or her wishful imagination. Every last inch of the dirty, smelly, and haggard personification of the war-ravaged Perry Adams stood at her threshold. With one arm he held Constable Dan's black leather vest and tin star. In his outstretched right arm was a bouquet of wild sunflowers gathered from a ditch outside of town.

Millie flew across the room, feet barely touching the floor. She collapsed in tears and fell into Perry's arms.

Perry looked at her with a grin as dusty and gritty as it was wide.

"If I had known you were goin' to serenade the genteel citizens of Lowland with such a boisterous barroom song, I never would have bought you the piano."

CHAPTER 26

Early Fall 1863

ROUTE TO RECOVERY

As much as they wanted to stay under the same roof that night, Perry spent that night at the Lowland boarding house, lest townsfolk think poorly of the new schoolteacher at the mission school. It was late September and the holler beckoned. As much as he needed to unload the stress of war, and as much as he wanted to be by Millie's side, he had to report to Moses about Gabe's bravery and his current condition. He also wanted to check on his animals and his corn crop. He begged for Millie's understanding.

Millie had been a careful steward of the money Perry left her prior to riding off to war. Perry used a bit of those funds along with the proceeds from the sale of Buck to the Union Army to purchase a spotted Appaloosa in Lowland. The horse was saddle broke and ready to ride. He named the horse Appy. The first stop of his maiden ride in the saddle with Appy was Moses's farm.

From a distance, Perry saw Moses look toward him and break into a full sprint uphill toward him. Perry knew that Gabe's absence would cause Moses great turmoil.

"My son! My son! Tell me, Perry. My son has not perished on the battle-field," Moses shrieked as he drew near.

"Gabe is safe," Perry shouted. "Your son is a war hero."

"But where is he? Why did he not accompany you?"

"He was injured."

"Injured? How bad is he?"

"Never fear," Perry said as Moses reached his side. "Gabe is going to be fine in due time. He took a bullet to the thigh. But that rascal fought on, at least as long as he could. It was incredible. The bullet did not hit any major vessels or bone, but he lost quite a bit of blood. It was precarious for a while, but with some rehab of his muscle, he's going to be ducky. Colonel Anthony himself decided Gabe worthy of receiving the Jayhawker Medal for Bravery. Your son is a war hero."

"Oh, thank you, Jesus. And what about you, Perry?"

"I'm fine, Watty," Perry said. "I wish I could say the say the same of Constable Dan."

"I heard."

Perry recounted some of the horrors he experienced at the Battle of Leavenworth, including how despite Gabe's shot to spare Dan from immediate death, the constable had become a casualty of war as the result of a rebel bullet. Still haunted by guilt, Perry continued to bury in his heart the truth about the act of mercy he delivered. Of all the sordid details of war gripping the edges of his soul, that was the one that spooked Perry the most.

"I am so proud of Gabe, but I mourn for Dan. He was a good man," Moses said. "They'll never be able to find a finer constable. I hope the man who killed Dan will face the eternal fires of hell."

Perry labored to picture the image of the Confederate soldier who fired the gutshot at Dan as being the target of Moses's scorn. He had not witnessed that shot, but he certainly witnessed his own fateful shot that delivered mercy. That image was burned in his mind forever.

"I buried Dan atop a bluff overlooking the river on the edge of the city. The Colonel told me they would mark the grave with a slab of granite. Dan was a hero that day. He saved my life."

"It sounds like you were quite the hero yourself," Moses said. "Judging by all the terrors you encountered on that hilltop, releasing you to home was the right and honorable thing to do."

"We weren't all heroes. It was an ambush. We were trying to survive. A man can undergo transformation in a bad way when faced with that kind of adversity. But I now know it's through desperation that a man also discovers the metal from which his heart is forged."

"Thanks for looking after Gabe. I knew I could count on you to keep my son as safe as was possible."

"Oh, Gabe was quite capable of doing that himself. You should have seen him in action. I am thankful he will be coming home soon."

"Almost makes me sorry I missed it . . . almost," Moses said. "I will be glad to have Gabe home."

Sensing a need to draw Perry's mind back to the present, Moses continued, "So, tell me about this new horse. What happened to Buck?"

"I am hopeful by now Buck is galloping across the prairies of Kansas. Lost him in the battle as soon as the opening volleys were fired. Gabe's horse also bolted for safer ground. Appy here has been a good mount so far, but this is our first ride together."

"Speaking of horses, Beulah, Barney and their colt are doing great. And that calf of Butter's is growing like a bush of wild hemp."

"I can't wait to see them. I think it's time to visit the Lowland stable to see what offers they might extend for those two young'ens. I have a piano debt to pay off. And where's old Archibald?"

The floppy-eared dog, hearing his name in Perry's voice, came bounding out the door of Watty's house.

"*Uh-roo-roo-roo,*" Archibald barked. He jumped into Perry's arms and licked him across the face.

"I'm glad to see you too, old boy," Perry said. "And Watty, how's the corn looking?"

"It's high as an elephant's tail. After a dry-down, you ought to be able to harvest, if you're up to it. And if you aren't, I'll come over and lend a hand."

"I think I can manage, Watty. It will be good rehabilitation for my spirit. You have done more than enough."

"You are the one who has delivered beyond measure. You kept Gabe safe, and you pushed those Rebel bastards back beyond the edge of hell, which is exactly where they belong. I pray one day we will be a nation forever free."

"We share that common wish, my friend. But it may take a while. While I think Gabe was an exception, I witnessed men of your race not being treated as equals at the Fort hospital. I still believe deeply that our cause is just and will work by your side in that endeavor, but my fighting days are over. I've put my life on hold for too many months. It's time to move forward."

Perry shared with Moses what he had heard of the ongoing campaigns between the forces of the Union and Confederacy at battlefields such as Gettysburg, Vicksburg, and Chickamauga. He recounted the words etched in his memory delivered by President Lincoln at Gettysburg and, in particular, the phrase that concluded the speech:

> "From these honored dead we take increased devotion to that cause for which they gave the last full measure of devotion—that we here highly resolve that these dead shall not have died in vain—that this nation, under God, shall have a new birth of freedom—and that government of the people, by the people, for the people, shall not perish from the earth."

"I am confident, Watty, this great conflict will pass with a most favorable outcome," Perry said. "But the inner discord of all those who have been touched both directly and indirectly, including you and Gabe, and the ultimate healing of a unified free nation, is my utmost concern. There doesn't seem to be any middle ground. All the statesmen have flown the coop."

Reconnecting with his land in Jawbone Holler was Perry's catalyst to draw out the lingering venom of war, if not the burdensome guilt and horrific memories.

Perry, Appy, and Archibald hit the trail north to Jawbone Holler. Perry immediately checked on his animals and went to inspect his corn crop. A bit weedier than usual, but Moses had done an admirable job of coaxing the crop toward harvest. Perry drew a quilt tightly around his body that first night. He slept like a baby for the first time in weeks.

After several days, Perry headed back to Lowland. He had some marketing to tend to for the colt and calf. After receiving a satisfactory offer for the off-spring from the Lowland livestock trader that was sufficient to settle his piano debt with Pete and Lucy, he stuffed the money into his pocket.

Perry also had a more pressing matter to discuss with Father Carrigan. He rode Appy to the church and tethered him to a post outside. He walked with a sense of dread toward the church door.

"Good morning, Father," Perry said.

"Good morning, Perry," Father Carrigan said as he restocked candles around the periphery of the big stone church. "I already heard from Millie about your return. I am thankful to God and St. Michael, the Archangel, for his intercession."

"Pardon me, Father, but even with Michael's holy intervention, the battle was hell. It scarred me in ways not seen by the human eye. I have many deeds to confess. I pray you will be open to petitioning God to lift the anchor of this burden from my soul."

"There is nothing to forgive regarding the desperate acts of a soldier. You were doing your job as ordained by God, as much as members of the Rebel force believed they were. As long as you did not go beyond the bounds of assignment and kill out of hate, I am sure God will consider your soul to be spotless. Were not all the casualties you dealt on the battlefield out of survival and self-defense?"

"Yes," Perry said. "Almost all. But there is one in particular for which I fear I will require absolution."

Father Carrigan entered the dark walnut confessional as Perry shut the door.

"Father, forgive me, for I have sinned. This is my first confession since I went to battle, and upon the examination of my remorseful soul, I ask you for absolution for the sin of killing Constable Dan."

"Oh, my son, surely there were extenuating circumstances."

"There were, Father. Constable Dan was gutshot. He was paralyzed at the nerve, laying on the field of battle as life was leaking from his body. He would have done the deed himself but was afraid it would be a sin for which he could seek no forgiveness. He begged me for mercy, not once, but three times before I sent him to heavenly peace."

Perry continued, "I have come to realize I have killed two of the most important living beings in my life, though my Old Lukey was merely a mule. This time it wasn't a mule I ushered to the other side of existence."

"Under the circumstance of war, only God can judge. But by committing such an action, you dethroned the authority of God. Killing is a sin. Due to the circumstance surrounding this act, and your decision to not send Constable Dan to eternal damnation due to a desperate act of his own hand, it was an honorable thing to do for a friend. But this act will require absolution, which I will extend to you through the authority vested in me by God."

Perry wept unrestrained in the darkness of the adjacent booth.

"Perry, what you have done represents a decision no man should have to make. It is never our place to decide the time or manner of death not related to the defense of our own mortal body, but you should not let yourself be tormented by this act of mercy. God knows all the details."

Perry continued to wash his soul through repentant tears.

"Perry Adams, child of God, I lift up your spirit to God, the Father of mercies. Through the death and resurrection of His Son, God has reconciled the world to Himself and sent the Holy Spirit among us for the forgiveness of sins. Through the ministry of the Church, may God give you pardon and peace. I absolve you from your sins, in the name of the Father, and of the Son, and of the Holy Spirit."

Father Carrigan continued, "Living out the rest of your life in a manner of honoring God's creations—man, beast, and nature—is your fitting act of contrition."

Perry found solace in his forgiveness. It would take additional time for him to forgive himself.

After Perry exited the confessional, Father Carrigan sat at his side and wrapped his arms around Perry's shoulders. The two men sat speechless in the front pew of the church. Perry gasped with sorrow and pain for a full hour. He collected his inner strength and raised a far different topic with Father Carrigan.

"Father, I want to spend the rest of my earthly life, and what I hope and pray will also be my eternal life, with Millicent Longworth."

"I may have to find a new teacher for the school, but it shall be done, my son," Father Carrigan said. "When can we put this blessed event on the schedule?"

"I need to ask her first. You and God are the first to know."

"God knows you better than you know the back of your own hand. That makes me the second being to know this exceptionally good news. Go to Millie with the knowledge there is no reason on Earth or in heaven for your union not to occur. And Perry, know you are a good and worthy man."

"Every day's a blessing, Father," Perry said. "Every. Single. Day."

With the burden of guilt at least partially lifted from his soul, Perry rode his new horse Appy across town and waited for Millie to return from her new teaching duties at school.

As she arrived home, Millie soaked in a more discerning look at Perry. Much of the Perry she grew to love had been left on that bloody hillside at Leavenworth. His shoulders were not as straight and commanding. His chin was not as high. His eyes were empty.

"Perry, I pledge every ounce of energy I possess to help you reclaim the spirit and countenance of the man I have grown to love and cherish," Millie said.

"I just visited with Father Carrigan, but I continue to fear I might not be able to turn the corner myself, Miss Millie. It would be a huge burden to place on your fair shoulders."

Perry paused. Would it be fair to ask Millie to help him carry the burden he bore regarding the act of mercy he delivered to Constable Dan? He could not tolerate the weight of his action alone. Millie was the woman he loved. Between them there should be no enigmas to separate their bonding. Perry needed to declare the matter that stood in the way of reuniting his earthy and ethereal beings.

"Millie, please sit," Perry said. "I must share with you a burden that is mine alone to carry but one I cannot keep concealed as you weigh the worthiness of the wretched man I have become."

Millie looked deeply into Perry's azure eyes. She braced herself for whatever words might be forthcoming.

"Millie, I killed Constable Dan," Perry said.

Perry could see that the words hit Millie full-on like the blast of a hostile cannonade.

"Perry, what does this mean? How could you, the soulful man I have grown to love, deliver such a deed of hatred upon an ally? Has your gentle spirit been a façade all these years?"

"Father Carrigan told me it was an act of mercy," Perry explained. "But, Millie, the guilt is still unbearable. I know an enemy rifle delivered the tragic shot that sealed Constable Dan's fate. Dan begged for my intercession to save his soul from an ultimate act of self-destruction. He asked me to lift that weight from his soul. He saved my life. Every fiber of my presence before you today is in his debt. My last act of kinship was to excise the earthly barricade between himself and life hereafter. It was me, not the Rebel bullet, that sealed his fate. In spite of my absolution, the guilt remains unbearable."

"Oh, Perry!" Millie said. "I know the action you took was out of your bond with Dan. What you did was an expression of self-sacrifice, not one of malice. I beg your forgiveness for initially misunderstanding otherwise. Loyalty and devotion drove your decision. It was a request motivated by the trust Dan had in you to cease the suffering that befell him. His fate was determined by the Rebel gunshot, not by yours. I will devote every speck of my energy to resurrect you in body, mind, and spirit, even if it takes the rest of my life."

CHAPTER 27

Winter 1863-1864

THE GREAT
REDEMPTION

PERRY HATED TO THINK WHERE HIS SPIRIT might be had he not been afforded a couple of days of isolation on his walk north from Leavenworth. Even now he was a shell of his former self. One of the healing tasks he promised before leaving camp was to wire his estranged father back in Indiana. A small measure of making that connection might still be less than repentant, but it was time to mend fences with the old man.

Perry minimized the cost of the telegram. He chose his words carefully. Short and to the point. It kept his emotions in check for the message to Stew Adams in the town now known as French Lick.

Esteemed Pappy . . . Hope my message finds you well . . . Now residing on Kansas farm . . . Raising corn . . . Saw action in war with Kansas Jayhawkers . . . Hope to marry soon . . . Will let you know the date . . . Working to fulfill homestead agreement near town of Lowland . . . Sorrow for my departure years ago, but only choice . . . Please forgive me . . .

Will make full restitution for items I took . . . Best wishes for your cattle
venture . . . Greetings from Joe Henderson, formerly of Seymour . . . He's
carrying on your cattle line in Kansas Flint Hills . . . Hope our paths cross
again . . . Sincerely, Perry.

While at the telegraph office, Perry sent off a quick note to his friends in
Roubideaux, which could now be considered, due to the influence of border
ruffians, enemy territory. Not knowing Pete's status, he sent the wire to the
attention of Marcus Mixon, owner and proprietor, Roubideaux Trading Post.

When Stewart Adams received his telegram, his reaction was one of astonish-
ment. He was fairly confident his only offspring, Perry, was surely dead at this
point, either from the challenges presented by the world or from self-destruction
due to overconsumption of rum. He had been an unruly shit as a young man, an
embarrassment, really. And the reason Salt Spring was no more. Stew was genuinely pleased to read that his son turned his life around and was now asking for
forgiveness. He took some pride in Perry's success. His strict directives to the
younger Perry might have spurred a small degree of that achievement. He was
also proud Perry took up arms against the infidels of the Confederacy. Whether
it would actually be a matter of follow-up, Stew found comfort in Perry's promise
to make restitution for the items he pilfered the night he left back in '57. He sent
a telegram back to his son via the telegraph office in Lowland.

Dear Son . . . I have many reasons to be a proud father . . . I do not harbor
hatred . . . Also realize the past pattern of my own harshness . . . It was
tough to lose your mother . . . I'll never recover. . . Took it out on you
. . . Love the woman you met with your whole heart . . . Even more than
your land . . . Let me know the date . . . Cherish every day, for each is a
blessing . . . Glad to hear Joe is doing well with my cattle . . . No restitu-
tion required . . . Best wishes from pappy . . . Stew Adams.

When Perry read his father's wire, the thing that stuck out to him the most was a reminder that for all these years, he had been using his father's favorite phrase, and he had not even realized it. Every day is indeed a blessing.

When Marcus received his telegram, he was in the middle of accepting delivery of some new beer mugs Pete ordered from Saint Louie. Being of service age for both armies in the internally conflicted Missouri, Pete patiently waited for a conscription notice from one side or the other. No such order arrived. Passion for neither side burned in Pete's soul. He was perfectly happy serving out his time by Lucy's side, keeping the folks of Roubideaux lubricated with drink and song from his duty location of The Outpost Tavern. Pete considered it his duty to help folks think about anything else besides the hatred of war.

Upon Marcus's arrival at the bar, Pete was busy preparing for that evening's activities.

"Pete, I bring you a double-barrel delivery today," Marcus said. "Not only do I have a couple crates of brand-new beer mugs, but I also bring news about Perry."

"Let's get these beauties unloaded first, and we can chat," Pete said. "These new mugs might make the Smit's taste a little better. Any updates on my new piano? The one I borrowed is not as melodic."

"Your piano's on the way. But I think the problem you are noticing with the borrowed one is more about the player than the instrument. You were simply spoiled by the quality of your previous player."

"Don't remind me."

"But I have a more important message to share with you, Pete. Sarsaparilla!"

The two men engaged the help of several of the bar regulars to carry the crates of new beer mugs down a ramp from the wagon and move them into place behind the bar.

Marcus continued, "Perry wants some Sarsaparilla. Said he would come to the Missouri side to get it. Said he had been involved in some of the war action on his side of the river. He must mean the incursion at Leavenworth. Perry was one of the Jayhawkers. But it sounds like he's returned to Jawbone Holler as a former Jayhawker."

"I'm guessing as far as Perry's concerned, it's once a Jayhawker, always a Jayhawker," Pete said. "Since it sounds like he was one of the confirmed survivors in Leavenworth, I am guessing he's dealing with some significant issues. It sounded like a bloody mess on both sides. From the descriptions I read, even the rocks and trees were shedding blood. I'm glad he made it home."

"You and me both. If there's such a thing as an honorable Jayhawker, Perry would be it. While their hearts are in the right place in regard to slavery, most of those fellas are little more than thieves and murderers. If March 1st works out for you, Pete, I'll confirm with a wire back to our Kansas friend."

"Works for me, Marcus," Pete said. "Tell Perry my sarsaparilla syrup is ready to stir at the riverbank. Awesome possum."

Given the reputation of Marcus as a notorious cheapskate, the return wire to Perry was short and to the point.

Perry . . . Pete says awesome possum. He's ready to stir the sarsaparilla . . . the date works for us . . . High noon . . . See you then . . . Marcus.

Perry was uplifted by both replies he received. He placed his hand over his heart at the thought that his father might have grown softer over the last several years. He was elated to hear Pete and Marcus were willing to meet him on their side of the river. Though Missouri was still a Union state, the pro-slavery sentiments of many of their citizens could make crossing the river during wartime a bit of a risk. At this point, however, Perry was little more than a Kansas corn farmer, and if pushed, a Kansas corn farmer who was contemplating a move to Missouri due to its friendlier political climate for agriculture.

The date for meeting with Pete and Marcus was only weeks away. Perry moved with the determination of an ant before a downpour. Perry stopped at the Lowland general store and asked to see the jewelry on hand, though all that time he wished it were Marcus he was dealing with for this particular transaction.

Perry ran his eyes up and down the display case for a good ten minutes. He narrowed his choice, though, exuding an attitude of disinterest in any of the offerings. The ring of choice was a thin gold band with a single glimmering diamond.

"How much for that one?" he said, pointing to a simple setting resembling a runt in a litter of otherwise fine pigs. The clerk was privately questioning Perry's judgment, but he was just a hillbilly farmer.

"Oh, Mr. Adams, that setting is extremely humble. It's been in the store for more than six months. Nobody who has been serious about winning the heart of a future spouse has even considered that ring."

"Anyone who's counting on a piece of jewelry to win the heart of a fair maiden is playing the game all wrong. It's as perfect as she is."

Visiting Millie on the afternoon of Feb. 1st, Perry hatched a plan to surprise her. While she stepped away, Perry dug into his pocket and placed the ring inside her rosary box, which was located on a bookshelf next to Constable Dan's black leather vest and tin star. As the afternoon melted into evening, Perry asked Millie for a prayer.

"Miss Millie, I am feeling a bit melancholy this evening and perhaps in need of healing intercession," he said. "Would you mind fetching your rosary? Father Carrigan told me when it feels like I'm about to go over the edge of a life crisis, I should always seek out The Almighty for counsel."

"Yes, sir, Mr. Adams," Millie said, walking across the room to retrieve her boxed rosary.

"Would you open it for me, Millie?"

As Millie reached into the box to produce the rosary, the sparkling ring popped out and landed at her feet.

"What's that Millie? It looks like some kind of fancy ring. Have you been seeing suitors behind my back?"

"Why, no I have not," Millie said, as serious as a court order hand-delivered by Judge Merriweather himself.

"I am glad to hear it."

Perry kneeled to pick up the shimmering band. In one motion, he presented it to her in the open palm of his hand.

"Miss Millie Longworth, you are the essence of my heartbeat, the sparkle in my spirit and the stars in my heaven. I love you with all my heart. Would you bless me for the rest of my life by giving me your hand in marriage?"

Millie's emotions and words were jumbled.

"I-I-I . . . " she stuttered.

Millie waited for such a question all her life, biding her time to ensure that if it came from anyone, it would be the right man. One edge of her faith grew weary, while the other edge was honed to seek another life path with God. But she was pulled back to Roubideaux by a magnetism toward the stranger she could not get out of her mind. Perry Adams was that man. Tears of joy flooded from Millie's eyes as she extended her hand.

Perry slipped the ring on Millie's finger, and they fell together in a tender embrace.

Before departing for a night at the boarding house, Perry and Millie toasted their promise with the bottle of sweet red wine Perry had bought years before during the night of their first date. The couple waited a lifetime for the blessed event, so they wasted little time to set the date of Friday, March 25th, 1864. The date coincided with The Feast of Annunciation, the date of commemoration for the angel Gabriel's visit to the Virgin Mary announcing she would give birth to Jesus Christ.

While there was no such grand announcement pending for Millie and Perry, they considered the date a blessing for their future prospects. Millie set the date with Father Carrigan.

Before leaving town the next morning, Perry sent a telegram to his father.

Wedding day approaching . . . March 25th, Lowland, Kansas . . . Sorry for late notice . . . Hope you can make it. Perry.

Perry hit the trail north to the holler. He made a quick stop at Moses's farm. He wanted Moses to hear the news first.

"Watty, I come bearing good news."

"Has President Lincoln bettered Jefferson Davis in a spirited match of arm rasslin'?"

"It's even better news than that."

"Better than that? Has the Union trounced the slave masters once and for all?"

"Even better, Watty. I have asked Miss Millie for her hand and, believe it or not, she accepted."

"I am so elated by this news, Perry. Congratulations."

"I am sorry you and Miss Sally never had the opportunity."

"She was my wife in every aspect of the word. We jumped the broom together. She blessed me with three sons. My only regret is that she and two of my sons were taken from me. We were slaves. While I know I may never set eyes on her in this life, I know I will in the hereafter. But I will never end my search. This war won't last forever. That's what keeps me going, that and my current condition to enjoy the freedom of a farmer."

"You are indeed a blessed man, Watty. And you have blessed us all with your kind spirit, despite the fact everything about your past logically points you toward hate. I am proud to have you as my bartering partner."

"The feeling is quite mutual."

"One other question for you, Watty. Would you do me the honor of standing with me at the altar? The friendships I have with you, Pete, and Marcus are among the greatest blessings God has bestowed on me, after Millie, of course."

"Of course, I will, Perry. As long as Pete and Marcus don't refer to me as Willie Jefferson."

"They know the full story, Watty. But don't be surprised if Pete calls you that. He's a pesky fella, like a nest of yellowjackets. But his heart is in the right place. Pete and Marcus have gone through quite a powerful conversion of thought."

Marcus did not require conversion, but Moses kept that knowledge to himself.

"A man is truly blessed who transforms himself through honest discernment and opens the gate of his mind to matters that before were impossible for him to even consider. Those changes stick. I look forward to meeting Pete and Marcus again. I know you would not associate with them if they were not great men. It's too bad that not all the men in their state hold themselves to such enlightened standards."

Moses continued, "Perry, there's one more thing you should know."

He shouted toward the house.

"Gabe, come out here. There's a man who wants to see you."

Gabe came to the doorway. He jogged with a noticeable limp to greet his fellow Jayhawker.

"Mr. Adams, I have made it home, and I'm practically as perfect as I ever was. I'm still on the mend but caring for our animals is as healing as any remedy I ever got at the Fort hospital."

"No doubt, Gabe," Perry said.

"And Mr. Adams has delivered me some most welcome news," Moses said. "He and Miss Millie are tying the knot of matrimony."

"I expect you to be there, Gabe," Perry said. "Your papa might need some encouragement to stand as my witness."

"I would not miss it for anything, Mr. Adams," Gabe said. "Papa will be delivered to your altar, even if I have to coax him by the shirt collar."

CHAPTER 28

Winter 1864

STAIN OF PREJUDICE

QUICKLY AGREEING TO STAND WITH PERRY at the altar as one of the chosen groomsmen, Moses was not sure how his appearance might be perceived by others who would attend the ceremony. Prejudice based on race was rampant, even in the most enlightened communities. Moses had sensed it in Lowland when Constable Dan asked him to serve as a deputy during the town meeting. Moses saw a few chilling stares. He was aware of some fingers pointing out the Black man wearing a badge. He had seen it all before, but that was the first time he had perceived these feelings as a freedman in the free state of Kansas.

Moses immediately had second thoughts.

"Perry, I am a proud man," Moses said. "Some might interpret my pride as stubbornness or worse, as an outright contemptuous threat to their being. For some men predisposed with prejudice, that might lead them to actions of desperation. If any hatred-fueled action were taken against me or Gabe, I am more than capable of dealing with any consequences that might come. Your friendship means that much to me. What concerns me even more is that hatred might be directed at you, simply for being my friend. Are you sure you want me to stand witness to your character at your matrimonial altar?"

"I would not have it any other way, Watty. I would rather opt not to join my true love in matrimony than to compromise to any degree the respect and admiration I have for you. That represents the depth of my beliefs on this topic."

"I know you are only asking me to stand as your friend, but it's a public event and I would be front and center with you, instead of cowering in the back row," Moses said. "Black men have been lynched for less."

Moses's words hung in the air like a spiderweb on the stillness of a muggy morning.

"You need to see something, Perry."

Moses went inside his home and quickly retrieved a recent copy of the *Lowland Ledger* he had picked up in town the week before. He unfolded the paper and pointed to a headline. "Stain of Hatred Runs Deep Against Freed Men."

The item recounted in detail an epidemic of atrocities against both slaves and freedmen of African heritage. The acts were fueled by desperate whites who feared their lives would crumble if the war to end slavery succeeded. Outside the Deep South, the highest number of lynchings and murders was in the Union, Pro-Slavery State of Missouri.

The newspaper story focused in detail on the death of Joe Campbell, a freedman and a married father of six children, four girls and two boys. The family lived in a rural area outside of Cobbler Junction, Missouri, a mere forty miles east of Roubideaux. Campbell was a hard-working man who toiled on his own small farm as well as for white farmers in the area.

"This happened just two months ago," Moses said. "Out of jealousy, some of those farmers Joe Campbell worked for wanted him dead. They wanted his land and everything that went with it. They accused him of raping the daughter of one of his farmer bosses."

Molly Young was thirteen years old. She reported the rape to her daddy in brutal detail, according to the story.

"Joe accounted for his whereabouts when the crime was to have taken place," Moses said. "He was working on a farm some five miles away. But the farmer who hired him refused to corroborate Joe's alibi."

The story stated Campbell was arrested and hauled to the Ruby County Courthouse jail. As he was taken into custody, rumors flew that Molly Young died as a result of the attack. The local newspaper printed the accusations without challenge. The newspaper further fanned the flames by reporting Campbell was expected to serve a mere twenty-five years for the crime.

Whites in the area, including many of the farmers for whom Campbell worked, were enraged. Powered by the lies and their own thirst for blood, they called on the county judge to swiftly impose the death penalty. The judge refused and the sheriff and his deputies guarded their prisoner amid the growing mob mentality.

Days later the angry crowd outside the jail grew to some three hundred. Their size emboldened their shouts of racial slurs. The sheriff and the judge ordered the mob to disperse, but their anger boiled over. In the early morning hours, they firebombed the jail and flushed out the judge, the sheriff and three deputies. The men were dragged into the street, beaten to a pulp, and tied together with barbed fencing wire. The burnt-out threshold of the jail was all that stood between the crowd and their desire to deliver their sentence upon Campbell.

They rushed the jail, where they found Campbell cowering in a cell fortified with hardened steel bars. They spat at him and urinated into the cell. Men chiseled their way into the cell and grabbed Campbell by the neck. After delivering a beating even more dire than the ones they administered to the white county officials, they placed a noose around his neck and dragged him to the town square. They flung the rope around a sturdy branch of a massive oak tree and lynched him in front of a crowd of revelers who gathered for the spectacle they considered a fair application of justice.

Members of the mob pontificated about the justness of their sentence against Campbell and how it sent a clear message about their intolerance for crimes against their community.

After hearing about the arrest and detention of her husband, the now-widowed Mrs. Campbell and her two teenage sons broke through the crowd to claim the body of their husband and father. After her audible and angry protest about the execution of her innocent husband, members of the mob circled the three like a pack of wolves.

"Hang them all. Hang them all. Hang them all." The chant grew with intensity. After beating them senseless, nooses were placed around their necks, and they were hung on branches opposite Joe Campbell.

After the vigilantes noticed the dead body of Mrs. Campbell was heavy with child, one member of the mob took a knife to her stomach and excised the baby, who was lifeless from the trauma. Other members of the mob, enraged by Mrs. Campbell's uppity tone, threw the infant against the rock wall of the Ruby County Courthouse until it was indistinguishable. They deposited all the broken bodies of their victims on a wagon and transported them to a desolate countryside location for a quick and hush-hush burning. There was no evidence left behind.

One day after the mob lynched Joe Campbell, it was learned Mollie Young was alive and well. She fabricated the story with her father to cover for a consensual physical engagement between herself and a neighbor boy. The local newspapers did not retract.

Several members of the mob were questioned, but the county never pressed a single charge against any of the perpetrators. The incident was swept under the rug like a dusting of springtime pollen. It was an event the locals never recounted. The images many of them saw that day left a stain on their souls, even on those who merely heard about the crime.

"That could have been me on the end of that noose," Moses said. "Perry, there are several crimes for which lynching has become an acceptable and appropriate penalty—horse thieving, cattle rustling, murder, and being a Black man not willing to descend to what folks consider our proper submissive profile in society. All those crimes are subject to the same sentence—death resulting from a tall tree and a shorter rope. I am truly afraid my struggle has only begun, and I do not wish for any spillover on to you."

Perry rubbed his forehead in shock. "I'm aghast knowing the status I enjoy as a free and independent citizen might be a peril to you if viewed through the jaundiced eyes of small-minded people. I will defend your every right as a human being, Watty, not white, not black, but human. While it's a shame, from this day forward, I will protect you and Gabe with every fiber of my being. You are my friend, and this duty is a cross I will bear freely. The stain of hatred demands a good scrubbing, but I fear it has set stubbornly into the long fibers of our desecrated societal cloth."

"I would never ask you to put yourself in harm's way to defend me or Gabe for actions that are cultural norms for a good many Americans. I shall not and will not expect such protection at your hand."

"While your agreement to stand beside me at the altar might rub people of extreme opinion the wrong way, I will not tolerate even that thought. Our friendship is thicker than water and deeper than blood itself. I will defend you to my own death."

The story Moses shared of Joe Campbell and his family haunted Perry. He suspected Ruby counties existed in every state across the entire nation.

Meanwhile, the war waged on. In mid-February of 1864, the Union army captured and occupied Meridian, Mississippi—a critical supply point for Confederate forces. At about the same time, the Confederates played a wild card, launching the war's first effective submarine attack. Near Charleston Harbor, the USS Housatonic was broadsided by a torpedo fired by the CSS H.L. Hunley. Both vessels were lost as a result of the battle. It was more a stalemate than success.

Regardless of how fate might decide the ultimate victor, Perry noted symbolism in the submarine attack. He began to build a massive wall of doubt that even a positive outcome in the Union's favor could heal the nation's lingering scar of slavery. Both sides could just as likely sink into the murky depths of doom.

Perry could only control what was within his reach, preparing for his corn crop of 1864. He took advantage of favorable weather to prepare his seedbed, but this year, instead of hills, he would experiment with planting the corn in rows.

Beulah was still missing her colt. She snorted and lurched as Perry brought the pair from the barn to hitch to the John Deere plow.

Once the team was in tandem with Perry in position to push them along in the crisscross pattern to level the field's furrows, his world felt misaligned. As he and his horses worked to prepare their little patch of earth, Perry's mind was flooded by insignificance. His existence took on a hollow sense despite the major steps he was about to take. Farming felt much like a task and less like a passion.

Perry scooted his boots through the ridges of the soil, his steps shorter and less directed. His delights and desires rested elsewhere, and thoughts of indisputable injustice swirled about him. At a time when others suffered so gravely, why did he deserve the happiness he expected would come in the weeks ahead? Why was he floored by guilt? What more could he have done or do in the future? Perry could not overcome the fact that he was a selected survivor. The feeling of helplessness anchored each stride across the field.

Moving deliberately was all he could do. Deserving of favor or not, Perry chased away emotional clouds of uncertainty by drawing from his faith and his adopted philosophy of "work and pray." Also in his favor were several providential truths, each supplying a comfort of confidence. He was assured in the preordination of his pairing with Millie. He was engaged in farming, the vocation he considered God's work. He was certain he had been placed in the situations he faced through the force of a higher hand. Through the gloom, Perry plowed on.

CHAPTER 29

Spring 1864

AWESOME POSSUM

Two weeks passed, and time erected a protective honeycomb to shield Perry from the hostile buzzing of his anxious misgivings. It was time to leave for the sarsaparilla showdown on Roubideaux's side of the river. The Roubideaux gang would surely expect a worthy story. Perry was thankful he had a narrative of jubilation to share with them about his engagement with Millie that, at least on the personal level, overshadowed the tale of tribulation he also shared about the bleeding bluffs at Leavenworth.

He stuffed the piano money into his pocket, strapped his pistol to his leg, saddled up Appy and slid his rifle into his saddle's leather scabbard. Perry rode over hill and dell before he reached the main road east. He headed toward the ferry that would deposit him on the Roubideaux side of the muddy Missouri River. The level of danger had eroded from previous weeks, so Perry hopped aboard the steam ferry with the twin smokestacks and hit the Missouri side of the riverbank at right around 11 a.m.

Perry led Appy to the shade of a bankside willow tree and waited for the appointed hour when his friends would arrive. The river was running high, and it smelled but not as deathly as usual. Perry chalked that up to the melting of massive snowfalls in regions upstream.

The sun was high in the sky, but it was a full ten minutes past noon when the weeds rustled along the river path. Marcus and Pete were shooting wise-cracks back and forth as they approached the riverbank.

"I believe old Perry must have chickened-out," Marcus said loud enough that Perry could hear. "I think a streak of yella' runs down his spine."

"Me too, Marcus," Pete said as loudly. "I guess this here sarsaparilla syrup is just going to waste. I shall dump it into the river and wish for a friend with a bit more courage and commitment to principle."

Out of the bushes, Perry stood up.

"And I think I might try to find some new friends on this godforsaken side of the river who have a better sense of time. You two rascals are late. You suffer from anemic senses of humor to boot."

The three men gathered at the river's edge amid smiles, handshakes and bear hugs.

"I wasn't sure if I would ever see you two again," Perry said.

"Nor we, you," Pete replied.

"How are tensions on this side?" Perry asked.

"Awesome possum," Pete chimed in.

"Things are as calm as a church mouse on a Monday morning," Marcus said. "Business is as brisk as ever. People seem to want to get on with life. They are growing weary of all that has happened over the last several months. The tenets that once drove extreme action have cooled. People are starting to see the chalk writing on the board. The Confederacy is drawing its final breaths."

"So, what's new with you?" Pete asked.

"Quite a bit, actually," Perry said. "You want the good news or the bad news?"

"Hit us with the bad news first," Pete said. "I like to finish off conversations on a high note."

Perry stared across the river, searching the creases of his mind for a good place to start.

"You both know of my decision to volunteer after hearing about Quantrill's raid on Lawrence. I volunteered for the Jayhawkers. Joined them in Leavenworth at an inopportune time."

"We heard about the Battle of Leavenworth," Marcus said. "We were hoping that did not involve you. It sounded like a bloody mess."

"It was. You'll have to take my word for it. I still have nightmares."

Perry explained the action blow for blow, as best he could, even though he could tell his mind already was trying to blot it out. He explained how Constable Dan met his demise from a rebel bullet, but nothing about his last minutes. Perry recalled the heroics of his young friend Gabe Watson. He recounted his walk home from Leavenworth, his run-in with the cyclone, sleeping in the corn shock and the semi-dazed encounter with the world around him.

"It was just a blessing to be alive," Perry said. "After everything I faced in those days, I know God isn't done with Perry Adams."

"So, if your survival is the unwelcome news, the good news really must be fantastic," Pete said.

"It is. Miss Millie and I are going to be united in matrimony."

"Congratulations, you old hermit! I always knew she had a dubious taste in men," Pete said. "I could never prove it until that unfortunate day when I formally introduced the two of you."

"So, when is the date of this blessed event?" Marcus asked.

"Fellas, that's kind of the main reason I am here. The date is set for Friday, March 25th. It's also the date of The Feast of Annunciation, which, in case you heathens don't know, is the date when we celebrate the archangel Gabriel's announcement to the Virgin Mary that she would give birth to our savior."

"So, is there some hidden meaning there?" Marcus asked sheepishly. "Did the archangel Gabriel visit Miss Millie? Is she on the nest?"

"No, sir, you blasphemer." Perry laughed. "Miss Millie is still as innocent as the day I first saw her sitting at Pete's ratty old piano."

"So, are we invited?" Pete asked. "Do you have room in the pews for a couple of disrespectful Missouri gentlemen?"

"You sure are. I am delivering the invitation to you in first person. And fellas, I would be honored if you both agreed to stand with me at the altar as groomsmen. I'm sure Millie has already delivered the message, so I'll spill the beans. She wants Lucy to be her matron of honor."

"What the hell? Don't you too have any worthy friends in Kansas? Thought you were a popular guy over there in Lowland," Pete said.

"Yes. I have a third groomsman, a man I have grown to respect and consider a brother as much as I do you two," Perry said. "You initially heard of him under the pseudonym of Willie Jefferson. It's my neighbor, Moses Watson. His son Gabe, the war hero I told you about, he will be an usher."

"I would be honored to stand by Moses's side and attest to your high character," Pete said.

"Likewise," Marcus added, "despite the fact you mislead us about Moses for so long. Time for me to come clean among friends. I've already met Moses and Gabe. They spent the night in my stable before hopping the river to their new life in Kansas. Your fears about me squealing to Charlie Wilson cut me deeply, but I could not mention anything about it while that bastard was still kicking."

"Holy crap, so that's the deeply held secret Pete has hinted about. You're an engineer on the Underground Railroad. I'll be damned."

"Pete has known it all along. But now it's your secret to hold tight as well . . . at least until this bullshit is all over."

"There's a surprise around every damn corner with you guys, isn't there?" Perry asked. "All of a sudden, I feel like the rogue here."

"But since Moses considers you close enough to be his brother in spirit, you must be a decent fella after all." Pete laughed. "And if you and Moses are brothers, we all shall be, and that also makes us uncles of a war hero. We might have to bring a bigger wagon because even though Jep isn't quite sure who you are, he is going to want to tag along. As for Lucy and me, we will relish the chance to get all fancied up."

Perry, Pete, and Marcus sat bankside for several more minutes talking about life along the border in their little corner of the world. It was decided that Roubideaux was sufficiently calm for a quick trip to Marcus' trading post, followed by a quick drink for old time's sake at The Outpost Tavern. They walked up the riverbank with Perry leading Appy along the trail.

At Marcus's, Perry stocked up on peppermint sticks for Millie, a couple bricks of plug tobacco for Moses and a couple of construction essentials, a hand-crank drill and a box of nails. Perry was adding a room to his home to accommodate a piano and another two-legged being who soon would join him and Archibald at the house in Jawbone Holler. He also stocked up on a few food staples that fit into his saddle bag.

Pete walked on toward The Outpost, donned his bar apron, and started serving his thirsty customers.

Sitting at the end of the bar was a fair-faced young man, in his late teens, with high cheek bones, a sharply pronounced jawline and a head of neatly parted dark hair. Drinking age was not a big issue. Anyone who looked old enough to consume with a modicum of control was extended that privilege. The handsome young man was finishing a mug of Smit's—The Frontier's Finest brew.

"Can I fetch you another, sir?" Pete asked.

"Sure thing," the young man replied.

After loading the goods he'd bought from Marcus's Trading Post, Perry walked Appy up the street and tied him to a hitching post outside of The Outpost. Perry walked through the swinging doors as Pete slid another brew to the young man at the end of the bar.

Pete's new piano sat in the old familiar spot where Millie's piano formerly was. It was a fancy upright model with burled walnut veneer. The dark swirls of the exterior panels would be quite a match for Millie's stunning coal-black hair. Perry doubted, however, that the new piano carried tunes in the same quality as Miss Millie Longworth tickling the keys.

After he admired Pete's new piano, Perry reminded himself to remain vigilant in both action and words. He had been assured by his friends that Roubideaux was calm, but it was always better to be safe than sorry. He chose a barstool a couple of spots down the bar from the young man.

"Seeing your new piano reminds me, Pete. Here's the money for your beat-up old piano," Perry said as he slid the money to Pete across the bar. "And

I happen to know a young woman who could break in that new keyboard of yours in a right, proper manner."

"Don't remind me. I'm afraid her tenure was the gilded age of piano music in The Outpost. But the damn thing cost me an arm and a leg. I ain't gonna say how much."

The young man at the bar perked up when he heard that.

"It sure looks like a valuable piece of musical art," he said.

"Yeh, it is," Pete said. "I put as many resources back into this place as possible and that's my latest investment. But I'm not worried about it from a security standpoint. I could not imagine someone trying to pilfer such a big unwieldy piece of musical furniture. I figure my money's safer here than in any bank."

"I think you are right about that, sir," the young man said. "Banks are pretty much like a ripe crimson raspberry waiting to be bootlegged by a blue jay."

"Oh, trust me, it's not nearly as valuable as it would be with the right set of hands floating across the keyboard," Perry said. "But what's past is passed. I am fairly sure I could talk that certain piano player to deliver an occasional guest performance."

"You do that, my friend, and the 'mater beers are on the house."

"Now that you remind me, Pete, set me up. It's been far too long, and you mix them up to perfection."

The reddish liquid caught the attention of the young man.

"What is that you're drinking, sir?" he asked Perry.

"It's a delectable mix of tomato juice and Smit's," Perry said. "Pete says he invented it. We call it 'mater beer. Some folks call it bloody beer, but you order it by either name and Pete will know exactly what you mean."

"I like the way bloody beer sounds," the young man said. "It seems fittin' for the times we live in and the company we are forced to keep. I think I'll try one."

The young man's tone set off an alarm with Perry. He proceeded with caution.

"You must not be from these parts because Pete serves these 'mater beers on a pretty regular basis," Perry said. "I think he does it to disguise the objectionable taste of Smit's."

"Sounds about right to me," the young man said as Pete slid a 'mater beer down the bar. "Not sure this trend has hit my hometown yet. It's about a half-day ride to the south and east. It was time to expand my horizons a bit, so I decided to go on a trek of exploration. Roubideaux seems like a pleasant town. I might think about settling here someday."

"I have grown fond of this town myself," Perry said. "I will be glad when this war is over, and the border can reclaim a more peaceable nature."

"The way things look right now, it might be a good spell before the border reclaims a more harmonious demeanor," the young man said. "I've seen a lot of injustice committed against folks on this side of the river by aggressors from the west."

"As have I," Perry said. "But I have seen the exact same situation from a perspective on the other side of the river. There are belligerents aplenty in both camps."

"Not sure if you've heard of a group of thieves and murderers called the Jayhawkers," the young man said. "I have experienced their burning and butchering firsthand while visiting relatives several years back in a small town called Osceola. The Jayhawkers came whooping into town, burning, looting, and killing. I was too young to take up arms or I surely would have. Instead, I hid like a coward in a cornfield. But I set that record straight a couple of years ago during a brief visit to a dog-shit town they call Lawrence. I was fifteen, but old enough to pull a trigger."

Perry was shocked at what he heard. Had this young man really ridden with the murderous devil named Quantrill?

"I cannot address the atrocities you experienced at the hands of those early Jayhawkers, but I can assuredly say they have been forced to change their ways by the Union forces," Perry said. "There's a lot of truth about one rotten apple spoiling the whole bushel."

"And how do you know that, sir?" the young man asked.

"I rode with the Jayhawkers at the Battle of Leavenworth," the sentence escaped Perry's mouth before he could even think.

"Isn't that interesting?" the young man mused. "Heard it was a bloody battle. I respect you for surviving and I have no quarrel with you, being on the other side and all. We are all serving the causes we considered worth dying for. Seeing how we both appear to be law-abiding civilians at present, I am hopeful you do not judge me for my past actions as well. Plus, you have introduced me to bloody beer, which I find quite quenching and delightful."

Sensing a de-escalation from a few seconds before, Perry introduced himself.

"Glad you like the beer," Perry said. "On this day that's affinity enough for me. The name's Perry Adams. I farm west of here about twenty miles or so."

Perry tipped his mug toward the young man in a friendly gesture.

The young man responded with a devilish smirk.

"The last name's James."

The two men finished their 'mater beers in silence. The young man tipped his hat, took one last look to size-up Pete's expensive piano, and left the bar without a farewell. He mounted his horse and continued his trek of exploration.

CHAPTER 30

Spring 1864

THE BETTER ANGEL

IN THE DAYS LEADING UP THE DATE OF THE WEDDING, the war between the states took another swing toward the Union side as President Lincoln appointed a fearless and hard-charging man named Ulysses S. Grant as commander of all Union armies. Lincoln admired his commitment to defeating the Confederate Army on the field of battle and the way people in the north referred to him as Unconditional Surrender Grant.

After reading about the new commander, Perry knew that marriage was much like the terms expected by Grant—unconditional surrender. He expressed his sentiments as such to both Millie and to Father Carrigan as the appointed day approached.

"I don't expect you to surrender any single aspect of what makes you, you," Millie told him. "If you did, you would no longer be the man for which I fell head over heels."

Their life together would not be free of compromise. Millie gave up her house in town for a less refined lifestyle in Jawbone Holler. And when she did,

Perry ensured her piano followed.

Due to her new home's distance from Lowland, and the fact she would be a married woman, she had to resign from her teaching job at the mission school. There was a chance she might be able to teach at the new one-room school now under construction three miles from the holler, but that all depended on whether an unmarried teacher was available. But even if one were, she could always help. She might enjoy ringing the bell to call the students to class, something Father Carrigan never allowed her to do. He insisted on the shepherd calling the flock.

One flock Father Carrigan could not assemble was Perry's appointed groomsmen. Only Perry could bring such a diverse cast of characters together for the blessed event. He recalled a quote he read from President Lincoln's newly appointed lieutenant general. Ulysses Grant measured his friendships the same way Perry did.

"The friend in adversity I shall always cherish most. I can better trust those who helped to relieve the gloom of my dark hours than those who are so ready to enjoy with me the sunshine of my prosperity."

Moses had been with him during that visit from the Missouri ruffians, and Moses lifted him up after the hailstorm. Pete had certainly seen both ends of the friendship scale, the sunshine of having introduced Perry to Millie and the gloom when Perry needed to be nursed back to health after being shot by Charlie Wilson. Dealing with Marcus, of course, always presented adversity, but the dedicated trading post proprietor also helped Perry secure his self-scouring steel John Deere plow and the spiffy duds he wore on his first date with Millie.

When thinking about Grant's quote in regard to Watty, Marcus, and Pete, Perry could not help but think of his missing friend, Constable Dan. Certainly, there had been times of emotional prosperity, like the arm rasslin' match, but also the height of adversity experienced on the bloody bluffs of Leavenworth. The three surviving friends would make perfect groomsmen, albeit a disparate bunch. He laughed at the idea of seeing the three men standing together at the foot of the altar.

In preparation for the journey down the aisle over which he would preside, Father Carrigan called Millie and Perry together for several discussions about the serious nature of the sacrament they were about to share. He talked to them about common commitment, overcoming disagreements, and raising children to honor both church and community.

"I do not expect either of you to take on the role of sacrificial lamb for the furtherance of the other," Father Carrigan said. "A tranquil home requires a united front in all matters, financial, spiritual and familial."

For their part, both Perry and Millie expected even more from themselves than the other about holding true to Father Carrigan's directives.

While Perry had lofty expectations leading up to the wedding, part of his mind remained focused on ensuring his readiness to drop seed corn into the ground in the days following the event. His seed was ready. Beulah and Barney were in prime springtime shape. The seedbed was soaking in the warmth and moisture needed for germination.

As he was inspecting all aspects of the farm, something was missing. Where was Archibald? Perry whistled for his floppy-eared dog from one side of the property to the other. It was rare that Archibald ever strayed too far from either the house or the barn, but he was nowhere to be found.

As Perry was about to give up, thinking Archibald might have gone off into the woods to chase a rabbit or deer, he spotted a rumpled lump of fur under a tree near the yard's edge. On closer inspection, he could see Archibald was in distress. Archibald labored with every breath. His left hind leg was puffy, and blood trickled down it. Two puncture wounds were as clear as day. A rattler had bitten Perry's floppy-eared buddy.

Perry picked up Archibald as gently as possible and carried him to the house. Snake bites were often fatal, and this was anything but a good harbinger of the near-term future. Archibald was a big dog, however, and that was a positive aspect in his favor. Perry surmised the bite occurred within the last several hours, but Archibald was a fighter. If any dog could survive a rattler bite, it would be Archibald. Perry acted quickly.

Perry placed Archibald in a comfortable position atop the dog's favorite blanket. He elevated Archibald's head so his heart was above the wound's location. He drew a pale of water, and as thoroughly as he could, he washed the wounded area to draw out as much venom as possible. After that, all he could do was wait.

Perry left Archibald in the house with a bowl of water within reach of his tongue. He saddled up Appy and went to see Moses and Gabe, who were tending their hog herd as Perry approached.

"Watty, I have a problem," Perry said. "Archibald has been snake-bit, and I am not sure what I can do. I brought him inside and washed the wound, but I fear beside that I am helpless."

"I've seen many snake bites," Moses said. "Some are fatal but most amount to little more than temporary flesh wounds. I assure you that your actions have been appropriate. Archibald's fate is now in more authoritative hands."

"I hope our kind and generous God is as fond of dogs as I am," Perry said as he reached into his saddlebag and brought out the two bricks of plug chewing tobacco he'd bought for Moses at Marcus's Trading Post. "I picked these up for you during my last visit over to Roubideaux. Marcus and Pete are anxious to meet you both. It's only a week away, so I hope you are preparing yourself for this duty beyond the call of friendship."

"Oh, I am quite ready," Moses said.

"I will make sure he lives up to that promise," Gabe said. "I only hope Archibald is able to attend the ceremony as well."

Upon returning home, Perry saw little change in Archibald, but at least the wound had not gotten any worse. It was clear he consumed some of the water Perry had left in the bowl by his head. The wound itself was no longer bleeding, but the puffiness remained. Only time would tell.

There was hardly any change in Archibald's condition during the second and third days as well. There was a slight decrease in swelling and the site of the bite itself became a dark red patch where the two fang marks had previously been seen.

Perry left Archibald and drove his wagon into town, both to see Millie but also to collect some of her belongings for her move to Jawbone Holler.

"Millie, I have some shocking news," Perry said.

"Mr. Adams, that's the last thing a woman wants to hear days before her wedding," Millie said.

"It's Archibald, three or four days ago a rattler bit him," Perry said. "He is holding his own, but it's still haphazard whether he will pull through it. I was hoping he would attend this Friday as part of our celebration."

"I did not want to mention it, but I was hoping so as well," Millie said.

"Millie, you know the black leather vest Constable Dan wore so well that I left in your caretaking; I wish to place it on our matrimonial altar as a remembrance of my friend who is not here to stand beside me," Perry said. "I also ask your permission to have one more item at the altar that is precious to me. I would like to place Old Luke's jawbone on a pedestal off to one side of the altar. If not for him and his being, this event would not be happening. I owe my existence in large degree to Luke and Constable Dan. I want to honor them both."

"If you raise no objection to the presence of my two persnickety older sisters as bridesmaids, along with Lucy as my matron of honor, there is no reason for me to object to these items that are so important to you," Millie said. "I also pray Archibald will be able to join us."

Perry and Millie loaded a few items into the wagon for his trip back to the holler. The piano, for now, stayed behind. It would soon be making the trip to a new room Perry built on the back side of the house.

Before leaving town, Perry fired off a telegram to Marcus and Pete to ensure they were preparing for Friday's event.

Marcus and Pete . . . Almost sarsaparilla time over here in Lowland . . . Hope you are preparing for Friday . . . Please bring Jep if he is sober and up for the trip . . . He would be a most welcome guest . . . Moses and Gabe looking forward to meeting you. Best, Perry.

Perry returned to the holler. After unloading Millie's belongings into the house, Perry's intention was to spend Wednesday night alone with Archibald.

He would travel to Lowland on Thursday, overnighting at the boarding house, in preparation for the Friday afternoon wedding. He would drive his wagon pulled by Beulah and Barney into town and put them up at the Lowland stable Thursday evening.

Perry and Millie both agreed to wear the clothes they wore on their first date for the wedding itself. Each considered the other to own the look of perfection that first night. There was no need to switch things up. The last thing Perry did on this Wednesday evening was to fold and pack his wedding clothes as best as he could.

That evening, there was still no major sign of improvement in Archibald's condition, but the dog opened his eyes and wagged his tail slightly. Perry was concerned if Archibald did not make it, a pall would be cast over the otherwise blessed event that was rapidly approaching.

That night, kneeling bedside, he prayed for Millie, for his friends who would be in transit from Roubideaux, and for healing for his floppy-eared hound dog. He did all he could do in preparation for the big day.

At the break of dawn, Perry was startled awake by a warm, wet sensation on his cheek. It was Archibald. Awake and hungry. He limped across the floor, but it was clear Archibald walked through the valley of rattler death and survived.

"*Uh-roo-roo-roo!*" Archibald barked.

"Praise God!" Perry shouted so loudly even the squirrels up the holler might be startled awake.

Perry hitched up the wagon, with Beulah and Barney taking the lead. He lifted Archibald into the wagon and headed south.

The morning of the wedding, the entire town was shutting its doors to attend the ceremony of the young man they once scorned as a wild-eyed oddball who had lived in a hole in the ground and ate his mule to survive the winter.

As the big day approached, Miss Millie became the lady of the town everybody wanted to know and to be seen with. This clearly was a match of two incredibly good people brought together by destiny.

At the mission church, Perry was glad to see an approaching wagon that included four passengers: Lucy, Pete, Marcus, and Jep. Lucy wore a long, luxurious gown. Pete was gussied up in his best bartender garb and Marcus looked quite like a man-about-town, complete with a conspicuous gray toupee perched atop his head. Even Old Jep was looking debonair in a matching pin-stripe suit. It looked a bit tight around the belly and was worn by him as a younger man, when he had the world by the tail.

"Howdy, Mister Jerry," Jep said with a sober tone Perry had never seen before. "I wouldn't have missed this day for the world. Plus, I wanted to be here in person so I could grant you the magical wishes you so rightly deserve."

Jep, still very much a genie, trailed Perry into the church. Perry tackled the final preparations, and Jep dove into the first row.

A perfectly matched pair of horses pulled a wagon from the north. Gabe was decked out in a military uniform, adorned with his Jayhawker medal. Moses was ready to take his place of honor alongside Marcus and Pete, dressed in a black suit, white shirt, and black ribbon tie.

The two Missouri friends greeted Gabe and Moses as they climbed from the wagon and tied the team to a hitching post.

"Moses and Gabe, it's good to see you again," Marcus said. "When this war's over, you'll have to come visit me in Roubideaux, and when you do, this time you'll stay in my house."

"We'll do that, Mr. Mixon," Moses replied. "And it's great to see you under less stressful terms, at least for us. I'm not so sure about the bride and groom."

"This here is Lucy and Pete Fontaine. They are the purveyors at Perry's favorite watering hole over in Roubideaux. They've kept our little secret as well about your last night in Missouri."

"And you must be the war hero, Gabe Watson," Pete said.

"I got a Jayhawker medal to prove it," Gabe said.

"Moses, we look forward to the relationship we have ahead as brothers of Perry," Pete said. "That makes us all brothers."

"If that's the case, you guys are going to have to spiff up a bit," Moses laughed. "Don't want you tarnishing the family reputation."

"And, young Gabe, from now on, you can just call me Uncle Pete," Pete said.

Pete reached into the breast pocket of his jacket and pulled out a silver flask. That was when Lucy knew it was time to find Millie for final preparations.

"Nice to meet you gentlemen," she said, walking into the church.

"The finest rum west of the Mississippi," Pete said, holding the flask high above his head. "Before we join as a united force to vouch for the honor of our notorious buddy, I suggest we bolster our constitutions with a swig of the spirit responsible for bringing Perry and Millie together. If rum had not given him the gumption to sing that song on the night they'd first laid eyes on each other, we might still be dealing with a bachelor brother forever to be a holler-dwelling hermit."

"So, here's to Perry," Pete said, as he raised the flask and passed it to Gabe for first-drink honors.

"War heroes go first," Pete continued.

"Don't mind if I do," said Gabe, as he drank down a swallow before passing the flask to Moses.

"Don't usually touch the stuff, gentlemen, but on this occasion, I'll make an exception," Moses said.

He raised the flask to his mouth and sucked down a generous drink. He hacked to regain his breath.

"Oh, that's harmful stuff," Moses said as he handed the flask to Marcus.

Marcus raised a toast to the war hero and the other two bothers-of-Perry.

"Here's to you, and here's to me, best of friends we'll always be. And if we ever disagree, screw you, and here's to me."

Marcus sucked down several gurgles, straightened his toupee and returned the flask to Pete.

Pete raised the flask and in one long gulp drained the remaining rum.

Unaware of the debauchery that took place among the four men, at exactly 2 p.m., Father Carrigan rang the church bell as a last call for any and all latecomers.

After being fortified for the event, the three groomsmen took their places in the wedding party. On the opposite side stood Lucy and Millie's two older sisters, each attractive in their own way, but they could not hold a candle to Millie in all her beautiful splendor, or for that matter, even Lucy. Gabe found a seat next to Jep in the front row, the place reserved for the groom's family, as did Judge Merriweather and good old floppy-eared Archibald.

Unseen by the wedding party, sliding into the last available pew at the rear of the church was Stewart Adams, who had journeyed all the way from French Lick, Indiana. Beside him, in the last vacant spot of the last available pew, Stew unfolded a piece of white, lace-trimmed cloth. It was his late wife Mary Katherine's bonnet.

At the front of the church, on the right side of the altar was the tribute to Constable Dan, his black leather vest and tin star hanging over the back of an oak chair. On the left side, atop a marble pedestal, was the bleached, white, long jawbone of Perry's much renowned mule, Luke.

Father Carrigan began the ceremony.

Everyone in attendance stood in a show of respect and support for the couple. Father Carrigan addressed the couple directly.

"Dearly beloved, we have come together into the house of the Church so that in the presence of the Church's minister and the community, your intention to enter into marriage may be strengthened by the Lord with a sacred seal," he said. "Christ abundantly blesses the love that binds you. Through a special Sacrament, he enriches and strengthens those he has already consecrated by Holy Baptism, that they may be faithful to each other forever and assume all the responsibilities of married life. And so, in the presence of the Church, I ask you to state your intentions."

Father Carrigan continued to address the couple.

"Perry and Millicent, have you come here to enter into marriage without coercion, freely and wholeheartedly?" he asked.

"I have," they said in unison.

Perry and Millie joined their right hands and pledged their faith in good times and bad, in sickness and health, and promised to love and honor each other all the days of their lives.

"May the Lord, in his kindness, strengthen the consent you have declared before the Church and graciously bring to fulfillment his blessings within you," Father Carrigan continued. "May the God of Abraham, the God of Isaac, the God of Jacob, the God who joined together our first parents in paradise, strengthen and bless in Christ the consent you have declared before the Church, so that what God joins together, no one may put asunder."

After the blessing of rings, the celebration of a Latin mass and communion, Father Carrigan spoke his final ceremonial words to seal the sacramental event.

"By the holy authority granted by the Church and the power vested in me by the State of Kansas, I pronounce you husband and wife. And may almighty God bless all of you, who are gathered here, in the name of the Father, the Son and the Holy Spirit. Perry, you may kiss your bride."

Perry lifted the veil from Millie's face and did just that. The crowd applauded.

Archibald let out a loud and celebratory, "*Uh-roo-roo-roo!*"

Father Carrigan smiled at the dog and continued, "Go in peace, glorifying the Lord by your life."

Perry shook hands with Father Carrigan before he and Millie walked arm-in-arm down the aisle, followed closely by Archibald. Perry saw Stew in the last row. He ran up and hugged the old man.

"It's great to see you again, son, but one of my priorities is to see Joe Henderson's herd of Adams cattle in the Flint Hills," Stew said, still wrestling with admitting pride in his son.

Looking down at the church pew where Stew had been seated, Perry saw his mother's bonnet. He knew in an instant the old man could not have cared less about seeing Joe's cattle herd. This trip was about seeing his son and meeting his new daughter-in-law. Perry smiled, knowing part of his mother was in his presence.

"Glad you could make it, Pappy," Perry said. "I'd like you to meet Millie."

Mille extended her hand in a graceful manner. Stew greeted her hand with both of his.

"Nice to meet you, Millie."

"If you might be staying around a couple days, I'd like to show you my farm. Better introduce you to Millie. Repay what I took when I left," Perry added.

"I wouldn't miss it for the world, son. But first, I think you two have a honeymoon to attend. Sorry I couldn't make it even more special, but I seem to have misplaced the bag of coins I was hoping one day to give you for that purpose.

Maybe they'll show up some day."

Perry turned his head to face Millie and smiled again.

As the couple reached the doorway of the church entrance hall, Perry noticed a strange new posting on the bulletin board typically devoted to welcoming parishioners. In bold lettering, the headline shouted, "Misplaced and Lost Families." Under it was a long list of freed slaves now residing in Kansas who had lost track of family members during their journey to liberty. Perry scanned the alphabetical list. Under "W", he saw the name Sally Watson and sons.

Perry made a mental note and a promise to himself that very moment, but he did not have time to linger in the entryway. There were hands to shake and cheeks to kiss.

Perry and Millie waited outside the doors of the church, greeting each guest as they filed out. First, the bridesmaids and groomsmen. They lined up across from each other along a stone sidewalk leading to the street. Soon, there was no sidewalk left and guests began to pile in two-deep. Each guest held a little burlap bag.

Jep stumbled out of the church. He was the last guest in line. "I grant a happily ever after to both of you," his eyes twinkling.

After Jep joined his place in line, Perry and Millie counted to three and made a mad dash for the buckboard wagon, down the stone sidewalk between the two lines of well-wishers. The guests stuck their hands into their burlap bags and pelted the young couple with a slightly nontraditional wedding send-off— handfuls of yellow kernels of corn.

Archibald had already leaped into the wagon's bed as Perry and Millie jumped into the seat of their buckboard. The guests applauded and the young couple glowed. Perry shook the reins and Beulah and Barney headed east toward Main Street for a celebratory ride.

"You've made me the happiest man in the world," Perry said.

"I hope you're right, husband, but I'm not sure that's possible. I don't think you saw the happiness in your pappy's eyes."

"Family, that's what it's all about, Millie. Life without one, at least away from one, can be rough. I'm glad Pappy came. A father and son should never lose connection, and I'll not let that happen again. I can't wait to introduce you."

Perry continued, "After seeing that poster in the entryway of the church, I am so glad Watty and Gabe have each other, but it reminded me they need to be reunited with their kin. Watty has the void of two missing sons and a wife that needs to be filled. You can see how it plagues his soul. After this war's over, I think Watty and I are going to have to go on a little expedition, with your permission, of course. I'm inclined to walk over mountains and through swamps to help Watty find his family."

"Of course, you have my permission, not that it's needed. You're a good man, Perry Adams. Now, how about we head home and start working on a family all our own?"

And so they did. Years prior this day, marriage was not even a far-off thought for a troubled young man who left Salt Spring, Indiana, and the patient young lady who pounded out after-hour bar tunes on a rickety old piano.

After dropping the seeds of the new year's corn crop into the soil, Perry hiked to the top of the highest bluff overlooking the holler named for Luke's relic. He retrieved from the bib of his overalls the brass pirate spyglass. Through its lens Perry beheld the magnificence of the meadows and his fields below. He read the inscription etched on the spyglass, "Avast! Pay attention." He wiped his brow and heeded the advice, knowing he had been blessed beyond measure.

With due respect to his pirate ancestry, after his hike up the bluff Perry belted out in the stillness of the serenity a new version of the old seafarer's verse, which he called a Kansas farm shanty.

"Now plow them fields my fair-faissd lad,
And ne'er a day will yau be sad.
So husk that corn till the day yau die.
Yaur saul 'twill float' to heaven nigh."

Luke's jawbone was preserved for posterity, as well as the stories behind it, always a reminder of life's adversity, yet also one of survival.

In the few episodes of turmoil awaiting Perry and Millie, and with the Civil War gasping its final wheezes over the next year, Perry drew inspiration from a section of President Abraham Lincoln's first inaugural address.

"The mystic chords of memory, stretching from every battle-field, and patriot grave, to every living heart and hearth-stone, all over this broad land, will yet swell the chorus of the Union, when again touched, as surely they will be, by the better angels of our nature."

Millie was heaven-sent, the better angel of Perry's nature.

Separated only during times when fulfilling promises to friends, Perry and Millie embarked on the journey of life. With unified spirits, they nurtured the land tucked into the fertile river bluffs of northeast Kansas. This place was not heaven, but it was close.

So together they pushed on, their steel plow cutting the furrows of time, pushing ever forward as they cultivated the legacy of Jawbone Holler.

THE END

ACKNOWLEDGMENTS

People I respect have told me I write with "a lot of flair," and at the time I heard it, I was not sure it was meant as a compliment, but now, I will move on and accept it as such. Writing a novel is a solitary journey, but it is not without the invaluable support and guidance of others. As the journey to complete and publish my novel, *Jawbone Holler*, has been realized, I feel compelled to express my deepest gratitude to those who kindled the flame of my love of writing.

I want to pay tribute to the late Martha Rockey, my high school journalism teacher, whose passion for the spoken and written word ignited a spark. I also want to thank my college journalism professor, John Lofflin, who pushed me beyond my limits and instilled in me the courage to explore new realms of storytelling . . . to invoke the reader's senses with the power of verbs and nouns, without resorting to too many adjectives and adverbs. Mother Dog!

I am thankful for all the lessons I learned from the Benedictine professors during college in Atchison, Kansas, including the monks and sisters who were drawn to the vocation of education. The transformation, intellectually and spiritually, I experienced at Benedictine College fueled me for a lifetime.

Then there's my lifelong writing shaman, John Schlageck. His wisdom, guidance, and unyielding belief in my abilities have been a constant source of inspiration. John helped me polish my voice and navigate the intricacies of storytelling. His influence on my writing cannot be overstated.

A special shout-out to my dear friend Darryl Chatman. His coaching and insights have been instrumental in making *Jawbone Holler* relevant in today's world. Darryl pushed me to explore the depth of racial issues and because of him one of my characters, Gabe, was born. He helped me weave a narrative that resonates with the struggles faced by our nation today and through his own story of inspiration.

I would also like to thank my friend Chris Chinn for her continued faith in everything I do, and for pointing out the need for an additional character, and, boom, Lucy was brought to life.

I owe a debt of gratitude to each of my children, Trace Thornton, Troy Thornton and Taylor McCord, for believing in the old man each step of the way. And specifically, I want to thank Tater Bugs for her keen editing insights. Even after five other professional editors, she was still able to tighten the flow. Her discerning eye and meticulous attention to detail transformed my jagged sections into smooth serenity. The unwavering support from all three of these "kids" was a driving force throughout this journey.

To my wife, Denise Brazier Thornton, your love, support, and guidance have been my anchor in the stormy seas of writing. Her belief in me, even during the moments of self-doubt, gave me the strength to persevere. During the lunacy of my month-long quest to complete my first draft, Denise was gone for two weeks visiting one of our kids. While any amount of time away from her disrupts my soul, I used the time to my advantage. After a full day of work, I was able to crank out a chapter during the evening hours, which I then read to her over the phone in the late evening. Her presence in the process, even from a distance, made all the difference.

I also want to express my appreciation to my dear friend and talented photographer and author Paul Mobley. His advocacy and unwavering belief in my manuscript were a constant source of motivation. Paul was dedicated to the mission of finding this story a home. I am eternally grateful for your friendship and for introducing me to the incredible team at Mascot Books.

I wish I could express my gratitude to my departed parents, Dorothy and Marion Thornton, for the unwavering support and love they bestowed on me throughout my life. While neither graduated from high school, they were both brilliant in their own ways but were held back by the inevitable circumstance of life. From the earliest days, they drilled into my brain the importance of education and exploration, pushing the bounds of my capabilities to chase dreams without fear of failure.

It was my dad who shared with me the captivating thoughts of the real Perry, an early Kansas pioneer who, according to lore, settled in the ragged Missouri River Hills. According to legend, he resorted to eating his mule during the depths of a cruel winter in a real place called Rawhide Holler, where I was born and raised. Perry's story is one I have forever remembered. The hard lessons embedded within it left an indelible mark on my soul, and on his fictional perils rests the foundation of this book.

I am also grateful to all five of my sisters for influencing my life toward the positive side, but especially to my loving sister Marilyn Anderson who devoted her career to teaching and has always had my back, including teaching me to read as a Rawhide Holler hillbilly kid who, for some reason, skipped kindergarten.

While the places mentioned in the story are mostly fictional, a few might recognize a point or two shared by Lowland and Troy, Kansas, the undeniable garden spot of the universe, and a few shared by Roubideaux and St. Joe, Missouri. To all those mentioned here and countless others who have read it or provided counsel, especially my author friend, Mike Matson, I extend my deepest gratitude.

Writing *Jawbone Holler* has been a labor of love, and it would not have been possible without your belief in me and your unwavering support. May my words honor the gifts you have all shared, and may they serve as a testament to the loving power of the human spirit.

With heartfelt appreciation,
Mace Thornton

ABOUT THE AUTHOR

Mace Thornton is a recovering journalist, an author, and strategic communications specialist. A native of Troy, Kansas, he grew up on a small farm in the Missouri River Hills of northeast Kansas. With a degree in journalism from Benedictine College in Atchison, Kansas, among his passions are writing, sports, and the people of agriculture. His award-winning journalism and commentaries have been published across the nation. His career took him far away from his home state for more than three decades, but he now lives a little closer, in the St. Louis area with his wife, Denise, and their spirited rescue pup, Anna Mae. In addition to writing, he is a partner at Stratovation Group, a research, marketing, and communications firm headquartered in Columbus, Ohio. The soul of his first novel, *Jawbone Holler*, is drawn from the hills where he was raised and the stories that echo through the people who embrace them. The Thorntons have three adult children scattered to the corners of our great nation: Trace (and Amy) in Virginia, Troy (and Katrina) in Washington state, and Taylor (and Shawn) in Georgia. The Thorntons also have one grandchild, Grace DeAnn McCord, born just prior to *Jawbone Holler*'s publication. She resides with her parents, Taylor and Shawn.